PENGUIN CLASSICS

OSCAR WILDE: COMPLETE SHORT FICTION

OSCAR FINGAL O'FLAHERTIE WILLS WILDE, was born in Dublin in 1854, the son of an eminent eye-surgeon and a nationalist poetess who wrote under the pseudonym of 'Speranza'. He went to Trinity College, Dublin and then to Magdalen College, Oxford, where he began to propagandize the new Aesthetic (or 'Art for Art's sake') Movement. Despite winning a first and the Newdigate Prize for poetry, Wilde failed to obtain an Oxford fellowship, and was forced to earn a living by lecturing and writing for periodicals. He published a largely unsuccessful volume of poems in 1881 and in the next year undertook a lecture tour of the United States in order to promote the D'Oyly Carte production of Gilbert and Sullivan's comic opera *Patience*. After his marriage to Constance Lloyd in 1884, he tried to establish himself as a writer, but with little initial success. However, his three volumes of short fiction, *The Happy Prince* (1888), *Lord Arthur Savile's Crime* (1891) and *A House of Pomegranates* (1891), together with his only novel, *The Picture of Dorian Gray* (1891), gradually won him a reputation as a modern writer with an original talent, a reputation confirmed and enhanced by the phenomenal success of his Society Comedies – *Lady Windermere's Fan*, *A Woman of No Importance*, *An Ideal Husband* and *The Importance of Being Earnest*, all performed on the West End stage between 1892 and 1895.

Success, however, was short-lived. In 1891 Wilde had met and fallen extravagantly in love with Lord Alfred Douglas. In 1895, when his success as a dramatist was at its height, Wilde brought an unsuccessful libel action against Douglas's father, the Marquess of Queensberry. Wilde lost the case and two trials later was sentenced to two years' imprisonment for acts of gross indecency. As a result of this experience he wrote *The Ballad of Reading Gaol*. He was released from prison in 1897 and went into an immediate self-imposed exile on the Continent. He died in Paris in ignominy in 1900.

IAN SMALL is professor of English Literature at the University of Birmingham. His publications include *Conditions for Criticism: Authority, Knowledge, and Literature in the Late Nineteenth Century* (1991), *Oscar Wilde Revalued* (1993), and (with Josephine Guy) *Politics and Value in English Studies* (1993) and *Oscar Wilde's Profession: Writing and the Culture Industry in the Late Nineteenth Century* (2001). In 1992 he edited (with Marcus Walsh) *The Theory and Practice of Text-Editing*.

OSCAR WILDE

Complete
Short Fiction

Edited by IAN SMALL

PENGUIN BOOKS

PENGUIN BOOKS

Published by the Penguin Group
Penguin Books Ltd, 80 Strand, London, WC2R ORL, England
Penguin Putnam Inc., 375 Hudson Street, New York, New York 10014, USA
Penguin Books Australia Ltd, 250 Camberwell Road, Camberwell, Victoria 3124, Australia
Penguin Books Canada Ltd, 10 Alcorn Avenue, Toronto, Ontario, Canada M4V 3B2
Penguin Books India (P) Ltd, 11 Community Centre, Panchsheel Park, New Delhi – 110 017, India
Penguin Books (NZ) Ltd, Cnr Rosedale and Airborne Roads, Albany, Auckland, New Zealand
Penguin Books (South Africa) (Pty) Ltd, 24 Sturdee Avenue, Rosebank 2196, South Africa

Penguin Books Ltd, Registered Offices: 80 Strand, London, WC2R ORL, England

www.penguin.com

This edition first published 1994
Reprinted with minor revisions 2003

020

Copyright © Ian Small, 1994, 2003
All rights reserved

The moral right of the editor has been asserted

Printed in England by Clays Ltd, St Ives plc

ISBN-13: 978-0-141-43969-3

www.greenpenguin.co.uk

Penguin Books is committed to a sustainable
future for our business, our readers and our planet.
This book is made from Forest Stewardship
Council™ certified paper.

THE STORY OF PENGUIN CLASSICS

Before 1946 ...'Classics' are mainly the domain of academics and students, without readable editions for everyone else. This all changes when a little-known classicist, E. V. Rieu, presents Penguin founder Allen Lane with the translation of Homer's *Odyssey* that he has been working on and reading to his wife Nelly in his spare time.

1946 *The Odyssey* becomes the first Penguin Classic published, and promptly sells three million copies. Suddenly, classic books are no longer for the privileged few.

1950s Rieu, now series editor, turns to professional writers for the best modern, readable translations, including Dorothy L. Sayers's *Inferno* and Robert Graves's *The Twelve Caesars*, which revives the salacious original.

1960s The Classics are given the distinctive black jackets that have remained a constant throughout the series's various looks. Rieu retires in 1964, hailing the Penguin Classics list as 'the greatest educative force of the 20th century'.

1970s A new generation of translators arrives to swell the Penguin Classics ranks, and the list grows to encompass more philosophy, religion, science, history and politics.

1980s The Penguin American Library joins the Classics stable, with titles such as *The Last of the Mohicans* safeguarded. Penguin Classics now offers the most comprehensive library of world literature available.

1990s The launch of Penguin Audiobooks brings the classics to a listening audience for the first time, and in 1999 the launch of the Penguin Classics website takes them online to a larger global readership than ever before.

The 21st Century Penguin Classics are rejacketed for the first time in nearly twenty years. This world famous series now consists of more than 1300 titles, making the widest range of the best books ever written available to millions – and constantly redefining the meaning of what makes a 'classic'.

The Odyssey continues ...

The best books ever written

PENGUIN 🐧 CLASSICS

SINCE 1946

Find out more at www.penguinclassics.com

Contents

Chronology

1854   Oscar Fingal O'Flahertie Wilde born (he added 'Wills' in the 1870s) on 16 October at 21 Westland Row, Dublin.

1855   His family move to 1 Merrion Square in Dublin.

1857   Birth of Isola Wilde, Oscar's sister.

1858   Birth of Constance Mary Lloyd, Wilde's future wife.

1864   Wilde's father is knighted following his appointment as Queen Victoria's 'Surgeon Oculist' the previous year. Wilde attends Portora Royal School, Enniskillen.

1867   Death of Isola Wilde.

1871–4 At Trinity College, Dublin, reading Classics and Ancient History.

1874–8 At Magdalen College, Oxford, reading Classics and Ancient History ('Greats').

1875   Travels in Italy with his tutor from Dublin, J. P. Mahaffy.

1876   First poems published in Dublin University Magazine. Death of Sir William Wilde.

1877   Further travels in Italy, and in Greece.

1878   Wins the Newdigate Prize for Poetry in Oxford with 'Ravenna'. Takes a double first from Oxford. Moves to London and starts to establish himself as a popularizer of Aestheticism.

1879   Meets Constance Lloyd.

1881   *Poems* published at his own expense; not well received critically.

1882   Lecture tour of North America, speaking on art, aesthetics and decoration. Revised edition of *Poems* published.

1883   His first play, *Vera; or, The Nihilists* performed in New York; it is not a success.

1884   Marries Constance Lloyd in London, honeymoon in Paris and Dieppe.

1885   Moves into 16 Tite Street, Chelsea. Cyril Wilde born.

1886   Vyvyan Wilde born. Meets Robert Ross, to become his lifelong friend and, in 1897, his literary executor. Ross might have been Wilde's first homosexual lover.

1887   Becomes the editor of *Lady's World: A Magazine of Fashion and Society*, and changes its name to *Woman's World*. Publication of 'The Canterville Ghost' and 'Lord Arthur Savil's Crime'.

1888   *The Happy Prince and Other Tales* published; on the whole well-received.

1889   'Pen, Pencil and Poison' (on the forger and poisoner Thomas Griffiths Wainewright), 'The Decay of Lying' (a dialogue in praise of artifice over nature and art over morality), 'The Portrait of Mr W.H.' (on the supposed identity of the dedicatee of Shakespeare's sonnets) all published.

1890   *The Picture of Dorian Gray* published in the July number of *Lippincott's Monthly Magazine*; fierce debate between Wilde and hostile critics ensues. 'The True Function and Value of Criticism' (later revised and included in *Intentions* as 'The Critic as Artist') published.

1891   Wilde's first meeting with Lord Alfred Douglas ('Bosie'). *The Duchess of Padua* performed in New York. 'The Soul of Man Under Socialism' and 'Preface to Dorian Gray' published in February and March in the *Fortnightly Review*. The revised and extended edition of *The Picture of Dorian Gray* published by Ward, Lock and Company in April. *Intentions* (collection of critical essays), *Lord Arthur Savile's Crime and Other Stories* and *A House of Pomegranates* (fairy-tales) published.

1892   *Lady Windermere's Fan* performed at St James's Theatre, London (February to July).

1893   *Salomé* published in French. *A Woman of No Importance* performed at Haymarket Theatre, London.

1894   *Salome* published in English with illustrations by Aubrey Beardsley; Douglas is the dedicatee. *The Sphinx*, a poem with illustrations by Charles Ricketts, published.

1895   *An Ideal Husband* opens at Haymarket Theatre in January; it is followed by the hugely successful *The Importance of Being Earnest* at St James's Theatre in February. On 28 February Wilde returns to his club, the Albemarle, to find a card from Douglas's father, the Marquess of Queensberry, accusing Wilde of 'posing as a somdomite' (sodomite). Wilde quickly takes out an action accusing Queensberry of criminal libel. In April Queensberry appears at the Old Bailey and is acquitted, following a successful plea of justification on the basis that Wilde was guilty of homosexual behaviour. Wilde is immediately arrested, after ignoring his friends' advice to flee the country. In May he is tried twice at the Old Bailey, and on 25 May sentenced to two years' imprisonment with hard labour for 'acts of gross indecency with another male person'. In July he is sent to Wandsworth Prison. In November he is declared bankrupt, and shortly afterwards transferred to Reading Gaol.

1896   Death of Wilde's mother, Lady Jane Francesca Wilde ('Speranza').

1897   Wilde writes the long letter to Douglas that would be later entitled 'De Profundis'. In May Wilde is released from prison, and sails for Dieppe by the night ferry. He never returns to Britain.

1898   *The Ballad of Reading Gaol* published pseudonymously as C.3.3, Wilde's cell-number in Reading Gaol. Wilde moves to Paris in February. Constance Wilde (who had by now changed her name to Holland) dies.

1899   Willie (b. 1852), Wilde's elder brother, dies.

1900   In January Queensberry dies. By July Wilde himself is very ill with a blood infection. On 29 November he is received into the Roman Catholic Church, and dies on 30 November in the Hôtel d'Alsace in Paris.

1905   An abridged version of *De Profundis*, edited by Robert Ross, published.

1908   The *Collected Works*, edited by Robert Ross, are published.

Introduction

This volume of Oscar Wilde's short fiction collects those stories originally published in the late 1880s and early 1890s. Most appeared first in periodicals and were then collected in three separate books: *The Happy Prince and Other Tales* (1888), *Lord Arthur Savile's Crime and Other Stories* (1891) and *A House of Pomegranates* (1891). This volume prints in addition Wilde's 'Poems in Prose' and 'The Portrait of Mr. W. H.' – a periodical essay, part-fiction and part-literary criticism, published in *Blackwood's Edinburgh Magazine* in 1889.[1] These works are some of Wilde's earliest, written during his middle thirties when he was still trying to establish himself as a serious writer in the London literary world. Indeed, Wilde found his first volume of fiction, *The Happy Prince*, difficult to place; in 1888 he submitted the manuscript to Macmillan, one of the most distinguished literary publishers of the time. At Oxford Wilde knew a son of the family, George Macmillan, and he assiduously used this undergraduate connection to try to sell his early work to the firm. The report of Macmillan's anonymous reader, however, was less than favourable, and it contained what has proved to be one of the least perspicacious judgements in nineteenth-century literary history:

There is undoubtedly point and cleverness in the way in wh[ich] these stories are told. The writer has, no doubt, the literary knack – the point and finish. You feel at once the hand of the man who knows how to write. Two or three of the stories are very pretty, but I can hardly say as a whole that they have any striking imaginative brilliance – nor do I think that they would be likely to rush into marked popularity. They are pretty and bright, but they hardly strike into the reader's mind. They are good and respectable. Whether they are more than that, I doubt.[2]

Not surprisingly, Macmillan refused the volume, and in June 1890 Alexander, George's brother, also rejected Wilde's famous novel, *The Picture of Dorian Gray*, returning the manuscript of it with almost indecent haste. *Dorian Gray* was finally brought out by Ward Locke, one of the less reputable Victorian publishing houses; *The Happy Prince and Other Tales* had been published earlier by David Nutt, another minor firm. It is ironic that today both pieces are considered to be among the most distinguished and popular works of late nineteenth-century fiction: *Dorian Gray* has been dramatized and filmed, and 'The Happy Prince' is frequently anthologized and has been turned into an animated film. The idea of Wilde hawking his manuscripts from publisher to publisher fits uneasily with the image of him which has been transmitted to the twentieth century, one associated with accomplished but effortless achievement. In fact, this myth – of a Wilde who, in his own words, put his genius into his life and his talent into his works – is far from the truth. Wilde was successful as a writer for only a relatively short period in his life, and then as a dramatist, rather than as a writer of fiction. Fame, and the financial and social success which accompanied it, came only in 1892, with the enormously successful first production of *Lady Windermere's Fan*, and it lasted until the middle of 1895 when the run of *The Importance of Being Earnest* was halted by the scandal surrounding Wilde's trials and subsequent imprisonment. On his release from prison in 1897 Wilde lived in self-imposed exile in France and Italy, begging from friends and never recapturing his former reputation. He died in 1900 in relative obscurity.

At the point in his career when Wilde began writing his short fiction, what reputation he did possess was that which attached to what we should now call a 'media personality' rather than a writer. He had been born and brought up in Dublin, the second son of Sir William and Lady Wilde. His father was an eminent eye surgeon and his mother an Irish nationalist who wrote poetry under the pseudonym of 'Speranza'. Oscar was educated at Portora Royal School and Trinity College, Dublin, where he was taught by the eminent classicist John Pentland Mahaffy and from where he won a scholarship to Magdalen College, Oxford, taking in 1878 a first-class honours degree in *Literae Humaniores* (in, that is, Greek and Latin literature, history and philosophy). He also distinguished himself by winning the Newdigate Prize for his poem 'Ravenna'. The Oxford years were not, however, a complete success, for although Wilde succeeded in impressing dedicated friends, such as George Macmillan, he was also becoming adept at making lifelong enemies. His relationships would continue to follow this pattern of 'friend or foe' right up until the first of his trials when he found that the counsel for his opponent, the Marquess of Queensberry, was none other than Edward Carson, an old enemy from his days at Trinity. Another setback at Oxford, but one which had more immediate and serious consequences, was Wilde's failure to secure a fellowship at Magdalen College: with it one possible route to literary fame was closed. A contemporary – such as Walter Pater – could support a modestly successful literary career by virtue of a fellowship at Brasenose College; Wilde, however, was forced to build a literary career in a different way. In the absence of the relative financial security of an academic post, he moved to London, and set about making himself known to the rich and powerful in London Society.

Much of his effort was spent on cultivating an image that would distinguish him in the fashionable milieu of London literary life. At Trinity, and later at Oxford, Wilde had become interested in the literary movement known as Aestheticism. Associated initially with French writers such as Théophile Gautier and Charles Baudelaire, and later in Britain with the work of Algernon Swinburne and Walter Pater, Aestheticism, or the 'Art for Art's Sake' movement, advocated the separation of artistic from ethical concerns. Followers of this movement were known popularly as Aesthetes and were generally the subject of public disapproval, if not outright contempt. In his search for a suitable image to engage literary society, Wilde fixed upon that of the Aesthete; indeed he perfected the role to such an extent that in the late 1870s and early 1880s he enjoyed modest celebrity as the prototypical 'Aesthete'. He adopted a special 'Aesthetic' dress and hair cut which had their origins in a fancy-dress ball which he had attended as an undergraduate. Distinguished by this flamboyant appearance, and later by the witty conversation for which he was to become renowned, Wilde socialized conscientiously, attending fashionable parties, first nights and private views. On the strength of his new-found celebrity, he undertook in December 1881 a highly successful lecture tour in the United States in order to promote Richard D'Oyly Carte's production of Gilbert and Sullivan's comic opera *Patience*, which was taken by some to be a satire on Wilde's own 'Aesthetic' posing. The lecture tour made Wilde money, and brought him further celebrity as the spokesman for what the press (and Wilde himself) had called a 'new Renaissance' of art, a concern that we can now identify with the broadly based revival of interest in the applied and decorative arts which occurred in Britain in the last half of Victoria's reign. However, during this season of celebrity, success as a writer continued to elude him. In 1881 he had published a collection of poems, but at his own expense; moreover the volume attracted mainly hostile criticism.

Wilde returned briefly to New York in 1883 to see the first night of his melodrama *Vera; Or, the Nihilists*, but the play was not well received. In 1884 he married Constance Lloyd. They moved to 16 (now 33) Tite Street, Chelsea, a house which had been designed for them by the fashionable architect, E. W. Godwin. The couple had two sons, Cyril and Vyvyan, born in 1885 and 1886 respectively. Like so many other late nineteenth-century writers, including Rudyard Kipling and George Bernard Shaw, Wilde, finding himself with a wife and young family to support, was forced to turn his hand to journalism. In the early 1880s, he earned his money through book reviewing for periodicals such as the *Pall Mall Gazette* and the *Dramatic Review*; and for a period in the mid-eighties he even edited the periodical *Woman's World*.

Wilde published *The Happy Prince and Other Tales* in 1888, but literary success eluded him really until 1891, when four of his books appeared in the same year. All consisted of earlier material, some of it in a revised form: *Lord Arthur Savile's Crime and Other Stories*, *Intentions* (a collection of four critical dialogues or essays), *The Picture of Dorian Gray*, and *A House of Pomegranates*. His play *The Duchess of Padua* was also produced in New York under the title *Guido Ferranti*. But most significantly, 1891 saw Wilde begin work on the first of his Society Comedies, *Lady Windermere's Fan*. The play was staged by George Alexander at the St James's

Theatre in 1892. It was a considerable artistic and financial success; indeed it is estimated to have earned Wilde in excess of £11,000, a sum worth much more then than it is now. In the same year *Salome*, Wilde's biblical drama, was refused a licence by the Lord Chamberlain's Office, but the final three Society Comedies, which established Wilde's literary fame, followed in quick succession: *A Woman of No Importance* and *A Ideal Husband* were produced by Herbert Beerbohm Tree at the Haymarket Theatre in April 1893 and January 1895 respectively; and Wilde's masterpiece, *The Importance of Being Earnest*, opened at the St James's Theatre in February 1895, making Wilde the toast of the fashionable theatres of the West End.

The story of how this dazzling success was transformed into disgrace, imprisonment and destitution in a matter of weeks is one of the best-known narratives in literary history. In 1891 the poet Lionel Johnson had introduced Wilde to Lord Alfred Douglas, the third son of the Marquess of Queensberry, then, as Wilde had been a decade or so earlier, an undergraduate at Magdalen College, Oxford. Wilde fell deeply and tragically in love, and the affair with 'Bosie' (as Douglas was known to his family) is the most exhaustively moralized of all nineteenth-century male – male relationships. Perhaps its two most important aspects were its very public nature and the violent and unpredictable reaction of Douglas's father. Douglas insisted upon flaunting his relationship with Wilde, possibly with the intention of hurting his father, and he cared little how his behaviour affected any of the parties concerned. Matters were further complicated by the mysterious death in 1894 of Viscount Drumlanrig, Douglas's half-brother, and by the rumour that he had been involved in a homosexual scandal implicating prominent members of British public life, including perhaps the Prime Minister himself, Lord Rosebery. Partly as a consequence of the death of Drumlanrig and partly because of the public nature of the affair with Lord Alfred, Queensberry prosecuted what amounted to a vendetta against Wilde. He tried to create a public scene on the first night of *The Importance of Being Earnest*, but was thwarted by the timely intervention of the theatre's management. Two weeks later, on 28 February 1895, he left at the Albemarle Club a card that carried the inaccurately spelt but mortifyingly exact inscription 'For Oscar Wilde posing as a somdomite'. Despite the advice of most of his friends, Wilde sued Queensberry for criminal libel. Under cross-examination Wilde made a number of compromising revelations, and the case went against him. He was soon arrested on charges made under the Criminal Law Amendment Act of 1885, which made both private and public homosexual relationships between men illegal. The specific accusations concerned acts of gross indecency with young, lower-class male prostitutes. The jury at what was effectively Wilde's second trial failed to agree. A retrial took place, and on 25 May 1895 Wilde was convicted, receiving a sentence of two years' imprisonment with hard labour, one which could involve a regime of both solitary confinement and repetitive, debilitating manual tasks. Wilde movingly described this prison regime in letters on prison reform written to the *Morning Chronicle* and in a long bitter letter of recrimination written to Douglas which was later published under the title of *De Profundis*. During his time in prison Wilde was declared bankrupt and his possessions were sold. After his release he led a nomadic existence on the Continent. Constance died in 1898, leaving him a small annuity of £150 a year, but he was denied access to his children. In November 1900 Wilde grew ill and underwent an operation to his ear. This last illness was diagnosed at the time as cerebral meningitis; a more recent account has suggested tertiary syphilis. Whatever the cause, Wilde died in obscurity and poverty in Paris on 30 November.

The stories in Wilde's volumes *The Happy Prince* and *A House of Pomegranates* are *fairy* stories – they are stories written for parents to tell to their children. Moreover filial and parental relationships – particularly, the idea of adult responsibility to children – form an important theme within the stories. So, for example, in 'The Selfish Giant', the role of the child is to educate the giant into the art of good parenting, and the giant's reward for learning the values of tolerance and altruism is a divine death-bed revelation: the child he has cared for becomes mysteriously and magically transformed into an image of Christ offering His hand to lead the giant to heaven. It is also significant that in the early stories

Wilde always sees parenting from a child's point of view; so the narrative focus is always the child's perception of a good parent, and not the parent's perception of a good child. Wilde goes further by suggesting that to be a good parent – that is, to show tolerance and kindness towards children – is a moral education for the adult, and as such, is as necessary for the adult as for the child. All of this represents a thoroughgoing if simple reversal of the conventional fairy tale form, for Wilde's stories run directly counter to the nineteenth-century tradition of moral tales for children that emphasize the role of parents in educating recalcitrant children into the norms and values of *adult* culture. Good examples of this tradition are to be found in the characters of Mrs Do-as-you-would-be-done-by and Mrs Be-done-by-as-you-did, both of whom are agents in the moral re-education of the chimney-sweep Tom in Charles Kingsley's *The Water Babies* (1862–3), a work which had as its subtitle 'A Fairy Story for a Land-Baby'. In fact the strategy of reversal is a key to understanding the whole of Wilde's work, and in the stories it can be seen in both their thematic concerns and formal structures.

The sympathy and tenderness with which Wilde describes the child's world was unusual in Victorian Britain, and it obviously derived from his own experience as a son and a father. Here it is worth noting that he had a particularly close relationship with his mother, Lady Jane Wilde. From the moment he left Ireland for Oxford right up to her death in 1896, Wilde was in regular contact with her; over a hundred of her letters to him survive. Most are familiar, conversational accounts of friends and neighbours and of common interests. Some reveal Lady Wilde to be in what she describes as trouble, and not infrequently she asks Oscar for financial support. So, for example, in 1894 she can be found writing to him that 'You are always good & kind & generous, & have ever been my best aid and companion'.[3] That Wilde should have preserved such a copious correspondence from his mother is in itself revealing; more significant, however, is that after his father's death Wilde willingly took on a protective filial role. Interestingly, though, in this role-reversal Lady Wilde did not relinquish all of her maternal authority, for there is some evidence that Wilde's refusal to flee to France to avoid arrest after the failure of his prosecution of Queensberry was made at the insistence of his mother who wished him to stand trial to clear his name.

Given Wilde's attachment to his mother, it should be unsurprising that he took his own role as parent equally seriously: indeed the evidence suggests that he was a loving and devoted father. For example, in a letter to Robert Ross (reputedly Wilde's first homosexual lover, certainly a lifelong faithful friend and his painstaking literary executor) Wilde reveals the importance of his children in his life – so much so that even his gay relationships had to be accommodated to them: in this instance Wilde's lover (and as such, interloper into his family matters) becomes a friend to his children, Cyril and Vyvyan, here through the present of a kitten:

> 16, Tite Street,
> Chelsea, S.W.
>
> My Dear Bobbie,
>   The kitten is quite lovely – it does not *look* white, indeed it looks a sort of tortoise-shell colour . . . with velvety dark [patches?] but as you said it was white I have given orders that it is always to be spoken of as the 'white kitten' – the children are enchanted with it, and sit, one on each side of its basket, worshipping – It seems pensive – perhaps it is thinking of some dim rose-garden in Persia, and wondering why it is kept in this chill England.
>   I hope you are enjoying yourself at Cambridge – whatever people may say against Cambridge, it is certainly the best preparatory school for Oxford that I know.
>   After this insult I better stop.
>   Yours ever
>   Oscar Wilde.[4]

Devotion to his children continued through Wilde's disgrace and up to his death. After his release from prison and despite his protests, Constance forbade Wilde to see Cyril and Vyvyan. Wilde persuaded several of his friends, principally More Adey and Ada Leverson, to act as intermediaries, but Constance was never reconciled to Wilde re-establishing contact with the children, and he died without ever seeing them again. In *Time Remembered*, Vyvyan (Wilde's second son) described receiving a letter from a Frenchman called Ernest Lajeunesse. Lajeunesse recalled an encounter with Wilde in a French hotel in the late 1890s – that is, after the trials, imprisonment and self-imposed exile:

One autumn evening, while putting on my overcoat after finishing my meal, I clumsily upset something, perhaps a salt-cellar, on Monsieur Sébastien's [i.e., Sebastian Melmoth, the pseudonym by which Wilde was known in France] table. He said nothing, but my mother scolded me and told me to apologize, which I did, distressed by my clumsiness. But Monsieur Sébastien turned to my mother and said: 'Be patient with your little boy. One must always be patient with them. If, one day, you should find yourself separated from him . . .' I did not give him time to finish his sentence, but asked him: 'Have you got a little boy?' 'I've got two', he said. 'Why don't you bring them here with you?' My mother interrupted . . . 'It doesn't matter; it doesn't matter at all,' he said with a sad smile. 'They don't come here with me because they are too far away . . .' Then he took my hand, drew me to him and kissed me on both cheeks. I bade him farewell, and then I saw that he was crying. And we left.

While kissing me he had said a few words which I did not understand. But on the following day we arrived before him and a bank employee who used to sit at a table on the other side of us asked us: 'Did you understand what Monsieur Sébastien said last evening?' 'No,' we replied. 'He said, in English: "Oh, my poor dear boys!"'[5]

There is no external evidence to support Lajeunesse's anecdote, but nor is there any reason to doubt its truthfulness. In fact it affirms all that we do know about the constancy of Wilde's affection towards his children, a sentiment which in turn goes some way towards explaining that initial decision to write fairy stories, and why the themes of love and self-denial figure so strongly in them.

There were, however, other, more pragmatic reasons for Wilde's decision to write fiction. One of the most striking qualities of his short stories is that they can be read both as simple and satisfying narratives for children and as self-conscious literary exercises. This combination of naivety and complexity largely derives from Wilde's exploitation of a number of popular sub-genres that had grown up in the second half of the nineteenth century in response to changes in the audiences and markets for literature. Developments in printing technologies in the 1860s and 1870s had substantially reduced the cost of book production, making it possible to print books relatively cheaply for the first time. Together with a new impetus towards universal adult literacy, formalized in John Forster's 1870 Education Act, and a new focus on leisure brought about through greater prosperity and legislation limiting working hours, this new availability of cheap books led to a dramatic increase in the potential readership for literature. New sub-genres were developed to exploit the interests of these new groups of readers, whose tastes and backgrounds were different from the limited and exclusive readership addressed by writers earlier in the century. The most popular of the new sub-genres included ghost stories, detective fiction, the sensation novel, and the fairy tale. Authors who successfully exploited these new topics and sub-genres – such as Arthur Conan Doyle, Mary Elizabeth Braddon, Wilkie Collins and J. S. Le Fanu – became household names; and demand for new kinds of stories was so strong that it fuelled a succession of new monthly and fortnightly magazines, the best known of which included *Temple Bar*, *London Society*, *Tit Bits*, *The Argosy*, *Tinsley's Magazine* and *Belgravia*.

In the late 1880s, when he had made the transition from writing journalism to writing fiction, a literary reputation was not Wilde's only concern; he also required financial security. Earlier works, such as the *Poems* and his first plays, *The Duchess of Padua* and *Vera; Or, the Nihilists* had failed on both counts. When Wilde tried again to establish a literary career, this time more attuned to the twin imperatives of creative and commercial success, he struck out in a new and altogether more modern direction: that of the short story. In choosing to try his hand at fairy tales, and subsequently at ghost and detective stories, Wilde was no doubt attempting to emulate the fame (and indeed fortune) of popular writers such as Collins, Braddon and Conan Doyle. Moreover, he was not the only 'serious' writer to entertain such ambitions; a few years later, Henry James also tried his hand at writing in a popular genre, and the result proved to be one of his most successful works, *The Turn of the Screw*. However, Wilde was also very keen to keep himself aloof from those writers who merely pandered to what he would later refer to scathingly as 'Public Opinion'. The result of this dilemma was the emergence of Wilde's most distinctive stylistic device, that of parody. Almost all of his short stories represent parodies of the sub-genres which he appropriated. Sometimes these parodies are overt and witty – in, for example, 'Sir Arthur Savile's Crime' or 'The Canterville Ghost'. On other occasions, as in 'The Fisherman and his Soul', they are more subtle and complex, and the line between the parodic and the serious is deliberately blurred. This last kind of story is the most self-consciously 'literary', and it is in this group that we find the strongest prefiguring of the complexity of Wilde's later work.

Whether overt or subtle, Wilde's parodies are never simply playful: to appreciate their serious and subversive edge we need to understand the *social* dimension of the popular genres which he was exploiting. Ghost stories, detective fiction and fairy stories all deploy a number of stock literary devices, the most important of which include an emphasis on plot, rather than character; the use of character types such as heroes and heroines, villains and cads; and the adoption of a simple moral framework in which good and evil are rigidly and unambiguously defined, so much so that the qualities constituting good and evil are not in question. These elements are most visible in the endings to such stories where the most important function of plot is to reward good and punish evil: so princesses marry their princes, detectives catch their villains, and ghosts are finally and successfully laid to rest. All these actions represent a restoration of the social order, and through it, a reaffirmation of the status quo. In this sense the tendency of ghost stories, detective fiction and fairy stories is always towards a conservatism: they dramatize the triumph and cohesiveness of society's values when they are threatened by an outside evil force, whether it comes in the shape of a wicked witch, criminal, or malevolent ghost. Here it is worth remembering that fairy stories were originally told to children, and so their primary social function was to educate children into the values of a culture, in particular its moral values.

The effect of Wilde's stories could not be more different. While they seem to adhere to the stock literary devices of a genre –

the simple plotting, the use of given character-types, the deployment of a rigid moral framework, and so on – they nevertheless invest those devices with a very different significance. Evil and the threats which it poses are certainly present in Wilde's stories: they come as the vengeful Canterville ghost, or in Lord Arthur's attempts to commit murder, or in the fisherman's decision to cut away his soul (and so his moral conscience). But the threat that evil presents typically functions to *expose* the corruption and poverty of society's values, rather than – as with the conventional moral tale – to reaffirm their intrinsic rightness. In this way Wilde subverts the traditional moralizing function of such fiction; or, as he says rather more forcefully in the 'Preface' to *The Picture of Dorian Gray*: 'There is no such thing as a moral or an immoral book. Books are well written, or badly written. That is all.' Indeed, rather than socialize readers into the given values of a culture, Wilde's stories subtly criticize the nature of those values, and the ways in which they bring about social cohesion in the first place. Some examples will make this strategy a little clearer.

'Lord Arthur Savile's Crime' parodies elements of both detective and sensation fiction. The story is set in the fashionable salon of Lady Windermere, and it concerns a visiting palmist's prediction to the young Lord Arthur Savile that he will commit a murder. Savile, who is engaged to be married, decides that, out of gentlemanly duty to his future wife, he must fulfil his destiny before his marriage takes place, and the story relates his various attempts to find a suitable murder victim. After a string of failures, one night by chance he comes across the same palmist leaning over the railings of the Thames. Lord Arthur seizes his opportunity and pushes the palmist into the river. The murder committed, and his destiny fulfilled, Savile returns home in relief, marries his bride and lives happily ever after. The whole plot represents a comic inversion of the traditional devices of moral justice, for here it is the act of murder (rather than the unmasking of the murderer) which brings about the restoration of social order: the murderer becomes the hero (and ironically is rewarded through a happy marriage) and the victim becomes the villain (and equally ironically is punished by death). The consequence of this inversion is that the reader's attention is focused not on the traditional triumph of good over evil, but rather on the kind of society where murder is justified on the grounds of right conduct, where 'right' means observing the codes of gentlemanly behaviour. So Wilde's narrator ironically muses on the nature of duty:

[Arthur] recognised none the less clearly where his duty lay, and was fully conscious of the fact that he had no right to marry until he had committed the murder. This done, he could stand before the altar with Sybil Merton, and give his life into her hands without terror of wrongdoing. This done, he could take her to his arms, knowing that she would never have to blush for him, never have to hang her head in shame . . .

Many men in his position would have preferred the primrose path of dalliance to the steep heights of duty; but Lord Arthur was too conscientious to set pleasure above principle. (pp. 180–81)

This comic discrepancy between manners and morals is a theme that preoccupied Wilde for the rest of his creative life, and it is central to his best-known works, the Society Comedies.

The plot of 'The Canterville Ghost' works by means of a similar series of inversions. Once again it is the evil avenging ghost which turns out to be the hero, and the members of the bourgeois family he taunts become the villains. The plot is relatively simple: it concerns the ghost's varied but failed attempts to frighten a new American family that has recently taken up residence in his house. The problem for the ghost lies in the family's matter-of-fact sensibilities: they refuse to believe in the supernatural, and always find a perfectly rational explanation for the ghost's manifestations and the disruption it causes, such as strange noises and stains on the floor. In the dénouement of the story, the ghost is finally laid to rest by the youngest daughter, for she alone has the imagination to understand him, and it is her sympathy with his suffering which finally allows him to find peace. Like 'Lord Arthur Savile's Crime', the story reserves its censure not for the ghost and the murder he committed, but rather for the family (and by extension the society) responsible for criminalizing him. So when Virginia, the young girl, complains that 'it is very wrong to kill anyone', the ghost interjects:

'Oh, I hate the cheap severity of abstract ethics! My wife was very plain, never had my ruffs properly starched, and knew nothing about cookery. Why, there was a buck I had shot in Hogley Woods, a magnificent pricket, and do you know how she had it sent up to table? However, it is no matter now, for it is all over, and I don't think it was very nice of her brothers to starve me to death, though I did kill her.'

'Starve you to death? Oh, Mr Ghost, I mean Sir Simon, are you hungry? I have a sandwich in my case. Would you like it?' (p. 224)

The implication is that criminal behaviour is produced by society's lack of moral imagination and sympathy – a theme Wilde was to take up in his essay 'The Soul of Man under Socialism' and, in relation to his own imprisonment, in *De Profundis*. There Wilde charges his society with responsibility for his suffering:

Society takes upon itself the right to inflict appalling punishments on the individual, but it also has the supreme vice of shallowness, and fails to realise what it has done. When the man's punishment is over, it leaves him to himself: that is to say it abandons him at the very moment when its highest duty towards him begins. It is really ashamed of its own actions, and shuns those whom it has punished, as people shun a creditor whose debt they cannot pay, or one on whom they have inflicted an irreparable, an irredeemable wrong. I claim on my side that if I realise what I have suffered, Society should realise what it has inflicted on me: and that there should be no bitterness or hate on either side.[6]

Interestingly, very shortly after this passage, Wilde describes the way events in his own life had been 'prefigured' in his 'art'. 'Some of it,' he observes, 'is in "The Happy Prince": some of it is in "The Young King".'[7]

'The Fisherman and his Soul' represents the most complex kind of parody. The tale itself is reminiscent of Hans Christian Andersen's 'The Little Mermaid' and Matthew Arnold's poem 'The Forsaken Merman'. In both of these examples, the moral of the tale centres on the familiar Christian opposition between the spiritual (represented by the conscience and the soul) and the material (represented by worldly attractions and the body), which is in turn presented in terms of the equally familiar opposition between selfless love and selfish desire. Needless to say, both Andersen's fairy tale and Arnold's poem describe the corrupting influence of the material world and sexual desire, and the ultimate triumph of the power of selfless spiritual love whose reward is immortality. In Wilde's tale, however, these moral dichotomies are not nearly so clear cut. Most obviously, the roles of soul and body seem to be reversed: so when Wilde's fisherman cuts away his soul from his body, the soul embarks upon a life of dedicated immorality which parodies and inverts the three temptations of Christ. Paradoxically, it is the soul which expresses a fascination with the sins of the flesh and the world, rather than the other way around:

And ever did his Soul tempt him with evil, and whisper of terrible things. Yet did it not prevail against him, so great was the power of his love.

And after the year was over, the Soul thought within himself, 'I have tempted my master with evil, and his love is stronger than I am.' (p. 144)

Wilde seems to suggest that the fisherman's ability to withstand temptation derives from the power of his love. Usually love is considered to be the prerogative of the soul or spirit, but in Wilde's story, love (and the values associated with it, such as fidelity) reside in the *body*. The implication is that for Wilde 'true love' is exclusively of the body and is therefore (sexual) desire, a conclusion which completely reverses the traditional Christian understanding of the relationship between body and soul, where soul is the regulating conscience of the body.

The society and its values which Wilde implicates in his stories (and in his other works, including the comedies and *De Profundis*) is always fashionable Society, with a capital 'S' – that is, the world of privilege, of rich salons and country houses. London 'Society', as this group was more formally known, was composed of the upper middle-class or the aristocracy, that Victorian and Edwardian group which Max Beerbohm later called the 'upper ten thousand' of British society. In Wilde's work this group is characterized in terms of its philistinism and materialism: they know, in the words of Lord Darlington in *Lady Windermere's Fan*, 'the price of everything and the value of nothing'. The group is represented in the stories by characters such as the daughter of the professor in 'The Nightingale and the Rose', who prefers material objects – the Chamberlain's nephew's gift of jewels – to the rose created at the cost of the nightingale's life; or the Town Councillors in 'The Happy Prince' who, unlike the swallow (and, finally, unlike God), can recognize only the material worth of the prince, and who ensure that when his statue is stripped of its gold and its precious jewels it is discarded for scrap; or the spoilt Infanta and her entourage who value the faithful dwarf only in terms of his ability to entertain them. In all these stories the worldly materialism of society is set against the values of selfless love and fidelity. That opposition is not in itself unusual; what marks out Wilde's tales is that such values are always vulnerable to society's vulgar self-interest. In traditional fairy tales, love and constancy are rewarded in this world; in Wilde's tales love and constancy lead generally to the destruction of the individual (the one possible exception is 'The Model Millionaire'). Some of the tales compensate for this destruction with the reward of a Christian afterlife: so the Happy Prince and the swallow are taken to 'God's garden of Paradise'; and the Selfish Giant dies after being vouchsafed a beatific vision of Christ. But in general terms the most striking feature of the tales is the impotence of good – a conclusion which is again reiterated in the Society Comedies. For example in a play such as *Lady Windermere's Fan*, selfless love (couched in terms of maternal devotion) is powerful enough to 'save' the reputation of Lady Windermere, but impotent in the face of the hypocrisy of London Society. Similarly, in *A Woman of No Importance*, the selfless charity of Mrs Arbuthnot is only a source of humour for the social circles that ultimately reject her. In the stories the most forceful statement of the impotence of selfless love occurs in the final sentence of 'The Star-Child', where the child's realization of the value of selflessness is followed by a death which renders that love ineffectual:

Yet ruled he not long, so great had been his suffering, and so bitter the fire of his testing, for after the space of three years he died. And he who came after him ruled evilly. (p. 164)

It is also worth noting that the society Wilde describes is always recognizably Victorian, and that the archetypal themes of suffering that he appropriates are given a specific Victorian character. So the temptation of the Soul in 'The Fisherman and his Soul' is described in terms of the lure of the Orient, a favourite motif in late Victorian culture, strikingly articulated in works such as Gustave Flaubert's *Salammbô*, Sir Richard Burton's translation of *The Arabian Nights* and Edward Fitzgerald's *The Rubáiyát of Omar Khayyám*. (Indeed the exoticism of the East figures in other stories by Wilde – in 'The Young King', and 'The Birthday of the Infanta', for example.) Similarly, suffering in 'The Happy Prince' is given a specific Victorian cast. The Swallow notices

the rich making merry in their beautiful houses, while the beggars were sitting at the gates. He flew into dark lanes, and saw the white faces of starving children looking out listlessly at the black streets. Under the archway of a bridge two little boys were lying in one another's arms to try and keep themselves warm. (pp. 9–10)

The pattern is repeated in 'The Young King', where the misery which the King witnesses is reminiscent of Victorian social-problem novels – those novels, such as Elizabeth Gaskell's *Mary Barton*, written in middle years of the nineteenth century and which dwell upon the misery of the urban poor:

The meagre daylight peered in through the grated windows, and showed him the gaunt figures of the weavers bending over their cases. Pale, sickly-looking children were crouched on the huge crossbeams. As the shuttles dashed through the warp they lifted up the heavy battens, and when the shuttles stopped they let the battens fall and pressed the threads together. Their faces were pinched with famine, and their thin hands shook and trembled. Some haggard women were seated at a table sewing. A horrible odour filled the place. The air was foul and heavy, and the walls dripped and streamed with damp. (p. 87)

In these ways the stories are topical, and they point to a potential audience more sophisticated and knowing than the child desiring to be told a good story. In letters to *The Speaker* and *The Pall Mall Gazette* in 1891 Wilde ridiculed the idea that 'the extremely limited vocabulary at the disposal of the British child' should be 'the standard by which the prose of an artist is to be judged'.

Indeed, it is the simultaneous appeal to both child and adult that explains what is perhaps the most striking and modern element in all the stories – those themes to which their subtexts allude.

In the last decade there has been a trend among critics of Wilde's work to see submerged concerns in his fiction and drama, particularly that of nineteenth-century sexual politics. So some critics read the representation of marriage and sexual ethics in the Society Comedies in terms of a covert discussion of the politics of male–male desire. For example, the plot of *A Woman of No Importance* appears to be concerned with a familiar tension between child and parents: Lord Illingworth, the father of the illegitimate Gerald Arbuthnot, competes for his affections with his mother. However, cancelled drafts of the play confirm the suspicions of some gay critics that Wilde's original concern was with plotting the dynamics of male–male desire between an older and powerful man (here Lord Illingworth) and a younger, attractive *ingénu* (Gerald Arbuthnot). Vestiges of this concern remain in the stereotyped character of Mrs Arbuthnot, whose emotions have little interest in the play, despite the fact that in terms of the plot, she is the central character. More tangible evidence for the existence of this submerged gay politics exists in a scene maintained throughout the drafts of the play. It concerns a group of middle-aged women discussing their 'ideal man'. In their conversation the dowagers emphasize qualities such as physical beauty, idleness and fecklessness, thereby self-consciously overturning Victorian stereotypes that value duty, work and protectiveness. It is significant that precisely these qualities are attributed to Dorian Gray and are features of the way in which Wilde describes the object of desire in homosexual relationships. Equally significant is the fact that these qualities are attributed to an ideal *man*, and not an ideal husband. By divorcing the terms 'man' and 'husband', Wilde resists the Victorian practice of defining men by means of their relationships with women.

It is possible to see the existence of exactly the same kind of subtexts in some of the short stories. For example, when Wilde's narrator in 'The Model Millionaire' describes Hughie Erskine, he does so in a particularly loaded way: Erskine is a 'delightful ineffectual young man with a perfect profile and no profession'. Wilde re-used the terms of the description in an epigram published in 'Phrases and Philosophies for the Use of the Young':

There is something tragic about the enormous number of young men there are in England at the present moment who start life with a perfect profile, and end by adopting some useful profession.[8]

The same epigram was read out by Edward Carson in court in Wilde's first trial, and the connection with Wilde's own homosexuality was thereby made explicit. Lord Arthur Savile shares some of the physical characteristics of Hughie Erskine: he is described as having led the 'delicate and luxurious life of a young man of birth and fortune, a life exquisite in its freedom from sordid care, its beautiful boyish insouciance'. The motivation for Lord Arthur's actions is of course his relationship with his fiancée, but the story itself completely disregards her feelings: indeed its interest is firmly with Lord Arthur and not, as might be expected, with the force of heterosexual desire.

However the most elaborate of all of Wilde's coded references to a gay double life occurs in the 'Portrait of Mr. W. H.' There Wilde's character (once again called Erskine) describes his relationship with Cyril Graham which is reminiscent of Wilde's representation of male–male desire, and uncannily prophetic of his own relationship with Bosie and Bosie's father, the Marquess of Queensberry:

I don't think that Lord Crediton cared very much for Cyril ... Cyril had very little affection for him, and was only too glad to spend most of his holidays with us in Scotland. They never really got on together at all. Cyril thought him a bear, and he thought Cyril effeminate. He was effeminate, I suppose, in some things, though he was a very good rider and a capital fencer. In fact he got the foils before he left Eton. But he was very languid in his manner, and not a little vain of his good looks, and had a strong objection to football. The two things that really gave him pleasure were poetry and acting. At Eton he was always dressing up and reciting Shakespeare ... I was absurdly devoted to him ... he always set an absurdly high value on personal appearance, and once read a paper before our debating society to prove that it was better to be good-looking than to be good. He certainly was wonderfully handsome. People who did not like him, Philistines and college tutors, and young men reading for the Church, used to say that he was merely pretty; but there was a great deal more in his face than mere prettiness. I think he was the most splendid creature I ever saw, and nothing could exceed the grace of his movements, the charm of his manner. He fascinated everybody who was worth fascinating, and a great many people who were not. He was often wilful and petulant, and I used to think him dreadfully insincere. (pp. 52-3)

It is significant that the main theme of this story is forgery and deception: what matters in it is not the distinction between truth and lies, but the ability to sustain a falsehood – a topic which Wilde explored more fully in his critical essay 'The Decay of Lying' in *Intentions* (1891). Other stories provide variations on this basic theme. For example, the plots of both 'The Sphinx Without a Secret' and 'The Model Millionaire' involve a sustained deception. In the first story a widow so desires mystery that she literally invents a secret life; the irony of Wilde's tale is that the heroine is only living the appearance of a double life. What matters is not the 'reality' behind the secret, but the woman's ability to sustain a belief in secrecy. In the second story, a millionaire wants to be painted as a pauper. During the course of the story the millionaire fails to keep his real identity secret, but his lie is maintained by the work of art – his portrait. In both these examples the emphasis is not upon truth-telling, for the revelation of truth is seen as a mark of failure; success, rather, is an ability to sustain a deception. At one level this reversal of the traditional truth-telling functions of ghost and mystery stories is part of Wilde's larger strategy of parody, but the interest in revaluing deception is also part of the sexual subtexts of the stories. The idea of deception in Wilde's own life was linked to an emerging homosexual consciousness, and the need to maintain secrets, as his trials later revealed, was both urgent and necessary. Indeed nearly all of Wilde's writing is obsessed with the parallel themes of secrecy, unmasking and love, and an enduring element of many of the stories is the power of a love which society either ignores or sees as illicit: the dwarf's inappropriate love for the

Infanta; the Fisherman's profane love for the Mermaid; the invisibility of the Prince's benevolent love of children, and so on. In this way the archetypal themes of the stories, those of love and its vulnerability, are placed in very specific contexts. So, on the one hand, the stories fulfil the demands of their respective genres by being accessible to a very wide audience; but the contexts they use invariably work in a coded way, and are to be recognized only by a coterie audience. This dual function makes for the stories' paradoxical qualities – their simplicity and complexity, their heterodoxy and orthodoxy, their appeal to adults and children.

In the century since Wilde's short stories were first published, literary critics have had little to say about them: either they are dismissed as juvenilia, or they are simply overlooked. However, many of the themes and character-types so well known from Wilde's comedies were first established in the stories. Like his drama the stories are inhabited by witty dandies who keep their social world at a distance with a well-turned epigram, by the imperious dowagers who run London Society and by innocents who suffer for their honesty in a corrupt world. In the stories we see Wilde developing the parodic style that the plays were to make famous. The stories also reveal his early interest in the devices of melodrama, the ability of paradox to shock the reader and the power of irony to subvert stock literary forms. Most importantly, the stories are also the first expression of Wilde's preoccupation with the oppositions that were to dominate his life and thought. They include love and desire; art and life; sincerity and insincerity; innocence and sin; honesty and deceit; altruism and greed; self-sacrifice and self-aggrandizement. Wilde spent the years between 1889 and 1895, the main creative period of his life, trying to overturn and revalue the basis of these oppositions and the moral and social values which gave them force. In his own life, Wilde tragically failed in this ambition; but the fiction, by contrast and despite the negativism of Macmillan's anonymous reader, has proved remarkably successful.

Notes to the Introduction

1 I also print as an appendix one fugitive text by Wilde; see 'A Note on the Texts'.

2 The reader's report survives in the Macmillan archive in the British Library. See Macmillan Add. 5594; 16 Feb. 1888.

3 The unpublished sequence of letters is housed in the William Andrews Clark Memorial Library, The University of California at Los Angeles (ALS W67126 W6721: 1894. Sept? 27).

4 Letter to Ross (c. 1888), also in the Clark Library; published in Ian Small, *Oscar Wilde Revalued: An Essay on New Materials and Methods of Research* (Greensboro, NC, 1993), p. 45.

5 Vyvyan Holland, *Time Remembered* (1966), pp. 11–12.

6 Wilde, *De Profundis* (letter to Lord Alfred Douglas, Jan–March. 1897) in *The Letters of Oscar Wilde*, ed. Sir Rupert Hart-Davis (London, 1963), p. 470.

7 Ibid. 475.

8 'Phrases and Philosophies for the Use of the Young', in *The Oxford Authors: Oscar Wilde*, ed. Isobel Murray (Oxford, 1989), p. 573.

Further Reading

Biography

Richard Ellmann, *Oscar Wilde* (London, 1987).
Merlin Holland, *The Wilde Album* (1997).
E. H. Mikhail, ed., *Oscar Wilde: Interviews and Recollections* 2 vols. (London, 1979).
H. Montgomery Hyde, *The Trials of Oscar Wilde* (London, 1948).
Richard Pine, *Oscar Wilde* (Dublin, 1983).

Editions

The Picture of Dorian Gray, ed. Donald E. Lawler (New York, 1988).
Lady Windermere's Fan, ed. Ian Small (London, 1980).
A Woman of No Importance, ed. Ian Small (London, 1993)
An Ideal Husband, ed. Russell Jackson (London, 1993).
The Importance of Being Earnest and Other Plays, ed. Richard Allen Cave (Harmondsworth, 2000)
The Importance of Being Earnest, ed. Russell Jackson (London, 1980; revd edn, 1993).
Vera; Or, the Nihilists, ed. Frances Miriam Reed (Dyfed, 1989).
Oscar Wilde: Poems and Poems in Prose (*The Complete Works of Oscar Wilde*, Vol. I), eds. Bobby Fong and Karl Beckson (Oxford, 2000).
Oscar Wilde's Oxford Notebooks, eds. Philip E. Smith, II, and Michael S. Helfand (New York, 1989).
Isobel Murray, ed., *The Oxford Authors: Oscar Wilde* (Oxford, 1989).
Robert Ross, ed., *The First Collected Edition of the Works of Oscar Wilde* (London, 1908–22).

Collections of Criticism

Karl Beckson, ed., *Oscar Wilde: The Critical Heritage* (London, 1970).

Richard Ellmann, ed., *Oscar Wilde: A Collection of Critical Essays* (Englewood Cliffs, NJ, 1969; repr., 1986).

Regenia Gagnier, ed., *Critical Essays on Oscar Wilde* (New York, 1991).

Peter Raby, ed., *The Cambridge Companion to Oscar Wilde* (Cambridge, 1997).

Willliam Tydeman, ed., *Wilde: Comedies* (London, 1982).

Criticism

Karl Beckson, *The Oscar Wilde Encyclopedia* (New York, 1998).

Alan Bird, *The Plays of Oscar Wilde* (London, 1977).

Regenia Gagnier, *Idylls of the Marketplace: Oscar Wilde and the Victorian Public* (London, 1987).

Josephine M. Guy and Ian Small, *Oscar Wilde's Profession: Writing and the Culture Industry in the Late Nineteenth Century* (Oxford, 2000).

Norbert Kohl, *Oscar Wilde: The Works of a Conformist Rebel* (Cambridge, 1991).

Christopher Nassaar, *Into The Demon Universe: A Literary Exploration of Oscar Wilde* (New Haven, Conn., 1974).

Kerry Powell, *Oscar Wilde and the Theatre of the 1890s* (Cambridge, 1990).

Peter Raby, *Oscar Wilde* (Cambridge, 1988).

Rodney Shewan, *Oscar Wilde: Art and Egotism* (London, 1977).

Alan Sinfield, *The Wilde Century* (London, 1994).

Letters

The Letters of Oscar Wilde, ed., Rupert Hart-Davis (London, 1963).

More Letters of Oscar Wilde, ed., Rupert Hart-Davis (London, 1985).

The Complete Letters of Oscar Wilde, eds. Merlin Holland and Rupert Hart-Davis (London, 2000).

Bibliography

Ian Fletcher and John Stokes, 'Oscar Wilde', in *Anglo-Irish Literature: A Review of Research*, ed. Richard J. Finneran (New York, 1976), 48–137.

Ian Fletcher and John Stokes, 'Oscar Wilde', in *Recent Research on Anglo-Irish Writers: A Supplement to Anglo-Irish Literature: A Review of Research*, ed. Richard J. Finneran (New York, 1983), 21–47.

Stuart Mason, [C. S. Millard], *A Bibliography of Oscar Wilde* (London, 1914).

E. H. Mikhail, *Oscar Wilde: An Annotated Bibliography of Criticism* (London, 1978).

Ian Small, *Oscar Wilde: Recent Research* (Gerrards Cross, Bucks., 2000).

—, *Oscar Wilde Revalued: An Essay on New Materials and Methods of Research* (Greensboro, NC, 1993).

A Note on the Texts

The present edition prints the first book-version of the stories contained in *The Happy Prince and Other Tales* (London: David Nutt, 1888), *A House of Pomegranates* (London: Osgood, McIlvaine and Co., 1891), and *Lord Arthur Savile's Crime* (London: Osgood, McIlvaine and Co., 1891). In all three cases there were very few editions in Wilde's lifetime. There were only two of *The Happy Prince*; *A House of Pomegranates* was printed in only one edition, and unsold copies of it were remaindered around the time of Wilde's death. *Lord Arthur Savile's Crime*, too, was printed in only one British and one American edition. In most cases, and in keeping with much nineteenth-century writing practice, the first publication of the stories had in fact been in the periodical press. However, the argument for reprinting the stories as they were collected in book-form is two-fold. In the first instance, the act of collecting, arranging and revising the stories represented an artistic judgement and reveals Wilde's mature attitude towards his texts. The second reason involves the pragmatics of nineteenth-century publishing. Generally speaking, once their work had passed out of their hands authors had little control over it; however, book publishing offered significantly more artistic and authorial control than the periodical press, which had to answer to much narrower constraints. Moreover, the three volumes of stories were reprinted in their book-form in the collected edition of Wilde's works published by Robert Ross, his literary executor, and Ross clearly had access to authorial material not available to the modern editor. I have collated Ross's edition with the first book editions; the only differences are of punctuation, but these have not been noted. As with Ross, in printing the first book editions I have made some silent corrections to obvious printers' errors.

This volume also reprints 'The Portrait of Mr. W. H.' and the 'Poems in Prose'. The identity of both works presents the editor with a problem. 'The Portrait of Mr. W. H.' is an anomalous text; it hovers between Wilde's stories and his literary criticism (as it is represented in *Intentions*). The decision to include it here is based on what I have judged to be its basic narrative impetus, together with its clear relationship with popular sub-genres which Wilde explored in his other stories. The difficulty over categorizing the 'Poems in Prose' is similar in that they can be seen either as poems or prose-narratives. My decision to include them here is largely pragmatic: there is no modern edition of Wilde's poems, and the 'Poems in Prose' (in their entirety) are relatively inaccessible for the general reader. Moreover, all are informed by a strong narrative structure and have a generic relationship with some of the stories.

Unlike the volumes of stories, the texts for both 'The Portrait of Mr. W. H.' and the 'Poems in Prose' are taken from periodicals. ('The Portrait of Mr. W. H.' is from *Blackwood's Edinburgh Magazine*, July, 1889, and the six 'Poems in Prose' from *The Fortnightly Review*, July, 1894.) There is a second and much longer version of 'The Portrait of Mr. W. H.', which was printed posthumously. The reasons for not taking this work as base-text are two-fold. In the first instance it is much more literary criticism than prose fiction; more importantly, although there is clear evidence that Wilde wished to extend the original periodical essay of 'The Portrait of Mr. W. H.' into a book, we have no way of knowing whether the posthumous text in fact does represent that intention. (For details of this issue, see Horst Schroeder, *Oscar Wilde, 'The Portrait of Mr. W. H.' – Its Composition, Publication and Reception*, Braunschweig, 1984.)

Finally I print one fugitive text as an appendix. It is a fragment of a hitherto unknown poem in prose, 'Elder-tree'; the manuscript of it is in the William Andrews Clark Memorial Library at the University of California, Los Angeles. It was first published in my *Oscar Wilde Revalued* (1993).

The Happy Prince and
Other Tales

To Carlos Blacker[1]

The Happy Prince

High above the city, on a tall column, stood the statue of the Happy Prince. He was gilded all over with thin leaves of fine gold, for eyes he had two bright sapphires, and a large red ruby glowed on his sword-hilt.

He was very much admired indeed. 'He is as beautiful as a weathercock,' remarked one of the Town Councillors who wished to gain a reputation for having artistic tastes; 'only not quite so useful,' he added, fearing lest people should think him unpractical, which he really was not.

'Why can't you be like the Happy Prince?' asked a sensible mother of her little boy who was crying for the moon. 'The Happy Prince never dreams of crying for anything.'

'I am glad there is some one in the world who is quite happy,' muttered a disappointed man as he gazed at the wonderful statue.

'He looks just like an angel,' said the Charity Children[1] as they came out of the cathedral in their bright scarlet cloaks, and their clean white pinafores.

'How do you know?' said the Mathematical Master, 'you have never seen one.'

'Ah! but we have, in our dreams,' answered the children; and the Mathematical Master frowned and looked very severe, for he did not approve of children dreaming.

One night there flew over the city a little Swallow. His friends had gone away to Egypt six weeks before, but he had stayed behind, for he was in love with the most beautiful Reed. He had met her early in the spring as he was flying down the river after a big yellow moth, and had been so attracted by her slender waist that he had stopped to talk to her.

'Shall I love you?' said the Swallow, who liked to come to the point at once, and the Reed made him a low bow. So he flew round and round her, touching the water with his wings, and making silver ripples. This was his courtship, and it lasted all through the summer.

'It is a ridiculous attachment,' twittered the other Swallows, 'she has no money, and far too many relations;' and indeed the river was quite full of Reeds. Then, when the autumn came, they all flew away.

After they had gone he felt lonely, and began to tire of his lady-love. 'She has no conversation,' he said, 'and I am afraid that she is a coquette, for she is always flirting with the wind.' And certainly, whenever the wind blew, the Reed made the most graceful curtsies. 'I admit that she is domestic,' he continued, 'but I love travelling, and my wife, consequently, should love travelling also.'

'Will you come away with me?' he said finally to her; but the Reed shook her head, she was so attached to her home.

'You have been trifling with me,' he cried, 'I am off to the Pyramids. Good-bye!' and he flew away.

All day long he flew, and at night-time he arrived at the city. 'Where shall I put up?' he said; 'I hope the town has made preparations.'

Then he saw the statue on the tall column. 'I will put up there,' he cried; 'it is a fine position with plenty of fresh air.' So he alighted just between the feet of the Happy Prince.

'I have a golden bedroom,' he said softly to himself as he looked round, and he prepared to go to sleep; but just as he was putting his head under his wing a large drop of water fell on him. 'What a curious thing!' he cried, 'there is not a single cloud in the sky, the stars are quite clear and bright, and yet it is raining. The climate in the north of Europe is really dreadful. The Reed used to like the rain, but that was merely her selfishness.'

Then another drop fell.

'What is the use of a statue if it cannot keep the rain off?' he said; 'I must look for a good chimney-pot,' and he determined to fly away.

But before he had opened his wings, a third drop fell, and he looked up, and saw – Ah! what did he see?

The eyes of the Happy Prince were filled with tears, and tears were running down his golden cheeks. His face was so beautiful in the moonlight that the little Swallow was filled with pity.

'Who are you?' he said.

'I am the Happy Prince.'

'Why are you weeping then?' asked the Swallow; 'you have quite drenched me.'

'When I was alive and had a human heart,' answered the statue, 'I did not know what tears were, for I lived in the Palace of Sans-Souci[2] where sorrow is not allowed to enter. In the daytime I played with my companions in the garden, and in the evening I led the dance in the Great Hall. Round the garden ran a very lofty wall, but I never cared to ask what lay beyond it, everything about me was so beautiful. My courtiers called me the Happy Prince, and happy indeed I was, if pleasure be happiness. So I lived, and so I died. And now that I am dead they have set me up here so high that I can see all the ugliness and all the misery of my city, and though my heart is made of lead yet I cannot choose but weep.'

'What, is he not solid gold?' said the Swallow to himself. He was too polite to make any personal remarks out loud.

'Far away,' continued the statue in a low musical voice, 'far away in a little street there is a poor house. One of the windows is open, and through it I can see a woman seated at a table. Her face is thin and worn, and she has coarse, red hands, all pricked by the needle, for she is a seamstress. She is embroidering passion-flowers on a satin gown for the loveliest of the Queen's maids-of-honour to wear at the next Court-ball. In a bed in the corner of the room her little boy is lying ill. He has a fever, and is asking for oranges. His mother has nothing to give him but river water, so he is crying. Swallow, Swallow, little Swallow, will you not bring her the ruby out of my sword-hilt? My feet are fastened to this pedestal and I cannot move.'

'I am waited for in Egypt,' said the Swallow. 'My friends are flying up and down the Nile, and talking to the large lotus-flowers. Soon they will go to sleep in the tomb of the great King.

The King is there himself in his painted coffin. He is wrapped in yellow linen, and embalmed with spices. Round his neck is a chain of pale green jade, and his hands are like withered leaves.'

'Swallow, Swallow, little Swallow,' said the Prince, 'will you not stay with me for one night, and be my messenger? The boy is so thirsty, and the mother so sad.'

'I don't think I like boys,' answered the Swallow. 'Last summer, when I was staying on the river, there were two rude boys, the miller's sons, who were always throwing stones at me. They never hit me, of course; we swallows fly far too well for that, and besides, I come of a family famous for its agility; but still, it was a mark of disrespect.'

But the Happy Prince looked so sad that the little Swallow was sorry. 'It is very cold here,' he said; 'but I will stay with you for one night, and be your messenger.'

'Thank you, little Swallow,' said the Prince.

So the Swallow picked out the great ruby from the Prince's sword, and flew away with it in his beak over the roofs of the town.

He passed by the cathedral tower, where the white marble angels were sculptured. He passed by the palace and heard the sound of dancing. A beautiful girl came out on the balcony with her lover. 'How wonderful the stars are,' he said to her, 'and how wonderful is the power of love!' 'I hope my dress will be ready in time for the State-ball,' she answered; 'I have ordered passion-flowers to be embroidered on it; but the seamstresses are so lazy.'

He passed over the river, and saw the lanterns hanging to the masts of the ships. He passed over the Ghetto, and saw the old Jews bargaining with each other, and weighing out money in copper scales. At last he came to the poor house and looked in. The boy was tossing feverishly on his bed, and the mother had fallen asleep, she was so tired. In he hopped, and laid the great ruby on the table beside the woman's thimble. Then he flew gently round the bed, fanning the boy's forehead with his wings. 'How cool I feel,' said the boy, 'I must be getting better;' and he sank into a delicious slumber.

Then the Swallow flew back to the Happy Prince, and told

him what he had done. 'It is curious,' he remarked, 'but I feel quite warm now, although it is so cold.'

'That is because you have done a good action,' said the Prince. And the little Swallow began to think, and then he fell asleep. Thinking always made him sleepy.

When day broke he flew down to the river and had a bath.

'What a remarkable phenomenon,' said the Professor of Ornithology as he was passing over the bridge. 'A swallow in winter!' And he wrote a long letter about it to the local newspaper. Every one quoted it, it was full of so many words that they could not understand.

'To-night I go to Egypt,' said the Swallow, and he was in high spirits at the prospect. He visited all the public monuments, and sat a long time on top of the church steeple. Wherever he went the Sparrows chirruped, and said to each other, 'What a distinguished stranger!' so he enjoyed himself very much.

When the moon rose he flew back to the Happy Prince. 'Have you any commissions for Egypt?' he cried; 'I am just starting.'

'Swallow, Swallow, little Swallow,' said the Prince, 'will you not stay with me one night longer?'

'I am waited for in Egypt,' answered the Swallow. To-morrow my friends will fly up to the Second Cataract.[3] The river-horse couches there among the bulrushes, and on a great granite throne sits the God Memnon.[4] All night long he watches the stars, and when the morning star shines he utters one cry of joy, and then he is silent. At noon the yellow lions come down to the water's edge to drink. They have eyes like green beryls,[5] and their roar is louder than the roar of the cataract.'

'Swallow, Swallow, little Swallow,' said the Prince, 'far away across the city I see a young man in a garret. He is leaning over a desk covered with papers, and in a tumbler by his side there is a bunch of withered violets. His hair is brown and crisp, and his lips are red as a pomegranate, and he has large and dreamy eyes. He is trying to finish a play for the Director of the Theatre, but he is too cold to write any more. There is no fire in the grate, and hunger has made him faint.'

'I will wait with you one night longer,' said the Swallow, who really had a good heart. 'Shall I take him another ruby?'

'Alas! I have no ruby now,' said the Prince; 'my eyes are all that I have left. They are made of rare sapphires, which were brought out of India a thousand years ago. Pluck out one of them and take it to him. He will sell it to the jeweller, and buy food and firewood, and finish his play.'

'Dear Prince,' said the Swallow, 'I cannot do that;' and he began to weep.

'Swallow, Swallow, little Swallow,' said the Prince, 'do as I command you.'

So the Swallow plucked out the Prince's eye, and flew away to the student's garret. It was easy enough to get in, as there was a hole in the roof. Through this he darted, and came into the room. The young man had his head buried in his hands, so he did not hear the flutter of the bird's wings, and when he looked up he found the beautiful sapphire lying on the withered violets.

'I am beginning to be appreciated,' he cried; 'this is from some great admirer. Now I can finish my play,' and he looked quite happy.

The next day the Swallow flew down to the harbour. He sat on the mast of a large vessel and watched the sailors hauling big chests out of the hold with ropes. 'Heave a-hoy!' they shouted as each chest came up. 'I am going to Egypt!' cried the Swallow, but nobody minded, and when the moon rose he flew back to the Happy Prince.

'I am come to bid you good-bye,' he cried.

'Swallow, Swallow, little Swallow,' said the Prince, 'will you not stay with me one night longer?'

'It is winter,' answered the Swallow, 'and the chill snow will soon be here. In Egypt the sun is warm on the green palm-trees, and the crocodiles lie in the mud and look lazily about them. My companions are building a nest in the Temple of Baalbec, and the pink and white doves are watching them, and cooing to each other. Dear Prince, I must leave you, but I will never forget you, and next spring I will bring you back two beautiful jewels in place of those you have given away. The ruby shall be redder than a red rose, and the sapphire shall be as blue as the great sea.'

'In the square below,' said the Happy Prince, 'there stands a little match-girl. She has let her matches fall in the gutter, and they are all spoiled. Her father will beat her if she does not bring home some money, and she is crying. She has no shoes or stockings, and her little head is bare. Pluck out my other eye, and give it to her, and her father will not beat her.'

'I will stay with you one night longer,' said the Swallow, 'but I cannot pluck out your eye. You would be quite blind then.'

'Swallow, Swallow, little Swallow,' said the Prince, 'do as I command you.'

So he plucked out the Prince's other eye, and darted down with it. He swooped past the match-girl, and slipped the jewel into the palm of her hand. 'What a lovely bit of glass,' cried the little girl; and she ran home, laughing.

Then the Swallow came back to the Prince. 'You are blind now,' he said, 'so I will stay with you always.'

'No, little Swallow,' said the poor Prince, 'you must go away to Egypt.'

'I will stay with you always,' said the Swallow, and he slept at the Prince's feet.

All the next day he sat on the Prince's shoulder, and told him stories of what he had seen in strange lands. He told him of the red ibises, who stand in long rows on the banks of the Nile, and catch gold fish in their beaks; of the Sphinx, who is as old as the world itself, and lives in the desert, and knows everything; of the merchants, who walk slowly by the side of their camels, and carry amber beads in their hands; of the King of the Mountains of the Moon,[6] who is as black as ebony, and worships a large crystal; of the great green snake that sleeps in a palm-tree, and has twenty priests to feed it with honey-cakes; and of the pygmies who sail over a big lake on large flat leaves, and are always at war with the butterflies.

'Dear little Swallow,' said the Prince, 'you tell me of marvellous things, but more marvellous than anything is the suffering of men and of women. There is no Mystery so great as Misery. Fly over my city, little Swallow, and tell me what you see there.'

So the Swallow flew over the great city, and saw the rich making merry in their beautiful houses, while the beggars were sitting at the gates. He flew into dark lanes, and saw the white faces of starving children looking out listlessly at the black streets. Under the archway of a bridge two little boys were lying in one another's arms to try and keep themselves warm. 'How hungry we are!' they said. 'You must not lie here,' shouted the Watchman, and they wandered out into the rain.

Then he flew back and told the Prince what he had seen.

'I am covered with fine gold,' said the Prince, 'you must take it off, leaf by leaf, and give it to my poor; the living always think that gold can make them happy.'

Leaf after leaf of the fine gold the Swallow picked off, till the Happy Prince looked quite dull and grey. Leaf after leaf of the fine gold he brought to the poor, and the children's faces grew rosier, and they laughed and played games in the street. 'We have bread now!' they cried.

Then the snow came, and after the snow came the frost. The streets looked as if they were made of silver, they were so bright and glistening; long icicles like crystal daggers hung down from the eaves of the houses, everybody went about in furs, and the little boys wore scarlet caps and skated on the ice.

The poor little Swallow grew colder and colder, but he would not leave the Prince, he loved him too well. He picked up crumbs outside the baker's door when the baker was not looking, and tried to keep himself warm by flapping his wings.

But at last he knew that he was going to die. He had just strength to fly up to the Prince's shoulder once more. 'Good-bye, dear Prince!' he murmured, 'will you let me kiss your hand?'

'I am glad that you are going to Egypt at last, little Swallow,' said the Prince, 'you have stayed too long here; but you must kiss me on the lips, for I love you.'

'It is not to Egypt that I am going,' said the Swallow. 'I am going to the House of Death. Death is the brother of Sleep, is he not?'

And he kissed the Happy Prince on the lips, and fell down dead at his feet.

At that moment a curious crack sounded inside the statue, as if something had broken. The fact is that the leaden heart had snapped right in two. It certainly was a dreadfully hard frost.

Early the next morning the Mayor was walking in the square

below in company with the Town Councillors. As they passed the column he looked up at the statue: 'Dear me! how shabby the Happy Prince looks!' he said.

'How shabby indeed!' cried the Town Councillors, who always agreed with the Mayor, and they went up to look at it.

'The ruby has fallen out of his sword, his eyes are gone, and he is golden no longer,' said the Mayor; 'in fact, he is little better than a beggar!'

'Little better than a beggar,' said the Town Councillors.

'And here is actually a dead bird at his feet!' continued the Mayor. 'We must really issue a proclamation that birds are not to be allowed to die here.' And the Town Clerk made a note of the suggestion.

So they pulled down the statue of the Happy Prince. 'As he is no longer beautiful he is no longer useful,'[7] said the Art Professor at the University.

Then they melted the statue in a furnace, and the Mayor held a meeting of the Corporation to decide what was to be done with the metal. 'We must have another statue, of course,' he said, 'and it shall be a statue of myself.'

'Of myself,' said each of the Town Councillors, and they quarrelled. When I last heard of them they were quarrelling still.

'What a strange thing!' said the overseer of the workmen at the foundry. 'This broken lead heart will not melt in the furnace. We must throw it away.' So they threw it on a dust-heap where the dead Swallow was also lying.

'Bring me the two most precious things in the city,' said God to one of His Angels; and the Angel brought Him the leaden heart and the dead bird.

'You have rightly chosen,' said God, 'for in my garden of Paradise this little bird shall sing for evermore, and in my city of gold the Happy Prince shall praise me.'

The Nightingale and the Rose

'She said that she would dance with me if I brought her red roses,' cried the young Student; 'but in all my garden there is no red rose.'

From her nest in the holm-oak tree the Nightingale heard him, and she looked out through the leaves, and wondered.

'No red rose in all my garden!' he cried, and his beautiful eyes filled with tears. 'Ah, on what little things does happiness depend! I have read all that the wise men have written, and all the secrets of philosophy are mine, yet for want of a red rose is my life made wretched.'

'Here at last is a true lover,' said the Nightingale. 'Night after night have I sung of him, though I knew him not: night after night have I told his story to the stars, and now I see him. His hair is dark as the hyacinth-blossom, and his lips are red as the rose of his desire; but passion has made his face like pale ivory, and sorrow has set her seal upon his brow.'

'The Prince gives a ball to-morrow night,' murmured the young Student, 'and my love will be of the company. If I bring her a red rose she will dance with me till dawn. If I bring her a red rose, I shall hold her in my arms, and she will lean her head upon my shoulder, and her hand will be clasped in mine. But there is no red rose in my garden, so I shall sit lonely, and she will pass me by. She will have no heed of me, and my heart will break.'

'Here indeed is the true lover,' said the Nightingale. 'What I sing of, he suffers: what is joy to me, to him is pain. Surely Love is a wonderful thing. It is more precious than emeralds, and dearer than fine opals. Pearls and pomegranates cannot buy it, nor is it set forth in the market-place. It may not be purchased of the merchants, nor can it be weighed out in the balance for gold.'

'The musicians will sit in their gallery,' said the young Student, 'and play upon their stringed instruments, and my love will dance to the sound of the harp and the violin. She will dance so lightly that her feet will not touch the floor, and the courtiers in their gay dresses will throng round her. But with me she will not dance, for I have no red rose to give her;' and he flung himself down on the grass, and buried his face in his hands, and wept.

'Why is he weeping?' asked a little Green Lizard, as he ran past him with his tail in the air.

'Why, indeed?' said a Butterfly, who was fluttering about after a sunbeam.

'Why, indeed?' whispered a Daisy to his neighbour, in a soft, low voice.

'He is weeping for a red rose,' said the Nightingale.

'For a red rose!' they cried; 'how very ridiculous!' and the little Lizard, who was something of a cynic, laughed outright.

But the Nightingale understood the secret of the Student's sorrow, and she sat silent in the oak-tree, and thought about the mystery of Love.

Suddenly she spread her brown wings for flight, and soared into the air. She passed through the grove like a shadow, and like a shadow she sailed across the garden.

In the centre of the grass-plot was standing a beautiful Rose-tree, and when she saw it, she flew over to it, and lit upon a spray.

'Give me a red rose,' she cried, 'and I will sing you my sweetest song.'

But the Tree shook its head.

'My roses are white,' it answered; 'as white as the foam of the sea, and whiter than the snow upon the mountain. But go to my brother who grows round the old sun-dial, and perhaps he will give you what you want.'

So the Nightingale flew over to the Rose-tree that was growing round the old sun-dial.

'Give me a red rose,' she cried, 'and I will sing you my sweetest song.'

But the Tree shook its head.

'My roses are yellow,' it answered; 'as yellow as the hair of the mermaiden who sits upon an amber throne, and yellower than the daffodil that blooms in the meadow before the mower comes with his scythe. But go to my brother who grows beneath the Student's window, and perhaps he will give you what you want.'

So the Nightingale flew over to the Rose-tree that was growing beneath the Student's window.

'Give me a red rose,' she cried, 'and I will sing you my sweetest song.'

But the Tree shook its head.

'My roses are red,' it answered, 'as red as the feet of the dove, and redder than the great fans of coral that wave and wave in the ocean-cavern. But the winter has chilled my veins, and the frost has nipped my buds, and the storm has broken my branches, and I shall have no roses at all this year.'

'One red rose is all I want,' cried the Nightingale, 'only one red rose! Is there no way by which I can get it?'

'There is a way,' answered the Tree; 'but it is so terrible that I dare not tell it to you.'

'Tell it to me,' said the Nightingale, 'I am not afraid.'

'If you want a red rose,' said the Tree, 'you must build it out of music by moonlight, and stain it with your own heart's-blood. You must sing to me with your breast against a thorn. All night long you must sing to me, and the thorn must pierce your heart, and your life-blood must flow into my veins, and become mine.'

'Death is a great price to pay for a red rose,' cried the Nightingale, 'and Life is very dear to all. It is pleasant to sit in the green wood, and to watch the Sun in his chariot of gold, and the Moon in her chariot of pearl. Sweet is the scent of the hawthorn, and sweet are the bluebells that hide in the valley, and the heather that blows on the hill. Yet Love is better than Life, and what is the heart of a bird compared to the heart of a man?'

So she spread her brown wings for flight, and soared into the air. She swept over the garden like a shadow, and like a shadow she sailed through the grove.

The young Student was still lying on the grass, where she had left him, and the tears were not yet dry in his beautiful eyes.

'Be happy,' cried the Nightingale, 'be happy; you shall have your red rose. I will build it out of music by moonlight, and stain it with my own heart's-blood. All that I ask of you in return is that you will be a true lover, for Love is wiser than Philosophy, though she is wise, and mightier than Power, though he is mighty. Flame-coloured are his wings, and coloured like flame is his body. His lips are sweet as honey, and his breath is like frankincense.'

The Student looked up from the grass, and listened, but he could not understand what the Nightingale was saying to him, for he only knew the things that are written down in books.

But the Oak-tree understood, and felt sad, for he was very fond of the little Nightingale who had built her nest in his branches.

'Sing me one last song,' he whispered; 'I shall feel very lonely when you are gone.'

So the Nightingale sang to the Oak-tree, and her voice was like water bubbling from a silver jar.

When she had finished her song the Student got up, and pulled a note-book and a lead-pencil out of his pocket.

'She has form,' he said to himself, as he walked away through the grove – 'that cannot be denied to her; but has she got feeling? I am afraid not. In fact, she is like most artists; she is all style, without any sincerity.' She would not sacrifice herself for others. She thinks merely of music, and everybody knows that the arts are selfish. Still, it must be admitted that she has some beautiful notes in her voice. What a pity it is that they do not mean anything, or do any practical good.' And he went into his room, and lay down on his little pallet-bed, and began to think of his love; and, after a time, he fell asleep.

And when the Moon shone in the heavens the Nightingale flew to the Rose-tree, and set her breast against the thorn. All night long she sang with her breast against the thorn, and the cold crystal Moon leaned down and listened. All night long she sang, and the thorn went deeper and deeper into her breast, and her life-blood ebbed away from her.

She sang first of the birth of love in the heart of a boy and a girl. And on the topmost spray of the Rose-tree there blossomed a marvellous rose, petal following petal, as song followed song. Pale was it, at first, as the mist that hangs over the river – pale as the feet of the morning, and silver as the wings of the dawn. As the shadow of a rose in a mirror of silver, as the shadow of a rose in a water-pool, so was the rose that blossomed on the topmost spray of the Tree.

But the Tree cried to the Nightingale to press closer against the thorn. 'Press closer, little Nightingale,' cried the Tree, 'or the Day will come before the rose is finished.'

So the Nightingale pressed closer against the thorn, and louder and louder grew her song, for she sang of the birth of passion in the soul of a man and a maid.

And a delicate flush of pink came into the leaves of the rose, like the flush in the face of the bridegroom when he kisses the lips of the bride. But the thorn had not yet reached her heart, so the rose's heart remained white, for only a Nightingale's heart's-blood can crimson the heart of a rose.

And the Tree cried to the Nightingale to press closer against the thorn. 'Press closer, little Nightingale,' cried the Tree, 'or the Day will come before the rose is finished.'

So the Nightingale pressed closer against the thorn, and the thorn touched her heart, and a fierce pang of pain shot through her. Bitter, bitter was the pain, and wilder and wilder grew her song, for she sang of the Love that is perfected by Death, of the Love that dies not in the tomb.

And the marvellous rose became crimson, like the rose of the eastern sky. Crimson was the girdle of petals, and crimson as a ruby was the heart.

But the Nightingale's voice grew fainter, and her little wings began to beat, and a film came over her eyes. Fainter and fainter grew her song, and she felt something choking her in her throat.

Then she gave one last burst of music. The white Moon heard it, and she forgot the dawn, and lingered on in the sky. The red rose heard it, and it trembled all over with ecstasy, and opened its petals to the cold morning air. Echo[2] bore it to her purple cavern in the hills, and woke the sleeping shepherds from their dreams. It floated through the reeds of the river, and they carried its message to the sea.

'Look, look!' cried the Tree, 'the rose is finished now;' but the Nightingale made no answer, for she was lying dead in the long grass, with the thorn in her heart.

And at noon the Student opened his window and looked out.

'Why, what a wonderful piece of luck!' he cried; 'here is a red rose! I have never seen any rose like it in all my life. It is so beautiful that I am sure it has a long Latin name;' and he leaned down and plucked it.

Then he put on his hat, and ran up to the Professor's house with the rose in his hand.

The daughter of the Professor was sitting in the doorway winding blue silk on a reel, and her little dog was lying at her feet.

'You said that you would dance with me if I brought you a red rose,' cried the Student. 'Here is the reddest rose in all the world. You will wear it to-night next your heart, and as we dance together it will tell you how I love you.'

But the girl frowned.

'I am afraid it will not go with my dress,' she answered; 'and, besides, the Chamberlain's nephew has sent me some real jewels, and everybody knows that jewels cost far more than flowers.'

'Well, upon my word, you are very ungrateful,' said the Student angrily; and he threw the rose into the street, where it fell into the gutter, and a cart-wheel went over it.

'Ungrateful!' said the girl. 'I tell you what, you are very rude; and, after all, who are you? Only a Student. Why, I don't believe you have even got silver buckles to your shoes as the Chamberlain's nephew has;' and she got up from her chair and went into the house.

'What a silly thing Love is,' said the Student as he walked away. 'It is not half as useful as Logic, for it does not prove anything, and it is always telling one of things that are not going to happen, and making one believe things that are not true. In fact, it is quite unpractical, and, as in this age to be practical is everything, I shall go back to Philosophy and study Meta-physics.'

So he returned to his room and pulled out a great dusty book, and began to read.

The Selfish Giant

Every afternoon, as they were coming from school, the children used to go and play in the Giant's garden.

It was a large lovely garden, with soft green grass. Here and there over the grass stood beautiful flowers like stars, and there were twelve peach-trees that in the spring-time broke out into delicate blossoms of pink and pearl, and in the autumn bore rich fruit. The birds sat on the trees and sang so sweetly that the children used to stop their games in order to listen to them. 'How happy we are here!' they cried to each other.

One day the Giant came back. He had been to visit his friend the Cornish ogre, and had stayed with him for seven years. After the seven years were over he had said all that he had to say, for his conversation was limited, and he determined to return to his own castle. When he arrived he saw the children playing in the garden.

'What are you doing here?' he cried in a very gruff voice, and the children ran away.

'My own garden is my own garden,' said the Giant; 'any one can understand that, and I will allow nobody to play in it but myself.' So he built a high wall all round it, and put up a notice-board.

> TRESPASSERS
> WILL BE
> PROSECUTED

He was a very selfish Giant.

The poor children had now nowhere to play. They tried to play on the road, but the road was very dusty and full of hard stones, and they did not like it. They used to wander round the high wall when their lessons were over, and talk about the beautiful garden inside.

'How happy we were there,' they said to each other.

Then the Spring came, and all over the country there were little blossoms and little birds. Only in the garden of the Selfish Giant it was still Winter. The birds did not care to sing in it as there were no children, and the trees forgot to blossom. Once a beautiful flower put its head out from the grass, but when it saw the notice-board it was so sorry for the children that it slipped back into the ground again, and went off to sleep. The only people who were pleased were the Snow and the Frost. 'Spring has forgotten this garden,' they cried, 'so we will live here all the year round.' The Snow covered up the grass with her great white cloak, and the Frost painted all the trees silver. Then they invited the North Wind to stay with them, and he came. He was wrapped in furs, and he roared all day about the garden, and blew the chimney-pots down. 'This is a delightful spot,' he said, 'we must ask the Hail on a visit.' So the Hail came. Every day for three hours he rattled on the roof of the castle till he broke most of the slates, and then he ran round and round the garden as fast as he could go. He was dressed in grey, and his breath was like ice.

'I cannot understand why the Spring is so late in coming,' said the Selfish Giant, as he sat at the window and looked out at his cold white garden; 'I hope there will be a change in the weather.'

But the Spring never came, nor the Summer. The Autumn gave golden fruit to every garden, but to the Giant's garden she gave none. 'He is too selfish,' she said. So it was always Winter there, and the North Wind, and the Hail, and the Frost, and the Snow danced about through the trees.

One morning the Giant was lying awake in bed when he heard some lovely music. It sounded so sweet to his ears that he thought it must be the King's musicians passing by. It was really only a little linnet singing outside his window, but it was so long since he had heard a bird sing in his garden that it seemed to him to be the most beautiful music in the world. Then the Hail stopped dancing over his head, and the North Wind ceased roaring, and a delicious perfume came to him through the open casement. 'I believe the Spring has come at last,' said the Giant; and he jumped out of bed and looked out.

What did he see?

He saw a most wonderful sight. Through a little hole in the wall the children had crept in, and they were sitting in the branches of the trees. In every tree that he could see there was a little child. And the trees were so glad to have the children back again that they had covered themselves with blossoms, and were waving their arms gently above the children's heads. The birds were flying about and twittering with delight, and the flowers were looking up through the green grass and laughing. It was a lovely scene, only in one corner it was still Winter. It was the farthest corner of the garden, and in it was standing a little boy. He was so small that he could not reach up to the branches of the tree, and he was wandering all round it, crying bitterly. The poor tree was still quite covered with frost and snow, and the North Wind was blowing and roaring above it. 'Climb up! little boy,' said the Tree, and it bent its branches down as low as it could; but the boy was too tiny.

And the Giant's heart melted as he looked out. 'How selfish I have been!' he said; 'now I know why the Spring would not come here. I will put that poor little boy on the top of the tree, and then I will knock down the wall, and my garden shall be the children's playground for ever and ever.' He was really very sorry for what he had done.

So he crept downstairs and opened the front door quite softly, and went out into the garden. But when the children saw him they were so frightened that they all ran away, and the garden became Winter again. Only the little boy did not run, for his eyes were so full of tears that he did not see the Giant coming. And the Giant stole up behind him and took him gently in his hand, and put him up into the tree. And the tree broke at once into blossom, and the birds came and sang on it, and the little boy stretched out his two arms and flung them round the Giant's neck, and kissed him. And the other children, when they saw that the Giant was not wicked any longer, came running back, and with them came the Spring. 'It is your garden now, little children,' said the Giant, and he took a great axe and knocked down the wall. And when the people were going to market at twelve o'clock they found the Giant playing with the children in the most beautiful garden they had ever seen.

All day long they played, and in the evening they came to the Giant to bid him good-bye.

'But where is your little companion?' he said: 'the boy I put into the tree.' The Giant loved him the best because he had kissed him.

'We don't know,' answered the children; 'he has gone away.'

'You must tell him to be sure and come here to-morrow,' said the Giant. But the children said that they did not know where he lived, and had never seen him before; and the Giant felt very sad.

Every afternoon, when school was over, the children came and played with the Giant. But the little boy whom the Giant loved was never seen again. The Giant was very kind to all the children, yet he longed for his first little friend, and often spoke of him. 'How I would like to see him!' he used to say.

Years went over, and the Giant grew very old and feeble. He could not play about any more, so he sat in a huge armchair, and watched the children at their games, and admired his garden. 'I have many beautiful flowers,' he said; 'but the children are the most beautiful flowers of all.'

One winter morning he looked out of his window as he was dressing. He did not hate the Winter now, for he knew that it was merely the Spring asleep, and that the flowers were resting.

Suddenly he rubbed his eyes in wonder, and looked and looked. It certainly was a marvellous sight. In the farthest corner of the garden was a tree quite covered with lovely white blossoms. Its branches were all golden, and silver fruit hung down from them, and underneath it stood the little boy he had loved.

Downstairs ran the Giant in great joy, and out into the garden. He hastened across the grass, and came near to the child. And when he came quite close his face grew red with anger, and he said, 'Who hath dared to wound thee?' For on the palms of the child's hands were the prints of two nails, and the prints of two nails were on the little feet.

'Who hath dared to wound thee?' cried the Giant; 'tell me, that I may take my big sword and slay him.'

'Nay!' answered the child; 'but these are the wounds of Love.'

'Who art thou?' said the Giant, and a strange awe fell on him, and he knelt before the little child.

And the child smiled on the Giant, and said to him, 'You let me play once in your garden, to-day you shall come with me to my garden, which is Paradise.'

And when the children ran in that afternoon, they found the Giant lying dead under the tree, all covered with white blossoms.

The Devoted Friend

One morning the old Water-rat put his head out of his hole. He had bright beady eyes and stiff grey whiskers, and his tail was like a long bit of black india-rubber. The little ducks were swimming about in the pond, looking just like a lot of yellow canaries, and their mother, who was pure white with real red legs, was trying to teach them how to stand on their heads in the water.

'You will never be in the best society unless you can stand on your heads,' she kept saying to them; and every now and then she showed them how it was done. But the little ducks paid no attention to her. They were so young that they did not know what an advantage it is to be in society at all.

'What disobedient children!' cried the old Water-rat; 'they really deserve to be drowned.'

'Nothing of the kind,' answered the Duck, 'every one must make a beginning, and parents cannot be too patient.'

'Ah! I know nothing about the feelings of parents,' said the Water-rat; 'I am not a family man. In fact, I have never been married, and I never intend to be. Love is all very well in its way, but friendship is much higher. Indeed, I know of nothing in the world that is either nobler or rarer than a devoted friendship.'

'And what, pray, is your idea of the duties of a devoted friend?' asked a Green Linnet, who was sitting in a willow-tree hard by, and had overheard the conversation.

'Yes, that is just what I want to know,' said the Duck, and she swam away to the end of the pond, and stood upon her head, in order to give her children a good example.

'What a silly question!' cried the Water-rat. 'I should expect my devoted friend to be devoted to me, of course.'

'And what would you do in return?' said the little bird, swinging upon a silver spray, and flapping his tiny wings.

'I don't understand you,' answered the Water-rat.

'Let me tell you a story on the subject,' said the Linnet.

'Is the story about me?' asked the Water-rat. 'If so, I will listen to it, for I am extremely fond of fiction.'

'It is applicable to you,' answered the Linnet; and he flew down, and alighting upon the bank, he told the story of The Devoted Friend.

'Once upon a time,' said the Linnet, 'there was an honest little fellow named Hans.'

'Was he very distinguished?' asked the Water-rat.

'No,' answered the Linnet, 'I don't think he was distinguished at all, except for his kind heart, and his funny round good-humoured face. He lived in a tiny cottage all by himself, and every day he worked in his garden. In all the country-side there was no garden so lovely as his. Sweet-william grew there, and Gilly-flowers, and Shepherds'-purses, and Fair-maids of France. There were damask Roses, and yellow Roses, lilac Crocuses, and gold, purple Violets and white. Columbine and Ladysmock, Marjoram and Wild Basil, the Cowslip and the Flower-de-luce,[1] the Daffodil and the Clove-Pink bloomed or blossomed in their proper order as the months went by, one flower taking another flower's place, so that there were always beautiful things to look at, and pleasant odours to smell.

'Little Hans had a great many friends, but the most devoted friend of all was big Hugh the Miller. Indeed, so devoted was the rich Miller to little Hans, that he [Hans] would never go by his garden without leaning over the wall and plucking a large nosegay, or a handful of sweet herbs, or filling his pockets with plums and cherries if it was the fruit season.

'"Real friends should have everything in common," the Miller used to say, and little Hans nodded and smiled, and felt very proud of having a friend with such noble ideas.

'Sometimes, indeed, the neighbours thought it strange that the rich Miller never gave little Hans anything in return, though he had a hundred sacks of flour stored away in his mill, and six milch cows, and a large flock of woolly sheep; but Hans never troubled his head about these things, and nothing gave him greater pleasure than to listen to all the wonderful things the Miller used to say about the unselfishness of true friendship.

'So little Hans worked away in his garden. During the spring, the summer, and the autumn he was very happy, but when the winter came, and he had no fruit or flowers to bring to the market, he suffered a good deal from cold and hunger, and often had to go to bed without any supper but a few dried pears or some hard nuts. In the winter, also, he was extremely lonely, as the Miller never came to see him then.

'"There is no good in my going to see little Hans as long as the snow lasts," the Miller used to say to his wife, "for when people are in trouble they should be left alone, and not be bothered by visitors. That at least is my idea about friendship, and I am sure I am right. So I shall wait till the spring comes, and then I shall pay him a visit, and he will be able to give me a large basket of primroses, and that will make him so happy."

'"You are certainly very thoughtful about others," answered the Wife, as she sat in her comfortable armchair by the big pinewood fire; "very thoughtful indeed. It is quite a treat to hear you talk about friendship. I am sure the clergyman himself could not say such beautiful things as you do, though he does live in a three-storied house, and wears a gold ring on his little finger."

'"But could we not ask little Hans up here?" said the Miller's youngest son. "If poor Hans is in trouble I will give him half my porridge, and show him my white rabbits."

'"What a silly boy you are!" cried the Miller; "I really don't know what is the use of sending you to school. You seem not to learn anything. Why, if little Hans came up here, and saw our warm fire, and our good supper, and our great cask of red wine, he might get envious, and envy is a most terrible thing, and would spoil anybody's nature. I certainly will not allow Hans's nature to be spoiled. I am his best friend, and I will always watch over him, and see that he is not led into any temptations. Besides, if Hans came here, he might ask me to let him have some flour on credit, and that I could not do. Flour is one thing, and friendship is another, and they should not be confused. Why, the words are spelt differently, and mean quite different things. Everybody can see that."

'"How well you talk!" said the Miller's Wife, pouring herself out a large glass of warm ale; "really I feel quite drowsy. It is just like being in church."

'"Lots of people act well," answered the Miller; "but very few people talk well, which shows that talking is much the more difficult thing of the two,[2] and much the finer thing also;" and he looked sternly across the table at his little son, who felt so ashamed of himself that he hung his head down, and grew quite scarlet, and began to cry into his tea. However, he was so young that you must excuse him.'

'Is that the end of the story?' asked the Water-rat.

'Certainly not,' answered the Linnet, 'that is the beginning.'

'Then you are quite behind the age,' said the Water-rat. 'Every good story-teller nowadays starts with the end, and then goes on to the beginning, and concludes with the middle. That is the new method. I heard all about it the other day from a critic who was walking round the pond with a young man. He spoke of the matter at great length, and I am sure he must have been right, for he had blue spectacles and a bald head, and whenever the young man made any remark, he always answered "Pooh!" But pray go on with your story. I like the Miller immensely. I have all kinds of beautiful sentiments myself, so there is a great sympathy between us.'

'Well,' said the Linnet, hopping now on one leg and now on the other, 'as soon as the winter was over, and the primroses began to open their pale yellow stars, the Miller said to his wife that he would go down and see little Hans.

'"Why, what a good heart you have!" cried his wife; "you are always thinking of others. And mind you take the big basket with you for the flowers."

'So the Miller tied the sails of the windmill together with a strong iron chain, and went down the hill with the basket on his arm.

'"Good morning, little Hans," said the Miller.

'"Good morning," said Hans, leaning on his spade, and smiling from ear to ear.

'"And how have you been all the winter?" said the Miller.

'"Well, really," cried Hans, "it is very good of you to ask, very good indeed. I am afraid I had rather a hard time of it, but now the spring has come, and I am quite happy, and all my flowers are doing well."

'"We often talked of you during the winter, Hans," said the Miller, "and wondered how you were getting on."

'"That was kind of you," said Hans; "I was half afraid you had forgotten me."

'"Hans, I am surprised at you," said the Miller; "friendship never forgets. That is the wonderful thing about it, but I am afraid you don't understand the poetry of life. How lovely your primroses are looking, by-the-bye!"

'"They are certainly very lovely," said Hans, "and it is a most lucky thing for me that I have so many. I am going to bring them into the market and sell them to the Burgomaster's daughter, and buy back my wheelbarrow with the money."

'"Buy back your wheelbarrow? You don't mean to say you have sold it? What a very stupid thing to do!"

'"Well, the fact is," said Hans, "that I was obliged to. You see the winter was a very bad time for me, and I really had no money at all to buy bread with. So I first sold the silver buttons off my Sunday coat, and then I sold my silver chain, and then I sold my big pipe, and at last I sold my wheelbarrow. But I am going to buy them all back again now."

'"Hans," said the Miller, "I will give you my wheelbarrow. It is not in very good repair; indeed, one side is gone, and there is something wrong with the wheel-spokes; but in spite of that I will give it to you. I know it is very generous of me, and a great many people would think me extremely foolish for parting with it, but I am not like the rest of the world. I think that generosity is the essence of friendship, and, besides, I have got a new wheelbarrow for myself. Yes, you may set your mind at ease, I will give you my wheelbarrow."

'"Well, really, that is generous of you," said little Hans, and his funny round face glowed all over with pleasure. "I can easily put it in repair, as I have a plank of wood in the house."

'"A plank of wood!" said the Miller; "why, that is just what I want for the roof of my barn. There is a very large hole in it, and the corn will all get damp if I don't stop it up. How lucky you mentioned it! It is quite remarkable how one good action always breeds another. I have given you my wheelbarrow, and now you are going to give me your plank. Of course, the wheelbarrow is worth far more than the plank, but true friendship never notices things like that. Pray get it at once, and I will set to work at my barn this very day."

'"Certainly," cried little Hans, and he ran into the shed and dragged the plank out.

'"It is not a very big plank," said the Miller, looking at it, "and I am afraid that after I have mended my barn-roof there won't be any left for you to mend the wheelbarrow with; but, of course, that is not my fault. And now, as I have given you my wheelbarrow, I am sure you would like to give me some flowers in return. Here is the basket, and mind you fill it quite full."

'"Quite full?" said little Hans, rather sorrowfully, for it was really a very big basket, and he knew that if he filled it he would have no flowers left for the market, and he was very anxious to get his silver buttons back.

'"Well, really," answered the Miller, "as I have given you my wheelbarrow, I don't think that it is much to ask you for a few flowers. I may be wrong, but I should have thought that friend-ship, true friendship, was quite free from selfishness of any kind."

'"My dear friend, my best friend," cried little Hans, "you are welcome to all the flowers in my garden. I would much sooner have your good opinion than my silver buttons, any day;" and he ran and plucked all his pretty primroses, and filled the Miller's basket.

'"Good-bye, little Hans," said the Miller, as he went up the hill with the plank on his shoulder, and the big basket in his hand.

'"Good-bye," said little Hans, and he began to dig away quite merrily, he was so pleased about the wheelbarrow.

'The next day he was nailing up some honeysuckle against the porch, when he heard the Miller's voice calling to him from the road. So he jumped off the ladder, and ran down the garden, and looked over the wall.

'There was the Miller with a large sack of flour on his back.

'"Dear little Hans," said the Miller, "would you mind carrying this sack of flour for me to market?"

'"Oh, I am so sorry," said Hans, "but I am really very busy to-day. I have got all my creepers to nail up, and all my flowers to water, and all my grass to roll."

'"Well, really," said the Miller, "I think that, considering that I am going to give you my wheelbarrow, it is rather unfriendly of you to refuse."

'"Oh, don't say that," cried little Hans, "I wouldn't be unfriendly for the whole world;" and he ran in for his cap, and trudged off with the big sack on his shoulders.

'It was a very hot day, and the road was terribly dusty, and before Hans had reached the sixth milestone he was so tired that he had to sit down and rest. However, he went on bravely, and at last he reached the market. After he had waited there some time, he sold the sack of flour for a very good price, and then he returned home at once, for he was afraid that if he stopped too late he might meet some robbers on the way.

'"It has certainly been a hard day," said little Hans to himself as he was going to bed, "but I am glad I did not refuse the Miller, for he is my best friend, and, besides, he is going to give me his wheelbarrow."

'Early the next morning the Miller came down to get the money for his sack of flour, but little Hans was so tired that he was still in bed.

'"Upon my word," said the Miller, "you are very lazy. Really, considering that I am going to give you my wheelbarrow, I think you might work harder. Idleness is a great sin, and I certainly don't like any of my friends to be idle or sluggish. You must not mind my speaking quite plainly to you. Of course I should not dream of doing so if I were not your friend. But what is the good of friendship if one cannot say exactly what one means? Anybody can say charming things and try to please and to flatter, but a true friend always says unpleasant things, and does not mind giving pain. Indeed, if he is a really true friend he prefers it, for he knows that then he is doing good."

'"I am very sorry," said little Hans, rubbing his eyes and

pulling off his night-cap, "but I was so tired that I thought I would lie in bed for a little time, and listen to the birds singing. Do you know that I always work better after hearing the birds sing?"

'"Well, I am glad of that," said the Miller, clapping little Hans on the back, "for I want you to come up to the mill as soon as you are dressed, and mend my barn-roof for me."

'Poor little Hans was very anxious to go and work in his garden, for his flowers had not been watered for two days, but he did not like to refuse the Miller, as he was such a good friend to him.

'"Do you think it would be unfriendly of me if I said I was busy?" he inquired in a shy and timid voice.

'"Well, really," answered the Miller, "I do not think it is much to ask of you, considering that I am going to give you my wheelbarrow; but of course if you refuse I will go and do it myself."

'"Oh! on no account," cried little Hans; and he jumped out of bed, and dressed himself, and went up to the barn.

'He worked there all day long, till sunset, and at sunset the Miller came to see how he was getting on.

'"Have you mended the hole in the roof yet, little Hans?" cried the Miller in a cheery voice.

'"It is quite mended," answered little Hans, coming down the ladder.

'"Ah!" said the Miller, "there is no work so delightful as the work one does for others."

'"It is certainly a great privilege to hear you talk," answered little Hans, sitting down and wiping his forehead, "a very great privilege. But I am afraid I shall never have such beautiful ideas as you have."

'"Oh! they will come to you," said the Miller, "but you must take more pains. At present you have only the practice of friendship; some day you will have the theory also."

'"Do you really think I shall?" asked little Hans.

'"I have no doubt of it," answered the Miller; "but now that you have mended the roof, you had better go home and rest, for I want you to drive my sheep to the mountain to-morrow."

'Poor little Hans was afraid to say anything to this, and early the next morning the Miller brought his sheep round to the cottage, and Hans started off with them to the mountain. It took him the whole day to get there and back; and when he returned he was so tired that he went off to sleep in his chair, and did not wake up till it was broad daylight.

'"What a delightful time I shall have in my garden," he said, and he went to work at once.

'But somehow he was never able to look after his flowers at all, for his friend the Miller was always coming round and sending him off on long errands, or getting him to help at the mill. Little Hans was very much distressed at times, as he was afraid his flowers would think he had forgotten them, but he consoled himself by the reflection that the Miller was his best friend. "Besides," he used to say, "he is going to give me his wheelbarrow, and that is an act of pure generosity."

'So little Hans worked away for the Miller, and the Miller said all kinds of beautiful things about friendship, which Hans took down in a note-book, and used to read over at night, for he was a very good scholar.

'Now it happened that one evening little Hans was sitting by his fireside when a loud rap came at the door. It was a very wild night, and the wind was blowing and roaring round the house so terribly that at first he thought it was merely the storm. But a second rap came, and then a third, louder than either of the others.

'"It is some poor traveller," said little Hans to himself, and he ran to the door.

'There stood the Miller with a lantern in one hand and a big stick in the other.

'"Dear little Hans," cried the Miller, "I am in great trouble. My little boy has fallen off a ladder and hurt himself, and I am going for the Doctor. But he lives so far away, and it is such a bad night, that it has just occurred to me that it would be much better if you went instead of me. You know I am going to give you my wheelbarrow, and so it is only fair that you should do something for me in return."

'"Certainly," cried little Hans, "I take it quite as a compliment your coming to me, and I will start off at once. But you must lend me your lantern, as the night is so dark that I am afraid I might fall into the ditch."

'"I am very sorry," answered the Miller, "but it is my new lantern, and it would be a great loss to me if anything happened to it."

'"Well, never mind, I will do without it," cried little Hans, and he took down his great fur coat, and his warm scarlet cap, and tied a muffler round his throat, and started off.

'What a dreadful storm it was! The night was so black that little Hans could hardly see, and the wind was so strong that he could scarcely stand. However, he was very courageous, and after he had been walking about three hours, he arrived at the Doctor's house, and knocked at the door.

'"Who is there?" cried the Doctor, putting his head out of his bedroom window.

'"Little Hans, Doctor."

'"What do you want, little Hans?"

'"The Miller's son has fallen from a ladder, and has hurt himself, and the Miller wants you to come at once."

'"All right!" said the Doctor; and he ordered his horse, and his big boots, and his lantern, and came downstairs, and rode off in the direction of the Miller's house, little Hans trudging behind him.

'But the storm grew worse and worse, and the rain fell in torrents, and little Hans could not see where he was going, or keep up with the horse. At last he lost his way, and wandered off on the moor, which was a very dangerous place, as it was full of deep holes, and there poor little Hans was drowned. His body was found the next day by some goatherds, floating in a great pool of water, and was brought back by them to the cottage.

'Everybody went to little Hans's funeral, as he was so popular, and the Miller was the chief mourner.

'"As I was his best friend," said the Miller, "it is only fair that I should have the best place;" so he walked at the head of the procession in a long black cloak, and every now and then he wiped his eyes with a big pocket-handkerchief.

'"Little Hans is certainly a great loss to every one," said the

Blacksmith, when the funeral was over, and they were all seated comfortably in the inn, drinking spiced wine and eating sweet cakes.

'"A great loss to me at any rate," answered the Miller; "why, I had as good as given him my wheelbarrow, and now I really don't know what to do with it. It is very much in my way at home, and it is in such bad repair that I could not get anything for it if I sold it. I will certainly take care not to give away anything again. One always suffers for being generous."'

'Well?' said the Water-rat, after a long pause.

'Well, that is the end,' said the Linnet.

'But what became of the Miller?' asked the Water-rat.

'Oh! I really don't know,' replied the Linnet; 'and I am sure that I don't care.'

'It is quite evident then that you have no sympathy in your nature,' said the Water-rat.

'I am afraid you don't quite see the moral of the story,' remarked the Linnet.

'The what?' screamed the Water-rat.

'The moral.'

'Do you mean to say that the story has a moral?'

'Certainly,' said the Linnet.

'Well, really,' said the Water-rat, in a very angry manner, 'I think you should have told me that before you began. If you had done so, I certainly would not have listened to you; in fact, I should have said "Pooh," like the critic. However, I can say it now;' so he shouted out 'Pooh' at the top of his voice, gave a whisk with his tail, and went back into his hole.

'And how do you like the Water-rat?' asked the Duck, who came paddling up some minutes afterwards. 'He has a great many good points, but for my own part I have a mother's feelings, and I can never look at a confirmed bachelor without the tears coming into my eyes.'

'I am rather afraid that I have annoyed him,' answered the Linnet. 'The fact is, that I told him a story with a moral.'

'Ah! that is always a very dangerous thing to do,'[3] said the Duck.

And I quite agree with her.

The Remarkable Rocket

The King's son was going to be married, so there were general rejoicings. He had waited a whole year for his bride, and at last she had arrived. She was a Russian Princess, and had driven all the way from Finland in a sledge drawn by six reindeer. The sledge was shaped like a great golden swan, and between the swan's wings lay the little Princess herself. Her long ermine cloak reached right down to her feet, on her head was a tiny cap of silver tissue, and she was as pale as the Snow Palace in which she had always lived. So pale was she that as she drove through the streets all the people wondered. 'She is like a white rose!' they cried, and they threw down flowers on her from the balconies.

At the gate of the Castle the Prince was waiting to receive her. He had dreamy violet eyes, and his hair was like fine gold. When he saw her he sank upon one knee, and kissed her hand.

'Your picture was beautiful,' he murmured, 'but you are more beautiful than your picture;' and the little Princess blushed.

'She was like a white rose before,' said a young Page to his neighbour, 'but she is like a red rose now;' and the whole Court was delighted.

For the next three days everybody went about saying, 'White rose, Red rose, Red rose, White rose;' and the King gave orders that the Page's salary was to be doubled. As he received no salary at all this was not of much use to him, but it was considered a great honour, and was duly published in the Court Gazette.

When the three days were over the marriage was celebrated. It was a magnificent ceremony, and the bride and bridegroom walked hand in hand under a canopy of purple velvet embroidered with little pearls. Then there was a State Banquet, which lasted for five hours. The Prince and Princess sat at the top of the

Great Hall and drank out of a cup of clear crystal. Only true lovers could drink out of this cup, for if false lips touched it, it grew grey and dull and cloudy.

'It is quite clear that they love each other,' said the little Page, 'as clear as crystal!' and the King doubled his salary a second time. 'What an honour!' cried all the courtiers.

After the banquet there was to be a Ball. The bride and bridegroom were to dance the Rose-dance together, and the King had promised to play the flute. He played very badly, but no one had ever dared to tell him so, because he was the King. Indeed, he only knew two airs, and was never quite certain which one he was playing; but it made no matter, for, whatever he did, everybody cried out, 'Charming! charming!'

The last item on the programme was a grand display of fireworks, to be let off exactly at midnight. The little Princess had never seen a firework in her life, so the King had given orders that the Royal Pyrotechnist[1] should be in attendance on the day of her marriage.

'What are fireworks like?' she had asked the Prince, one morning, as she was walking on the terrace.

'They are like the Aurora Borealis,' said the King, who always answered questions that were addressed to other people, 'only much more natural.[2] I prefer them to stars myself, as you always know when they are going to appear, and they are as delightful as my own flute-playing. You must certainly see them.'

So at the end of the King's garden a great stand had been set up, and as soon as the Royal Pyrotechnist had put everything in its proper place, the fireworks began to talk to each other.

'The world is certainly very beautiful,' cried a little Squib. 'Just look at those yellow tulips. Why! if they were real crackers they could not be lovelier. I am very glad I have travelled. Travel improves the mind wonderfully, and does away with all one's prejudices.'

'The King's garden is not the world, you foolish squib,' said a big Roman Candle; 'the world is an enormous place, and it would take you three days to see it thoroughly.'

'Any place you love is the world to you,' exclaimed a pensive Catharine Wheel, who had been attached to an old deal box in early life, and prided herself on her broken heart; 'but love is not fashionable any more, the poets have killed it. They wrote so much about it that nobody believed them, and I am not surprised. True love suffers, and is silent. I remember myself once – But it is no matter now. Romance is a thing of the past.'

'Nonsense!' said the Roman Candle, 'Romance never dies. It is like the moon, and lives for ever. The bride and bridegroom, for instance, love each other very dearly. I heard all about them this morning from a brown-paper cartridge, who happened to be staying in the same drawer as myself, and knew the latest Court news.'

But the Catharine Wheel shook her head. 'Romance is dead, Romance is dead, Romance is dead,' she murmured. She was one of those people who think that, if you say the same thing over and over a great many times, it becomes true in the end.

Suddenly, a sharp, dry cough was heard, and they all looked round.

It came from a tall, supercilious-looking Rocket, who was tied to the end of a long stick. He always coughed before he made any observation, so as to attract attention.

'Ahem! ahem!' he said, and everybody listened except the poor Catharine Wheel, who was still shaking her head, and murmuring, 'Romance is dead.'

'Order! order!' cried out a Cracker. He was something of a politician, and had always taken a prominent part in the local elections, so he knew the proper Parliamentary expressions to use.

'Quite dead,' whispered the Catharine Wheel, and she went off to sleep.

As soon as there was perfect silence, the Rocket coughed a third time and began. He spoke with a very slow, distinct voice, as if he was dictating his memoirs, and always looked over the shoulder of the person to whom he was talking. In fact, he had a most distinguished manner.

'How fortunate it is for the King's son,' he remarked, 'that he is to be married on the very day on which I am to be let off. Really, if it had been arranged beforehand, it could not have turned out better for him; but Princes are always lucky.'

'Dear me!' said the little Squib, 'I thought it was quite the other way, and that we were to be let off in the Prince's honour.'

'It may be so with you,' he answered; 'indeed, I have no doubt that it is, but with me it is different. I am a very remarkable Rocket, and come of remarkable parents. My mother was the most celebrated Catharine Wheel of her day, and was renowned for her graceful dancing. When she made her great public appearance she spun round nineteen times before she went out, and each time that she did so she threw into the air seven pink stars. She was three feet and a half in diameter, and made of the very best gunpowder. My father was a Rocket like myself, and of French extraction. He flew so high that the people were afraid that he would never come down again. He did, though, for he was of a kindly disposition, and he made a most brilliant descent in a shower of golden rain. The newspapers wrote about his performance in very flattering terms. Indeed, the Court Gazette called him a triumph of Pylotechnic[3] art.'

'Pyrotechnic, Pyrotechnic, you mean,' said a Bengal Light;[4] 'I know it is Pyrotechnic, for I saw it written on my own canister.'

'Well, I said Pylotechnic,' answered the Rocket, in a severe tone of voice, and the Bengal Light felt so crushed that he began at once to bully the little squibs, in order to show that he was still a person of some importance.

'I was saying,' continued the Rocket, 'I was saying – What was I saying?'

'You were talking about yourself,' replied the Roman Candle.

'Of course; I knew I was discussing some interesting subject when I was so rudely interrupted. I hate rudeness and bad manners of every kind, for I am extremely sensitive. No one in the whole world is so sensitive as I am, I am quite sure of that.'

'What is a sensitive person?' said the Cracker to the Roman Candle.

'A person who, because he has corns himself, always treads on other people's toes,' answered the Roman Candle in a low whisper; and the Cracker nearly exploded with laughter.

'Pray, what are you laughing at?' inquired the Rocket; 'I am not laughing.'

'I am laughing because I am happy,' replied the Cracker.

'That is a very selfish reason,' said the Rocket angrily. 'What right have you to be happy? You should be thinking about others. In fact, you should be thinking about me. I am always thinking about myself, and I expect everybody else to do the same. That is what is called sympathy. It is a beautiful virtue, and I possess it in a high degree. Suppose, for instance, anything happened to me to-night, what a misfortune that would be for every one! The Prince and Princess would never be happy again, their whole married life would be spoiled; and as for the King, I know he would not get over it. Really, when I begin to reflect on the importance of my position, I am almost moved to tears.'

'If you want to give pleasure to others,' cried the Roman Candle, 'you had better keep yourself dry.'

'Certainly,' exclaimed the Bengal Light, who was now in better spirits; 'that is only common sense.'

'Common sense, indeed!' said the Rocket indignantly; 'you forget that I am very uncommon, and very remarkable. Why, anybody can have common sense, provided that they have no imagination. But I have imagination, for I never think of things as they really are; I always think of them as being quite different. As for keeping myself dry, there is evidently no one here who can at all appreciate an emotional nature. Fortunately for myself, I don't care. The only thing that sustains one through life is the consciousness of the immense inferiority of everybody else, and this is a feeling that I have always cultivated. But none of you have any hearts. Here you are laughing and making merry just as if the Prince and Princess had not just been married.'

'Well, really,' exclaimed a small Fire-balloon, 'why not? It is a most joyful occasion, and when I soar up into the air I intend to tell the stars all about it. You will see them twinkle when I talk to them about the pretty bride.'

'Ah! what a trivial view of life!' said the Rocket; 'but it is only what I expected. There is nothing in you; you are hollow and empty. Why, perhaps the Prince and Princess may go to live in a country where there is a deep river, and perhaps they may have one only son, a little fair-haired boy with violet eyes like the Prince himself; and perhaps some day he may go out to walk with his nurse; and perhaps the nurse may go to sleep under a great elder-tree; and perhaps the little boy may fall into the deep river and be drowned. What a terrible misfortune! Poor people, to lose their only son! It is really too dreadful! I shall never get over it.'

'But they have not lost their only son,' said the Roman Candle; 'no misfortune has happened to them at all.'

'I never said that they had,' replied the Rocket; 'I said that they might. If they had lost their only son there would be no use in saying anything more about the matter. I hate people who cry over spilt milk. But when I think that they might lose their only son, I certainly am very much affected.'

'You certainly are!' cried the Bengal Light. 'In fact, you are the most affected person I ever met.'

'You are the rudest person I ever met,' said the Rocket, 'and you cannot understand my friendship for the Prince.'

'Why, you don't even know him,' growled the Roman Candle.

'I never said I knew him,' answered the Rocket. 'I dare say that if I knew him I should not be his friend at all. It is a very dangerous thing to know one's friends.'

'You had really better keep yourself dry,' said the Fire-balloon. 'That is the important thing.'

'Very important for you, I have no doubt,' answered the Rocket, 'but I shall weep if I choose;' and he actually burst into real tears, which flowed down his stick like rain-drops, and nearly drowned two little beetles, who were just thinking of setting up house together, and were looking for a nice dry spot to live in.

'He must have a truly romantic nature,' said the Catharine Wheel, 'for he weeps when there is nothing at all to weep about;' and she heaved a deep sigh, and thought about the deal box.

But the Roman Candle and the Bengal Light were quite indignant, and kept saying, 'Humbug! humbug!' at the top of their voices. They were extremely practical, and whenever they objected to anything they called it humbug.

Then the moon rose like a wonderful silver shield; and the stars began to shine, and a sound of music came from the palace.

The Prince and Princess were leading the dance. They danced so beautifully that the tall white lilies peeped in at the window and watched them, and the great red poppies nodded their heads and beat time.

Then ten o'clock struck, and then eleven, and then twelve, and at the last stroke of midnight every one came out on the terrace, and the King sent for the Royal Pyrotechnist.

'Let the fireworks begin,' said the King; and the Royal Pyrotechnist made a low bow, and marched down to the end of the garden. He had six attendants with him, each of whom carried a lighted torch at the end of a long pole.

It was certainly a magnificent display.

Whizz! Whizz! went the Catharine Wheel, as she spun round and round. Boom! Boom! went the Roman Candle. Then the Squibs danced all over the place, and the Bengal Lights made everything look scarlet. 'Good-bye,' cried the Fire-balloon, as he soared away dropping tiny blue sparks. Bang! Bang! answered the Crackers, who were enjoying themselves immensely. Every one was a great success except the Remarkable Rocket. He was so damp with crying that he could not go off at all. The best thing in him was the gunpowder, and that was so wet with tears that it was of no use. All his poor relations, to whom he would never speak, except with a sneer, shot up into the sky like wonderful golden flowers with blossoms of fire. Huzza! Huzza! cried the Court; and the little Princess laughed with pleasure.

'I suppose they are reserving me for some grand occasion,' said the Rocket; 'no doubt that is what it means,' and he looked more supercilious than ever.

The next day the workmen came to put everything tidy. 'This is evidently a deputation,' said the Rocket; 'I will receive them with becoming dignity:' so he put his nose in the air, and began to frown severely as if he were thinking about some very important subject. But they took no notice of him at all till they were just going away. Then one of them caught sight of him. 'Hallo!' he cried, 'what a bad rocket!' and he threw him over the wall into the ditch.

'BAD Rocket? BAD Rocket?' he said, as he whirled through the air; 'impossible! GRAND Rocket, that is what the man said. BAD and GRAND sound very much the same, indeed they often are the same;' and he fell into the mud.

'It is not comfortable here,' he remarked, 'but no doubt it is some fashionable watering-place, and they have sent me away to recruit my health. My nerves are certainly very much shattered, and I require rest.'

Then a little Frog, with bright jewelled eyes, and a green mottled coat, swam up to him.

'A new arrival, I see!' said the Frog. 'Well, after all there is nothing like mud. Give me rainy weather and a ditch, and I am quite happy. Do you think it will be a wet afternoon? I am sure I hope so, but the sky is quite blue and cloudless. What a pity!'

'Ahem! ahem!' said the Rocket, and he began to cough.

'What a delightful voice you have!' cried the Frog. 'Really it is quite like a croak, and croaking is of course the most musical sound in the world. You will hear our glee-club[5] this evening. We sit in the old duck-pond close by the farmer's house, and as soon as the moon rises we begin. It is so entrancing that everybody lies awake to listen to us. In fact, it was only yesterday that I heard the farmer's wife say to her mother that she could not get a wink of sleep at night on account of us. It is most gratifying to find oneself so popular.'

'Ahem! ahem!' said the Rocket angrily. He was very much annoyed that he could not get a word in.

'A delightful voice, certainly,' continued the Frog; 'I hope you will come over to the duck-pond. I am off to look for my daughters. I have six beautiful daughters, and I am so afraid the Pike may meet them. He is a perfect monster, and would have no hesitation in breakfasting off them. Well, good-bye: I have enjoyed our conversation very much, I assure you.'

'Conversation, indeed!' said the Rocket. 'You have talked the whole time yourself. That is not conversation.'

'Somebody must listen,' answered the Frog, 'and I like to do all the talking myself. It saves time, and prevents arguments.'

'But I like arguments,' said the Rocket.

'I hope not,' said the Frog complacently. 'Arguments are extremely vulgar, for everybody in good society holds exactly the same opinions. Good-bye a second time; I see my daughters in the distance;' and the little Frog swam away.

'You are a very irritating person,' said the Rocket, 'and very ill-bred. I hate people who talk about themselves, as you do, when one wants to talk about oneself, as I do. It is what I call selfishness, and selfishness is a most detestable thing, especially to any one of my temperament, for I am well known for my sympathetic nature. In fact, you should take example by me, you could not possibly have a better model. Now that you have the chance you had better avail yourself of it, for I am going back to Court almost immediately. I am a great favourite at Court; in fact, the Prince and Princess were married yesterday in my honour. Of course you know nothing of these matters, for you are a provincial.'

'There is no good talking to him,' said a Dragon-fly, who was sitting on the top of a large brown bulrush; 'no good at all, for he has gone away.'

'Well, that is his loss, not mine,' answered the Rocket. 'I am not going to stop talking to him merely because he pays no attention. I like hearing myself talk. It is one of my greatest pleasures. I often have long conversations all by myself, and I am so clever that sometimes I don't understand a single word of what I am saying.'[6]

'Then you should certainly lecture on Philosophy,' said the Dragon-fly; and he spread a pair of lovely gauze wings and soared away into the sky.

'How very silly of him not to stay here!' said the Rocket. 'I am sure that he has not often got such a chance of improving his mind. However, I don't care a bit. Genius like mine is sure to be appreciated some day;' and he sank down a little deeper into the mud.

After some time a large White Duck swam up to him. She had yellow legs, and webbed feet, and was considered a great beauty on account of her waddle.

'Quack, quack, quack,' she said. 'What a curious shape you are! May I ask were you born like that, or is it the result of an accident?'

'It is quite evident that you have always lived in the country,' answered the Rocket, 'otherwise you would know who I am. However, I excuse your ignorance. It would be unfair to expect other people to be as remarkable as oneself. You will no doubt be surprised to hear that I can fly up into the sky, and come down in a shower of golden rain.'

'I don't think much of that,' said the Duck, 'as I cannot see what use it is to any one. Now, if you could plough the fields like the ox, or draw a cart like the horse, or look after the sheep like the collie-dog, that would be something.'

'My good creature,' cried the Rocket in a very haughty tone of voice, 'I see that you belong to the lower orders. A person of my position is never useful. We have certain accomplishments, and that is more than sufficient. I have no sympathy myself with industry of any kind, least of all with such industries as you seem to recommend. Indeed, I have always been of opinion that hard work is simply the refuge of people who have nothing whatever to do."[7]

'Well, well,' said the Duck, who was of a very peaceable disposition, and never quarrelled with any one, 'everybody has different tastes. I hope, at any rate, that you are going to take up your residence here.'

'Oh! dear no,' cried the Rocket. 'I am merely a visitor, a distinguished visitor. The fact is that I find this place rather tedious. There is neither society here, nor solitude. In fact, it is essentially suburban. I shall probably go back to Court, for I know that I am destined to make a sensation in the world.'

'I had thoughts of entering public life once myself,' remarked the Duck; 'there are so many things that need reforming. Indeed, I took the chair at a meeting some time ago, and we passed resolutions condemning everything that we did not like. However, they did not seem to have much effect. Now I go in for domesticity, and look after my family.'

'I am made for public life,' said the Rocket, 'and so are all my relations, even the humblest of them. Whenever we appear we excite great attention. I have not actually appeared myself, but when I do so it will be a magnificent sight. As for domesticity, it ages one rapidly, and distracts one's mind from higher things.'

'Ah! the higher things of life, how fine they are!' said the Duck; 'and that reminds me how hungry I feel:' and she swam away down the stream, saying, 'Quack, quack, quack.'

'Come back! come back!' screamed the Rocket, 'I have a great deal to say to you;' but the Duck paid no attention to him. 'I am glad that she has gone,' he said to himself, 'she has a decidedly middle-class mind;' and he sank a little deeper still into the mud, and began to think about the loneliness of genius, when suddenly two little boys in white smocks came running down the bank, with a kettle and some faggots.

'This must be the deputation,' said the Rocket, and he tried to look very dignified.

'Hallo!' cried one of the boys, 'look at this old stick! I wonder how it came here;' and he picked the Rocket out of the ditch.

'OLD Stick!' said the Rocket, 'impossible! GOLD Stick, that is what he said. Gold Stick is very complimentary. In fact, he mistakes me for one of the Court dignitaries!'[8]

'Let us put it into the fire!' said the other boy, 'it will help to boil the kettle.'

So they piled the faggots together, and put the Rocket on top, and lit the fire.

'This is magnificent,' cried the Rocket, 'they are going to let me off in broad daylight, so that every one can see me.'

'We will go to sleep now,' they said, 'and when we wake up the kettle will be boiled;' and they lay down on the grass, and shut their eyes.

The Rocket was very damp, so he took a long time to burn. At last, however, the fire caught him.

'Now I am going off!' he cried, and he made himself very stiff and straight. 'I know I shall go much higher than the stars, much higher than the moon, much higher than the sun. In fact, I shall go so high that –'

Fizz! Fizz! Fizz! and he went straight up into the air.

'Delightful!' he cried, 'I shall go on like this for ever. What a success I am!'

But nobody saw him.

Then he began to feel a curious tingling sensation all over him.

'Now I am going to explode,' he cried. 'I shall set the whole world on fire, and make such a noise, that nobody will talk about anything else for a whole year.' And he certainly did explode. Bang! Bang! Bang! went the gunpowder. There was no doubt about it.

But nobody heard him, not even the two little boys, for they were sound asleep.

Then all that was left of him was the stick, and this fell down on the back of a Goose who was taking a walk by the side of the ditch.

'Good heavens!' cried the Goose. 'It is going to rain sticks;' and she rushed into the water.

'I knew I should create a great sensation,' gasped the Rocket, and he went out.

The Portrait of Mr. W. H.

The Portrait of Mr. W. H.

I had been dining with Erskine in his pretty little house in Birdcage Walk,[1] and we were sitting in the library over our coffee and cigarettes, when the question of literary forgeries happened to turn up in conversation. I cannot at present remember how it was that we stuck upon this somewhat curious topic, as it was at that time, but I know that we had a long discussion about Macpherson, Ireland, and Chatterton,[2] and that with regard to the last I insisted that his so-called forgeries were merely the result of an artistic desire for perfect representation; that we had no right to quarrel with an artist for the conditions under which he chooses to present his work; and that all Art being to a certain degree a mode of acting, an attempt to realise one's own personality on some imaginative plane[3] out of reach of the trammelling accidents and limitations of real life, to censure an artist for a forgery was to confuse an ethical with an aesthetical problem.

Erskine, who was a good deal older than I was, and had been listening to me with the amused deference of a man of forty, suddenly put his hand upon my shoulder and said to me, 'What would you say about a young man who had a strange theory about a certain work of art, believed in his theory, and committed a forgery in order to prove it?'

'Ah! that is quite a different matter,' I answered.

Erskine remained silent for a few moments, looking at the thin grey threads of smoke that were rising from his cigarette. 'Yes,' he said, after a pause, 'quite different.'

There was something in the tone of his voice, a slight touch of bitterness perhaps, that excited my curiosity. 'Did you ever know anybody who did that?' I cried.

'Yes,' he answered, throwing his cigarette into the fire, – 'a great friend of mine, Cyril Graham.[4] He was very fascinating, and very foolish, and very heartless. However, he left me the only legacy I ever received in my life.'

'What was that?' I exclaimed. Erskine rose from his seat, and going over to a tall inlaid cabinet that stood between the two windows, unlocked it, and came back to where I was sitting, holding in his hand a small panel picture set in an old and somewhat tarnished Elizabethan frame.

It was a full-length portrait of a young man in late sixteenth-century costume, standing by a table, with his right hand resting on an open book. He seemed about seventeen years of age, and was of quite extraordinary personal beauty, though evidently somewhat effeminate. Indeed, had it not been for the dress and the closely cropped hair, one would have said that the face, with its dreamy wistful eyes, and its delicate scarlet lips, was the face of a girl. In manner, and especially in the treatment of the hands, the picture reminded one of François Clouet's later work.[5] The black velvet doublet with its fantastically gilded points, and the peacock-blue background against which it showed up so pleasantly, and from which it gained such luminous value of colour, were quite in Clouet's style; and the two masks of Tragedy and Comedy that hung somewhat formally from the marble pedestal had that hard severity of touch – so different from the facile grace of the Italians – which even at the Court of France the great Flemish master never completely lost, and which in itself has always been a characteristic of the northern temper.

'It is a charming thing,' I cried; 'but who is this wonderful young man, whose beauty Art has so happily preserved for us?'

'This is the portrait of Mr. W. H.,' said Erskine, with a sad smile. It might have been a chance effect of light, but it seemed to me that his eyes were quite bright with tears.

'Mr. W. H.!' I exclaimed; 'who was Mr. W. H.?'

'Don't you remember?' he answered; 'look at the book on which his hand is resting.'

'I see there is some writing there, but I cannot make it out,' I replied.

'Take this magnifying-glass and try,' said Erskine, with the same sad smile still playing about his mouth.

I took the glass, and moving the lamp a little nearer, I began to spell out the crabbed sixteenth-century handwriting. 'To the onlie begetter of these insuing sonnets' ... 'Good heavens!' I cried, 'is this Shakespeare's Mr. W. H.?'

'Cyril Graham used to say so,' muttered Erskine.

'But it is not a bit like Lord Pembroke,'[6] I answered. 'I know the Penshurst portraits[7] very well. I was staying near there a few weeks ago.'

'Do you really believe then that the Sonnets are addressed to Lord Pembroke?' he asked.

'I am sure of it,' I answered. 'Pembroke, Shakespeare, and Mrs. Mary Fitton[8] are the three personages of the Sonnets; there is no doubt at all about it.'

'Well, I agree with you,' said Erskine, 'but I did not always think so. I used to believe – well, I suppose I used to believe in Cyril Graham and his theory.'

'And what was that?' I asked, looking at the wonderful portrait, which had already begun to have a strange fascination for me.

'It is a long story,' said Erskine, taking the picture away from me – rather abruptly I thought at the time – 'a very long story; but if you care to hear it, I will tell it to you.'

'I love theories about the Sonnets,' I cried; 'but I don't think I am likely to be converted to any new idea. The matter has ceased to be a mystery to any one. Indeed, I wonder that it ever was a mystery.'

'As I don't believe in the theory, I am not likely to convert you to it,' said Erskine, laughing; 'but it may interest you.'

'Tell it to me, of course,' I answered. 'If it is half as delightful as the picture, I shall be more than satisfied.'

'Well,' said Erskine, lighting a cigarette, 'I must begin by telling you about Cyril Graham himself. He and I were at the same house at Eton. I was a year or two older than he was, but we were immense friends, and did all our work and all our play together. There was, of course, a good deal more play than work, but I cannot say that I am sorry for that. It is always an advantage not to have received a sound commercial education, and what I learned in the playing fields at Eton[9] has been quite as useful to me as anything I was taught at Cambridge. I should tell you that Cyril's father and mother were both dead. They had been drowned in a horrible yachting accident off the Isle of Wight. His father had been in the diplomatic service, and had married a daughter, the only daughter, in fact, of old Lord Crediton, who became Cyril's guardian after the death of his parents. I don't think that Lord Crediton cared very much for Cyril. He had never really forgiven his daughter for marrying a man who had no title. He was an extraordinary old aristocrat, who swore like a costermonger, and had the manners of a farmer. I remember seeing him once on Speech-day. He growled at me, gave me a sovereign, and told me not to grow up "a damned Radical" like my father. Cyril had very little affection for him, and was only too glad to spend most of his holidays with us in Scotland. They never really got on together at all. Cyril thought him a bear, and he thought Cyril effeminate. He was effeminate, I suppose, in some things, though he was a very good rider and a capital fencer. In fact he got the foils before he left Eton. But he was very languid in his manner, and not a little vain of his good looks, and had a strong objection to football. The two things that really gave him pleasure were poetry and acting. At Eton he was always dressing up and reciting Shakespeare, and when we went up to Trinity he became a member of the A.D.C.[10] his first term. I remember I was always very jealous of his acting. I was absurdly devoted to him; I suppose because we were so different in some things. I was a rather awkward, weakly lad, with huge feet, and horribly freckled. Freckles run in Scotch families just as gout does in English families. Cyril used to say that of the two he preferred the gout; but he always set an absurdly high value on personal appearance, and once read a paper before our debating society to prove that it was better to be good-looking than to be good.[11] He certainly was wonderfully handsome. People who did not like him, Philistines[12] and college tutors, and young men reading for the Church, used to say that he was merely pretty; but there was a great deal more in his face than mere prettiness. I think he was the most splendid creature I ever saw, and nothing could exceed the grace of his movements, the charm of his manner. He fascinated everybody who was worth fascinating, and a great many people who were not. He was often wilful and petulant, and I used to think him dreadfully insincere. It was due, I think, chiefly to his inordinate desire to please. Poor Cyril! I told him once that he was contented with very cheap triumphs, but he only laughed. He was horribly spoiled. All charming people, I fancy, are spoiled. It is the secret of their attraction.

'However, I must tell you about Cyril's acting. You know that no actresses are allowed to play at the A.D.C. At least they were not in my time. I don't know how it is now. Well, of course Cyril was always cast for the girls' parts, and when *As You Like It* was produced he played Rosalind. It was a marvellous performance. In fact, Cyril Graham was the only perfect Rosalind I have ever seen. It would be impossible to describe to you the beauty, the delicacy, the refinement of the whole thing. It made an immense sensation, and the horrid little theatre, as it was then, was crowded every night. Even when I read the play now I can't help thinking of Cyril. It might have been written for him. The next term he took his degree, and came to London to read for the diplomatic.[13] But he never did any work. He spent his days in reading Shakespeare's Sonnets, and his evenings at the theatre. He was, of course, wild to go on the stage. It was all that I and Lord Crediton could do to prevent him. Perhaps if he had gone on the stage he would be alive now. It is always a silly thing to give advice, but to give good advice is absolutely fatal.[14] I hope you will never fall into that error. If you do, you will be sorry for it.

'Well, to come to the real point of the story, one day I got a letter from Cyril asking me to come round to his rooms that evening. He had charming chambers in Piccadilly overlooking the Green Park,[15] and as I used to go to see him every day, I was rather surprised at his taking the trouble to write. Of course I went, and when I arrived I found him in a state of great excitement. He told me that he had at last discovered the true secret of Shakespeare's Sonnets; that all the scholars and critics had been entirely on the wrong tack; and that he was the first who, working purely by internal evidence, had found out who Mr. W. H. really was. He was perfectly wild with delight, and for a long time would not tell me his theory. Finally, he produced a bundle of notes, took his copy of the Sonnets off the mantelpiece, and sat down and gave me a long lecture on the whole subject.

'He began by pointing out that the young man to whom Shakespeare addressed these strangely passionate poems must have been somebody who was a really vital factor in the development of his dramatic art, and that this could not be said either of Lord Pembroke or Lord Southampton.[16] Indeed, whoever he was, he could not have been anybody of high birth, as was shown very clearly by the 25th Sonnet, in which Shakespeare contrasts himself with those who are "great princes' favourites;" says quite frankly —

> "Let those who are in favour with their stars
> Of public honour and proud titles boast,
> Whilst I, whom fortune of such triumph bars,
> Unlook'd for joy in that I honour most;"

and ends the sonnet by congratulating himself on the mean state of him he so adored:

> "Then happy I, that loved and am beloved
> Where I may not remove nor be removed."

This sonnet Cyril declared would be quite unintelligible if we fancied that it was addressed to either the Earl of Pembroke or the Earl of Southampton, both of whom were men of the highest position in England and fully entitled to be called "great princes"; and he in corroboration of his view read me Sonnets CXXIV and CXXV, in which Shakespeare tells us that his love is not "the child of state," that it "suffers not in smiling pomp," but is "builded far from accident." I listened with a good deal of interest, for I don't think the point had ever been made before; but what followed was still more curious, and seemed to me at the time to entirely dispose of Pembroke's claim. We know from Meres[17] that the Sonnets had been written before 1598, and Sonnet CIV informs us that Shakespeare's friendship for Mr. W. H. had been already in existence for three years. Now Lord Pembroke, who was born in 1580, did not come to London till he was eighteen years of age, that is to say till 1598, and Shakespeare's acquaintance with Mr. W. H. must have begun in 1594, or at the latest in 1595. Shakespeare, accordingly, could not have known Lord Pembroke till after the Sonnets had been written.

'Cyril pointed out also that Pembroke's father did not die till 1601; whereas it was evident from the line,

> "You had a father, let your son say so,"

that the father of Mr. W. H. was dead in 1598. Besides, it was absurd to imagine that any publisher of the time, and the preface is from the publisher's hand,[18] would have ventured to address William Herbert, Earl of Pembroke, as Mr. W. H.; the case of Lord Buckhurst being spoken of as Mr. Sackville[19] being not really a parallel instance, as Lord Buckhurst was not a peer, but merely the younger son of a peer, with a courtesy title, and the passage in *England's Parnassus*, where he is so spoken of, is not a formal and stately dedication, but simply a casual allusion. So far for Lord Pembroke, whose supposed claims Cyril easily demolished while I sat by in wonder. With Lord Southampton Cyril had even less difficulty. Southampton became at a very early age the lover of Elizabeth Vernon,[20] so he needed no entreaties to marry; he was not beautiful; he did not resemble his mother, as Mr. W. H. did –

> "Thou art thy mother's glass, and she in thee
> Calls back the lovely April of her prime;"

and, above all, his Christian name was Henry, whereas the punning sonnets (CXXXV and CXLIII) show that the Christian name of Shakespeare's friend was the same as his own – *Will*.

'As for the other suggestions of unfortunate commentators, that Mr. W. H. is a misprint for Mr. W. S., meaning Mr. William Shakespeare; that "Mr. W. H. all" should be read "Mr. W. Hall"; that Mr. W. H. is Mr. William Hathaway; and that a full stop should be placed after "wisheth," making Mr. W. H. the writer and not the subject of the dedication,[21] – Cyril got rid of them in a very short time; and it is not worth while to mention his reasons, though I remember he sent me off into a fit of laughter by reading to me, I am glad to say not in the original, some extracts from a German commentator called Barnstorff, who insisted that Mr. W. H. was no less a person than "Mr. William

Himself."[22] Nor would he allow for a moment that the Sonnets are mere satires on the work of Drayton[23] and John Davies of Hereford.[24] To him, as indeed to me, they were poems of serious and tragic import, wrung out of the bitterness of Shakespeare's heart, and made sweet by the honey of his lips. Still less would he admit that they were merely a philosophical allegory, and that in them Shakespeare is addressing his Ideal Self, or Ideal Manhood, or the Spirit of Beauty, or the Reason, or the Divine Logos, or the Catholic Church.[25] He felt, as indeed I think we all must feel, that the Sonnets are addressed to an individual, – to a particular young man whose personality for some reason seems to have filled the soul of Shakespeare with terrible joy and no less terrible despair.

'Having in this manner cleared the way as it were, Cyril asked me to dismiss from my mind any preconceived ideas I might have formed on the subject, and to give a fair and unbiassed hearing to his own theory. The problem he pointed out was this: Who was that young man of Shakespeare's day who, without being of noble birth or even of noble nature, was addressed by him in terms of such passionate adoration that we can but wonder at the strange worship, and are almost afraid to turn the key that unlocks the mystery of the poet's heart? Who was he whose physical beauty was such that it became the very corner-stone of Shakespeare's art; the very source of Shakespeare's inspiration; the very incarnation of Shakespeare's dreams? To look upon him as simply the object of certain love-poems is to miss the whole meaning of the poems: for the art of which Shakespeare talks in the Sonnets is not the art of the Sonnets themselves, which indeed were to him but slight and secret things – it is the art of the dramatist to which he is always alluding; and he to whom Shakespeare said –

> "Though art all my art, and dost advance
> As high as learning my rude ignorance," –

he to whom he promised immortality,

> "Where breath most breathes, even in the mouth of men," –

was surely none other than the boy-actor for whom he created

Viola and Imogen, Juliet and Rosalind, Portia and Desdemona, and Cleopatra[26] herself. This was Cyril Graham's theory, evolved as you see purely from the Sonnets themselves, and depending for its acceptance not so much on demonstrable proof or formal evidence, but on a kind of spiritual and artistic sense, by which alone he claimed could the true meaning of the poems be discerned. I remember his reading to me that fine sonnet –

> "How can my Muse want subject to invent,
> While thou dost breathe, that pour'st into my verse
> Thine own sweet argument, too excellent
> For every vulgar paper to rehearse?
> O, give thyself the thanks, if aught in me
> Worthy perusal stand against thy sight;
> For who's so dumb that cannot write to thee,
> When thou thyself dost give invention light?
> Be thou the tenth Muse, ten times more in worth
> Than those old nine which rhymers invocate;
> And he that calls on thee, let him bring forth
> Eternal numbers to outlive long date"

– and pointing out how completely it corroborated his theory; and indeed he went through all the Sonnets carefully, and showed, or fancied that he showed, that, according to his new explanation of their meaning, things that had seemed obscure, or evil, or exaggerated, became clear and rational, and of high artistic import, illustrating Shakespeare's conception of the true relations between the art of the actor and the art of the dramatist.

'It is of course evident that there must have been in Shakespeare's company some wonderful boy-actor of great beauty, to whom he intrusted the presentation of his noble heroines; for Shakespeare was a practical theatrical manager as well as an imaginative poet, and Cyril Graham had actually discovered the boy-actor's name. He was Will, or, as he preferred to call him, Willie Hughes.[27] The Christian name he found of course in the punning sonnets, CXXXV and CXLIII; the surname was, according to him, hidden in the eighth[28] line of the 20th Sonnet, where Mr. W. H. is described as –

"A man in hew, all *Hews* in his controwling."

'In the original edition of the Sonnets "Hews" is printed with a capital letter and in italics, and this, he claimed, showed clearly that a play on words was intended, his view receiving a good deal of corroboration from those sonnets in which curious puns are made on the words "use" and "usury." Of course I was converted at once, and Willie Hughes became to me as real a person as Shakespeare. The only objection I made to the theory was that the name of Willie Hughes does not occur in the list of the actors of Shakespeare's company as it is printed in the first folio. Cyril, however, pointed out that the absence of Willie Hughes's name from this list really corroborated the theory, as it was evident from Sonnet LXXXVI that Willie Hughes had abandoned Shakespeare's company to play at a rival theatre, probably in some of Chapman's plays.[29] It is in reference to this that in the great sonnet on Chapman Shakespeare said to Willie Hughes –

> "But when your countenance filled up his line,
> Then lacked I matter; that enfeebled mine" –

the expression "when your countenance filled up his line" referring obviously to the beauty of the young actor giving life and reality and added charm to Chapman's verse, the same idea being also put forward in the 79th Sonnet –

> "Whilst I alone did call upon thy aid,
> My verse alone had all thy gentle grace,
> But now my gracious numbers are decayed,
> And my sick Muse does give another place;"

and in the immediately preceding sonnet, where Shakespeare says –

> "Every alien pen has got my *use*
> And under thee their poesy disperse,"

the play upon words (use = Hughes) being of course obvious, and the phrase "under thee their poesy disperse," meaning "by your assistance as an actor bring their plays before the people."

'It was a wonderful evening, and we sat up almost till dawn reading and re-reading the Sonnets. After some time, however, I began to see that before the theory could be placed before the world in a really perfected form, it was necessary to get some independent evidence about the existence of this young actor Willie Hughes. If this could be once established, there could be no possible doubt about his identity with Mr. W. H.; but otherwise the theory would fall to the ground. I put this forward very strongly to Cyril, who was a good deal annoyed at what he called my Philistine[30] tone of mind, and indeed was rather bitter upon the subject. However, I made him promise that in his own interest he would not publish his discovery till he had put the whole matter beyond the reach of doubt; and for weeks and weeks we searched the registers of City churches, the Alleyn MSS at Dulwich, the Record Office, the papers of the Lord Chamberlain[31] – everything, in fact, that we thought might contain some allusion to Willie Hughes. We discovered nothing, of course, and every day the existence of Willie Hughes seemed to me to become more problematical. Cyril was in a dreadful state, and used to go over the whole question day after day, entreating me to believe; but I saw the one flaw in the theory, and I refused to be convinced till the actual existence of Willie Hughes, a boy-actor of Elizabethan days, had been placed beyond the reach of doubt or cavil.

'One day Cyril left town to stay with his grandfather, I thought at the time, but I afterwards heard from Lord Crediton that this was not the case; and about a fortnight afterwards I received a telegram from him, handed in at Warwick, asking me to be sure to come and dine with him that evening at eight o'clock. When I arrived, he said to me, "The only apostle who did not deserve proof was S. Thomas, and S. Thomas was the only apostle who got it." I asked him what he meant. He answered that he had not merely been able to establish the existence in the sixteenth century of a boy-actor of the name of Willie Hughes, but to prove by the most conclusive evidence that he was the Mr. W. H. of the Sonnets. He would not tell me anything more at the time; but after dinner he solemnly produced the picture I showed you, and told me that he had discovered it by the merest chance nailed to the side of an old chest that he had bought at a farmhouse in Warwickshire. The chest itself, which was a very fine example of Elizabethan work, he had, of course, brought with him, and in the centre of the front panel the initials W. H. were undoubtedly carved. It was this monogram that had attracted his attention, and he told me that it was not till he had had the chest in his possession for several days that he had thought of making any careful examination of the inside. One morning, however, he saw that one of the sides of the chest was much thicker than the other, and looking more closely, he discovered that a framed panel picture was clamped against it. On taking it out, he found it was the picture that is now lying on the sofa. It was very dirty, and covered with mould; but he managed to clean it, and, to his great joy, saw that he had fallen by mere chance on the one thing for which he had been looking. Here was an authentic portrait of Mr. W. H., with his hand resting on the dedicatory page of the Sonnets, and on the frame itself could be faintly seen the name of the young man written in black uncial letters on a faded gold ground, "Master Will. Hews."

'Well, what was I to say? It never occurred to me for a moment that Cyril Graham was playing a trick on me, or that he was trying to prove his theory by means of a forgery.'

'But is it a forgery?' I asked.

'Of course it is,' said Erskine. 'It is a very good forgery; but it is a forgery none the less. I thought at the time that Cyril was rather calm about the whole matter; but I remember he more than once told me that he himself required no proof of the kind, and that he thought the theory complete without it. I laughed at him, and told him that without it the theory would fall to the ground, and I warmly congratulated him on the marvellous discovery. We then arranged that the picture should be etched or facsimiled, and placed as the frontispiece to Cyril's edition of the Sonnets; and for three months we did nothing but go over each poem line by line, till we had settled every difficulty of text or meaning. One unlucky day I was in a print-shop in Holborn, when I saw upon the counter some extremely beautiful drawings in silver-point. I was so attracted by them that I bought them; and the proprietor of the place, a man called Rawlings, told me that they were done by a young painter of the name of Edward Merton, who was very clever, but as poor as a church mouse. I went to see Merton some days afterwards, having got his address from the print-seller, and found a pale, interesting young man, with a rather common-looking wife – his model, as I subsequently learned. I told him how much I admired his drawings, at which he seemed very pleased, and I asked him if he would show me some of his other work. As we were looking over a portfolio, full of really very lovely things, – for Merton had a most delicate and delightful touch, – I suddenly caught sight of a drawing of the picture of Mr. W. H. There was no doubt whatever about it. It was almost a facsimile – the only difference being that the two masks of Tragedy and Comedy were not suspended from the marble table as they are in the picture, but were lying on the floor at the young man's feet. "Where on earth did you get that?" I said. He grew rather confused, and said – "Oh, that is nothing. I did not know it was in this portfolio. It is not a thing of any value." "It is what you did for Mr. Cyril Graham," exclaimed his wife; "and if this gentleman wishes to buy it, let him have it." "For Mr. Cyril Graham?" I repeated. "Did you paint the picture of Mr. W. H.?" "I don't understand what you mean," he answered, growing very red. Well, the whole thing was quite dreadful. The wife let it all out. I gave her five pounds when I was going away. I can't bear to think of it now; but of course I was furious. I went off at once to Cyril's chambers, waited there for three hours before he came in, with that horrid lie staring me in the face, and told him I had discovered his forgery. He grew very pale, and said – "I did it purely for your sake. You would not be convinced in any other way. It does not affect the truth of the theory." "The truth of the theory!" – I exclaimed; "the less we talk about that the better. You never even believed in it yourself. If you had, you would not have committed a forgery to prove it." High words passed between us; we had a fearful quarrel. I daresay I was unjust. The next morning he was dead.'

'Dead!' I cried.

'Yes; he shot himself with a revolver. Some of the blood splashed upon the frame of the picture, just where the name had been painted. By the time I arrived – his servant had sent for me at once – the police were already there. He had left a letter for me, evidently written in the greatest agitation and distress of mind.'

'What was in it?' I asked.

'Oh, that he believed absolutely in Willie Hughes; that the forgery of the picture had been done simply as a concession to me, and did not in the slightest degree invalidate the truth of the theory; and that in order to show me how firm and flawless his faith in the whole thing was, he was going to offer his life as a sacrifice to the secret of the Sonnets. It was a foolish, mad letter. I remember he ended by saying that he intrusted to me the Willie Hughes theory, and that it was for me to present it to the world, and to unlock the secret of Shakespeare's heart.'

'It is a most tragic story,' I cried; 'but why have you not carried out his wishes?'

Erskine shrugged his shoulders. 'Because it is a perfectly unsound theory from beginning to end,' he answered.

'My dear Erskine,' I said, getting up from my seat, 'you are entirely wrong about the whole matter. It is the only perfect key to Shakespeare's Sonnets that has ever been made. It is complete in every detail. I believe in Willie Hughes.'

'Don't say that,' said Erskine gravely; 'I believe there is something fatal about the idea, and intellectually there is nothing to be said for it. I have gone into the whole matter, and I assure you the theory is entirely fallacious. It is plausible up to a certain point. Then it stops. For heaven's sake, my dear boy, don't take up the subject of Willie Hughes. You will break your heart over it.'

'Erskine,' I answered, 'it is your duty to give this theory to the world. If you will not do it, I will. By keeping it back you wrong the memory of Cyril Graham, the youngest and the most splendid of all the martyrs of literature. I entreat you to do him justice. He died for this thing, – don't let his death be in vain.'

Erskine looked at me in amazement. 'You are carried away by the sentiment of the whole story,' he said. 'You forget that a thing is not necessarily true because a man dies for it. I was devoted to Cyril Graham. His death was a horrible blow to me. I did not recover it for years. I don't think I have ever recovered it. But Willie Hughes? There is nothing in the idea of Willie Hughes.

No such person ever existed. As for bringing the whole thing before the world – the world thinks that Cyril Graham shot himself by accident. The only proof of his suicide was contained in the letter to me, and of this letter the public never heard anything. To the present day Lord Crediton thinks that the whole thing was accidental.'

'Cyril Graham sacrificed his life to a great idea,' I answered; 'and if you will not tell of his martyrdom, tell at least of his faith.'

'His faith,' said Erskine, 'was fixed in a thing that was false, in a thing that was unsound, in a thing that no Shakespearean scholar would accept for a moment. The theory would be laughed at. Don't make a fool of yourself, and don't follow a trail that leads nowhere. You start by assuming the existence of the very person whose existence is the thing to be proved. Besides, everybody knows that the Sonnets were addressed to Lord Pembroke. The matter is settled once for all.'

'The matter is not settled!' I exclaimed. 'I will take up the theory where Cyril Graham left it, and I will prove to the world that he was right.'

'Silly boy!' said Erskine. 'Go home: it is after two, and don't think about Willie Hughes any more. I am sorry I told you anything about it, and very sorry indeed that I should have converted you to a thing in which I don't believe.'

'You have given me the key to the greatest mystery of modern literature,' I answered; 'and I shall not rest till I have made you recognise, till I have made everybody recognise, that Cyril Graham was the most subtle Shakespearean critic of our day.'

As I walked home through St. James's Park the dawn was just breaking over London. The white swans were lying asleep on the polished lake, and the gaunt Palace[32] looked purple against the pale-green sky. I thought of Cyril Graham, and my eyes filled with tears.

II

It was past twelve o'clock when I awoke, and the sun was streaming in through the curtains of my room in long slanting beams of dusty gold. I told my servant that I would be at home to no one; and after I had had a cup of chocolate and a *petit-pain*,[33] I took down from the book-shelf my copy of Shakespeare's Sonnets, and began to go carefully through them. Every poem seemed to me to corroborate Cyril Graham's theory. I felt as if I had my hand upon Shakespeare's heart, and was counting each separate throb and pulse of passion. I thought of the wonderful boy-actor, and saw his face in every line.

Two sonnets, I remember, struck me particularly: they were the 53rd and the 67th. In the first of these, Shakespeare, complimenting Willie Hughes on the versatility of his acting, on his wide range of parts, a range extending from Rosalind to Juliet, and from Beatrice to Ophelia,[34] says to him –

> 'What is your substance, whereof are you made,
> That millions of strange shadows on you tend?
> Since every one hath, every one, one shade,
> And you, but one, can every shadow lend' –

lines that would be unintelligible if they were not addressed to an actor, for the word 'shadow' had in Shakespeare's day a technical meaning connected with the stage. 'The best in this kind are but shadows,' says Theseus of the actors, in the *Midsummer Night's Dream*, and there are many similar allusions in the literature of the day. These sonnets evidently belonged to the series in which Shakespeare discusses the nature of the actor's art, and of the strange and rare temperament that is essential to the perfect stage-player. 'How is it,' says Shakespeare to Willie Hughes, 'that you have so many personalities?' and then he goes on to point out that his beauty is such that it seems to realise every form and phase of fancy, to embody each dream of the creative imagination – an idea that is still further expanded in the sonnet that immediately follows, where, beginning with the fine thought,

> 'O, how much more doth beauty beauteous seem
> By that sweet ornament which *truth* doth give!'

Shakespeare invites us to notice how the truth of acting, the truth of visible presentation on the stage, adds to the wonder of poetry, giving life to its loveliness, and actual reality to its ideal form.

And yet, in the 67th Sonnet, Shakespeare calls upon Willie Hughes to abandon the stage with its artificiality, its false mimic life of painted face and unreal costume, its immoral influences and suggestions, its remoteness from the true world of noble action and sincere utterance.

> 'Ah! wherefore with infection should he live,
> And with his presence grace impiety,
> That sin by him advantage should achieve,
> And lace itself with his society?
> Why should false painting imitate his cheek
> And steal dead seeming of his living hue?
> Why should poor beauty indirectly seek
> Roses of shadow, since his rose is true?'

It may seem strange that so great a dramatist as Shakespeare, who realised his own perfection as an artist and his humanity as a man on the ideal plane of stage-writing and stage-playing, should have written in these terms about the theatre; but we must remember that in Sonnets CX and CXI Shakespeare shows us that he too was wearied of the world of puppets, and full of shame at having made himself 'a motley to the view.' The 111th Sonnet is especially bitter: –

> 'O, for my sake do you with Fortune chide
> The guilty goddess of my harmful deeds,
> That did not better for my life provide
> Than public means which public manners breeds.
> Thence comes it that my name receives a brand,
> And almost thence my nature is subdued
> To what it works in, like the dyer's hand:
> Pity me, then, and wish I were renewed' –

and there are many signs elsewhere of the same feeling, signs familiar to all real students of Shakespeare.

One point puzzled me immensely as I read the Sonnets, and it was days before I struck on the true interpretation, which indeed Cyril Graham himself seems to have missed. I could not understand how it was that Shakespeare set so high a value on his young friend marrying. He himself had married young, and the result had been unhappiness, and it was not likely that he would have asked Willie Hughes to commit the same error. The boy-player of Rosalind had nothing to gain from marriage, or from the passions of real life. The early sonnets, with their strange entreaties to have children, seemed to me a jarring note. The explanation of the mystery came on me quite suddenly, and I found it in the curious dedication. It will be remembered that the dedication runs as follows: –

> 'TO THE ONLIE BEGETTER OF
> THESE INSUING SONNETS
> MR W. H. ALL HAPPINESSE
> AND THAT ETERNITIE
> PROMISED BY
> OUR EVER-LIVING POET
> WISHETH
> THE WELL-WISHING
> ADVENTURER IN
> SETTING
> FORTH.
>
> T. T.

Some scholars have supposed that the word 'begetter' in this dedication means simply the procurer of the Sonnets for Thomas Thorpe[35] the publisher; but this view is now generally abandoned, and the highest authorities are quite agreed that it is to be taken in the sense of inspirer, the metaphor being drawn from the analogy of physical life. Now I saw that the same metaphor was used by Shakespeare himself all through the poems, and this set me on the right track. Finally I made my great discovery. The marriage that Shakespeare proposes for Willie Hughes is the 'marriage with his Muse,' an expression which is definitely put forward in the 82nd Sonnet, where, in the bitterness of his heart at the defection of the boy-actor for whom he had written his greatest parts, and whose beauty had indeed suggested them, he opens his complaint by saying –

'I'll grant thou wert not married to my Muse.'

The children he begs him to beget are no children of flesh and blood, but more immortal children of undying fame. The whole cycle of the early sonnets is simply Shakespeare's invitation to Willie Hughes to go upon the stage and become a player. How barren and profitless a thing, he says, is this beauty of yours if it be not used: –

> 'When forty winters shall besiege thy brow,
> And dig deep trenches in thy beauty's field,
> Thy youth's proud livery, so gazed on now,
> Will be a tattered weed, of small worth held:
> Then being asked where all thy beauty lies,
> Where all the treasure of thy lusty days,
> To say, within thine own deep-sunken eyes,
> Were an all-eating shame and thriftless praise.'

You must create something in art: my verse 'is thine, and *born* of thee;' only listen to me, and I will '*bring forth* eternal numbers to outlive long date,' and you shall people with forms of your own image the imaginary world of the stage. These children that you beget, he continues, will not wither away, as mortal children do, but you shall live in them and in my plays: do but –

> 'Make thee another self, for love of me,
> That beauty still may live in thine or thee!'

I collected all the passages that seemed to me to corroborate this view, and they produced a strong impression on me, and showed me how complete Cyril Graham's theory really was. I also saw that it was quite easy to separate those lines in which he speaks of the Sonnets themselves from those in which he speaks of his great dramatic work. This was a point that had been entirely overlooked by all critics up to Cyril Graham's day. And yet it was one of the most important points in the whole series of poems. To the Sonnets Shakespeare was more or less indifferent. He did not wish to rest his fame on them. They were to him his 'slight Muse,'[36] as he calls them, and intended, as Meres tells us, for private circulation only among a few, a very few, friends. Upon the other hand he was extremely conscious of the high artistic value of his plays, and shows a noble self-reliance upon his dramatic genius. When he says to Willie Hughes: –

> 'But thy eternal summer shall not fade,
> Nor lose possession of that fair thou owest;
> Nor shall Death brag thou wander'st in his shade,
> When in *eternal lines* to time thou growest;
>> So long as men can breathe or eyes can see,
>> So long lives this and this gives life to thee;' –

the expression 'eternal lines' clearly alludes to one of his plays that he was sending him at the time, just as the concluding couplet points to his confidence in the probability of his plays being always acted. In his address to the Dramatic Muse (Sonnets C and CI), we find the same feeling.

> 'Where art thou, Muse, that thou forget'st so long
> To speak of that which gives thee all thy might?
> Spends thou thy fury on some worthless song,
> Darkening thy power to lend base subjects light?'

he cries, and he then proceeds to reproach the mistress of Tragedy and Comedy for her 'neglect of Truth in Beauty dyed,' and says –

> 'Because he needs no praise, wilt thou be dumb?
> Excuse not silence so; for 't lies in thee
> To make him much outlive a gilded tomb,
> And to be praised of ages yet to be.
>> Then do thy office, Muse; I teach thee how
>> To make him seem long hence as he shows now.'

It is, however, perhaps in the 55th Sonnet that Shakespeare gives to this idea its fullest expression. To imagine that the 'powerful rhyme' of the second line refers to the sonnet itself, is to entirely mistake Shakespeare's meaning. It seemed to me that it was extremely likely, from the general character of the sonnet, that a particular play was meant, and that the play was none other but *Romeo and Juliet*.

> 'Not marble, nor the gilded monuments
> Of princes, shall outlive this powerful rhyme;
> But you shall shine more bright in these contents
> Than unswept stone besmeared with sluttish time.
> When wasteful wars shall statues overturn,
> And broils root out the work of masonry,

Not Mars his sword nor war's quick fire shall burn
The living record of your memory.
'Gainst death and all-oblivious enmity
Shall you pace forth; your praise shall still find room
Even in the eyes of all posterity
That wear this world out to the ending doom.
So, till the judgment that yourself arise,
You live in this, and dwell in lovers' eyes.'

It was also extremely suggestive to note how here as elsewhere Shakespeare promised Willie Hughes immortality in a form that appealed to men's eyes – that is to say, in a spectacular form, in a play that is to be looked at.

For two weeks I worked hard at the Sonnets, hardly ever going out, and refusing all invitations. Every day I seemed to be discovering something new, and Willie Hughes became to me a kind of spiritual presence, an ever-dominant personality. I could almost fancy that I saw him standing in the shadow of my room, so well had Shakespeare drawn him, with his golden hair, his tender flower-like grace, his dreamy deep-sunken eyes, his delicate mobile limbs, and his white lily hands. His very name fascinated me. Willie Hughes! Willie Hughes! How musically it sounded! Yes; who else but he could have been the master-mistress of Shakespeare's passion,[a] the lord of his love to whom he was bound in vassalage,[b] the delicate minion of pleasure,[c] the rose of the whole world,[d] the herald of the spring[e] decked in the proud livery of youth,[f] the lovely boy whom it was sweet music to hear,[g] and whose beauty was the very raiment of Shakespeare's heart,[h] as it was the keystone of his dramatic power? How bitter now seemed the whole tragedy of his desertion and his shame! – shame that he made sweet and lovely[i] by the mere magic of his personality, but that was none the less shame. Yet as Shakespeare forgave him, should not we forgive him also? I did not care to pry into the mystery of his sin.

His abandonment of Shakespeare's theatre was a different

---

[a] Sonnet xx, 2.
[b] Sonnet xxvi, 1.
[c] Sonnet cxxvi, 9.
[d] Sonnet cix, 14.
[e] Sonnet i, 10.
[f] Sonnet ii, 3.
[g] Sonnet viii, 1.
[h] Sonnet xxii, 6.
[i] Sonnet xcv, 1.

matter, and I investigated it at great length. Finally I came to the conclusion that Cyril Graham had been wrong in regarding the rival dramatist of the 80th Sonnet as Chapman. It was obviously Marlowe[37] who was alluded to. At the time the Sonnets were written, such an expression as 'the proud full sail of his great verse' could not have been used of Chapman's work, however applicable it might have been to the style of his later Jacobean plays. No: Marlowe was clearly the rival dramatist of whom Shakespeare spoke in such laudatory terms; and that

> 'Affable familiar ghost
> Which nightly gulls him with intelligence,'

was the Mephistopheles of his Doctor Faustus.[38] No doubt, Marlowe was fascinated by the beauty and grace of the boy-actor, and lured him away from the Blackfriars' Theatre,[39] that he might play the Gaveston of his *Edward II*.[40] That Shakespeare had the legal right to retain Willie Hughes in his own company is evident from Sonnet LXXXVII, where he says: –

> 'Farewell! thou are too dear for my possessing,
> And like enough thou know'st thy estimate:
> The *charter of thy worth* gives thee releasing;
> My *bonds* in thee are all determinate.
> For how do I hold thee but by thy granting?
> And for that riches where is my deserving?
> The cause of this fair gift in me is wanting,
> *And so my patent back again is swerving*.
> Thyself thou gavest, thy own work then not knowing,
> Or me, to whom thou gavest it, else mistaking;
> So thy great gift, upon misprision growing,
> Comes home again, on better judgment making.
>   Thus have I had thee, as a dream doth flatter,
>   In sleep a king, but waking no such matter.'

But him whom he could not hold by love, he would not hold by force. Willie Hughes became a member of Lord Pembroke's company, and, perhaps in the open yard of the Red Bull Tavern,[41] played the part of King Edward's delicate minion.[42] On Marlowe's death, he seems to have returned to Shakespeare, who, whatever his fellow-partners may have thought of the matter, was not slow to forgive the wilfulness and treachery of the young actor.

How well, too, had Shakespeare drawn the temperament of the stage-player! Willie Hughes was one of those

> 'That do not do the thing they most do show,
> Who, moving others, are themselves as stone.'

He could act love, but could not feel it, could mimic passion without realising it.

> 'In many's looks the false heart's history
> Is writ in moods and frowns and wrinkles strange,'

but with Willie Hughes it was not so. 'Heaven,' says Shakespeare, in a sonnet of mad idolatry –

> 'Heaven in thy creation did decree
> That in thy face sweet love should ever dwell;
> Whate'er thy thoughts or thy heart's workings be,
> Thy looks should nothing thence but sweetness tell.'

In his 'inconstant mind' and his 'false heart,' it was easy to recognise the insincerity and treachery that somehow seem inseparable from the artistic nature, as in his love of praise, that desire for immediate recognition that characterises all actors. And yet, more fortunate in this than other actors, Willie Hughes was to know something of immortality. Inseparably connected with Shakespeare's plays, he was to live in them.

> 'Your name from hence immortal life shall have,
> Though I, once gone, to all the world must die:
> The earth can yield me but a common grave,
> When you entombed in men's eyes shall lie.
> Your monument shall be my gentle verse,
> Which eyes not yet created shall o'er-read,
> And tongues to be your being shall rehearse
> When all the breathers of this world are dead.'

There were endless allusions, also, to Willie Hughes's power over his audience, – the 'gazers,' as Shakespeare calls them; but perhaps the most perfect description of his wonderful mastery over dramatic art was in *The Lover's Complaint*,[43] where Shakespeare says of him: –

'In him a plenitude of subtle matter,
Applied to cautels, all strange forms receives,
Of burning blushes, or of weeping water,
Or swooning paleness; and he takes and leaves,
In either's aptness, as it best deceives,
To blush at speeches rank, to weep at woes,
Or to turn white and swoon at tragic shows.

*

So on the tip of his subduing tongue,
All kinds of arguments and questions deep,
All replication prompt and reason strong,
For his advantage still did wake and sleep,
To make the weeper laugh, the laugher weep,
He had the dialect and the different skill,
Catching all passions in his craft of will.'

Once I thought that I had really found Willie Hughes in Elizabethan literature. In a wonderfully graphic account of the last days of the great Earl of Essex, his chaplain, Thomas Knell,[44] tells us that the night before the Earl died, 'he called William Hewes, which was his musician, to play upon the virginals and to sing. "Play," said he, "my song, Will Hewes, and I will sing it myself." So he did it most joyfully, not as the howling swan, which, still looking down, waileth her end, but as a sweet lark, lifting up his hands and casting up his eyes to his God, with this mounted the crystal skies, and reached with his unwearied tongue the top of highest heavens.' Surely the boy who played on the virginals to the dying father of Sidney's Stella[45] was none other but the Will Hews to whom Shakespeare dedicated the Sonnets, and whom he tells us was himself sweet 'music to hear.' Yet Lord Essex died in 1576, when Shakespeare himself was but twelve years of age. It was impossible that his musician could have been the Mr. W. H. of the Sonnets. Perhaps Shakespeare's young friend was the son of the player upon the virginals? It was at least something to have discovered that Will Hews was an Elizabethan name.[46] Indeed the name Hews seemed to have been closely connected with music and the stage. The first English actress was the lovely Margaret Hews, whom Prince Rupert so madly loved.[47] What more probable than that between her and Lord Essex's

72

musician had come the boy-actor of Shakespeare's plays? But the proofs, the links – where were they? Alas! I could not find them. It seemed to me that I was always on the brink of absolute verification, but that I could never really attain to it.

From Willie Hughes's life I soon passed to thoughts of his death. I used to wonder what had been his end.

Perhaps he had been one of those English actors who in 1604 went across sea to Germany and played before the great Duke Henry Julius of Brunswick, himself a dramatist of no mean order, and at the Court of that strange Elector of Brandenburg,[48] who was so enamoured of beauty that he was said to have bought for his weight in amber the young son of a travelling Greek merchant, and to have given pageants in honour of his slave all through that dreadful famine year of 1606–7, when the people died of hunger in the very streets of the town, and for the space of seven months there was no rain. We know at any rate that *Romeo and Juliet* was brought out at Dresden in 1613, along with *Hamlet* and *King Lear*, and it was surely to none other than Willie Hughes that in 1615 the death-mask of Shakespeare was brought by the hand of one of the suite of the English ambassador, pale token of the passing away of the great poet who had so dearly loved him. Indeed there would have been something peculiarly fitting in the idea that the boy-actor, whose beauty had been so vital an element in the realism and romance of Shakespeare's art, should have been the first to have brought to Germany the seed of the new culture, and was in his way the precursor of that *Aufklarung*[49] or Illumination of the eighteenth century, that splendid movement which, though begun by Lessing and Herder, and brought to its full and perfect issue by Goethe, was in no small part helped on by another actor – Friedrich Schroeder[50] – who awoke the popular consciousness, and by means of the feigned passions and mimetic methods of the stage showed the intimate, the vital, connection between life and literature. If this was so, – and there was certainly no evidence against it, – it was not improbable that Willie Hughes was one of those English comedians (*mimae quidam ex Britannia*, as the old chronicle calls them), who were slain at Nuremberg[51] in a sudden uprising of the people, and were secretly buried in a little vineyard outside the city by some young men 'who had found pleasure in their performances, and of whom some had sought to be instructed in the mysteries of the new art.' Certainly no more fitting place could there be for him to whom Shakespeare said, 'thou art all my art,' than this little vineyard outside the city walls. For was it not from the sorrows of Dionysos that Tragedy sprang?[52] Was not the light laughter of Comedy, with its careless merriment and quick replies, first heard on the lips of the Sicilian vine-dressers? Nay, did not the purple and red stain of the wine-froth on face and limbs give the first suggestion of the charm and fascination of disguise – the desire for self-concealment, the sense of the value of objectivity thus showing itself in the rude beginnings of the art? At any rate, wherever he lay – whether in the little vineyard at the gate of the Gothic town, or in some dim London churchyard amidst the roar and bustle of our great city – no gorgeous monument marked his resting-place. His true tomb, as Shakespeare saw, was the poet's verse, his true monument the permanence of the drama. So had it been with others whose beauty had given a new creative impulse to their age. The ivory body of the Bithynian slave rots in the green ooze of the Nile, and on the yellow hills of the Cerameicus is strewn the dust of the young Athenian; but Antinous lives in sculpture, and Charmides in philosophy.[53]

III

After three weeks had elapsed, I determined to make a strong appeal to Erskine to do justice to the memory of Cyril Graham, and to give to the world his marvellous interpretation of the Sonnets – the only interpretation that thoroughly explained the problem. I have not any copy of my letter, I regret to say, nor have I been able to lay my hand upon the original; but I remember that I went over the whole ground, and covered sheets of paper with passionate reiteration of the arguments and proofs that my study had suggested to me. It seemed to me that I was not merely restoring Cyril Graham to his proper place in literary history, but rescuing the honour of Shakespeare himself from the tedious memory of a commonplace intrigue. I put into the letter all my enthusiasm. I put into the letter all my faith.

No sooner, in fact, had I sent it off than a curious reaction came over me. It seemed to me that I had given away my capacity for belief in the Willie Hughes theory of the Sonnets, that something had gone out of me, as it were, and that I was perfectly indifferent to the whole subject. What was it that had happened? It is difficult to say. Perhaps, by finding perfect expression for a passion, I had exhausted the passion itself. Emotional forces, like the forces of physical life, have their positive limitations. Perhaps the mere effort to convert any one to a theory involves some form of renunciation of the power of credence. Perhaps I was simply tired of the whole thing, and, my enthusiasm having burnt out, my reason was left to its own unimpassioned judgment. However it came about, and I cannot pretend to explain it, there was no doubt that Willie Hughes suddenly became to me a mere myth, an idle dream, the boyish fancy of a young man who, like most ardent spirits, was more anxious to convince others than to be himself convinced.

As I had said some very unjust and bitter things to Erskine in my letter, I determined to go and see him at once, and to make my apologies to him for my behaviour. Accordingly, the next morning I drove down to Birdcage Walk, and found Erskine sitting in his library, with the forged picture of Willie Hughes in front of him.

'My dear Erskine!' I cried, 'I have come to apologise to you.'

'To apologise to me?' he said. 'What for?'

'For my letter,' I answered.

'You have nothing to regret in your letter,' he said. 'On the contrary, you have done me the greatest service in your power. You have shown me that Cyril Graham's theory is perfectly sound.'

'You don't mean to say that you believe in Willie Hughes?' I exclaimed.

'Why not?' he rejoined. 'You have proved the thing to me. Do you think I cannot estimate the value of evidence?'

'But there is no evidence at all,' I groaned, sinking into a chair. 'When I wrote to you I was under the influence of a perfectly silly enthusiasm. I had been touched by the story of Cyril Graham's death, fascinated by his romantic theory, enthralled by the wonder and novelty of the whole idea. I see now that the theory is based on a delusion. The only evidence for the existence of Willie Hughes is that picture in front of you, and the picture is a forgery. Don't be carried away by mere sentiment in this matter. Whatever romance may have to say about the Willie Hughes theory, reason is dead against it.'

'I don't understand you,' said Erskine, looking at me in amazement. 'Why, you yourself have convinced me by your letter that Willie Hughes is an absolute reality. Why have you changed your mind? Or is all that you have been saying to me merely a joke?'

'I cannot explain it to you,' I rejoined, 'but I see now that there is really nothing to be said in favour of Cyril Graham's interpretation. The Sonnets are addressed to Lord Pembroke. For heaven's sake don't waste your time in a foolish attempt to discover a young Elizabethan actor who never existed, and to make a phantom puppet the centre of the great cycle of Shakespeare's Sonnets.'

'I see that you don't understand the theory,' he replied.

'My dear Erskine,' I cried, 'not understand it! Why, I feel as if I had invented it. Surely my letter shows you that I not merely went into the whole matter, but that I contributed proofs of every kind. The one flaw in the theory is that it presupposes the existence of the person whose existence is the subject of dispute. If we grant that there was in Shakespeare's company a young actor of the name of Willie Hughes, it is not difficult to make him the object of the Sonnets. But as we know that there was no actor of this name in the company of the Globe Theatre,[54] it is idle to pursue the investigation further.'

'But that is exactly what we don't know,' said Erskine. 'It is quite true that his name does not occur in the list given in the first folio; but, as Cyril pointed out, that is rather a proof in favour of the existence of Willie Hughes than against it, if we remember his treacherous desertion of Shakespeare for a rival dramatist.'

We argued the matter over for hours, but nothing that I could say could make Erskine surrender his faith in Cyril Graham's interpretation. He told me that he intended to devote his life to proving the theory, and that he was determined to do justice to Cyril Graham's memory. I entreated him, laughed at him, begged of him, but it was of no use. Finally we parted, not exactly in anger, but certainly with a shadow between us. He thought me shallow, I thought him foolish. When I called on him again, his servant told me that he had gone to Germany.

Two years afterwards, as I was going into my club, the hall-porter handed me a letter with a foreign postmark. It was from Erskine, and written at the Hotel d'Angleterre, Cannes.[55] When I had read it I was filled with horror, though I did not quite believe that he would be so mad as to carry his resolve into execution. The gist of the letter was that he had tried in every way to verify the Willie Hughes theory, and had failed, and that as Cyril Graham had given his life for this theory, he himself had determined to give his own life also to the same cause. The concluding words of the letter were these: 'I still believe in Willie Hughes; and by the time you receive this, I shall have died by my own hand for Willie Hughes's sake: for his sake, and for the sake of Cyril Graham, whom I drove to his death by my shallow scepticism and ignorant lack of faith. The truth was once revealed to you, and you rejected it. It comes to you now stained with the blood of two lives, – do not turn away from it.'

It was a horrible moment. I felt sick with misery, and yet I could not believe it. To die for one's theological beliefs is the worst use a man can make of his life, but to die for a literary theory! It seemed impossible.

I looked at the date. The letter was a week old. Some unfortunate chance had prevented my going to the club for several days, or I might have got it in time to save him. Perhaps it was not too late. I drove off to my rooms, packed up my things, and started by the night-mail from Charing Cross.[56] The journey was intolerable. I thought I would never arrive. As soon as I did I drove to the Hotel d'Angleterre. They told me that Erskine had been buried two days before, in the English cemetery. There was something horribly grotesque about the whole tragedy. I said all kinds of wild things, and the people in the hall looked curiously at me.

Suddenly Lady Erskine, in deep mourning, passed across the vestibule. When she saw me she came up to me, murmured something about her poor son, and burst into tears. I led her into her sitting-room. An elderly gentleman was there waiting for her. It was the English doctor.

We talked a great deal about Erskine, but I said nothing about his motive for committing suicide. It was evident that he had not told his mother anything about the reason that had driven him to so fatal, so mad an act. Finally Lady Erskine rose and said, 'George left you something as a memento. It was a thing he prized very much. I will get it for you.'

As soon as she had left the room I turned to the doctor and said, 'What a dreadful shock it must have been to Lady Erskine! I wonder that she bears it as well as she does.'

'Oh, she knew for months past that it was coming,' he answered.

'Knew it for months past!' I cried. 'But why didn't she stop him? Why didn't she have him watched? He must have been mad.'

The doctor stared at me. 'I don't know what you mean,' he said.

'Well,' I cried, 'if a mother knows that her son is going to commit suicide –'

'Suicide!' he answered. 'Poor Erskine did not commit suicide. He died of consumption. He came here to die. The moment I saw him I knew that there was no hope. One lung was almost gone, and the other was very much affected. Three days before he died he asked me was there any hope. I told him frankly that there was none, and that he had only a few days to live. He wrote some letters, and was quite resigned, retaining his senses to the last.'

At that moment Lady Erskine entered the room with the fatal picture of Willie Hughes in her hand. 'When George was dying he begged me to give you this,' she said. As I took it from her, her tears fell on my hand.

The picture hangs now in my library, where it is very much admired by my artistic friends. They have decided that it is not a Clouet, but an Ouvry.[57] I have never cared to tell them its true history. But sometimes, when I look at it, I think that there is really a great deal to be said for the Willie Hughes theory of Shakespeare's Sonnets.

A House of Pomegranates

To Constance Mary Wilde[1]

The Young King

To Margaret, Lady Brooke[1]

It was the night before the day fixed for his coronation, and the
young King was sitting alone in his beautiful chamber. His
courtiers had all taken their leave of him, bowing their heads to
the ground, according to the ceremonious usage of the day, and
had retired to the Great Hall of the Palace, to receive a few last
lessons from the Professor of Etiquette; there being some of them
who had still quite natural manners, which in a courtier is, I
need hardly say, a very grave offence.

The lad – for he was only a lad, being but sixteen years of age
– was not sorry at their departure, and had flung himself back
with a deep sigh of relief on the soft cushions of his embroidered
couch, lying there, wild-eyed and open-mouthed, like a brown
woodland Faun,[2] or some young animal of the forest newly
snared by the hunters.

And, indeed, it was the hunters who had found him, coming
upon him almost by chance as, bare-limbed and pipe in hand, he
was following the flock of the poor goatherd who had brought
him up, and whose son he had always fancied himself to be. The
child of the old King's only daughter by a secret marriage with
one much beneath her in station – a stranger, some said, who, by
the wonderful magic of his lute-playing, had made the young
Princess love him; while others spoke of an artist from Rimini, to
whom the Princess had shown much, perhaps too much honour,
and who had suddenly disappeared from the city, leaving his
work in the Cathedral unfinished – he had been, when but a
week old, stolen away from his mother's side, as she slept, and
given into the charge of a common peasant and his wife, who
were without children of their own, and lived in a remote part of
the forest, more than a day's ride from the town. Grief, or the

plague, as the court physician stated, or, as some suggested, a swift Italian poison administered in a cup of spiced wine, slew, within an hour of her wakening, the white girl who had given him birth, and as the trusty messenger who bare the child across his saddle-bow stooped from his weary horse and knocked at the rude door of the goatherd's hut, the body of the Princess was being lowered into an open grave that had been dug in a deserted churchyard, beyond the city gates, a grave where, it was said, that another body was also lying, that of a young man of marvellous and foreign beauty, whose hands were tied behind him with a knotted cord, and whose breast was stabbed with many red wounds.

Such, at least, was the story that men whispered to each other. Certain it was that the old King, when on his death-bed, whether moved by remorse for his great sin, or merely desiring that the kingdom should not pass away from his line, had had the lad sent for, and, in the presence of the Council, had acknowledged him as his heir.

And it seems that from the very first moment of his recognition he had shown signs of that strange passion for beauty that was destined to have so great an influence over his life. Those who accompanied him to the suite of rooms set apart for his service, often spoke of the cry of pleasure that broke from his lips when he saw the delicate raiment and rich jewels that had been prepared for him, and of the almost fierce joy with which he flung aside his rough leathern tunic and coarse sheepskin cloak. He missed, indeed, at times the fine freedom of his forest life, and was always apt to chafe at the tedious Court ceremonies that occupied so much of each day, but the wonderful palace – *Joyeuse*,[3] as they called it – of which he now found himself lord, seemed to him to be a new world fresh-fashioned for his delight; and as soon as he could escape from the council-board or audience-chamber, he would run down the great staircase, with its lions of gilt bronze and its steps of bright porphyry, and wander from room to room, and from corridor to corridor, like one who was seeking to find in beauty an anodyne from pain, a sort of restoration from sickness.

Upon these journeys of discovery, as he would call them – and, indeed, they were to him real voyages through a marvellous land, he would sometimes be accompanied by the slim, fair-haired Court pages, with their floating mantles, and gay fluttering ribands; but more often he would be alone, feeling through a certain quick instinct, which was almost a divination, that the secrets of art are best learned in secret, and that Beauty, like Wisdom, loves the lonely worshipper.

Many curious stories were related about him at this period. It was said that a stout Burgomaster, who had come to deliver a florid oratorical address on behalf of the citizens of the town, had caught sight of him kneeling in real adoration before a great picture that had just been brought from Venice, and that seemed to herald the worship of some new gods. On another occasion he had been missed for several hours, and after a lengthened search had been discovered in a little chamber in one of the northern turrets of the palace gazing, as one in a trance, at a Greek gem carved with the figure of Adonis.[4] He had been seen, so the tale ran, pressing his warm lips to the marble brow of an antique statue that had been discovered in the bed of the river on the occasion of the building of the stone bridge, and was inscribed with the name of the Bithynian slave of Hadrian.[5] He had passed a whole night in noting the effect of the moonlight on a silver image of Endymion.[6]

All rare and costly materials had certainly a great fascination for him, and in his eagerness to procure them he had sent away many merchants, some to traffic for amber with the rough fisher-folk of the north seas, some to Egypt to look for that curious green turquoise which is found only in the tombs of kings, and is said to possess magical properties, some to Persia for silken carpets and painted pottery, and others to India to buy gauze and stained ivory, moonstones and bracelets of jade, sandalwood and blue enamel and shawls of fine wool.

But what had occupied him most was the robe he was to wear at his coronation, the robe of tissued gold, and the ruby-studded crown, and the sceptre with its rows and rings of pearls. Indeed, it was of this that he was thinking to-night, as he lay back on his luxurious couch, watching the great pinewood log that was burning itself out on the open hearth. The designs, which were from the hands of the most famous artists of the time, had been submitted to him many months before, and he had given orders that the artificers were to toil night and day to carry them out, and that the whole world was to be searched for jewels that would be worthy of their work. He saw himself in fancy standing at the high altar of the cathedral in the fair raiment of a King, and a smile played and lingered about his boyish lips, and lit up with a bright lustre his dark woodland eyes.

After some time he rose from his seat, and leaning against the carved penthouse of the chimney, looked round at the dimly-lit room. The walls were hung with rich tapestries representing the Triumph of Beauty. A large press, inlaid with agate and lapis-lazuli, filled one corner, and facing the window stood a curiously wrought cabinet with lacquer panels of powdered and mosaiced gold, on which were placed some delicate goblets of Venetian glass, and a cup of dark-veined onyx. Pale poppies were broidered on the silk coverlet of the bed, as though they had fallen from the tired hands of sleep, and tall reeds of fluted ivory bare up the velvet canopy, from which great tufts of ostrich plumes sprang, like white foam, to the pallid silver of the fretted ceiling. A laughing Narcissus[7] in green bronze held a polished mirror above its head. On the table stood a flat bowl of amethyst.

Outside he could see the huge dome of the cathedral, looming like a bubble over the shadowy houses, and the weary sentinels pacing up and down on the misty terrace by the river. Far away, in an orchard, a nightingale was singing. A faint perfume of jasmine came through the open window. He brushed his brown curls back from his forehead, and taking up a lute, let his fingers stray across the cords. His heavy eyelids drooped, and a strange languor came over him. Never before had he felt so keenly, or with such exquisite joy, the magic and the mystery of beautiful things.

When midnight sounded from the clock-tower he touched a bell, and his pages entered and disrobed him with much ceremony, pouring rose-water over his hands, and strewing flowers on his pillow. A few moments after that they had left the room, he fell asleep.

*

And as he slept he dreamed a dream, and this was his dream.

He thought that he was standing in a long, low attic, amidst the whirr and clatter of many looms. The meagre daylight peered in through the grated windows, and showed him the gaunt figures of the weavers bending over their cases. Pale, sickly-looking children were crouched on the huge crossbeams. As the shuttles dashed through the warp they lifted up the heavy battens, and when the shuttles stopped they let the battens fall and pressed the threads together. Their faces were pinched with famine, and their thin hands shook and trembled. Some haggard women were seated at a table sewing. A horrible odour filled the place. The air was foul and heavy, and the walls dripped and streamed with damp.

The young King went over to one of the weavers, and stood by him and watched him.

And the weaver looked at him angrily, and said, 'Why art thou watching me? Art thou a spy set on us by our master?'

'Who is thy master?' asked the young King.

'Our master!' cried the weaver, bitterly. 'He is a man like myself. Indeed, there is but this difference between us – that he wears fine clothes while I go in rags, and that while I am weak from hunger he suffers not a little from overfeeding.'

'The land is free,' said the young King, 'and thou art no man's slave.'

'In war,' answered the weaver, 'the strong make slaves of the weak, and in peace the rich make slaves of the poor. We must work to live, and they give us such mean wages that we die. We toil for them all day long, and they heap up gold in their coffers, and our children fade away before their time, and the faces of those we love become hard and evil. We tread out the grapes, and another drinks the wine. We sow the corn, and our own board is empty. We have chains, though no eye beholds them; and are slaves, though men call us free.'

'Is it so with all?' he asked.

'It is so with all,' answered the weaver, 'with the young as well as with the old, with the women as well as with the men, with the little children as well as with those who are stricken in years. The merchants grind us down, and we must needs do their bidding.

The priest rides by and tells his beads, and no man has care of us. Through our sunless lanes creeps Poverty with her hungry eyes, and Sin with his sodden face follows close behind her. Misery wakes us in the morning, and Shame sits with us at night. But what are these things to thee? Thou art not one of us. Thy face is too happy.' And he turned away scowling, and threw the shuttle across the loom, and the young King saw that it was threaded with a thread of gold.

And a great terror seized upon him, and he said to the weaver, 'What robe is this that thou art weaving?'

'It is the robe for the coronation of the young King,' he answered; 'what is that to thee?'

And the young King gave a loud cry and woke, and lo! he was in his own chamber, and through the window he saw the great honey-coloured moon hanging in the dusky air.

And he fell asleep again and dreamed, and this was his dream.

He thought that he was lying on the deck of a huge galley that was being rowed by a hundred slaves. On a carpet by his side the master of the galley was seated. He was black as ebony, and his turban was of crimson silk. Great earrings of silver dragged down the thick lobes of his ears, and in his hands he had a pair of ivory scales.

The slaves were naked, but for a ragged loincloth, and each man was chained to his neighbour. The hot sun beat brightly upon them, and the negroes ran up and down the gangway and lashed them with whips of hide. They stretched out their lean arms and pulled the heavy oars through the water. The salt spray flew from the blades.

At last they reached a little bay, and began to take soundings. A light wind blew from the shore, and covered the deck and the great lateen sail[8] with a fine red dust. Three Arabs mounted on wild asses rode out and threw spears at them. The master of the galley took a painted bow in his hand and shot one of them in the throat. He fell heavily into the surf, and his companions galloped away. A woman wrapped in a yellow veil followed slowly on a camel, looking back now and then at the dead body.

As soon as they had cast anchor and hauled down the sail, the negroes went into the hold and brought up a long rope-ladder, heavily weighted with lead. The master of the galley threw it over the side, making the ends fast to two iron stanchions. Then the negroes seized the youngest of the slaves, and knocked his gyves off, and filled his nostrils and his ears with wax, and tied a big stone round his waist. He crept wearily down the ladder, and disappeared into the sea. A few bubbles rose where he sank. Some of the other slaves peered curiously over the side. At the prow of the galley sat a shark-charmer, beating monotonously upon a drum.

After some time the diver rose up out of the water, and clung panting to the ladder with a pearl in his right hand. The negroes seized it from him, and thrust him back. The slaves fell asleep over their oars.

Again and again he came up, and each time that he did so he brought with him a beautiful pearl. The master of the galley weighed them, and put them into a little bag of green leather.

The young King tried to speak, but his tongue seemed to cleave to the roof of his mouth, and his lips refused to move. The negroes chattered to each other, and began to quarrel over a string of bright beads. Two cranes flew round and round the vessel.

Then the diver came up for the last time, and the pearl that he brought with him was fairer than all the pearls of Ormuz,[9] for it was shaped like the full moon, and whiter than the morning star. But his face was strangely pale, and as he fell upon the deck the blood gushed from his ears and nostrils. He quivered for a little, and then he was still. The negroes shrugged their shoulders, and threw the body overboard.

And the master of the galley laughed, and, reaching out, he took the pearl, and when he saw it he pressed it to his forehead and bowed. 'It shall be,' he said, 'for the sceptre of the young King,' and he made a sign to the negroes to draw up the anchor.

And when the young King heard this he gave a great cry, and woke, and through the window he saw the long grey fingers of the dawn clutching at the fading stars.

And he fell asleep again, and dreamed, and this was his dream.

He thought that he was wandering through a dim wood, hung with strange fruits and with beautiful poisonous flowers. The adders hissed at him as he went by, and the bright parrots flew screaming from branch to branch. Huge tortoises lay asleep upon the hot mud. The trees were full of apes and peacocks.

On and on he went, till he reached the outskirts of the wood, and there he saw an immense multitude of men toiling in the bed of a dried-up river. They swarmed up the crag like ants. They dug deep pits in the ground and went down into them. Some of them cleft the rocks with great axes; others grabbled in the sand. They tore up the cactus by its roots, and trampled on the scarlet blossoms. They hurried about, calling to each other, and no man was idle.

From the darkness of a cavern Death and Avarice watched them, and Death said, 'I am weary; give me a third of them and let me go.'

But Avarice shook her head. 'They are my servants,' she answered.

And Death said to her, 'What hast thou in thy hand?'

'I have three grains of corn,' she answered; 'what is that to thee?'

'Give me one of them,' cried Death, 'to plant in my garden; only one of them, and I will go away.'

'I will not give thee anything,' said Avarice, and she hid her hand in the fold of her raiment.

And Death laughed, and took a cup, and dipped it into a pool of water, and out of the cup rose Ague. She passed through the great multitude, and a third of them lay dead. A cold mist followed her, and the water-snakes ran by her side.

And when Avarice saw that a third of the multitude was dead she beat her breast and wept. She beat her barren bosom, and cried aloud. 'Thou hast slain a third of my servants,' she cried, 'get thee gone. There is war in the mountains of Tartary,[10] and the kings of each side are calling to thee. The Afghans have slain the black ox, and are marching to battle. They have beaten upon their shields with their spears, and have put on their helmets of iron. What is my valley to thee, that thou shouldst tarry in it? Get thee gone, and come here no more.'

'Nay,' answered Death, 'but till thou hast given me a grain of corn I will not go.'

But Avarice shut her hand, and clenched her teeth. 'I will not give thee anything,' she muttered.

And Death laughed, and took up a black stone, and threw it into the forest, and out of a thicket of wild hemlock came Fever in a robe of flame. She passed through the multitude, and touched them, and each man that she touched died. The grass withered beneath her feet as she walked.

And Avarice shuddered, and put ashes on her head. 'Thou art cruel,' she cried; 'thou art cruel. There is famine in the walled cities of India, and the cisterns of Samarcand have run dry. There is famine in the walled cities of Egypt, and the locusts have come up from the desert. The Nile has not overflowed its banks, and the priests have cursed Isis and Osiris.[11] Get thee gone to those who need thee, and leave me my servants.'

'Nay,' answered Death, 'but till thou hast given me a grain of corn I will not go.'

'I will not give thee anything,' said Avarice.

And Death laughed again, and he whistled through his fingers, and a woman came flying through the air. Plague was written upon her forehead, and a crowd of lean vultures wheeled round her. She covered the valley with her wings, and no man was left alive.

And Avarice fled shrieking through the forest, and Death leaped upon his red horse and galloped away,[12] and his galloping was faster than the wind.

And out of the slime at the bottom of the valley crept dragons and horrible things with scales, and the jackals came trotting along the sand, sniffing up the air with their nostrils.

And the young King wept, and said: 'Who were these men, and for what were they seeking?'

'For rubies for a king's crown,' answered one who stood behind him.

And the young King started, and, turning round, he saw a man habited as a pilgrim and holding in his hand a mirror of silver.

And he grew pale, and said: 'For what king?'

And the pilgrim answered: 'Look in this mirror, and thou shalt see him.'

And he looked in the mirror, and, seeing his own face, he gave a great cry and woke, and the bright sunlight was streaming into the room, and from the trees of the garden and pleasaunce[13] the birds were singing.

And the Chamberlain and the high officers of State came in and made obeisance to him, and the pages brought him the robe of tissued gold, and set the crown and the sceptre before him.

And the young King looked at them, and they were beautiful. More beautiful were they than aught that he had ever seen. But he remembered his dreams, and he said to his lords: 'Take these things away, for I will not wear them.'

And the courtiers were amazed, and some of them laughed, for they thought that he was jesting.

But he spake sternly to them again, and said: 'Take these things away, and hide them from me. Though it be the day of my coronation, I will not wear them. For on the loom of Sorrow, and by the white hands of Pain, has this my robe been woven. There is Blood in the heart of the ruby, and Death in the heart of the pearl.' And he told them his three dreams.

And when the courtiers heard them they looked at each other and whispered, saying: 'Surely he is mad; for what is a dream but a dream, and a vision but a vision? They are not real things that one should heed them. And what have we to do with the lives of those who toil for us? Shall a man not eat bread till he has seen the sower, nor drink wine till he has talked with the vinedresser?'

And the Chamberlain spake to the young King, and said, 'My lord, I pray thee set aside these black thoughts of thine, and put on this fair robe, and set this crown upon thy head. For how shall the people know that thou art a king, if thou hast not a king's raiment?'

And the young King looked at him. 'Is it so, indeed?' he questioned. 'Will they not know me for a king if I have not a king's raiment?'

'They will not know thee, my lord,' cried the Chamberlain.

'I had thought that there had been men who were kinglike,' he answered, 'but it may be as thou sayest. And yet I will not wear this robe, nor will I be crowned with this crown, but even as I came to the palace so will I go forth from it.'

And he bade them all leave him, save one page whom he kept as his companion, a lad a year younger than himself. Him he kept for his service, and when he had bathed himself in clear water, he opened a great painted chest, and from it he took the leathern tunic and rough sheepskin cloak that he had worn when he had watched on the hillside the shaggy goats of the goatherd. These he put on, and in his hand he took his rude shepherd's staff.

And the little page opened his big blue eyes in wonder, and said smiling to him, 'My lord, I see thy robe and thy sceptre, but where is thy crown?'

And the young King plucked a spray of wild briar that was climbing over the balcony, and bent it, and made a circlet of it, and set it on his own head.

'This shall be my crown,' he answered.

And thus attired he passed out of his chamber into the Great Hall, where the nobles were waiting for him.

And the nobles made merry, and some of them cried out to him, 'My lord, the people wait for their king, and thou showest them a beggar,' and others were wrath and said, 'He brings shame upon our state, and is unworthy to be our master.' But he answered them not a word, but passed on, and went down the bright porphyry staircase, and out through the gates of bronze, and mounted upon his horse, and rode towards the cathedral, the little page running beside him.

And the people laughed and said, 'It is the King's fool who is riding by,' and they mocked him.

And he drew rein and said, 'Nay, but I am the King.' And he told them his three dreams.

And a man came out of the crowd and spake bitterly to him, and said, 'Sir, knowest thou not that out of the luxury of the rich cometh the life of the poor? By your pomp we are nurtured, and your vices give us bread. To toil for a hard master is bitter, but to have no master to toil for is more bitter still. Thinkest thou that the ravens will feed us? And what cure hast thou for these things?

Wilt thou say to the buyer, "Thou shalt buy for so much," and to the seller, "Thou shalt sell at this price?" I trow not. Therefore go back to thy Palace and put on thy purple and fine linen. What hast thou to do with us, and what we suffer?'

'Are not the rich and the poor brothers?' asked the young King.

'Aye,' answered the man, 'and the name of the rich brother is Cain.'

And the young King's eyes filled with tears, and he rode on through the murmurs of the people, and the little page grew afraid and left him.

And when he reached the great portal of the cathedral, the soldiers thrust their halberts out and said, 'What dost thou seek here? None enters by this door but the King.'

And his face flushed with anger, and he said to them, 'I am the King,' and waved their halberts aside and passed in.

And when the old Bishop saw him coming in his goatherd's dress, he rose up in wonder from his throne, and went to meet him, and said to him, 'My son, is this a king's apparel? And with what crown shall I crown thee, and what sceptre shall I place in thy hand? Surely this should be to thee a day of joy, and not a day of abasement.'

'Shall Joy wear what Grief has fashioned?' said the young King. And he told him his three dreams.

And when the Bishop had heard them he knit his brows, and said, 'My son, I am an old man, and in the winter of my days, and I know that many evil things are done in the wide world. The fierce robbers come down from the mountains, and carry off the little children, and sell them to the Moors. The lions lie in wait for the caravans, and leap upon the camels. The wild boar roots up the corn in the valley, and the foxes gnaw the vines upon the hill. The pirates lay waste the sea-coast and burn the ships of the fishermen, and take their nets from them. In the salt-marshes live the lepers; they have houses of wattled reeds, and none may come nigh them. The beggars wander through the cities, and eat their food with the dogs. Canst thou make these things not to be? Wilt thou take the leper for thy bedfellow, and set the beggar at thy board? Shall the lion do thy bidding, and the wild boar obey thee? Is not He who made misery wiser than thou art? Wherefore I praise thee not for this that thou hast done, but I bid thee ride back to the Palace and make thy face glad, and put on the raiment that beseemeth a king, and with the crown of gold I will crown thee, and the sceptre of pearl will I place in thy hand. And as for thy dreams, think no more of them. The burden of this world is too great for one man to bear, and the world's sorrow too heavy for one heart to suffer.'

'Sayest thou that in this house?' said the young King, and he strode past the Bishop, and climbed up the steps of the altar, and stood before the image of Christ.

He stood before the image of Christ, and on his right hand and on his left were the marvellous vessels of gold, the chalice with the yellow wine, and the vial with the holy oil. He knelt before the image of Christ, and the great candles burned brightly by the jewelled shrine, and the smoke of the incense curled in thin blue wreaths through the dome. He bowed his head in prayer, and the priests in their stiff copes crept away from the altar.

And suddenly a wild tumult came from the street outside, and in entered the nobles with drawn swords and nodding plumes, and shields of polished steel. 'Where is this dreamer of dreams?'[14] they cried. 'Where is this King, who is apparelled like a beggar – this boy who brings shame upon our state? Surely we will slay him, for he is unworthy to rule over us.'

And the young King bowed his head again, and prayed, and when he had finished his prayer he rose up, and turning round he looked at them sadly.

And lo! through the painted windows came the sunlight streaming upon him, and the sunbeams wove round him a tissued robe that was fairer than the robe that had been fashioned for his pleasure. The dead staff blossomed,[15] and bare lilies that were whiter than pearls. The dry thorn blossomed, and bare roses that were redder than rubies. Whiter than fine pearls were the lilies, and their stems were of bright silver. Redder than male rubies were the roses, and their leaves were of beaten gold.

He stood there in the raiment of a king, and the gates of the jewelled shrine flew open, and from the crystal of the many-rayed monstrance[16] shone a marvellous and mystical light. He stood there in a king's raiment, and the Glory of God filled the place, and the saints in their carven niches seemed to move. In the fair raiment of a king he stood before them, and the organ pealed out its music, and the trumpeters blew upon their trumpets, and the singing boys sang.

And the people fell upon their knees in awe, and the nobles sheathed their swords and did homage, and the Bishop's face grew pale, and his hands trembled. 'A greater than I hath crowned thee,' he cried, and he knelt before him.

And the young King came down from the high altar, and passed home through the midst of the people. But no man dared look upon his face, for it was like the face of an angel.

The Birthday of the Infanta[1]

To Mrs William H. Grenfell,[2]
of Taplow Court

It was the birthday of the Infanta. She was just twelve years of age, and the sun was shining brightly in the gardens of the palace.

Although she was a real Princess and the Infanta of Spain, she had only one birthday every year, just like the children of quite poor people, so it was naturally a matter of great importance to the whole country that she should have a really fine day for the occasion. And a really fine day it certainly was. The tall striped tulips stood straight up upon their stalks, like long rows of soldiers, and looked defiantly across the grass at the roses, and said: 'We are quite as splendid as you are now.' The purple butterflies fluttered about with gold dust on their wings, visiting each flower in turn; the little lizards crept out of the crevices of the wall, and lay basking in the white glare; and the pomegranates split and cracked with the heat, and showed their bleeding red hearts. Even the pale yellow lemons, that hung in such profusion from the mouldering trellis and along the dim arcades, seemed to have caught a richer colour from the wonderful sunlight, and the magnolia trees opened their great globe-like blossoms of folded ivory, and filled the air with a sweet heavy perfume.

The little Princess herself walked up and down the terrace with her companions, and played at hide and seek round the stone vases and the old moss-grown statues. On ordinary days she was only allowed to play with children of her own rank, so she had always to play alone, but her birthday was an exception, and the King had given orders that she was to invite any of her young friends whom she liked to come and amuse themselves with her. There was a stately grace about these slim Spanish children as they glided about, the boys with their large-plumed hats and short fluttering cloaks, the girls holding up the trains of their long brocaded gowns, and shielding the sun from their eyes with huge fans of black and silver. But the Infanta was the most graceful of all, and the most tastefully attired, after the somewhat cumbrous fashion of the day. Her robe was of grey satin, the skirt and the wide puffed sleeves heavily embroidered with silver, and the stiff corset studded with rows of fine pearls. Two tiny slippers with big pink rosettes peeped out beneath her dress as she walked. Pink and pearl was her great gauze fan, and in her hair, which like an aureole of faded gold stood out stiffly round her pale little face, she had a beautiful white rose.

From a window in the palace the sad melancholy King watched them. Behind him stood his brother, Don Pedro of Aragon, whom he hated, and his confessor, the Grand Inquisitor of Granada, sat by his side. Sadder even than usual was the King, for as he looked at the Infanta bowing with childish gravity to the assembling courtiers, or laughing behind her fan at the grim Duchess of Albuquerque who always accompanied her, he thought of the young Queen, her mother, who but a short time before – so it seemed to him – had come from the gay country of France, and had withered away in the sombre splendour of the Spanish court, dying just six months after the birth of her child, and before she had seen the almonds blossom twice in the orchard, or plucked the second year's fruit from the old gnarled fig-tree that stood in the centre of the now grass-grown courtyard. So great had been his love for her that he had not suffered even the grave to hide her from him. She had been embalmed by a Moorish physician, who in return for this service had been granted his life, which for heresy and suspicion of magical practices had been already forfeited, men said, to the Holy Office, and her body was still lying on its tapestried bier in the black marble chapel of the Palace, just as the monks had borne her in on that windy March day nearly twelve years before. Once every month the King, wrapped in a dark cloak and with a muffled lantern in his hand, went in and knelt by her side, calling out,

'*Mi reina! Mi reina!*'[3] and sometimes breaking through the formal etiquette that in Spain governs every separate action of life, and sets limits even to the sorrow of a King, he would clutch at the pale jewelled hands in a wild agony of grief, and try to wake by his mad kisses the cold painted face.

To-day he seemed to see her again, as he had seen her first at the Castle of Fontainebleau, when he was but fifteen years of age, and she still younger. They had been formally betrothed on that occasion by the Papal Nuncio[4] in the presence of the French King and all the Court, and he had returned to the Escurial[5] bearing with him a little ringlet of yellow hair, and the memory of two childish lips bending down to kiss his hand as he stepped into his carriage. Later on had followed the marriage, hastily performed at Burgos, a small town on the frontier between the two countries, and the grand public entry into Madrid with the customary celebration of high mass at the Church of La Atocha, and a more than usually solemn *auto-da-fé*,[6] in which nearly three hundred heretics, amongst whom were many Englishmen, had been delivered over to the secular arm to be burned.

Certainly he had loved her madly, and to the ruin, many thought, of his country, then at war with England for the possession of the empire of the New World. He had hardly ever permitted her to be out of his sight; for her, he had forgotten, or seemed to have forgotten, all grave affairs of State; and, with that terrible blindness that passion brings upon its servants, he had failed to notice that the elaborate ceremonies by which he sought to please her did but aggravate the strange malady from which she suffered. When she died he was, for a time, like one bereft of reason. Indeed, there is no doubt but that he would have formally abdicated and retired to the great Trappist monastery at Granada, of which he was already titular Prior, had he not been afraid to leave the little Infanta at the mercy of his brother, whose cruelty, even in Spain, was notorious, and who was suspected by many of having caused the Queen's death by means of a pair of poisoned gloves that he had presented to her on the occasion of her visiting his castle in Aragon. Even after the expiration of the three years of public mourning that he had ordained throughout his whole dominions by royal edict, he would never suffer his ministers to speak about any new alliance, and when the Emperor himself sent to him, and offered him the hand of the lovely Archduchess of Bohemia, his niece, in marriage, he bade the ambassadors tell their master that the King of Spain was already wedded to Sorrow, and that though she was but a barren bride he loved her better than Beauty; an answer that cost his crown the rich provinces of the Netherlands, which soon after, at the Emperor's instigation, revolted against him under the leadership of some fanatics of the Reformed Church.

His whole married life, with its fierce, fiery-coloured joys and the terrible agony of its sudden ending, seemed to come back to him to-day as he watched the Infanta playing on the terrace. She had all the Queen's pretty petulance of manner, the same wilful way of tossing her head, the same proud curved beautiful mouth, the same wonderful smile – *vrai sourire de France*[7] indeed – as she glanced up now and then at the window, or stretched out her little hand for the stately Spanish gentlemen to kiss. But the shrill laughter of the children grated on his ears, and the bright pitiless sunlight mocked his sorrow, and a dull odour of strange spices, spices such as embalmers use, seemed to taint – or was it fancy? – the clear morning air. He buried his face in his hands, and when the Infanta looked up again the curtains had been drawn, and the King had retired.

She made a little *moue*[8] of disappointment, and shrugged her shoulders. Surely he might have stayed with her on her birthday. What did the stupid State-affairs matter? Or had he gone to that gloomy chapel, where the candles were always burning, and where she was never allowed to enter? How silly of him, when the sun was shining so brightly, and everybody was so happy! Besides, he would miss the sham bull-fight for which the trumpet was already sounding, to say nothing of the puppet show and the other wonderful things. Her uncle and the Grand Inquisitor were much more sensible. They had come out on the terrace, and paid her nice compliments. So she tossed her pretty head, and taking Don Pedro by the hand, she walked slowly down the steps towards a long pavilion of purple silk that had been erected at the end of the garden, the other children following in strict order of precedence, those who had the longest names going first.

A procession of noble boys, fantastically dressed as *toreadors*, came out to meet her, and the young Count of Tierra-Nueva, a wonderfully handsome lad of about fourteen years of age, uncovering his head with all the grace of a born hidalgo and grandee[9] of Spain, led her solemnly into a little gilt and ivory chair that was placed on a raised daïs above the arena. The children grouped themselves all round, fluttering their big fans and whispering to each other, and Don Pedro and the Grand Inquisitor stood laughing at the entrance. Even the Duchess – the Camerera-Mayor[10] she was called – a thin, hard-featured woman with a yellow ruff, did not look quite so bad-tempered as usual, and something like a chill smile flitted across her wrinkled face and twitched her thin bloodless lips.

It certainly was a marvellous bull-fight, and much nicer, the Infanta thought, than the real bull-fight that she had been brought to see at Seville, on the occasion of the visit of the Duke of Parma to her father. Some of the boys pranced about on richly-caparisoned hobby-horses brandishing long javelins with gay streamers of bright ribands attached to them; others went on foot waving their scarlet cloaks before the bull, and vaulting lightly over the barrier when he charged them; and as for the bull himself, he was just like a live bull, though he was only made of wicker-work and stretched hide, and sometimes insisted on running round the arena on his hind legs, which no live bull ever dreams of doing. He made a splendid fight of it too, and the children got so excited that they stood up upon the benches, and waved their lace handkerchiefs and cried out: *Bravo toro! Bravo toro!*[11] just as sensibly as if they had been grown-up people. At last, however, after a prolonged combat, during which several of the hobby-horses were gored through and through, and their riders dismounted, the young Count of Tierra-Nueva brought the bull to his knees, and having obtained permission from the Infanta to give the *coup de grâce*, he plunged his wooden sword into the neck of the animal with such violence that the head came right off, and disclosed the laughing face of little Monsieur de Lorraine, the son of the French Ambassador at Madrid.

The arena was then cleared amidst much applause, and the dead hobby-horses dragged solemnly away by two Moorish pages in yellow and black liveries, and after a short interlude, during which a French posture-master performed upon the tight-rope, some Italian puppets appeared in the semi-classical tragedy of *Sophonisba*[12] on the stage of a small theatre that had been built up for the purpose. They acted so well, and their gestures were so extremely natural, that at the close of the play the eyes of the Infanta were quite dim with tears. Indeed some of the children really cried, and had to be comforted with sweetmeats, and the Grand Inquisitor himself was so affected that he could not help saying to Don Pedro that it seemed to him intolerable that things made simply out of wood and coloured wax, and worked mechanically by wires, should be so unhappy and meet with such terrible misfortunes.

An African juggler followed, who brought in a large flat basket covered with a red cloth, and having placed it in the centre of the arena, he took from his turban a curious reed pipe, and blew through it. In a few moments the cloth began to move, and as the pipe grew shriller and shriller two green and gold snakes put out their strange wedge-shaped heads and rose slowly up, swaying to and fro with the music as a plant sways in the water. The children, however, were rather frightened at their spotted hoods and quick darting tongues, and were much more pleased when the juggler made a tiny orange-tree grow out of the sand and bear pretty white blossoms and clusters of real fruit; and when he took the fan of the little daughter of the Marquess de Las-Torres, and changed it into a blue bird that flew all round the pavilion and sang, their delight and amazement knew no bounds. The solemn minuet, too, performed by the dancing boys from the church of Nuestra Señora Del Pilar, was charming. The Infanta had never before seen this wonderful ceremony which takes place every year at May-time in front of the high altar of the Virgin, and in her honour; and indeed none of the royal family of Spain had entered the great cathedral of Saragossa since a mad priest, supposed by many to have been in the pay of Elizabeth of England, had tried to administer a poisoned wafer to the Prince of the Asturias. So she had known only by hearsay of 'Our Lady's Dance,' as it was called, and it certainly was a beautiful sight. The boys wore old-fashioned court dresses of white velvet, and their curious three-cornered hats were fringed with silver and surmounted with huge plumes of ostrich feathers, the dazzling whiteness of their costumes, as they moved about in the sunlight, being still more accentuated by their swarthy faces and long black hair. Everybody was fascinated by the grave dignity with which they moved through the intricate figures of the dance, and by the elaborate grace of their slow gestures, and stately bows, and when they had finished their performance and doffed their great plumed hats to the Infanta, she acknowledged their reverence with much courtesy, and made a vow that she would send a large wax candle to the shrine of Our Lady of Pilar in return for the pleasure that she had given her.

A troop of handsome Egyptians – as the gipsies were termed in those days – then advanced into the arena, and sitting down cross-legs, in a circle, began to play softly upon their zithers, moving their bodies to the tune, and humming, almost below their breath, a low dreamy air. When they caught sight of Don Pedro they scowled at him, and some of them looked terrified, for only a few weeks before he had had two of their tribe hanged for sorcery in the market-place at Seville, but the pretty Infanta charmed them as she leaned back peeping over her fan with her great blue eyes, and they felt sure that one so lovely as she was could never be cruel to anybody. So they played on very gently and just touching the cords of the zithers with their long pointed nails, and their heads began to nod as though they were falling asleep. Suddenly, with a cry so shrill that all the children were startled and Don Pedro's hand clutched at the agate pommel of his dagger, they leapt to their feet and whirled madly round the enclosure beating their tambourines, and chaunting some wild love-song in their strange guttural language. Then at another signal they all flung themselves again to the ground and lay there quite still, the dull strumming of the zithers being the only sound that broke the silence. After that they had done this several times, they disappeared for a moment and came back leading a brown shaggy bear by a chain, and carrying on their shoulders some little Barbary apes. The bear stood upon his head with the utmost gravity, and the wizened apes played all kinds of amusing tricks with two gipsy boys who seemed to be their masters, and fought with tiny swords, and fired off guns, and went through a regular soldier's drill just like the King's own bodyguard. In fact the gipsies were a great success.

But the funniest part of the whole morning's entertainment, was undoubtedly the dancing of the little Dwarf. When he stumbled into the arena, waddling on his crooked legs and wagging his huge misshapen head from side to side, the children went off into a loud shout of delight, and the Infanta herself laughed so much that the Camerera was obliged to remind her that although there were many precedents in Spain for a King's daughter weeping before her equals, there were none for a Princess of the blood royal making so merry before those who were her inferiors in birth. The Dwarf, however, was really quite irresistible, and even at the Spanish Court, always noted for its cultivated passion for the horrible, so fantastic a little monster had never been seen. It was his first appearance, too. He had been discovered only the day before, running wild through the forest, by two of the nobles who happened to have been hunting in a remote part of the great cork-wood that surrounded the town, and had been carried off by them to the Palace as a surprise for the Infanta, his father, who was a poor charcoal-burner, being but too well pleased to get rid of so ugly and useless a child. Perhaps the most amusing thing about him was his complete unconsciousness of his own grotesque appearance. Indeed he seemed quite happy and full of the highest spirits. When the children laughed, he laughed as freely and as joyously as any of them, and at the close of each dance he made them each the funniest of bows, smiling and nodding at them just as if he was really one of themselves, and not a little misshapen thing that Nature, in some humorous mood, had fashioned for others to mock at. As for the Infanta, she absolutely fascinated him. He could not keep his eyes off her, and seemed to dance for her alone, and when at the close of the performance, remembering how she had seen the great ladies of the Court throw bouquets to Caffarelli the famous Italian treble, whom the Pope had sent from his own chapel to Madrid that he might cure the King's melancholy by the sweetness of his voice, she took out of her hair the beautiful white rose, and partly for a jest and partly to tease the Camerera, threw it to him across the arena with her sweetest smile, he took the whole matter quite seriously, and pressing the flower to his rough coarse lips he put his hand upon his heart, and sank on one knee before her, grinning from ear to ear, and with his little bright eyes sparkling with pleasure.

This so upset the gravity of the Infanta that she kept on laughing long after the little Dwarf had run out of the arena, and expressed a desire to her uncle that the dance should be immediately repeated. The Camerera, however, on the plea that the sun was too hot, decided that it would be better that her Highness should return without delay to the Palace, where a wonderful feast had been already prepared for her, including a real birthday cake with her own initials worked all over it in painted sugar and a lovely silver flag waving from the top. The Infanta accordingly rose up with much dignity, and having given orders that the little dwarf was to dance again for her after the hour of siesta, and conveyed her thanks to the young Count of Tierra-Nueva for his charming reception, she went back to her apartments, the children following in the same order in which they had entered.

Now when the little Dwarf heard that he was to dance a second time before the Infanta, and by her own express command, he was so proud that he ran out into the garden, kissing the white rose in an absurd ecstasy of pleasure, and making the most uncouth and clumsy gestures of delight.

The Flowers were quite indignant at his daring to intrude into their beautiful home, and when they saw him capering up and down the walks, and waving his arms above his head in such a ridiculous manner, they could not restrain their feelings any longer.

'He is really far too ugly to be allowed to play in any place where we are,' cried the Tulips.

'He should drink poppy-juice, and go to sleep for a thousand years,' said the great scarlet Lilies, and they grew quite hot and angry.

'He is a perfect horror!' screamed the Cactus. 'Why, he is twisted and stumpy, and his head is completely out of proportion with his legs. Really he makes me feel prickly all over, and if he comes near me I will sting him with my thorns.'

'And he has actually got one of my best blooms,' exclaimed the White Rose-Tree. 'I gave it to the Infanta this morning myself, as a birthday present, and he has stolen it from her.' And she called out: 'Thief, thief, thief!' at the top of her voice.

Even the red Geraniums, who did not usually give themselves airs, and were known to have a great many poor relations themselves, curled up in disgust when they saw him, and when the Violets meekly remarked that though he was certainly extremely plain, still he could not help it, they retorted with a good deal of justice that that was his chief defect, and that there was no reason why one should admire a person because he was incurable; and, indeed, some of the Violets themselves felt that the ugliness of the little Dwarf was almost ostentatious, and that he would have shown much better taste if he had looked sad, or at least pensive, instead of jumping about merrily, and throwing himself into such grotesque and silly attitudes.

As for the old Sundial, who was an extremely remarkable individual, and had once told the time of day to no less a person than the Emperor Charles V himself, he was so taken aback by the little Dwarf's appearance, that he almost forgot to mark two whole minutes with his long shadowy finger, and could not help saying to the great milk-white Peacock, who was sunning herself on the balustrade, that every one knew that the children of Kings were Kings, and that the children of charcoal-burners were charcoal-burners, and that it was absurd to pretend that it wasn't so; a statement with which the Peacock entirely agreed, and indeed screamed out, 'Certainly, certainly,' in such a loud, harsh voice, that the gold-fish who lived in the basin of the cool splashing fountain put their heads out of the water, and asked the huge stone Tritons[13] what on earth was the matter.

But somehow the Birds liked him. They had seen him often in the forest, dancing about like an elf after the eddying leaves, or crouched up in the hollow of some old oak-tree, sharing his nuts with the squirrels. They did not mind his being ugly, a bit. Why, even the nightingale herself, who sang so sweetly in the orange groves at night that sometimes the Moon leaned down to listen, was not much to look at after all; and, besides, he had been kind to them, and during that terribly bitter winter, when there were no berries on the trees, and the ground was as hard as iron, and the wolves had come down to the very gates of the city to look for food, he had never once forgotten them, but had always given them crumbs out of his little hunch of black bread, and divided with them whatever poor breakfast he had.

So they flew round and round him, just touching his cheek with their wings as they passed, and chattered to each other, and the little Dwarf was so pleased that he could not help showing them the beautiful white rose, and telling them that the Infanta herself had given it to him because she loved him.

They did not understand a single word of what he was saying, but that made no matter, for they put their heads on one side, and looked wise, which is quite as good as understanding a thing, and very much easier.

The Lizards also took an immense fancy to him, and when he grew tired of running about and flung himself down on the grass to rest, they played and romped all over him, and tried to amuse him in the best way they could. 'Every one cannot be as beautiful as a lizard,' they cried; 'that would be too much to expect. And, though it sounds absurd to say so, he is really not so ugly after all, provided, of course, that one shuts one's eyes, and does not look at him.' The Lizards were extremely philosophical by nature, and often sat thinking for hours and hours together, when there was nothing else to do, or when the weather was too rainy for them to go out.

The Flowers, however, were excessively annoyed at their behaviour, and at the behaviour of the birds. 'It only shows,' they said, 'what a vulgarising effect this incessant rushing and flying about has. Well-bred people always stay exactly in the same place, as we do. No one ever saw us hopping up and down the walks, or galloping madly through the grass after dragon-flies. When we do want change of air, we send for the gardener, and he carries us to another bed. This is dignified, and as it should be. But birds and lizards have no sense of repose, and indeed birds have not even a permanent address. They are mere vagrants like the gipsies, and should be treated in exactly the same manner.' So they put their noses in the air, and looked very haughty, and were quite delighted when after some time they saw the little Dwarf scramble up from the grass, and make his way across the terrace to the palace.

'He should certainly be kept indoors for the rest of his natural life,' they said. 'Look at his hunched back, and his crooked legs,' and they began to titter.

But the little Dwarf knew nothing of all this. He liked the birds and the lizards immensely, and thought that the flowers were the most marvellous things in the whole world, except of course the Infanta, but then she had given him the beautiful white rose, and she loved him, and that made a great difference. How he wished that he had gone back with her! She would have put him on her right hand, and smiled at him, and he would have never left her side, but would have made her his playmate, and taught her all kinds of delightful tricks. For though he had never been in a palace before, he knew a great many wonderful things. He could make little cages out of rushes for the grasshoppers to sing in, and fashion the long-jointed bamboo into the pipe that Pan[14] loves to hear. He knew the cry of every bird, and could call the starlings from the tree-top, or the heron from the mere. He knew the trail of every animal, and could track the hare by its delicate footprints, and the boar by the trampled leaves. All the wild-dances he knew, the mad dance in red raiment with the autumn, the light dance in blue sandals over the corn, the dance with white snow-wreaths in winter, and the blossom-dance through the orchards in spring. He knew where the wood-pigeons built their nests, and once when a fowler had snared the parent birds, he had brought up the young ones himself, and had built a little dovecot for them in the cleft of a pollard elm. They were quite tame, and used to feed out of his hands every morning. She would like them, and the rabbits that scurried about in the long fern, and the jays with their steely feathers and black bills, and the hedgehogs that could curl themselves up into prickly balls, and the great wise tortoises that crawled slowly about, shaking their heads and nibbling at the young leaves. Yes, she must certainly come to the forest and play with him. He would give her his own little bed, and would watch outside the window till dawn, to see that the wild horned cattle did not harm her, nor the gaunt wolves creep too near the hut. And at dawn he would tap at the shutters and wake her, and they would go out and dance together all the day long. It was really not a bit lonely in the forest. Sometimes a Bishop rode through on his white mule, reading out of a painted book. Sometimes in their green velvet caps, and their jerkins of tanned deerskin, the falconers passed by, with hooded hawks on their wrists. At vintage time came the grape-treaders, with purple hands and feet, wreathed with glossy ivy and carrying dripping skins of wine; and the charcoal-burners sat round their huge braziers at night, watching the dry logs charring slowly in the fire, and roasting chestnuts in the ashes, and the robbers came out of their caves and made merry with them. Once, too, he had seen a beautiful procession winding up the long dusty road to Toledo. The monks went in front singing sweetly, and carrying bright banners and crosses of gold, and then, in silver armour, with matchlocks and pikes, came the soldiers, and in their midst walked three barefooted men, in strange yellow dresses painted all over with wonderful figures, and carrying lighted candles in their hands. Certainly there was a great deal to look at in the forest, and when she was tired he would find a soft bank of moss for her, or carry her in his arms, for he was very strong, though he knew that he was not tall. He would make her a necklace of red bryony berries, that would be quite as pretty as the white berries that she wore on her dress, and when she was tired of them, she could throw them away, and he would find her others. He would bring her acorn-cups and dew-drenched anemones, and tiny glow-worms to be stars in the pale gold of her hair.

But where was she? He asked the white rose, and it made him no answer. The whole palace seemed asleep, and even where the shutters had not been closed, heavy curtains had been drawn across the windows to keep out the glare. He wandered all round looking for some place through which he might gain an entrance, and at last he caught sight of a little private door that was lying open. He slipped through, and found himself in a splendid hall, far more splendid, he feared, than the forest, there was so much more gilding everywhere, and even the floor was made of great coloured stones, fitted together into a sort of geometrical pattern. But the little Infanta was not there, only some wonderful white statues that looked down on him from their jasper pedestals, with sad blank eyes and strangely smiling lips.

At the end of the hall hung a richly embroidered curtain of black velvet, powdered with suns and stars, the King's favourite devices, and broidered on the colour he loved best. Perhaps she was hiding behind that? He would try at any rate.

So he stole quietly across, and drew it aside. No; there was only another room, though a prettier room, he thought, than the one he had just left. The walls were hung with a many-figured green arras of needle-wrought tapestry representing a hunt, the work of some Flemish artists who had spent more than seven years in its composition. It had once been the chamber of *Jean le Fou*, as he was called, that mad King who was so enamoured of the chase, that he had often tried in his delirium to mount the huge rearing horses, and to drag down the stag on which the great hounds were leaping, sounding his hunting horn, and stabbing with his dagger at the pale flying deer. It was now used as the council-room, and on the centre table were lying the red portfolios of the ministers, stamped with the gold tulips of Spain, and with the arms and emblems of the house of Hapsburg.

The little Dwarf looked in wonder all round him, and was half-afraid to go on. The strange silent horsemen that galloped so swiftly through the long glades without making any noise, seemed to him like those terrible phantoms of whom he had heard the charcoal-burners speaking – the Comprachos, who hunt only at night, and if they meet a man, turn him into a hind, and chase him. But he thought of the pretty Infanta, and took courage. He wanted to find her alone, and to tell her that he too loved her. Perhaps she was in the room beyond.

He ran across the soft Moorish carpets, and opened the door. No! She was not here either. The room was quite empty.

It was a throne-room, used for the reception of foreign ambassadors, when the King, which of late had not been often, consented to give them a personal audience; the same room in which, many years before, envoys had appeared from England to make arrangements for the marriage of their Queen, then one of the Catholic sovereigns of Europe, with the Emperor's eldest son. The hangings were of gilt Cordovan leather, and a heavy gilt chandelier with branches for three hundred wax lights hung down from the black and white ceiling. Underneath a great canopy of gold cloth, on which the lions and towers of Castile were broidered in seed pearls, stood the throne itself, covered with a rich pall of black velvet studded with silver tulips and elaborately fringed with silver and pearls. On the second step of the throne was placed the kneeling-stool of the Infanta, with its cushion of cloth of silver tissue, and below that again, and beyond the limit of the canopy, stood the chair for the Papal Nuncio, who alone had the right to be seated in the King's presence on the occasion of any public ceremonial, and whose Cardinal's hat, with its tangled scarlet tassels, lay on a purple *tabouret*[15] in front. On the wall, facing the throne, hung a life-sized portrait of Charles V in hunting dress, with a great mastiff by his side, and a picture of Philip II receiving the homage of the Netherlands occupied the centre of the other wall. Between the windows stood a black ebony cabinet, inlaid with plates of ivory, on which the figures from Holbein's Dance of Death[16] had been graved – by the hand, some said, of that famous master himself.

But the little Dwarf cared nothing for all this magnificence. He would not have given his rose for all the pearls on the canopy, nor one white petal of his rose for the throne itself. What he wanted was to see the Infanta before she went down to the pavilion, and to ask her to come away with him when he had finished his dance. Here, in the Palace, the air was close and heavy, but in the forest the wind blew free, and the sunlight with wandering hands of gold moved the tremulous leaves aside. There were flowers, too, in the forest, not so splendid, perhaps, as the flowers in the garden, but more sweetly scented for all that; hyacinths in early spring that flooded with waving purple the cool glens, and grassy knolls; yellow primroses that nestled in little clumps round the gnarled roots of the oak-trees; bright celandine, and blue speedwell, and irises lilac and gold. There were grey catkins on the hazels, and the fox-gloves drooped with the weight of their dappled bee-haunted cells. The chestnut had its spires of white stars, and the hawthorn its pallid moons of beauty. Yes: surely she would come if he could only find her! She would come with him to the fair forest, and all day long he would dance for her delight. A smile lit up his eyes at the thought, and he passed into the next room.

Of all the rooms this was the brightest and the most beautiful. The walls were covered with a pink-flowered Lucca damask,[17] patterned with birds and dotted with dainty blossoms of silver; the furniture was of massive silver, festooned with florid wreaths, and swinging Cupids; in front of the two large fire-places stood great screens broidered with parrots and peacocks, and the floor, which was of sea-green onyx, seemed to stretch far away into the distance. Nor was he alone. Standing under the shadow of the doorway, at the extreme end of the room, he saw a little figure watching him. His heart trembled, a cry of joy broke from his lips, and he moved out into the sunlight. As he did so, the figure moved out also, and he saw it plainly.

The Infanta! It was a monster, the most grotesque monster he had ever beheld. Not properly shaped, as all other people were, but hunchbacked, and crooked-limbed, with huge lolling head and mane of black hair. The little Dwarf frowned, and the monster frowned also. He laughed, and it laughed with him, and held its hands to its sides, just as he himself was doing. He made it a mocking bow, and it returned him a low reverence. He went towards it, and it came to meet him, copying each step that he made, and stopping when he stopped himself. He shouted with amusement, and ran forward, and reached out his hand, and the hand of the monster touched his, and it was as cold as ice. He grew afraid, and moved his hand across, and the monster's hand followed it quickly. He tried to press on, but something smooth and hard stopped him. The face of the monster was now close to his own, and seemed full of terror. He brushed his hair off his eyes. It imitated him. He struck at it, and it returned blow for blow. He loathed it, and it made hideous faces at him. He drew back, and it retreated.

What is it? He thought for a moment, and looked round at the rest of the room. It was strange, but everything seemed to have its double in this invisible wall of clear water. Yes, picture for picture was repeated, and couch for couch. The sleeping Faun[18] that lay in the alcove by the doorway had its twin brother that slumbered, and the silver Venus[19] that stood in the sunlight held out her arms to a Venus as lovely as herself.

Was it Echo?[20] He had called to her once in the valley, and she had answered him word for word. Could she mock the eye, as she mocked the voice? Could she make a mimic world just like the real world? Could the shadows of things have colour and life and movement? Could it be that –?

He started, and taking from his breast the beautiful white rose, he turned round, and kissed it. The monster had a rose of its own, petal for petal the same! It kissed it with like kisses, and pressed it to its heart with horrible gestures.

When the truth dawned upon him, he gave a wild cry of despair, and fell sobbing to the ground. So it was he who was misshapen and hunchbacked, foul to look at and grotesque. He himself was the monster, and it was at him that all the children had been laughing, and the little Princess who he had thought loved him – she too had been merely mocking at his ugliness, and making merry over his twisted limbs. Why had they not left him in the forest, where there was no mirror to tell him how loathsome he was? Why had his father not killed him, rather than sell him to his shame? The hot tears poured down his cheeks, and he tore the white rose to pieces. The sprawling monster did the same, and scattered the faint petals in the air. It grovelled on the ground, and, when he looked at it, it watched him with a face drawn with pain. He crept away, lest he should see it, and covered his eyes with his hands. He crawled, like some wounded thing, into the shadow, and lay there moaning.

And at that moment the Infanta herself came in with her companions through the open window, and when they saw the ugly little dwarf lying on the ground and beating the floor with his clenched hands, in the most fantastic and exaggerated manner, they went off into shouts of happy laughter, and stood all round him and watched him.

'His dancing was funny,' said the Infanta; 'but his acting is funnier still. Indeed he is almost as good as the puppets, only of course not quite so natural.' And she fluttered her big fan, and applauded.

But the little Dwarf never looked up, and his sobs grew fainter and fainter, and suddenly he gave a curious gasp, and clutched his side. And then he fell back again, and lay quite still.

'That is capital,' said the Infanta, after a pause; 'but now you must dance for me.'

'Yes,' cried all the children, 'you must get up and dance, for you are as clever as the Barbary apes, and much more ridiculous.'

But the little Dwarf made no answer.

And the Infanta stamped her foot, and called out to her uncle, who was walking on the terrace with the Chamberlain, reading some despatches that had just arrived from Mexico where the Holy Office had recently been established. 'My funny little dwarf is sulking,' she cried, 'you must wake him up, and tell him to dance for me.'

They smiled at each other, and sauntered in, and Don Pedro stooped down, and slapped the Dwarf on the cheek with his embroidered glove. 'You must dance,' he said, '*petit monstre*.[21] You must dance. The Infanta of Spain and the Indies wishes to be amused.'

But the little Dwarf never moved.

'A whipping master should be sent for,' said Don Pedro wearily, and he went back to the terrace. But the Chamberlain looked grave, and he knelt beside the little dwarf, and put his hand upon his heart. And after a few moments he shrugged his shoulders, and rose up, and having made a low bow to the Infanta, he said:

'*Mi bella Princesa*, your funny little dwarf will never dance again. It is a pity, for he is so ugly that he might have made the King smile.'

'But why will he not dance again?' asked the Infanta, laughing.

'Because his heart is broken,' answered the Chamberlain.

And the Infanta frowned, and her dainty rose-leaf lips curled in pretty disdain. 'For the future let those who come to play with me have no hearts,' she cried, and she ran out into the garden.

The Fisherman and his Soul

To H. S. H. Alice, Princess of Monaco[1]

Every evening the young Fisherman went out upon the sea, and threw his nets into the water.

When the wind blew from the land he caught nothing, or but little at best, for it was a bitter and black-winged wind, and rough waves rose up to meet it. But when the wind blew to the shore, the fish came in from the deep, and swam into the meshes of his nets, and he took them to the market-place and sold them.

Every evening he went out upon the sea, and one evening the net was so heavy that hardly could he draw it into the boat. And he laughed, and said to himself, 'Surely I have caught all the fish that swim, or snared some dull monster that will be a marvel to men, or some thing of horror that the great Queen will desire,' and putting forth all his strength, he tugged at the coarse ropes till, like lines of blue enamel round a vase of bronze, the long veins rose up on his arms. He tugged at the thin ropes, and nearer and nearer came the circle of flat corks, and the net rose at last to the top of the water.

But no fish at all was in it, nor any monster or thing of horror, but only a little Mermaid lying fast asleep.

Her hair was as a wet fleece of gold, and each separate hair as a thread of fine gold in a cup of glass. Her body was as white ivory, and her tail was of silver and pearl. Silver and pearl was her tail, and the green weeds of the sea coiled round it; and like sea-shells were her ears, and her lips were like sea-coral. The cold waves dashed over her cold breasts, and the salt glistened upon her eyelids.

So beautiful was she that when the young Fisherman saw her

he was filled with wonder, and he put out his hand and drew the net close to him, and leaning over the side he clasped her in his arms. And when he touched her, she gave a cry like a startled sea-gull and woke, and looked at him in terror with her mauve-amethyst eyes, and struggled that she might escape. But he held her tightly to him, and would not suffer her to depart.

And when she saw that she could in no way escape from him, she began to weep, and said, 'I pray thee let me go, for I am the only daughter of a King, and my father is aged and alone.'

But the young Fisherman answered, 'I will not let thee go save thou makest me a promise that whenever I call thee, thou wilt come and sing to me, for the fish delight to listen to the song of the Sea-folk, and so shall my nets be full.'

'Wilt thou in very truth let me go, if I promise thee this?' cried the Mermaid.

'In very truth I will let thee go,' said the young Fisherman.

So she made him the promise he desired and sware it by the oath of the Sea-folk. And he loosened his arms from about her, and she sank down into the water, trembling with a strange fear.

Every evening the young Fisherman went out upon the sea, and called to the Mermaid, and she rose out of the water and sang to him. Round and round her swam the dolphins, and the wild gulls wheeled above her head.

And she sang a marvellous song. For she sang of the Sea-folk who drive their flocks from cave to cave, and carry the little calves on their shoulders; of the Tritons[2] who have long green beards, and hairy breasts, and blow through twisted conches when the King passes by; of the palace of the King which is all of amber, with a roof of clear emerald, and a pavement of bright pearl; and of the gardens of the sea where the great filigrane[3] fans of coral wave all day long and the fish dart about like silver birds, and the anemones cling to the rocks, and the pinks burgeon in the ribbed yellow sand. She sang of the big whales that come down from the north seas and have sharp icicles hanging to their fins; of the Sirens[4] who tell of such wonderful things that the merchants have to stop their ears with wax lest they should hear them, and leap into the water and be drowned; of the sunken galleys with their tall masts, and the frozen sailors clinging to the rigging, and the mackerel swimming in and out of the open portholes; of the little barnacles who are great travellers, and cling to the keels of the ships and go round and round the world; and of the cuttlefish who live in the sides of the cliffs and stretch out their long black arms, and can make night come when they will it. She sang of the nautilus[5] who has a boat of her own that is carved out of an opal and steered with a silken sail; of the happy Mermen who play upon harps and can charm the great Kraken[6] to sleep; of the little children who catch hold of the slippery porpoises and ride laughing upon their backs; of the Mermaids who lie in the white foam and hold out their arms to the mariners; and of the sea-lions with their curved tusks, and the sea-horses with their floating manes.

And as she sang, all the tunny-fish came in from the deep to listen to her, and the young Fisherman threw his nets round them and caught them, and others he took with a spear. And when his boat was well-laden, the Mermaid would sink down into the sea, smiling at him.

Yet would she never come near him that he might touch her. Oftentimes he called to her and prayed of her, but she would not; and when he sought to seize her she dived into the water as a seal might dive, nor did he see her again that day. And each day the sound of her voice became sweeter to his ears. So sweet was her voice that he forgot his nets and his cunning, and had no care of his craft. Vermilion-finned and with eyes of bossy gold, the tunnies went by in shoals, but he heeded them not. His spear lay by his side unused, and his baskets of plaited osier[7] were empty. With lips parted, and eyes dim with wonder, he sat idle in his boat and listened, listening till the sea-mists crept round him, and the wandering moon stained his brown limbs with silver.

And one evening he called to her, and said: 'Little Mermaid, little Mermaid, I love thee. Take me for thy bridegroom, for I love thee.'

But the Mermaid shook her head. 'Thou hast a human soul,' she answered. 'If only thou wouldst send away thy soul, then could I love thee.'

And the young Fisherman said to himself, 'Of what use is my

soul to me? I cannot see it. I may not touch it. I do not know it. Surely I will send it away from me, and much gladness shall be mine.' And a cry of joy broke from his lips, and standing up in the painted boat, he held out his arms to the Mermaid. 'I will send my soul away,' he cried, 'and you shall be my bride, and I will be thy bridegroom, and in the depth of the sea we will dwell together, and all that thou hast sung of thou shalt show me, and all that thou desirest I will do, nor shall our lives be divided.'

And the little Mermaid laughed for pleasure, and hid her face in her hands.

'But how shall I send my soul from me?' cried the young Fisherman. 'Tell me how I may do it, and lo! it shall be done.'

'Alas! I know not,' said the little Mermaid: 'the Sea-folk have no souls.' And she sank down into the deep, looking wistfully at him.

Now early on the next morning, before the sun was the span of a man's hand above the hill, the young Fisherman went to the house of the Priest and knocked three times at the door.

The novice looked out through the wicket, and when he saw who it was, he drew back the latch and said to him, 'Enter.'

And the young Fisherman passed in, and knelt down on the sweet-smelling rushes of the floor, and cried to the Priest who was reading out of the Holy Book and said to him, 'Father, I am in love with one of the Sea-folk, and my soul hindereth me from having my desire. Tell me how I can send my soul away from me, for in truth I have no need of it. Of what value is my soul to me? I cannot see it. I may not touch it. I do not know it.'

And the Priest beat his breast, and answered, 'Alack, alack, thou art mad, or hast eaten of some poisonous herb, for the soul is the noblest part of man, and was given to us by God that we should nobly use it. There is no thing more precious than a human soul, nor any earthly thing that can be weighed with it. It is worth all the gold that is in the world, and is more precious than the rubies of the kings. Therefore, my son, think not any more of this matter, for it is a sin that may not be forgiven. And as for the Sea-folk, they are lost, and they who would traffic with them are lost also. They are as the beasts of the field that know not good from evil, and for them the Lord has not died.'

The young Fisherman's eyes filled with tears when he heard the bitter words of the Priest, and he rose up from his knees and said to him, 'Father, the Fauns[8] live in the forest and are glad, and on the rocks sit the Mermen with their harps of red gold. Let me be as they are, I beseech thee, for their days are as the days of flowers. And as for my soul, what doth my soul profit me, if it stand between me and the thing that I love?'

'The love of the body is vile,' cried the Priest, knitting his brows, 'and vile and evil are the pagan things God suffers to wander through His world. Accursed be the Fauns of the woodland, and accursed be the singers of the sea! I have heard them at night-time, and they have sought to lure me from my beads. They tap at the window, and laugh. They whisper into my ears the tale of their perilous joys. They tempt me with temptations, and when I would pray they make mouths at me. They are lost, I tell thee, they are lost. For them there is no heaven nor hell, and in neither shall they praise God's name.'

'Father,' cried the young Fisherman, 'thou knowest not what thou sayest. Once in my net I snared the daughter of a King. She is fairer than the morning star, and whiter than the moon. For her body I would give my soul, and for her love I would surrender heaven. Tell me what I ask of thee, and let me go in peace.'

'Away! Away!' cried the Priest: 'thy leman[9] is lost, and thou shalt be lost with her.' And he gave him no blessing, but drove him from his door.

And the young Fisherman went down into the market-place, and he walked slowly, and with bowed head, as one who is in sorrow.

And when the merchants saw him coming, they began to whisper to each other, and one of them came forth to meet him, and called him by name, and said to him, 'What hast thou to sell?'

'I will sell thee my soul,' he answered: 'I pray thee buy it of me, for I am weary of it. Of what use is my soul to me? I cannot see it. I may not touch it. I do not know it.'

But the merchants mocked at him, and said, 'Of what use is a man's soul to us? It is not worth a clipped piece of silver. Sell us thy body for a slave, and we will clothe thee in sea-purple, and put a ring upon thy finger, and make thee the minion of the great Queen. But talk not of the soul, for to us it is nought, nor has it any value for our service.'

And the young Fisherman said to himself: 'How strange a thing this is! The Priest telleth me that the soul is worth all the gold in the world, and the merchants say that it is not worth a clipped piece of silver.' And he passed out of the market-place, and went down to the shore of the sea, and began to ponder on what he should do.

And at noon he remembered how one of his companions, who was a gatherer of samphire,[10] had told him of a certain young Witch who dwelt in a cave at the head of the bay and was very cunning in her witcheries. And he set to and ran, so eager was he to get rid of his soul, and a cloud of dust followed him as he sped round the sand of the shore. By the itching of her palm the young Witch knew his coming, and she laughed and let down her red hair. With her red hair falling around her, she stood at the opening of the cave, and in her hand she had a spray of wild hemlock that was blossoming.

'What d'ye lack? What d'ye lack?' she cried, as he came panting up the steep, and bent down before her. 'Fish for thy net, when the wind is foul? I have a little reed-pipe, and when I blow on it the mullet come sailing into the bay. But it has a price, pretty boy, it has a price. What d'ye lack? What d'ye lack? A storm to wreck the ships, and wash the chests of rich treasure ashore? I have more storms than the wind has, for I serve one who is stronger than the wind, and with a sieve and a pail of water I can send the great galleys to the bottom of the sea. But I have a price, pretty boy, I have a price. What d'ye lack? What d'ye lack? I know a flower that grows in the valley, none knows it but I. It has purple leaves, and a star in its heart, and its juice is as white as milk. Shouldst thou touch with this flower the hard lips of the Queen, she would follow thee all over the world. Out of the bed of the King she would rise, and over the whole world she would follow thee. And it has a price, pretty boy, it has a price. What d'ye lack? What d'ye lack? I can pound a toad in a mortar, and make broth of it, and stir the broth with a dead man's hand. Sprinkle it on thine enemy while he sleeps, and he will turn into a black viper, and his own mother will slay him. With a wheel I can draw the Moon from heaven, and in a crystal I can show thee Death. What d'ye lack? What d'ye lack? Tell me thy desire, and I will give it thee, and thou shalt pay me a price, pretty boy, thou shalt pay me a price.'

'My desire is but for a little thing,' said the young Fisherman, 'yet hath the Priest been wroth with me, and driven me forth. It is but for a little thing, and the merchants have mocked at me, and denied me. Therefore am I come to thee, though men call thee evil, and whatever be thy price I shall pay it.'

'What wouldst thou?' asked the Witch, coming near to him.

'I would send my soul away from me,' answered the young Fisherman.

The Witch grew pale, and shuddered, and hid her face in her blue mantle. 'Pretty boy, pretty boy,' she muttered, 'that is a terrible thing to do.'

He tossed his brown curls and laughed. 'My soul is nought to me,' he answered. 'I cannot see it. I may not touch it. I do not know it.'

'What wilt thou give me if I tell thee?' asked the Witch, looking down at him with her beautiful eyes.

'Five pieces of gold,' he said, 'and my nets, and the wattled house where I live, and the painted boat in which I sail. Only tell me how to get rid of my soul, and I will give thee all that I possess.'

She laughed mockingly at him, and struck him with the spray of hemlock. 'I can turn the autumn leaves into gold,' she answered, 'and I can weave the pale moonbeams into silver if I will it. He whom I serve is richer than all the kings of this world and has their dominions.'

'What then shall I give thee,' he cried, 'if thy price be neither gold nor silver?'

The Witch stroked his hair with her thin white hand. 'Thou must dance with me, pretty boy,' she murmured, and she smiled at him as she spoke.

'Nought but that?' cried the young Fisherman in wonder, and he rose to his feet.

'Nought but that,' she answered, and she smiled at him again.

'Then at sunset in some secret place we shall dance together,' he said, 'and after that we have danced thou shalt tell me the thing which I desire to know.'

She shook her head. 'When the moon is full, when the moon is full,' she muttered. Then she peered all round, and listened. A blue bird rose screaming from its nest and circled over the dunes, and three spotted birds rustled through the coarse grey grass and whistled to each other. There was no other sound save the sound of a wave fretting the smooth pebbles below. So she reached out her hand, and drew him near to her and put her dry lips close to his ear.

'To-night thou must come to the top of the mountain,' she whispered. 'It is a Sabbath, and He will be there.'

The young Fisherman started and looked at her, and she showed her white teeth and laughed. 'Who is He of whom thou speakest?' he asked.

'It matters not,' she answered. 'Go thou to-night, and stand under the branches of the hornbeam, and wait for my coming. If a black dog run towards thee, strike it with a rod of willow, and it will go away. If an owl speak to thee, make it no answer. When the moon is full I shall be with thee, and we will dance together on the grass.'

'But wilt thou swear to me to tell me how I may send my soul from me?' he made question.

She moved out into the sunlight, and through her red hair rippled the wind. 'By the hoofs of the goat I swear it,' she made answer.

'Thou art the best of the witches,' cried the young Fisherman, 'and I will surely dance with thee to-night on the top of the mountain. I would indeed that thou hadst asked of me either gold or silver. But such as thy price is thou shalt have it, for it is but a little thing.' And he doffed his cap to her, and bent his head low, and ran back to the town filled with a great joy.

And the Witch watched him as he went, and when he had passed from her sight she entered her cave, and having taken a mirror from a box of carved cedarwood, she set it up on a frame and burned vervain[11] on lighted charcoal before it, and peered through the coils of the smoke. And after a time she clenched her hands in anger. 'He should have been mine,' she muttered, 'I am as fair as she is.'

And that evening, when the moon had risen, the young Fisherman climbed up to the top of the mountain, and stood under the branches of the hornbeam. Like a targe[12] of polished metal the round sea lay at his feet, and the shadows of the fishing boats moved in the little bay. A great owl, with yellow sulphurous eyes, called to him by his name, but he made it no answer. A black dog ran towards him and snarled. He struck it with a rod of willow, and it went away whining.

At midnight the witches came flying through the air like bats. 'Phew!' they cried, as they lit upon the ground, 'there is some one here we know not!' and they sniffed about, and chattered to each other, and made signs. Last of all came the young Witch, with her red hair streaming in the wind. She wore a dress of gold tissue embroidered with peacocks' eyes, and a little cap of green velvet was on her head.

'Where is he, where is he?' shrieked the witches when they saw her, but she only laughed, and ran to the hornbeam, and taking the Fisherman by the hand she led him out into the moonlight and began to dance.

Round and round they whirled, and the young Witch jumped so high that he could see the scarlet heels of her shoes. Then right across the dancers came the sound of the galloping of a horse, but no horse was to be seen, and he felt afraid.

'Faster,' cried the Witch, and she threw her arms about his neck, and her breath was hot upon his face. 'Faster, faster!' she cried, and the earth seemed to spin beneath his feet, and his brain grew troubled, and a great terror fell on him, as of some evil thing that was watching him, and at last he became aware that under the shadow of a rock there was a figure that had not been there before.

It was a man dressed in a suit of black velvet, cut in the Spanish fashion. His face was strangely pale, but his lips were like a proud red flower. He seemed weary, and was leaning back toying in a listless manner with the pommel of his dagger. On the grass beside him lay a plumed hat, and a pair of riding gloves gauntleted with gilt lace, and sewn with seed-pearls wrought into a curious device. A short cloak lined with sables hung from his shoulder, and his delicate white hands were gemmed with rings. Heavy eyelids drooped over his eyes. The young Fisherman watched him, as one snared in a spell. At last their eyes met, and wherever he danced it seemed to him that the eyes of the man were upon him. He heard the Witch laugh, and caught her by the waist, and whirled her madly round and round. Suddenly a dog bayed in the wood, and the dancers stopped, and going up two by two, knelt down, and kissed the man's hands. As they did so, a little smile touched his proud lips, as a bird's wing touches the water and makes it laugh. But there was disdain in it. He kept looking at the young Fisherman.

'Come! let us worship,' whispered the Witch, and she led him up, and a great desire to do as she besought him seized on him, and he followed her. But when he came close, and without knowing why he did it, he made on his breast the sign of the Cross, and called upon the holy name.

No sooner had he done so than the witches screamed like hawks and flew away, and the pallid face that had been watching him twitched with a spasm of pain. The man went over to a little wood, and whistled. A jennet with silver trappings came running to meet him. As he leapt upon the saddle he turned round, and looked at the young Fisherman sadly.

And the Witch with the red hair tried to fly away also, but the Fisherman caught her by her wrists, and held her fast.

'Loose me,' she cried, 'and let me go. For thou hast named what should not be named, and shown the sign that may not be looked at.'

'Nay,' he answered, 'but I will not let thee go till thou hast told me the secret.'

'What secret?' said the Witch, wrestling with him like a wild cat, and biting her foam-flecked lips.

'Thou knowest,' he made answer.

Her grass-green eyes grew dim with tears, and she said to the Fisherman, 'Ask me anything but that!'

He laughed, and held her all the more tightly.

And when she saw that she could not free herself, she whispered to him, 'Surely I am as fair as the daughters of the sea, and as comely as those that dwell in the blue waters,' and she fawned on him and put her face close to his.

But he thrust her back frowning, and said to her, 'If thou keepest not the promise that thou madest to me I will slay thee for a false witch.'

She grew grey as a blossom of the Judas tree,[13] and shuddered. 'Be it so,' she muttered. 'It is thy soul and not mine. Do with it as thou wilt.' And she took from her girdle a little knife that had a handle of green viper's skin, and gave it to him.

'What shall this serve me?' he asked of her, wondering.

She was silent for a few moments, and a look of terror came over her face. Then she brushed her hair back from her forehead, and smiling strangely she said to him, 'What men call the shadow of the body is not the shadow of the body, but is the body of the soul. Stand on the sea-shore with thy back to the moon, and cut away from around thy feet thy shadow, which is thy soul's body, and bid thy soul leave thee, and it will do so.'

The young Fisherman trembled. 'Is this true?' he murmured.

'It is true, and I would that I had not told thee of it,' she cried, and she clung to his knees weeping.

He put her from him and left her in the rank grass, and going to the edge of the mountain he placed the knife in his belt, and began to climb down.

And his Soul that was within him called out to him and said, 'Lo! I have dwelt with thee for all these years, and have been thy servant. Send me not away from thee now, for what evil have I done thee?'

And the young Fisherman laughed. 'Thou hast done me no evil, but I have no need of thee,' he answered. 'The world is wide, and there is Heaven also, and Hell, and that dim twilight house that lies between. Go wherever thou wilt, but trouble me not, for my love is calling to me.'

And his Soul besought him piteously, but he heeded it not, but leapt from crag to crag, being sure-footed as a wild goat, and at last he reached the level ground and the yellow shore of the sea.

Bronze-limbed and well-knit, like a statue wrought by a Grecian, he stood on the sand with his back to the moon, and out of the foam came white arms that beckoned to him, and out of the waves rose dim forms that did him homage. Before him lay his shadow, which was the body of his soul, and behind him hung the moon in the honey-coloured air.

And his Soul said to him, 'If indeed thou must drive me from thee, send me not forth without a heart. The world is cruel, give me thy heart to take with me.'

He tossed his head and smiled. 'With what should I love my love if I gave thee my heart?' he cried.

'Nay, but be merciful,' said his Soul: 'give me thy heart, for the world is very cruel, and I am afraid.'

'My heart is my love's,' he answered, 'therefore tarry not, but get thee gone.'

'Should I not love also?' asked his Soul.

'Get thee gone, for I have no need of thee,' cried the young Fisherman, and he took the little knife with its handle of green viper's skin, and cut away his shadow from around his feet, and it rose up and stood before him, and looked at him, and it was even as himself.

He crept back, and thrust the knife into his belt, and a feeling of awe came over him. 'Get thee gone,' he murmured, 'and let me see thy face no more.'

'Nay, but we must meet again,' said the Soul. Its voice was low and flute-like, and its lips hardly moved while it spake.

'How shall we meet?' cried the young Fisherman. 'Thou wilt not follow me into the depths of the sea?'

'Once every year I will come to this place, and call to thee,' said the Soul. 'It may be that thou wilt have need of me.'

'What need should I have of thee?' cried the young Fisherman, 'but be it as thou wilt,' and he plunged into the water, and the Tritons blew their horns, and the little Mermaid rose up to meet him, and put her arms around his neck and kissed him on the mouth.

And the Soul stood on the lonely beach and watched them.

And when they had sunk down into the sea, it went weeping away over the marshes.

And after a year was over the Soul came down to the shore of the sea and called to the young Fisherman, and he rose out of the deep, and said, 'Why dost thou call to me?'

And the Soul answered, 'Come nearer, that I may speak with thee, for I have seen marvellous things.'

So he came nearer, and couched in the shallow water, and leaned his head upon his hand and listened.

And the Soul said to him, 'When I left thee I turned my face to the East and journeyed. From the East cometh everything that is wise. Six days I journeyed, and on the morning of the seventh day I came to a hill that is in the country of the Tartars.[14] I sat down under the shade of a tamarisk tree to shelter myself from the sun. The land was dry, and burnt up with the heat. The people went to and fro over the plain like flies crawling upon a disk of polished copper.

'When it was noon a cloud of red dust rose up from the flat rim of the land. When the Tartars saw it, they strung their painted bows, and having leapt upon their little horses they galloped to meet it. The women fled screaming to the waggons, and hid themselves behind the felt curtains.

'At twilight the Tartars returned, but five of them were missing, and of those that came back not a few had been wounded. They harnessed their horses to the waggons and drove hastily away. Three jackals came out of a cave and peered after them. Then they sniffed up the air with their nostrils, and trotted off in the opposite direction.

'When the moon rose I saw a camp-fire burning on the plain, and went towards it. A company of merchants were seated round it on carpets. Their camels were picketed behind them, and the negroes who were their servants were pitching tents of tanned skin upon the sand, and making a high wall of the prickly pear.

'As I came near them, the chief of the merchants rose up and drew his sword, and asked me my business.

'I answered that I was a Prince in my own land, and that I

had escaped from the Tartars, who had sought to make me their slave. The chief smiled, and showed me five heads fixed upon long reeds of bamboo.

'Then he asked me who was the prophet of God, and I answered him Mohammed.

'When he heard the name of the false prophet, he bowed and took me by the hand, and placed me by his side. A negro brought me some mare's milk in a wooden dish, and a piece of lamb's flesh roasted.

'At daybreak we started on our journey. I rode on a red-haired camel by the side of the chief, and a runner ran before us carrying a spear. The men of war were on either hand, and the mules followed with the merchandise. There were forty camels in the caravan, and the mules were twice forty in number.

'We went from the country of the Tartars into the country of those who curse the Moon. We saw the Gryphons[15] guarding their gold on the white rocks, and the scaled Dragons sleeping in their caves. As we passed over the mountains we held our breath lest the snows might fall on us, and each man tied a veil of gauze before his eyes. As we passed through the valleys the Pygmies shot arrows at us from the hollows of the trees, and at night time we heard the wild men beating on their drums. When we came to the Tower of Apes we set fruits before them, and they did not harm us. When we came to the Tower of Serpents we gave them warm milk in bowls of brass, and they let us go by. Three times in our journey we came to the banks of the Oxus. We crossed it on rafts of wood with great bladders of blown hide. The river-horses raged against us and sought to slay us. When the camels saw them they trembled.

'The kings of each city levied tolls on us, but would not suffer us to enter their gates. They threw us bread over the walls, little maize-cakes baked in honey and cakes of fine flour filled with dates. For every hundred baskets we gave them a bead of amber.

'When the dwellers in the villages saw us coming, they poisoned the wells and fled to the hill-summits. We fought with the Magadae who are born old, and grow younger and younger every year, and die when they are little children; and with the Laktroi who say that they are the sons of tigers, and paint themselves yellow and black; and with the Aurantes who bury their dead on the tops of trees, and themselves live in dark caverns lest the Sun, who is their god, should slay them; and with the Krimnians who worship a crocodile, and give it earrings of green glass, and feed it with butter and fresh fowls; and with the Agazonbae, who are dog-faced; and with the Sibans, who have horses' feet, and run more swiftly than horses. A third of our company died in battle, and a third died of want. The rest murmured against me, and said that I had brought them an evil fortune. I took a horned adder from beneath a stone and let it sting me. When they saw that I did not sicken they grew afraid.

'In the fourth month we reached the city of Illel. It was night time when we came to the grove that is outside the walls, and the air was sultry, for the Moon was travelling in Scorpion. We took the ripe pomegranates from the trees, and brake them and drank their sweet juices. Then we lay down on our carpets and waited for the dawn.

'And at dawn we rose and knocked at the gate of the city. It was wrought out of red bronze, and carved with sea-dragons and dragons that have wings. The guards looked down from the battlements and asked us our business. The interpreter of the caravan answered that we had come from the island of Syria with much merchandise. They took hostages, and told us that they would open the gate to us at noon, and bade us tarry till then.

'When it was noon they opened the gate, and as we entered in the people came crowding out of the houses to look at us, and a crier went round the city crying through a shell. We stood in the market-place, and the negroes uncorded the bales of figured cloths and opened the carved chests of sycamore. And when they had ended their task, the merchants set forth their strange wares, the waxed linen from Egypt and the painted linen from the country of the Ethiops, the purple sponges from Tyre and the blue hangings from Sidon, the cups of cold amber and the fine vessels of glass and the curious vessels of burnt clay. From the roof of a house a company of women watched us. One of them wore a mask of gilded leather.

'And on the first day the priests came and bartered with us, and on the second day came the nobles, and on the third day came the craftsmen and the slaves. And this is their custom with all merchants as long as they tarry in the city.

'And we tarried for a moon, and when the moon was waning, I wearied and wandered away through the streets of the city and came to the garden of its god. The priests in their yellow robes moved silently through the green trees, and on a pavement of black marble stood the rose-red house in which the god had his dwelling. Its doors were of powdered lacquer, and bulls and peacocks were wrought on them in raised and polished gold. The tiled roof was of sea-green porcelain, and the jutting eaves were festooned with little bells. When the white doves flew past, they struck the bells with their wings and made them tinkle.

'In front of the temple was a pool of clear water paved with veined onyx. I lay down beside it, and with my pale fingers I touched the broad leaves. One of the priests came towards me and stood behind me. He had sandals on his feet, one of soft serpent-skin and the other of birds' plumage. On his head was a mitre of black felt decorated with silver crescents. Seven yellows were woven into his robe, and his frizzed hair was stained with antimony.

'After a little while he spake to me, and asked me my desire.

'I told him that my desire was to see the god.

'"The god is hunting," said the priest, looking strangely at me with his small slanting eyes.

'"Tell me in what forest, and I will ride with him," I answered.

'He combed out the soft fringes of his tunic with his long pointed nails. "The god is asleep," he murmured.

'"Tell me on what couch, and I will watch by him," I answered.

'"The god is at the feast," he cried.

'"If the wine be sweet I will drink it with him, and if it be bitter I will drink it with him also," was my answer.

'He bowed his head in wonder, and, taking me by the hand, he raised me up, and led me into the temple.

'And in the first chamber I saw an idol seated on a throne of jasper bordered with great orient pearls. It was carved out of ebony, and in stature was of the stature of a man. On its forehead was a ruby, and thick oil dripped from its hair on to its thighs. Its feet were red with the blood of a newly-slain kid, and its loins girt with a copper belt that was studded with seven beryls.

'And I said to the priest, "Is this the god?" And he answered me, "This is the god."

'"Show me the god," I cried, "or I will surely slay thee." And I touched his hand, and it became withered.

'And the priest besought me, saying, "Let my lord heal his servant, and I will show him the god."

'So I breathed with my breath upon his hand, and it became whole again, and he trembled and led me into the second chamber, and I saw an idol standing on a lotus of jade hung with great emeralds. It was carved out of ivory, and in stature was twice the stature of a man. On its forehead was a chrysolite, and its breasts were smeared with myrrh and cinnamon. In one hand it held a crooked sceptre of jade, and in the other a round crystal. It ware buskins of brass, and its thick neck was circled with a circle of selenites.[16]

'And I said to the priest, "Is this the god?" And he answered me, "This is the god."

'"Show me the god," I cried, "or I will surely slay thee." And I touched his eyes, and they became blind.

'And the priest besought me, saying, "Let my lord heal his servant, and I will show him the god."

'So I breathed with my breath upon his eyes, and the sight came back to them, and he trembled again, and led me into the third chamber, and lo! there was no idol in it, nor image of any kind, but only a mirror of round metal set on an altar of stone.

'And I said to the priest, "Where is the god?"

'And he answered me: "There is no god but this mirror that thou seest, for this is the Mirror of Wisdom. And it reflecteth all things that are in heaven and on earth, save only the face of him who looketh into it. This it reflecteth not, so that he who looketh into it may be wise. Many other mirrors are there, but they are mirrors of Opinion. This only is the Mirror of Wisdom. And they who possess this mirror know everything, nor is there anything hidden from them. And they who possess it not have not Wisdom.

Therefore is it the god, and we worship it." And I looked into the mirror, and it was even as he had said to me.

'And I did a strange thing, but what I did matters not, for in a valley that is but a day's journey from this place have I hidden the Mirror of Wisdom. Do but suffer me to enter into thee again and be thy servant, and thou shalt be wiser than all the wise men, and Wisdom shall be thine. Suffer me to enter into thee, and none will be as wise as thou.'

But the young Fisherman laughed. 'Love is better than Wisdom,' he cried, 'and the little Mermaid loves me.'

'Nay, but there is nothing better than Wisdom,' said the Soul.

'Love is better,' answered the young Fisherman, and he plunged into the deep, and the Soul went weeping away over the marshes.

And after the second year was over the Soul came down to the shore of the sea, and called to the young Fisherman, and he rose out of the deep and said, 'Why dost thou call to me?'

And the Soul answered, 'Come nearer that I may speak with thee, for I have seen marvellous things.'

So he came nearer, and couched in the shallow water, and leaned his head upon his hand and listened.

And the Soul said to him, 'When I left thee, I turned my face to the South and journeyed. From the South cometh everything that is precious. Six days I journeyed along the highways that lead to the city of Ashter, along the dusty red-dyed highways by which the pilgrims are wont to go did I journey, and on the morning of the seventh day I lifted up my eyes, and lo! the city lay at my feet, for it is in a valley.

'There are nine gates to this city, and in front of each gate stands a bronze horse that neighs when the Bedouins come down from the mountains. The walls are cased with copper, and the watch-towers on the walls are roofed with brass. In every tower stands an archer with a bow in his hand. At sunrise he strikes with an arrow on a gong, and at sunset he blows through a horn of horn.

'When I sought to enter, the guards stopped me and asked of me who I was. I made answer that I was a Dervish and on my way to the city of Mecca, where there was a green veil on which the Koran was embroidered in silver letters by the hands of the angels. They were filled with wonder, and entreated me to pass in.

'Inside it is even as a bazaar. Surely thou shouldst have been with me. Across the narrow streets the gay lanterns of paper flutter like large butterflies. When the wind blows over the roofs they rise and fall as painted bubbles do. In front of their booths sit the merchants on silken carpets. They have straight black beards, and their turbans are covered with golden sequins, and long strings of amber and carved peach-stones glide through their cool fingers. Some of them sell galbanum and nard,[17] and curious perfumes from the islands of the Indian Sea, and the thick oil of red roses, and myrrh and little nail-shaped cloves. When one stops to speak to them, they throw pinches of frankincense upon a charcoal brazier and make the air sweet. I saw a Syrian who held in his hands a thin rod like a reed. Grey threads of smoke came from it, and its odour as it burned was as the odour of the pink almond in spring. Others sell silver bracelets embossed all over with creamy blue turquoise stones, and anklets of brass wire fringed with little pearls, and tigers' claws set in gold, and the claws of that gilt cat, the leopard, set in gold also, and earrings of pierced emerald, and finger-rings of hollowed jade. From the tea-houses comes the sound of the guitar, and the opium-smokers with their white smiling faces look out at the passers-by.

'Of a truth thou shouldst have been with me. The wine-sellers elbow their way through the crowd with great black skins on their shoulders. Most of them sell the wine of Schiraz,[18] which is as sweet as honey. They serve it in little metal cups and strew rose leaves upon it. In the market-place stand the fruitsellers, who sell all kinds of fruit: ripe figs, with their bruised purple flesh, melons, smelling of musk and yellow as topazes, citrons and rose-apples and clusters of white grapes, round red-gold oranges, and oval lemons of green gold. Once I saw an elephant go by. Its trunk was painted with vermilion and turmeric, and over its ears it had a net of crimson silk cord. It stopped opposite one of the booths and began eating the oranges, and the man only laughed. Thou canst not think how strange a people they are. When they are glad they go to the bird-sellers and buy of them a caged bird, and set it free that their joy may be greater, and when they are sad they scourge themselves with thorns that their sorrow may not grow less.

'One evening I met some negroes carrying a heavy palanquin[19] through the bazaar. It was made of gilded bamboo, and the poles were of vermilion lacquer studded with brass peacocks. Across the windows hung thin curtains of muslin embroidered with beetles' wings and with tiny seed-pearls, and as it passed by a pale-faced Circassian[20] looked out and smiled at me. I followed behind, and the negroes hurried their steps and scowled. But I did not care. I felt a great curiosity come over me.

'At last they stopped at a square white house. There were no windows to it, only a little door like the door of a tomb. They set down the palanquin and knocked three times with a copper hammer. An Armenian in a caftan of green leather peered through the wicket, and when he saw them he opened, and spread a carpet on the ground, and the woman stepped out. As she went in, she turned round and smiled at me again. I had never seen any one so pale.

'When the moon rose I returned to the same place and sought for the house, but it was no longer there. When I saw that, I knew who the woman was, and wherefore she had smiled at me.

'Certainly thou shouldst have been with me. On the feast of the New Moon the young Emperor came forth from his palace and went into the mosque to pray. His hair and beard were dyed with rose-leaves, and his cheeks were powdered with a fine gold dust. The palms of his feet and hands were yellow with saffron.

'At sunrise he went forth from his palace in a robe of silver, and at sunset he returned to it again in a robe of gold. The people flung themselves on the ground and hid their faces, but I would not do so. I stood by the stall of a seller of dates and waited. When the Emperor saw me, he raised his painted eyebrows and stopped. I stood quite still, and made him no obeisance. The people marvelled at my boldness, and counselled me to flee from the city. I paid no heed to them, but went and sat with the sellers of strange gods, who by reason of their craft are abominated. When I told them what I had done, each of them gave me a god and prayed me to leave them.

'That night, as I lay on a cushion in the tea-house that is in the Street of Pomegranates, the guards of the Emperor entered and led me to the palace. As I went in they closed each door behind me, and put a chain across it. Inside was a great court with an arcade running all round. The walls were of white alabaster, set here and there with blue and green tiles. The pillars were of green marble, and the pavement of a kind of peach-blossom marble. I had never seen anything like it before.

'As I passed across the court two veiled women looked down from a balcony and cursed me. The guards hastened on, and the butts of the lances rang upon the polished floor. They opened a gate of wrought ivory, and I found myself in a watered garden of seven terraces. It was planted with tulip-cups and moonflowers, and silver-studded aloes.[21] Like a slim reed of crystal a fountain hung in the dusky air. The cypress-trees were like burnt-out torches. From one of them a nightingale was singing.

'At the end of the garden stood a little pavilion. As we approached it two eunuchs came out to meet us. Their fat bodies swayed as they walked, and they glanced curiously at me with their yellow-lidded eyes. One of them drew aside the captain of the guard, and in a low voice whispered to him. The other kept munching scented pastilles, which he took with an affected gesture out of an oval box of lilac enamel.

'After a few moments the captain of the guard dismissed the soldiers. They went back to the palace, the eunuchs following slowly behind and plucking the sweet mulberries from the trees as they passed. Once the elder of the two turned round, and smiled at me with an evil smile.

'Then the captain of the guard motioned me towards the entrance of the pavilion. I walked on without trembling, and drawing the heavy curtain aside I entered in.

'The young Emperor was stretched on a couch of dyed lion skins, and a ger-falcon[22] perched upon his wrist. Behind him stood a brass-turbaned Nubian, naked down to the waist, and with heavy earrings in his split ears. On a table by the side of the couch lay a mighty scimitar of steel.

'When the Emperor saw me he frowned, and said to me, "What is thy name? Knowest thou not that I am Emperor of this city?" But I made him no answer.

'He pointed with his finger at the scimitar, and the Nubian seized it, and rushing forward struck at me with great violence. The blade whizzed through me, and did me no hurt. The man fell sprawling on the floor, and, when he rose up, his teeth chattered with terror and he hid himself behind the couch.

'The Emperor leapt to his feet, and taking a lance from a stand of arms, he threw it at me. I caught it in its flight, and brake the shaft into two pieces. He shot at me with an arrow, but I held up my hands and it stopped in mid-air. Then he drew a dagger from a belt of white leather, and stabbed the Nubian in the throat lest the slave should tell of his dishonour. The man writhed like a trampled snake, and a red foam bubbled from his lips.

'As soon as he was dead the Emperor turned to me, and when he had wiped away the bright sweat from his brow with a little napkin of purfled and purple silk, he said to me, "Art thou a prophet, that I may not harm thee, or the son of a prophet that I can do thee no hurt? I pray thee leave my city to-night, for while thou art in it I am no longer its lord."

'And I answered him, "I will go for half of thy treasure. Give me half of thy treasure, and I will go away."

'He took me by the hand, and led me out into the garden. When the captain of the guard saw me, he wondered. When the eunuchs saw me, their knees shook and they fell upon the ground in fear.

'There is a chamber in the palace that has eight walls of red porphyry,[23] and a brass-scaled ceiling hung with lamps. The Emperor touched one of the walls and it opened, and we passed down a corridor that was lit with many torches. In niches upon each side stood great wine-jars filled to the brim with silver pieces. When we reached the centre of the corridor the Emperor spake the word that may not be spoken, and a granite door swung back on a secret spring, and he put his hands before his face lest his eyes should be dazzled.

'Thou couldst not believe how marvellous a place it was. There were huge tortoise-shells full of pearls, and hollowed moonstones of great size piled up with red rubies. The gold was stored in coffers of elephant-hide, and the gold-dust in leather bottles. There were opals and sapphires, the former in cups of crystal, and the latter in cups of jade. Round green emeralds were ranged in order upon thin plates of ivory, and in one corner were silk bags filled, some with turquoise-stones, and others with beryls. The ivory horns were heaped with purple amethysts, and the horns of brass with chalcedonies and sards.[24] The pillars, which were of cedar, were hung with strings of yellow lynx-stones. In the flat oval shields there were carbuncles, both wine-coloured and coloured like grass. And yet I have told thee but a tithe of what was there.

'And when the Emperor had taken away his hands from before his face he said to me: "This is my house of treasure, and half that is in it is thine, even as I promised to thee. And I will give thee camels and camel drivers, and they shall do thy bidding and take thy share of the treasure to whatever part of the world thou desirest to go. And the thing shall be done to-night, for I would not that the Sun, who is my father, should see that there is in my city a man whom I cannot slay."

'But I answered him, "The gold that is here is thine, and the silver also is thine, and thine are the precious jewels and the things of price. As for me, I have no need of these. Nor shall I take aught from thee but that little ring that thou wearest on the finger of thy hand."

'And the Emperor frowned. "It is but a ring of lead," he cried, "nor has it any value. Therefore take thy half of the treasure and go from my city."

'"Nay," I answered, "but I will take nought but that leaden ring, for I know what is written within it, and for what purpose."

'And the Emperor trembled, and besought me and said, "Take all the treasure and go from my city. The half that is mine shall be thine also."

'And I did a strange thing, but what I did matters not, for in a cave that is but a day's journey from this place have I hidden the Ring of Riches. It is but a day's journey from this place, and it waits for thy coming. He who has this Ring is richer than all the kings of the world. Come therefore and take it, and the world's riches shall be thine.'

But the young Fisherman laughed. 'Love is better than Riches,' he cried, 'and the little Mermaid loves me.'

'Nay, but there is nothing better than Riches,' said the Soul.

'Love is better,' answered the young Fisherman, and he plunged into the deep, and the Soul went weeping away over the marshes.

And after the third year was over, the Soul came down to the shore of the sea, and called to the young Fisherman, and he rose out of the deep and said, 'Why dost thou call to me?'

And the Soul answered, 'Come nearer, that I may speak with thee, for I have seen marvellous things.'

So he came nearer, and couched in the shallow water, and leaned his head upon his hand and listened.

And the Soul said to him, 'In a city that I know of there is an inn that standeth by a river. I sat there with sailors who drank of two different coloured wines, and ate bread made of barley, and little salt fish served in bay leaves with vinegar. And as we sat and made merry, there entered to us an old man bearing a leathern carpet and a lute that had two horns of amber. And when he had laid out the carpet on the floor, he struck with a quill on the wire strings of his lute, and a girl whose face was veiled ran in and began to dance before us. Her face was veiled with a veil of gauze, but her feet were naked. Naked were her feet, and they moved over the carpet like little white pigeons. Never have I seen anything so marvellous, and the city in which she dances is but a day's journey from this place.'

Now when the young Fisherman heard the words of his Soul, he remembered that the little Mermaid had no feet and could not dance. And a great desire came over him, and he said to himself, 'It is but a day's journey, and I can return to my love,' and he laughed, and stood up in the shallow water, and strode towards the shore.

And when he had reached the dry shore he laughed again, and held out his arms to his Soul. And his Soul gave a great cry of joy and ran to meet him, and entered into him, and the young

Fisherman saw stretched before him upon the sand that shadow of the body that is the body of the Soul.

And his Soul said to him, 'Let us not tarry, but get hence at once, for the Sea-gods are jealous, and have monsters that do their bidding.'

So they made haste, and all that night they journeyed beneath the moon, and all the next day they journeyed beneath the sun, and on the evening of the day they came to a city.

And the young Fisherman said to his Soul, 'Is this the city in which she dances of whom thou didst speak to me?'

And his Soul answered him, 'It is not this city, but another. Nevertheless let us enter in.'

So they entered in and passed through the streets, and as they passed through the Street of the Jewellers the young Fisherman saw a fair silver cup set forth in a booth. And his Soul said to him, 'Take that silver cup and hide it.'

So he took the cup and hid it in the fold of his tunic, and they went hurriedly out of the city.

And after that they had gone a league from the city, the young Fisherman frowned, and flung the cup away, and said to his Soul, 'Why didst thou tell me to take this cup and hide it, for it was an evil thing to do?'

But his Soul answered him, 'Be at peace, be at peace.'

And on the evening of the second day they came to a city, and the young Fisherman said to his Soul, 'Is this the city in which she dances of whom thou didst speak to me?'

And his Soul answered him, 'It is not this city, but another. Nevertheless let us enter in.'

So they entered in and passed through the streets, and as they passed through the Street of the Sellers of Sandals, the young Fisherman saw a child standing by a jar of water. And his Soul said to him, 'Smite that child.' So he smote the child till it wept, and when he had done this they went hurriedly out of the city.

And after that they had gone a league from the city the young Fisherman grew wrath, and said to his Soul, 'Why didst thou tell me to smite the child, for it was an evil thing to do?'

But his Soul answered him, 'Be at peace, be at peace.'

And on the evening of the third day they came to a city, and the young Fisherman said to his Soul, 'Is this the city in which she dances of whom thou didst speak to me?'

And his Soul answered him, 'It may be that it is this city, therefore let us enter in.'

So they entered in and passed through the streets, but nowhere could the young Fisherman find the river or the inn that stood by its side. And the people of the city looked curiously at him, and he grew afraid and said to his Soul, 'Let us go hence, for she who dances with white feet is not here.'

But his Soul answered, 'Nay, but let us tarry, for the night is dark and there will be robbers on the way.'

So he sat him down in the market-place and rested, and after a time there went by a hooded merchant who had a cloak of cloth of Tartary, and bare a lantern of pierced horn at the end of a jointed reed. And the merchant said to him, 'Why dost thou sit in the market-place, seeing that the booths are closed and the bales corded?'

And the young Fisherman answered him, 'I can find no inn in this city, nor have I any kinsman who might give me shelter.'

'Are we not all kinsmen?' said the merchant. 'And did not one God make us? Therefore come with me, for I have a guest-chamber.'

So the young Fisherman rose up and followed the merchant to his house. And when he had passed through a garden of pomegranates and entered into the house, the merchant brought him rose-water in a copper dish that he might wash his hands, and ripe melons that he might quench his thirst, and set a bowl of rice and a piece of roasted kid before him.

And after that he had finished, the merchant led him to the guest-chamber, and bade him sleep and be at rest. And the young Fisherman gave him thanks, and kissed the ring that was on his hand, and flung himself down on the carpets of dyed goat's-hair. And when he had covered himself with a covering of black lamb's-wool he fell asleep.

And three hours before dawn, and while it was still night, his Soul waked him, and said to him, 'Rise up and go to the room of the merchant, even to the room in which he sleepeth, and slay him, and take from him his gold, for we have need of it.'

And the young Fisherman rose up and crept towards the room of the merchant, and over the feet of the merchant there was lying a curved sword, and the tray by the side of the merchant held nine purses of gold. And he reached out his hand and touched the sword, and when he touched it the merchant started and awoke, and leaping up seized himself the sword and cried to the young Fisherman, 'Dost thou return evil for good, and pay with the shedding of blood for the kindness that I have shown thee?'

And his Soul said to the young Fisherman, 'Strike him,' and he struck him so that he swooned, and he seized then the nine purses of gold, and fled hastily through the garden of pomegranates, and set his face to the star that is the star of morning.

And when they had gone a league from the city, the young Fisherman beat his breast, and said to his Soul, 'Why didst thou bid me slay the merchant and take his gold? Surely thou art evil.'

But his Soul answered him, 'Be at peace, be at peace.'

'Nay,' cried the young Fisherman, 'I may not be at peace, for all that thou hast made me to do I hate. Thee also I hate, and I bid thee tell me wherefore thou hast wrought with me in this wise.'

And his Soul answered him, 'When thou didst send me forth into the world thou gavest me no heart, so I learned to do all these things and love them.'

'What sayest thou?' murmured the young Fisherman.

'Thou knowest,' answered his Soul, 'thou knowest it well. Hast thou forgotten that thou gavest me no heart? I trow not. And so trouble not thyself nor me, but be at peace, for there is no pain that thou shalt not give away, nor any pleasure that thou shalt not receive.'

And when the young Fisherman heard these words he trembled and said to his Soul, 'Nay, but thou art evil, and hast made me forget my love, and hast tempted me with temptations, and hast set my feet in the ways of sin.'

And his Soul answered him, 'Thou hast not forgotten that when thou didst send me forth into the world thou gavest me no heart. Come, let us go to another city, and make merry, for we have nine purses of gold.'

But the young Fisherman took the nine purses of gold, and flung them down, and trampled on them.

'Nay,' he cried, 'but I will have nought to do with thee, nor will I journey with thee anywhere, but even as I sent thee away before, so will I send thee away now, for thou hast wrought me no good.' And he turned his back to the moon, and with the little knife that had the handle of green viper's skin he strove to cut from his feet that shadow of the body which is the body of the Soul.

Yet his Soul stirred not from him, nor paid heed to his command, but said to him, 'The spell that the Witch told thee avails thee no more, for I may not leave thee, nor mayest thou drive me forth. Once in his life may a man send his Soul away, but he who receiveth back his Soul must keep it with him for ever, and this is his punishment and his reward.'

And the young Fisherman grew pale and clenched his hands and cried, 'She was a false Witch in that she told me not that.'

'Nay,' answered his Soul, 'but she was true to Him she worships, and whose servant she will be ever.'

And when the young Fisherman knew that he could no longer get rid of his Soul, and that it was an evil Soul and would abide with him always, he fell upon the ground weeping bitterly.

And when it was day the young Fisherman rose up and said to his Soul, 'I will bind my hands that I may not do thy bidding, and close my lips that I may not speak thy words, and I will return to the place where she whom I love has her dwelling. Even to the sea will I return, and to the little bay where she is wont to sing, and I will call to her and tell her the evil I have done and the evil thou hast wrought on me.'

And his Soul tempted him and said, 'Who is thy love that thou shouldst return to her? The world has many fairer than she is. There are the dancing-girls of Samaris who dance in the manner of all kinds of birds and beasts. Their feet are painted with henna, and in their hands they have little copper bells. They laugh while they dance, and their laughter is as clear as the laughter of water. Come with me and I will show them to thee. For what is this trouble of thine about the things of sin? Is that which is pleasant to eat not made for the eater? Is there poison in that which is sweet to drink? Trouble not thyself, but come with me to another city. There is a little city hard by in which there is a garden of tulip-trees. And there dwell in this comely garden white peacocks and peacocks that have blue breasts. Their tails when they spread them to the sun are like disks of ivory and like gilt disks. And she who feeds them dances for their pleasure, and sometimes she dances on her hands and at other times she dances with her feet. Her eyes are coloured with stibium,[25] and her nostrils are shaped like the wings of a swallow. From a hook in one of her nostrils hangs a flower that is carved out of a pearl. She laughs while she dances, and the silver rings that are about her ankles tinkle like bells of silver. And so trouble not thyself any more, but come with me to this city.'

But the young Fisherman answered not his Soul, but closed his lips with the seal of silence and with a tight cord bound his hands, and journeyed back to the place from which he had come, even to the little bay where his love had been wont to sing. And ever did his Soul tempt him by the way, but he made it no answer, nor would he do any of the wickedness that it sought to make him to do, so great was the power of the love that was within him.

And when he had reached the shore of the sea, he loosed the cord from his hands, and took the seal of silence from his lips, and called to the little Mermaid. But she came not to his call, though he called to her all day long and besought her.

And his Soul mocked him and said, 'Surely thou hast but little joy out of thy love. Thou art as one who in time of dearth pours water into a broken vessel. Thou givest away what thou hast, and nought is given to thee in return. It were better for thee to come with me, for I know where the Valley of Pleasure lies, and what things are wrought there.'

But the young Fisherman answered not his Soul, but in a cleft of the rock he built himself a house of wattles, and abode there for the space of a year. And every morning he called to the Mermaid, and every noon he called to her again, and at night-time he spake her name. Yet never did she rise out of the sea to meet him, nor in any place of the sea could he find her, though he sought for her in the caves and in the green water, in the pools of the tide and in the wells that are at the bottom of the deep.

And ever did his Soul tempt him with evil, and whisper of terrible things. Yet did it not prevail against him, so great was the power of his love.

And after the year was over, the Soul thought within himself, 'I have tempted my master with evil, and his love is stronger than I am. I will tempt him now with good, and it may be that he will come with me.'

So he spake to the young Fisherman and said, 'I have told thee of the joy of the world, and thou hast turned a deaf ear to me. Suffer me now to tell thee of the world's pain, and it may be that thou wilt hearken. For of a truth, pain is the Lord of this world, nor is there anyone who escapes from its net. There be some who lack raiment, and others who lack bread. There be widows who sit in purple, and widows who sit in rags. To and fro over the fens go the lepers, and they are cruel to each other. The beggars go up and down on the highways, and their wallets are empty. Through the streets of the cities walks Famine, and the Plague sits at their gates. Come, let us go forth and mend these things, and make them not to be. Wherefore shouldst thou tarry here calling to thy love, seeing she comes not to thy call? And what is love, that thou shouldst set this high store upon it?'

But the young Fisherman answered it nought, so great was the power of his love. And every morning he called to the Mermaid, and every noon he called to her again, and at night-time he spake her name. Yet never did she rise out of the sea to meet him, nor in any place of the sea could he find him, though he sought for her in the rivers of the sea, and in the valleys that are under the waves, in the sea that the night makes purple, and in the sea that the dawn leaves grey.

And after the second year was over, the Soul said to the young Fisherman at night-time, and as he sat in the wattled house alone, 'Lo! now I have tempted thee with evil, and I have tempted thee with good, and thy love is stronger than I am. Wherefore will I tempt thee no longer, but I pray thee to suffer me to enter thy heart, that I may be one with thee even as before.'

'Surely thou mayest enter,' said the young Fisherman, 'for in the days when with no heart thou didst go through the world thou must have much suffered.'

'Alas!' cried his Soul, 'I can find no place of entrance, so compassed about with love is this heart of thine.'

'Yet I would that I could help thee,' said the young Fisherman.

And as he spake there came a great cry of mourning from the sea, even the cry that men hear when one of the Sea-folk is dead. And the young Fisherman leapt up, and left his wattled house, and ran down to the shore. And the black waves came hurrying to the shore, bearing with them a burden that was whiter than silver. White as the surf it was, and like a flower it tossed on the waves. And the surf took it from the waves, and the foam took it from the surf, and the shore received it, and lying at his feet the young Fisherman saw the body of the little Mermaid. Dead at his feet it was lying.

Weeping as one smitten with pain he flung himself down beside it, and he kissed the cold red of the mouth, and toyed with the wet amber of the hair. He flung himself down beside it on the sand, weeping as one trembling with joy, and in his brown arms he held it to his breast. Cold were the lips, yet he kissed them. Salt was the honey of the hair, yet he tasted it with a bitter joy. He kissed the closed eyelids, and the wild spray that lay upon their cups was less salt than his tears.

And to the dead thing he made confession. Into the shells of its ears he poured the harsh wine of his tale. He put the little hands round his neck, and with his fingers he touched the thin reed of the throat. Bitter, bitter was his joy, and full of strange gladness was his pain.

The black sea came nearer, and the white foam moaned like a leper. With white claws of foam the sea grabbled at the shore. From the palace of the Sea-King came the cry of mourning again, and far out upon the sea the great Tritons blew hoarsely upon their horns.

'Flee away,' said his Soul, 'for ever doth the sea come nigher, and if thou tarriest it will slay thee. Flee away, for I am afraid, seeing that thy heart is closed against me by reason of the greatness of thy love. Flee away to a place of safety. Surely thou wilt not send me without a heart into another world?'

But the young Fisherman listened not to his Soul, but called on the little Mermaid and said, 'Love is better than wisdom, and more precious than riches, and fairer than the feet of the daughters of men. The fires cannot destroy it, nor can the waters quench it. I called on thee at dawn, and thou didst not come to my call. The moon heard thy name, yet hadst thou no heed of me. For evilly had I left thee, and to my own hurt had I wandered away. Yet ever did thy love abide with me, and ever was it strong, nor did aught prevail against it, though I have looked upon evil and looked upon good. And now that thou art dead, surely I will die with thee also.'

And his Soul besought him to depart, but he would not, so great was his love. And the sea came nearer, and sought to cover him with its waves, and when he knew that the end was at hand he kissed with mad lips the cold lips of the Mermaid, and the heart that was within him brake. And as through the fulness of his love his heart did break, the Soul found an entrance and entered in, and was one with him even as before. And the sea covered the young Fisherman with its waves.

And in the morning the Priest went forth to bless the sea, for it had been troubled. And with him went the monks and the musicians, and the candle-bearers, and the swingers of censers, and a great company.

And when the Priest reached the shore he saw the young Fisherman lying drowned in the surf, and clasped in his arms was the body of the little Mermaid. And he drew back frowning, and having made the sign of the cross, he cried aloud and said, 'I will not bless the sea nor anything that is in it. Accursed be the Sea-folk, and accursed be all they who traffic with them. And as for him who for love's sake forsook God, and so lieth here with his leman slain by God's judgment, take up his body and the body of his leman, and bury them in the corner of the Field of the Fullers,[26] and set no mark above them, nor sign of any kind, that none may know the place of their resting. For accursed were they in their lives, and accursed shall they be in their deaths also.'

And the people did as he commanded them, and in the corner of the Field of the Fullers, where no sweet herbs grew, they dug a deep pit, and laid the dead things within it.

And when the third year was over, and on a day that was a holy day, the Priest went up to the chapel, that he might show to the people the wounds of the Lord, and speak to them about the wrath of God.

And when he had robed himself with his robes, and entered in and bowed himself before the altar, he saw that the altar was covered with strange flowers that never had he seen before. Strange were they to look at, and of curious beauty, and their beauty troubled him, and their odour was sweet in his nostrils. And he felt glad, and understood not why he was glad.

And after that he had opened the tabernacle, and incensed the monstrance[27] that was in it, and shown the fair wafer to the people, and hid it again behind the veil of veils, he began to speak to the people, desiring to speak to them of the wrath of God. But the beauty of the white flowers troubled him, and their odour was sweet in his nostrils, and there came another word into his lips, and he spake not of the wrath of God, but of the God whose name is Love. And why he so spake, he knew not.

And when he had finished his word the people wept, and the Priest went back to the sacristy, and his eyes were full of tears. And the deacons came in and began to unrobe him, and took from him the alb and the girdle, the maniple and the stole.[28] And he stood as one in a dream.

And after that they had unrobed him, he looked at them and said, 'What are the flowers that stand on the altar, and whence do they come?'

And they answered him, 'What flowers they are we cannot tell, but they come from the corner of the Fullers' Field.' And the Priest trembled, and returned to his own house and prayed.

And in the morning, while it was still dawn, he went forth with the monks and the musicians, and the candle-bearers and the swingers of censers, and a great company, and came to the shore of the sea, and blessed the sea, and all the wild things that are in it. The Fauns also he blessed, and the little things that dance in the woodland, and the bright-eyed things that peer through the leaves. All the things in God's world he blessed, and the people were filled with joy and wonder. Yet never again in the corner of the Fullers' Field grew flowers of any kind, but the field remained barren even as before. Nor came the Sea-folk into the bay as they had been wont to do, for they went to another part of the sea.

The Star-Child

To Miss Margot Tennant[1]

Once upon a time two poor Woodcutters were making their way home through a great pine-forest. It was winter, and a night of bitter cold. The snow lay thick upon the ground, and upon the branches of the trees: the frost kept snapping the little twigs on either side of them, as they passed: and when they came to the Mountain-Torrent she was hanging motionless in air, for the Ice-King had kissed her.

So cold was it that even the animals and the birds did not know what to make of it.

'Ugh!' snarled the Wolf, as he limped through the brushwood with his tail between his legs, 'this is perfectly monstrous weather. Why doesn't the Government look to it?'

'Weet! weet! weet!' twittered the green Linnets, 'the old Earth is dead, and they have laid her out in her white shroud.'

'The Earth is going to be married, and this is her bridal dress,' whispered the Turtle-doves to each other. Their little pink feet were quite frost-bitten, but they felt that it was their duty to take a romantic view of the situation.

'Nonsense!' growled the Wolf. 'I tell you that it is all the fault of the Government, and if you don't believe me I shall eat you.' The Wolf had a thoroughly practical mind, and was never at a loss for a good argument.

'Well, for my own part,' said the Woodpecker, who was a born philosopher, 'I don't care an atomic theory for explanations. If a thing is so, it is so, and at present it is terribly cold.'

Terribly cold it certainly was. The little Squirrels, who lived inside the tall fir-tree, kept rubbing each other's noses to keep themselves warm, and the Rabbits curled themselves up in their holes, and did not venture even to look out of doors. The only

149

people who seemed to enjoy it were the great horned Owls. Their feathers were quite stiff with rime, but they did not mind, and they rolled their large yellow eyes, and called out to each other across the forest, 'Tu-whit! Tu-whoo! Tu-whit! Tu-whoo! what delightful weather we are having!'

On and on went the two Woodcutters, blowing lustily upon their fingers, and stamping with their huge iron-shod boots upon the caked snow. Once they sank into a deep drift, and came out as white as millers are, when the stones are grinding; and once they slipped on the hard smooth ice where the marsh-water was frozen, and their faggots fell out of their bundles, and they had to pick them up and bind them together again; and once they thought that they had lost their way, and a great terror seized on them, for they knew that the Snow is cruel to those who sleep in her arms. But they put their trust in the good Saint Martin, who watches over all travellers, and retraced their steps, and went warily, and at last they reached the outskirts of the forest, and saw, far down in the valley beneath them, the lights of the village in which they dwelt.

So overjoyed were they at their deliverance that they laughed aloud, and the Earth seemed to them like a flower of silver, and the Moon like a flower of gold.

Yet, after that they had laughed they became sad, for they remembered their poverty, and one of them said to the other, 'Why did we make merry, seeing that life is for the rich, and not for such as we are? Better that we had died of cold in the forest, or that some wild beast had fallen upon us and slain us.'

'Truly,' answered his companion, 'much is given to some, and little is given to others. Injustice has parcelled out the world, nor is there equal division of aught save of sorrow.'

But as they were bewailing their misery to each other this strange thing happened. There fell from heaven a very bright and beautiful star. It slipped down the side of the sky, passing by the other stars in its course, and, as they watched it wondering, it seemed to them to sink behind a clump of willow-trees that stood hard by a little sheepfold no more than a stone's throw away.

'Why! there is a crock of gold for whoever finds it,' they cried, and they set to and ran, so eager were they for the gold.

And one of them ran faster than his mate, and outstripped him, and forced his way through the willows, and came out on the other side, and lo! there was indeed a thing of gold lying on the white snow. So he hastened towards it, and stooping down placed his hands upon it, and it was a cloak of golden tissue, curiously wrought with stars, and wrapped in many folds. And he cried out to his comrade that he had found the treasure that had fallen from the sky, and when his comrade had come up, they sat them down in the snow, and loosened the folds of the cloak that they might divide the pieces of gold. But, alas! no gold was in it, nor silver, nor, indeed, treasure of any kind, but only a little child who was asleep.

And one of them said to the other: 'This is a bitter ending to our hope, nor have we any good fortune, for what doth a child profit to a man? Let us leave it here, and go our way, seeing that we are poor men, and have children of our own whose bread we may not give to another.'

But his companion answered him: 'Nay, but it were an evil thing to leave the child to perish here in the snow, and though I am as poor as thou art, and have many mouths to feed, and but little in the pot, yet will I bring it home with me, and my wife shall have care of it.'

So very tenderly he took up the child, and wrapped the cloak around it to shield it from the harsh cold, and made his way down the hill to the village, his comrade marvelling much at his foolishness and softness of heart.

And when they came to the village, his comrade said to him, 'Thou hast the child, therefore give me the cloak, for it is meet that we should share.'

But he answered him: 'Nay, for the cloak is neither mine nor thine, but the child's only,' and he bade him Godspeed, and went to his own house and knocked.

And when his wife opened the door and saw that her husband had returned safe to her, she put her arms round his neck and kissed him, and took from his back the bundle of faggots, and brushed the snow off his boots, and bade him come in.

But he said to her, 'I have found something in the forest, and I have brought it to thee to have care of it,' and he stirred not from the threshold.

'What is it?' she cried. 'Show it to me, for the house is bare, and we have need of many things.' And he drew the cloak back, and showed her the sleeping child.

'Alack, goodman!' she murmured, 'have we not children of our own, that thou must needs bring a changeling to sit by the hearth? And who knows if it will not bring us bad fortune? And how shall we tend it?' And she was wroth against him.

'Nay, but it is a Star-Child,' he answered; and he told her the strange manner of the finding of it.

But she would not be appeased, but mocked at him, and spoke angrily, and cried: 'Our children lack bread, and shall we feed the child of another? Who is there who careth for us? And who giveth us food?'

'Nay, but God careth for the sparrows even, and feedeth them,' he answered.

'Do not the sparrows die of hunger in the winter?' she asked. 'And is it not winter now?' And the man answered nothing, but stirred not from the threshold.

And a bitter wind from the forest came in through the open door, and made her tremble, and she shivered, and said to him: 'Wilt thou not close the door? There cometh a bitter wind into the house, and I am cold.'

'Into a house where a heart is hard cometh there not always a bitter wind?' he asked. And the woman answered him nothing, but crept closer to the fire.

And after a time she turned round and looked at him, and her eyes were full of tears. And he came in swiftly, and placed the child in her arms, and she kissed it, and laid it in a little bed where the youngest of their own children was lying. And on the morrow the Woodcutter took the curious cloak of gold and placed it in a great chest, and a chain of amber that was round the child's neck his wife took and set it in the chest also.

So the Star-Child was brought up with the children of the Woodcutter, and sat at the same board with them, and was their playmate. And every year he became more beautiful to look at, so that all those who dwelt in the village were filled with wonder, for, while they were swarthy and black-haired, he was white and delicate as sawn ivory, and his curls were like the rings of the daffodil. His lips, also, were like the petals of a red flower, and his eyes were like violets by a river of pure water, and his body like the narcissus of a field where the mower comes not.

Yet did his beauty work him evil. For he grew proud, and cruel, and selfish. The children of the Woodcutter, and the other children of the village, he despised, saying that they were of mean parentage, while he was noble, being sprung from a Star, and he made himself master over them, and called them his servants. No pity had he for the poor, or for those who were blind or maimed or in any way afflicted, but would cast stones at them and drive them forth on to the highway, and bid them beg their bread elsewhere, so that none save the outlaws came twice to that village to ask for alms. Indeed, he was as one enamoured of beauty, and would mock at the weakly and ill-favoured, and make jest of them; and himself he loved, and in summer, when the winds were still, he would lie by the well in the priest's orchard and look down at the marvel of his own face, and laugh for the pleasure he had in his fairness.

Often did the Woodcutter and his wife chide him, and say: 'We did not deal with thee as thou dealest with those who are left desolate, and have none to succour them. Wherefore art thou so cruel to all who need pity?'

Often did the old priest send for him, and seek to teach him the love of living things, saying to him: 'The fly is thy brother. Do it no harm. The wild birds that roam through the forest have their freedom. Snare them not for thy pleasure. God made the blind-worm and the mole, and each has its place. Who art thou to bring pain into God's world? Even the cattle of the field praise Him.'

But the Star-Child heeded not their words, but would frown and flout, and go back to his companions, and lead them. And his companions followed him, for he was fair, and fleet of foot, and could dance, and pipe, and make music. And wherever the Star-Child led them they followed, and whatever the Star-Child bade them do, that did they. And when he pierced with a sharp reed the dim eyes of the mole, they laughed, and when he cast stones at the leper they laughed also. And in all things he ruled them, and they became hard of heart, even as he was.

Now there passed one day through the village a poor beggar-woman. Her garments were torn and ragged, and her feet were bleeding from the rough road on which she had travelled, and she was in very evil plight. And being weary she sat her down under a chestnut-tree to rest.

But when the Star-Child saw her, he said to his companions, 'See! There sitteth a foul beggar-woman under that fair and green-leaved tree. Come, let us drive her hence, for she is ugly and ill-favoured.'

So he came near and threw stones at her, and mocked her, and she looked at him with terror in her eyes, nor did she move her gaze from him. And when the Woodcutter, who was cleaving logs in a haggard[2] hard by, saw what the Star-Child was doing, he ran up and rebuked him, and said to him: 'Surely thou art hard of heart and knowest not mercy, for what evil has this poor woman done to thee that thou shouldst treat her in this wise?'

And the Star-Child grew red with anger, and stamped his foot upon the ground, and said, 'Who art thou to question me what I do? I am no son of thine to do thy bidding.'

'Thou speakest truly,' answered the Woodcutter, 'yet did I show thee pity when I found thee in the forest.'

And when the woman heard these words she gave a loud cry, and fell into a swoon. And the Woodcutter carried her to his own house, and his wife had care of her, and when she rose up from the swoon into which she had fallen, they set meat and drink before her, and bade her have comfort.

But she would neither eat nor drink, but said to the Wood-cutter, 'Didst thou not say that the child was found in the forest? And was it not ten years from this day?'

And the Woodcutter answered, 'Yea, it was in the forest that I found him, and it is ten years from this day.'

'And what signs didst thou find with him?' she cried. 'Bare he not upon his neck a chain of amber? Was not round him a cloak of gold tissue broidered with stars?'

'Truly,' answered the Woodcutter, 'it was even as thou sayest.'

And he took the cloak and the amber chain from the chest where they lay, and showed them to her.

And when she saw them she wept for joy, and said, 'He is my little son whom I lost in the forest. I pray thee send for him quickly, for in search of him have I wandered over the whole world.'

So the Woodcutter and his wife went out and called to the Star-Child, and said to him, 'Go into the house, and there shalt thou find thy mother, who is waiting for thee.'

So he ran in, filled with wonder and great gladness. But when he saw her who was waiting there, he laughed scornfully and said, 'Why, where is my mother? For I see none here but this vile beggar-woman.'

And the woman answered him, 'I am thy mother.'

'Thou art mad to say so,' cried the Star-Child angrily. 'I am no son of thine, for thou art a beggar, and ugly, and in rags. Therefore get thee hence, and let me see thy foul face no more.'

'Nay, but thou art indeed my little son, whom I bare in the forest,' she cried, and she fell on her knees, and held out her arms to him. 'The robbers stole thee from me, and left thee to die,' she murmured, 'but I recognised thee when I saw thee, and the signs also have I recognised, the cloak of golden tissue and the amber-chain. Therefore I pray thee come with me, for over the whole world have I wandered in search of thee. Come with me, my son, for I have need of thy love.'

But the Star-Child stirred not from his place, but shut the doors of his heart against her, nor was there any sound heard save the sound of the woman weeping for pain.

And at last he spoke to her, and his voice was hard and bitter. 'If in very truth thou art my mother,' he said, 'it had been better hadst thou stayed away, and not come here to bring me to shame, seeing that I thought I was the child of some Star, and not a beggar's child, as thou tellest me that I am. Therefore get thee hence, and let me see thee no more.'

'Alas! my son,' she cried, 'wilt thou not kiss me before I go? For I have suffered much to find thee.'

'Nay,' said the Star-Child, 'but thou art too foul to look at, and rather would I kiss the adder or the toad than thee.'

So the woman rose up, and went away into the forest weeping bitterly, and when the Star-Child saw that she had gone, he was glad, and ran back to his playmates that he might play with them.

But when they beheld him coming, they mocked him and said, 'Why, thou art as foul as the toad, and as loathsome as the adder. Get thee hence, for we will not suffer thee to play with us,' and they drave him out of the garden.

And the Star-Child frowned and said to himself, 'What is this that they say to me? I will go to the well of water and look into it, and it shall tell me of my beauty.'

So he went to the well of water and looked into it, and lo! his face was as the face of a toad, and his body was scaled like an adder. And he flung himself down on the grass and wept, and said to himself, 'Surely this has come upon me by reason of my sin. For I have denied my mother, and driven her away, and been proud, and cruel to her. Wherefore I will go and seek her through the whole world, nor will I rest till I have found her.'

And there came to him the little daughter of the Woodcutter, and she put her hand upon his shoulder and said, 'What doth it matter if thou hast lost thy comeliness? Stay with us, and I will not mock at thee.'

And he said to her, 'Nay, but I have been cruel to my mother, and as a punishment has this evil been sent to me. Wherefore I must go hence, and wander through the world till I find her, and she give me her forgiveness.'

So he ran away into the forest and called out to his mother to come to him, but there was no answer. All day long he called to her, and when the sun set he lay down to sleep on a bed of leaves, and the birds and the animals fled from him, for they remembered his cruelty, and he was alone save for the toad that watched him, and the slow adder that crawled past.

And in the morning he rose up, and plucked some bitter berries from the trees and ate them, and took his way through the great wood, weeping sorely. And of everything that he met he made inquiry if perchance they had seen his mother.

He said to the Mole, 'Thou canst go beneath the earth. Tell me, is my mother there?'

And the Mole answered, 'Thou hast blinded mine eyes. How should I know?'

He said to the Linnet, 'Thou canst fly over the tops of the tall trees, and canst see the whole world. Tell me, canst thou see my mother?'

And the Linnet answered, 'Thou hast clipt my wings for thy pleasure. How should I fly?'

And to the little Squirrel who lived in the fir-tree, and was lonely, he said, 'Where is my mother?'

And the Squirrel answered, 'Thou hast slain mine. Dost thou seek to slay thine also?'

And the Star-Child wept and bowed his head, and prayed forgiveness of God's things, and went on through the forest, seeking for the beggar-woman. And on the third day he came to the other side of the forest and went down into the plain.

And when he passed through the villages the children mocked him, and threw stones at him, and the carlots[3] would not suffer him even to sleep in the byres lest he might bring mildew on the stored corn, so foul was he to look at, and their hired men drave him away, and there was none who had pity on him. Nor could he hear anywhere of the beggar-woman who was his mother, though for the space of three years he wandered over the world, and often seemed to see her on the road in front of him, and would call to her, and run after her till the sharp flints made his feet to bleed. But overtake her he could not, and those who dwelt by the way did ever deny that they had seen her, or any like to her, and they made sport of his sorrow.

For the space of three years he wandered over the world, and in the world there was neither love nor loving-kindness nor charity for him, but it was even such a world as he had made for himself in the days of his great pride.

And one evening he came to the gate of a strong-walled city that stood by a river, and, weary and footsore though he was, he made to enter in. But the soldiers who stood on guard dropped their halberts across the entrance, and said roughly to him, 'What is thy business in the city?'

'I am seeking for my mother,' he answered, 'and I pray ye to suffer me to pass, for it may be that she is in this city.'

But they mocked at him, and one of them wagged a black beard, and set down his shield and cried, 'Of a truth, thy mother will not be merry when she sees thee, for thou art more ill-favoured than the toad of the marsh, or the adder that crawls in the fen. Get thee gone. Get thee gone. Thy mother dwells not in this city.'

And another, who held a yellow banner in his hand, said to him, 'Who is thy mother, and wherefore art thou seeking for her?'

And he answered, 'My mother is a beggar even as I am, and I have treated her evilly, and I pray ye to suffer me to pass that she may give me her forgiveness, if it be that she tarrieth in this city.' But they would not, and pricked him with their spears.

And, as he turned away weeping, one whose armour was inlaid with gilt flowers, and on whose helmet couched a lion that had wings, came up and made inquiry of the soldiers who it was who had sought entrance. And they said to him, 'It is a beggar and the child of a beggar, and we have driven him away.'

'Nay,' he cried, laughing, 'but we will sell the foul thing for a slave, and his price shall be the price of a bowl of sweet wine.'

And an old and evil-visaged man who was passing by called out, and said, 'I will buy him for that price,' and, when he had paid the price, he took the Star-Child by the hand and led him into the city.

And after that they had gone through many streets they came to a little door that was set in a wall that was covered with a pomegranate tree. And the old man touched the door with a ring of graved jasper and it opened, and they went down five steps of brass into a garden filled with black poppies and green jars of burnt clay. And the old man took then from his turban a scarf of figured silk, and bound with it the eyes of the Star-Child, and drave him in front of him. And when the scarf was taken off his eyes, the Star-Child found himself in a dungeon, that was lit by a lantern of horn.

And the old man set before him some mouldy bread on a trencher and said, 'Eat,' and some brackish water in a cup and said, 'Drink,' and when he had eaten and drunk, the old man went out, locking the door behind him and fastening it with an iron chain.

And on the morrow the old man, who was indeed the subtlest of the magicians of Libya and had learned his art from one who dwelt in the tombs of the Nile, came in to him and frowned at him, and said, 'In a wood that is nigh to the gate of this city of Giaours⁴ there are three pieces of gold. One is of white gold, and another is of yellow gold, and the gold of the third one is red. To-day thou shalt bring me the piece of white gold, and if thou bringest it not back, I will beat thee with a hundred stripes. Get thee away quickly, and at sunset I will be waiting for thee at the door of the garden. See that thou bringest the white gold, or it shall go ill with thee, for thou art my slave, and I have bought thee for the price of a bowl of sweet wine.' And he bound the eyes of the Star-Child with the scarf of figured silk, and led him through the house, and through the garden of poppies, and up the five steps of brass. And having opened the little door with his ring he set him in the street.

And the Star-Child went out of the gate of the city, and came to the wood of which the Magician had spoken to him.

Now this wood was very fair to look at from without, and seemed full of singing birds and of sweet-scented flowers, and the Star-Child entered it gladly. Yet did its beauty profit him little, for wherever he went harsh briars and thorns shot up from the ground and encompassed him, and evil nettles stung him, and the thistle pierced him with her daggers, so that he was in sore distress. Nor could he anywhere find the piece of white gold of which the Magician had spoken, though he sought for it from morn to noon, and from noon to sunset. And at sunset he set his face towards home, weeping bitterly, for he knew what fate was in store for him.

But when he had reached the outskirts of the wood, he heard from a thicket a cry as of someone in pain. And forgetting his own sorrow he ran back to the place, and saw there a little Hare caught in a trap that some hunter had set for it.

And the Star-Child had pity on it, and released it, and said to it, 'I am myself but a slave, yet may I give thee thy freedom.'

And the Hare answered him, and said: 'Surely thou hast given me freedom, and what shall I give thee in return?'

And the Star-Child said to it, 'I am seeking for a piece of white gold, nor can I anywhere find it, and if I bring it not to my master he will beat me.'

'Come thou with me,' said the Hare, 'and I will lead thee to it, for I know where it is hidden, and for what purpose.'

So the Star-Child went with the Hare, and lo! in the cleft of a great oak-tree he saw the piece of white gold that he was seeking. And he was filled with joy, and seized it, and said to the Hare, 'The service that I did to thee thou hast rendered back again many times over, and the kindness that I showed thee thou hast repaid a hundred fold.'

'Nay,' answered the Hare, 'but as thou dealt with me, so I did deal with thee,' and it ran away swiftly, and the Star-Child went towards the city.

Now at the gate of the city there was seated one who was a leper. Over his face hung a cowl of grey linen, and through the eyelets his eyes gleamed like red coals. And when he saw the Star-Child coming, he struck upon a wooden bowl, and clattered his bell, and called out to him, and said, 'Give me a piece of money, or I must die of hunger. For they have thrust me out of the city, and there is no one who has pity on me.'

'Alas!' cried the Star-Child, 'I have but one piece of money in my wallet, and if I bring it not to my master he will beat me, for I am his slave.'

But the leper entreated him, and prayed of him, till the Star-Child had pity, and gave him the piece of white gold.

And when he came to the Magician's house, the Magician opened to him, and brought him in, and said to him, 'Hast thou the piece of white gold?' And the Star-Child answered, 'I have it not.' So the Magician fell upon him, and beat him, and set before him an empty trencher, and said, 'Eat,' and an empty cup, and said, 'Drink,' and flung him again into the dungeon.

And on the morrow the Magician came to him, and said, 'If

to-day thou bringest me not the piece of yellow gold, I will surely keep thee as my slave, and give thee three hundred stripes.'

So the Star-Child went to the wood, and all day long he searched for the piece of yellow gold, but nowhere could he find it. And at sunset he sat him down and began to weep, and as he was weeping there came to him the little Hare that he had rescued from the trap.

And the Hare said to him, 'Why art thou weeping? And what dost thou seek in the wood?'

And the Star-Child answered, 'I am seeking for a piece of yellow gold that is hidden here, and if I find it not my master will beat me, and keep me as a slave.'

'Follow me,' cried the Hare, and it ran through the wood till it came to a pool of water. And at the bottom of the pool the piece of yellow gold was lying.

'How shall I thank thee?' said the Star-Child, 'for lo! this is the second time that you have succoured me.'

'Nay, but thou hadst pity on me first,' said the Hare, and it ran away swiftly.

And the Star-Child took the piece of yellow gold, and put it in his wallet, and hurried to the city. But the leper saw him coming, and ran to meet him, and knelt down and cried, 'Give me a piece of money or I shall die of hunger.'

And the Star-Child said to him, 'I have in my wallet but one piece of yellow gold, and if I bring it not to my master he will beat me and keep me as his slave.'

But the leper entreated him sore, so that the Star-Child had pity on him, and gave him the piece of yellow gold.

And when he came to the Magician's house, the Magician opened to him, and brought him in, and said to him, 'Hast thou the piece of yellow gold?' And the Star-Child said to him, 'I have it not.' So the Magician fell upon him, and beat him, and loaded him with chains, and cast him again into the dungeon.

And on the morrow the Magician came to him, and said, 'If to-day thou bringest me the piece of red gold I will set thee free, but if thou bringest it not I will surely slay thee.'

So the Star-Child went to the wood, and all day long he searched for the piece of red gold, but nowhere could he find it.

And at evening he sat him down, and wept, and as he was weeping there came to him the little Hare.

And the Hare said to him, 'The piece of red gold that thou seekest is in the cavern that is behind thee. Therefore weep no more but be glad.'

'How shall I reward thee,' cried the Star-Child, 'for lo! this is the third time thou hast succoured me.'

'Nay, but thou hadst pity on me first,' said the Hare, and it ran away swiftly.

And the Star-Child entered the cavern, and in its farthest corner he found the piece of red gold. So he put it in his wallet, and hurried to the city. And the leper seeing him coming, stood in the centre of the road, and cried out, and said to him, 'Give me the piece of red money, or I must die,' and the Star-Child had pity on him again, and gave him the piece of red gold, saying, 'Thy need is greater than mine.' Yet was his heart heavy, for he knew what evil fate awaited him.

But lo! as he passed through the gate of the city, the guards bowed down and made obeisance to him, saying, 'How beautiful is our lord!' and a crowd of citizens followed him, and cried out, 'Surely there is none so beautiful in the whole world!' so that the Star-Child wept, and said to himself, 'They are mocking me, and making light of my misery.' And so large was the concourse of the people, that he lost the threads of his way, and found himself at last in a great square, in which there was a palace of a King.

And the gate of the palace opened, and the priests and the high officers of the city ran forth to meet him, and they abased themselves before him, and said, 'Thou art our lord for whom we have been waiting, and the son of our King.'

And the Star-Child answered them and said, 'I am no king's son, but the child of a poor beggar-woman. And how say ye that I am beautiful, for I know that I am evil to look at?'

Then he, whose armour was inlaid with gilt flowers, and on whose helmet couched a lion that had wings, held up a shield, and cried, 'How saith my lord that he is not beautiful?'

And the Star-Child looked, and lo! his face was even as it had been, and his comeliness had come back to him, and he saw that in his eyes which he had not seen there before.

And the priests and the high officers knelt down and said to him, 'It was prophesied of old that on this day should come he who was to rule over us. Therefore, let our lord take this crown and this sceptre, and be in his justice and mercy our King over us.'

But he said to them, 'I am not worthy, for I have denied the mother who bare me, nor may I rest till I have found her, and known her forgiveness. Therefore, let me go, for I must wander again over the world, and may not tarry here, though ye bring me the crown and the sceptre.'

And as he spake he turned his face from them towards the street that led to the gate of the city, and lo! amongst the crowd that pressed round the soldiers, he saw the beggar-woman who was his mother, and at her side stood the leper, who had sat by the road.

And a cry of joy broke from his lips, and he ran over, and kneeling down he kissed the wounds on his mother's feet, and wet them with his tears. He bowed his head in the dust, and sobbing, as one whose heart might break, he said to her: 'Mother, I denied thee in the hour of my pride. Accept me in the hour of my humility. Mother, I gave thee hatred. Do thou give me love. Mother, I rejected thee. Receive thy child now.' But the beggar-woman answered him not a word.

And he reached out his hands, and clasped the white feet of the leper, and said to him: 'Thrice did I give thee of my mercy. Bid my mother speak to me once.' But the leper answered him not a word.

And he sobbed again, and said: 'Mother, my suffering is greater than I can bear. Give me thy forgiveness, and let me go back to the forest.' And the beggar-woman put her hand on his head, and said to him, 'Rise,' and the leper put his hand on his head, and said to him 'Rise,' also.

And he rose up from his feet, and looked at them, and lo! they were a King and a Queen.

And the Queen said to him, 'This is thy father whom thou hast succoured.'

And the King said, 'This is thy mother, whose feet thou hast washed with thy tears.'

And they fell on his neck and kissed him, and brought him into the palace, and clothed him in fair raiment, and set the crown upon his head, and the sceptre in his hand, and over the city that stood by the river he ruled, and was its lord. Much justice and mercy did he show to all, and the evil Magician he banished, and to the Woodcutter and his wife he sent many rich gifts, and to their children he gave high honour. Nor would he suffer any to be cruel to bird or beast, but taught love and loving-kindness and charity, and to the poor he gave bread, and to the naked he gave raiment, and there was peace and plenty in the land.

Yet ruled he not long, so great had been his suffering, and so bitter the fire of his testing, for after the space of three years he died. And he who came after him ruled evilly.

Lord Arthur Savile's Crime
and Other Stories

Lord Arthur Savile's Crime

A study of duty

I

It was Lady Windermere's[1] last reception before Easter, and
Bentinck House was even more crowded than usual. Six Cabinet
Ministers had come on from the Speaker's Levée[2] in their stars
and ribands, all the pretty women wore their smartest dresses,
and at the end of the picture-gallery stood the Princess Sophia
of Carlsrühe, a heavy Tartar-looking lady, with tiny black eyes
and wonderful emeralds, talking bad French at the top of her
voice, and laughing immoderately at everything that was said
to her. It was certainly a wonderful medley of people. Gorgeous
peeresses chatted affably to violent Radicals, popular preachers
brushed coat-tails with eminent sceptics, a perfect bevy of bishops
kept following a stout prima-donna from room to room, on
the staircase stood several Royal Academicians, disguised as
artists, and it was said that at one time the supper-room was
absolutely crammed with geniuses. In fact, it was one of Lady
Windermere's best nights, and the Princess stayed till nearly half-
past eleven.

As soon as she had gone, Lady Windermere returned to the
picture-gallery, where a celebrated political economist[3] was solemnly explaining the scientific theory of music to an indignant
virtuoso from Hungary, and began to talk to the Duchess of
Paisley. She looked wonderfully beautiful with her grand ivory
throat, her large blue forget-me-not eyes, and her heavy coils of
golden hair. *Or pur*[4] they were − not that pale straw colour that
nowadays usurps the gracious name of gold, but such gold as is

woven into sunbeams or hidden in strange amber; and they gave to her face something of the frame of a saint, with not a little of the fascination of a sinner.[5] She was a curious psychological study. Early in life she had discovered the important truth that nothing looks so like innocence as an indiscretion; and by a series of reckless escapades, half of them quite harmless, she had acquired all the privileges of a personality. She had more than once changed her husband; indeed, Debrett credits her with three marriages; but as she had never changed her lover, the world had long ago ceased to talk scandal about her. She was now forty years of age, childless, and with that inordinate passion for pleasure which is the secret of remaining young.

Suddenly she looked eagerly round the room, and said, in her clear contralto voice, 'Where is my cheiromantist?'[6]

'Your what, Gladys?' exclaimed the Duchess, giving an involuntary start.

'My cheiromantist, Duchess; I can't live without him at present.'

'Dear Gladys! you are always so original,' murmured the Duchess, trying to remember what a cheiromantist really was, and hoping it was not the same as a cheiropodist.

'He comes to see my hand twice a week regularly,' continued Lady Windermere, 'and is most interesting about it.'

'Good heavens!' said the Duchess to herself, 'he is a sort of cheiropodist after all. How very dreadful. I hope he is a foreigner at any rate. It wouldn't be quite so bad then.'

'I must certainly introduce him to you.'

'Introduce him!' cried the Duchess; 'you don't mean to say he is here?' and she began looking about for a small tortoise-shell fan and a very tattered lace shawl, so as to be ready to go at a moment's notice.

'Of course he is here, I would not dream of giving a party without him. He tells me I have a pure psychic hand, and that if my thumb had been the least little bit shorter, I should have been a confirmed pessimist, and gone into a convent.'

'Oh, I see!' said the Duchess, feeling very much relieved; 'he tells fortunes, I suppose?'

'And misfortunes, too,' answered Lady Windermere, 'any

amount of them. Next year, for instance, I am in great danger, both by land and sea, so I am going to live in a balloon, and draw up my dinner in a basket every evening. It is all written down on my little finger, or on the palm of my hand, I forget which.'

'But surely that is tempting Providence, Gladys.'

'My dear Duchess, surely Providence can resist temptation by this time.' I think every one should have their hands told once a month, so as to know what not to do. Of course, one does it all the same, but it is so pleasant to be warned. Now, if some one doesn't go and fetch Mr. Podgers at once, I shall have to go myself.'

'Let me go, Lady Windermere,' said a tall handsome young man, who was standing by, listening to the conversation with an amused smile.

'Thanks so much, Lord Arthur; but I am afraid you wouldn't recognise him.'

'If he is as wonderful as you say, Lady Windermere, I couldn't well miss him. Tell me what he is like, and I'll bring him to you at once.'

'Well, he is not a bit like a cheiromantist. I mean he is not mysterious, or esoteric, or romantic-looking. He is a little, stout man, with a funny, bald head, and great gold-rimmed spectacles; something between a family doctor and a country attorney. I'm really very sorry, but it is not my fault. People are so annoying. All my pianists look exactly like poets, and all my poets look exactly like pianists; and I remember last season asking a most dreadful conspirator to dinner, a man who had blown up ever so many people, and always wore a coat of mail, and carried a dagger up his shirt-sleeve; and do you know that when he came he looked just like a nice old clergyman, and cracked jokes all the evening? Of course, he was very amusing, and all that, but I was awfully disappointed; and when I asked him about the coat of mail, he only laughed, and said it was far too cold to wear in England. Ah, here is Mr. Podgers! Now, Mr. Podgers, I want you to tell the Duchess of Paisley's hand. Duchess, you must take your glove off. No, not the left hand, the other.'

'Dear Gladys, I really don't think it is quite right,' said the Duchess, feebly unbuttoning a rather soiled kid glove.

'Nothing interesting ever is,' said Lady Windermere: '*on a fait le monde ainsi*.[8] But I must introduce you. Duchess, this is Mr. Podgers, my pet cheiromantist. Mr. Podgers, this is the Duchess of Paisley, and if you say that she has a larger mountain of the moon than I have, I will never believe in you again.'

'I am sure, Gladys, there is nothing of the kind in my hand,' said the Duchess gravely.

'Your Grace is quite right,' said Mr. Podgers, glancing at the little fat hand with its short square fingers, 'the mountain of the moon is not developed. The line of life, however, is excellent. Kindly bend the wrist. Thank you. Three distinct lines on the *rascette*![9] You will live to a great age, Duchess, and be extremely happy. Ambition – very moderate, line of intellect not exaggerated, line of heart –'

'Now, do be indiscreet, Mr. Podgers,' cried Lady Windermere.

'Nothing would give me greater pleasure,' said Mr. Podgers, bowing, 'if the Duchess ever had been, but I am sorry to say that I see great permanence of affection, combined with a strong sense of duty.'

'Pray go on, Mr. Podgers,' said the Duchess, looking quite pleased.

'Economy is not the least of your Grace's virtues,' continued Mr. Podgers, and Lady Windermere went off into fits of laughter.

'Economy is a very good thing,' remarked the Duchess complacently; 'when I married Paisley he had eleven castles, and not a single house fit to live in.'

'And now he has twelve houses, and not a single castle,' cried Lady Windermere.

'Well, my dear,' said the Duchess, 'I like –'

'Comfort,' said Mr. Podgers, 'and modern improvements, and hot water laid on in every bedroom. Your Grace is quite right. Comfort is the only thing our civilisation can give us.'

'You have told the Duchess's character admirably, Mr. Podgers, and now you must tell Lady Flora's;' and in answer to a nod from the smiling hostess, a tall girl, with sandy Scotch hair, and high shoulder-blades, stepped awkwardly from behind the sofa, and held out a long, bony hand with spatulate[10] fingers.

'Ah, a pianist! I see,' said Mr. Podgers, 'an excellent pianist, but perhaps hardly a musician. Very reserved, very honest, and with a great love of animals.'

'Quite true!' exclaimed the Duchess, turning to Lady Windermere, 'absolutely true! Flora keeps two dozen collie dogs at Macloskie, and would turn our town house into a menagerie if her father would let her.'

'Well, that is just what I do with my house every Thursday evening,' cried Lady Windermere, laughing, 'only I like lions better than collie dogs.'[11]

'Your one mistake, Lady Windermere,' said Mr. Podgers, with a pompous bow.

'If a woman can't make her mistakes charming, she is only a female,' was the answer. 'But you must read some more hands for us. Come, Sir Thomas, show Mr. Podgers yours;' and a genial-looking old gentleman, in a white waistcoat, came forward, and held out a thick rugged hand, with a very long third finger.

'An adventurous nature; four long voyages in the past, and one to come. Been shipwrecked three times. No, only twice, but in danger of a shipwreck your next journey. A strong Conservative, very punctual, and with a passion for collecting curiosities. Had a severe illness between the ages of sixteen and eighteen. Was left a fortune when about thirty. Great aversion to cats and Radicals.'

'Extraordinary!' exclaimed Sir Thomas; 'you must really tell my wife's hand, too.'

'Your second wife's,' said Mr. Podgers quietly, still keeping Sir Thomas's hand in his. 'Your second wife's. I shall be charmed;' but Lady Marvel, a melancholy-looking woman, with brown hair and sentimental eyelashes, entirely declined to have her past or her future exposed; and nothing that Lady Windermere could do would induce Monsieur de Koloff, the Russian Ambassador, even to take his gloves off. In fact, many people seemed afraid to face the odd little man with his stereotyped smile, his gold spectacles, and his bright, beady eyes; and when he told poor Lady Fermor, right out before every one, that she did not care a bit for music, but was extremely fond of musicians, it was generally felt that cheiromancy was a most dangerous science, and one that ought not to be encouraged, except in a *tête-à-tête*.

Lord Arthur Savile, however, who did not know anything about Lady Fermor's unfortunate story, and who had been watching Mr. Podgers with a great deal of interest, was filled with an immense curiosity to have his own hand read, and feeling somewhat shy about putting himself forward, crossed over the room to where Lady Windermere was sitting, and, with a charming blush, asked her if she thought Mr. Podgers would mind.

'Of course, he won't mind,' said Lady Windermere, 'that is what he is here for. All my lions, Lord Arthur, are performing lions, and jump through hoops whenever I ask them. But I must warn you beforehand that I shall tell Sybil everything. She is coming to lunch with me to-morrow, to talk about bonnets, and if Mr. Podgers finds out that you have a bad temper, or a tendency to gout, or a wife living in Bayswater,[12] I shall certainly let her know all about it.'

Lord Arthur smiled, and shook his head. 'I am not afraid,' he answered. 'Sybil knows me as well as I know her.'

'Ah! I am a little sorry to hear you say that. The proper basis for marriage is a mutual misunderstanding.[13] No, I am not at all cynical, I have merely got experience, which, however, is very much the same thing. Mr. Podgers, Lord Arthur Savile is dying to have his hand read. Don't tell him that he is engaged to one of the most beautiful girls in London, because that appeared in the *Morning Post*[14] a month ago.'

'Dear Lady Windermere,' cried the Marchioness of Jedburgh, 'do let Mr. Podgers stay here a little longer. He has just told me I should go on the stage, and I am so interested.'

'If he has told you that, Lady Jedburgh, I shall certainly take him away. Come over at once, Mr. Podgers, and read Lord Arthur's hand.'

'Well,' said Lady Jedburgh, making a little *moue*[15] as she rose from the sofa, 'if I am not to be allowed to go on the stage, I must be allowed to be part of the audience at any rate.'

'Of course; we are all going to be part of the audience,' said Lady Windermere; 'and now, Mr. Podgers, be sure and tell us something nice. Lord Arthur is one of my special favourites.'

But when Mr. Podgers saw Lord Arthur's hand he grew curiously pale, and said nothing. A shudder seemed to pass through him, and his great bushy eyebrows twitched convulsively, in an odd, irritating way they had when he was puzzled. Then some huge beads of perspiration broke out on his yellow forehead, like a poisonous dew, and his fat fingers grew cold and clammy.

Lord Arthur did not fail to notice these strange signs of agitation, and, for the first time in his life, he himself felt fear. His impulse was to rush from the room, but he restrained himself. It was better to know the worst, whatever it was, than to be left in this hideous uncertainty.

'I am waiting, Mr. Podgers,' he said.

'We are all waiting,' cried Lady Windermere, in her quick, impatient manner, but the cheiromantist made no reply.

'I believe Arthur is going on the stage,' said Lady Jedburgh, 'and that, after your scolding, Mr. Podgers is afraid to tell him so.'

Suddenly Mr. Podgers dropped Lord Arthur's right hand, and seized hold of his left, bending down so low to examine it that the gold rims of his spectacles seemed almost to touch the palm. For a moment his face became a white mask of horror, but he soon recovered his *sang-froid*, and looking up at Lady Windermere, said with a forced smile, 'It is the hand of a charming young man.'

'Of course it is!' answered Lady Windermere, 'but will he be a charming husband? That is what I want to know.'

'All charming young men are,' said Mr. Podgers.

'I don't think a husband should be too fascinating,' murmured Lady Jedburgh pensively, 'it is so dangerous.'

'My dear child, they never are too fascinating,' cried Lady Windermere. 'But what I want are details. Details are the only things that interest. What is going to happen to Lord Arthur?'

'Well, within the next few months Lord Arthur will go on a voyage –'

'Oh yes, his honeymoon, of course!'

'And lose a relative.'

'Not his sister, I hope?' said Lady Jedburgh, in a piteous tone of voice.

'Certainly not his sister,' answered Mr. Podgers, with a deprecating wave of the hand, 'a distant relative merely.'

'Well, I am dreadfully disappointed,' said Lady Windermere. 'I have absolutely nothing to tell Sybil to-morrow. No one cares about distant relatives nowadays. They went out of fashion years ago. However, I suppose she had better have a black silk by her; it always does for church, you know. And now let us go to supper. They are sure to have eaten everything up, but we may find some hot soup. François used to make excellent soup once, but he is so agitated about politics at present, that I never feel quite certain about him. I do wish General Boulanger[16] would keep quiet. Duchess, I am sure you are tired?'

'Not at all, dear Gladys,' answered the Duchess, waddling towards the door. 'I have enjoyed myself immensely, and the cheiropodist, I mean the cheiromantist, is most interesting. Flora, where can my tortoise-shell fan be? Oh, thank you, Sir Thomas, so much. And my lace shawl, Flora? Oh, thank you, Sir Thomas, very kind, I'm sure;' and the worthy creature finally managed to get downstairs without dropping her scent-bottle more than twice.

All this time Lord Arthur Savile had remained standing by the fireplace, with the same feeling of dread over him, the same sickening sense of coming evil. He smiled sadly at his sister, as she swept past him on Lord Plymdale's arm, looking lovely in her pink brocade and pearls, and he hardly heard Lady Windermere when she called to him to follow her. He thought of Sybil Merton, and the idea that anything could come between them made his eyes dim with tears.

Looking at him, one would have said that Nemesis had stolen the shield of Pallas, and shown him the Gorgon's head.[17] He seemed turned to stone, and his face was like marble in its melancholy. He had lived the delicate and luxurious life of a young man of birth and fortune, a life exquisite in its freedom from sordid care, its beautiful boyish insouciance; and now for the first time he became conscious of the terrible mystery of Destiny, of the awful meaning of Doom.

How mad and monstrous it all seemed! Could it be that written on his hand, in characters that he could not read himself, but that another could decipher, was some fearful secret of sin, some blood-red sign of crime? Was there no escape possible? Were we no better than chessmen, moved by an unseen power, vessels the potter fashions at his fancy, for honour or for shame? His reason revolted against it, and yet he felt that some tragedy was hanging over him, and that he had been suddenly called upon to bear an intolerable burden. Actors are so fortunate. They can choose whether they will appear in tragedy or in comedy, whether they will suffer or make merry, laugh or shed tears. But in real life it is different. Most men and women are forced to perform parts for which they have no qualifications. Our Guildensterns play Hamlet for us, and our Hamlets have to jest like Prince Hal.[18] The world is a stage, but the play is badly cast.

Suddenly Mr. Podgers entered the room. When he saw Lord Arthur he started, and his coarse, fat face became a sort of greenish-yellow colour. The two men's eyes met, and for a moment there was silence.

'The Duchess has left one of her gloves here, Lord Arthur, and has asked me to bring it to her,' said Mr. Podgers finally. 'Ah, I see it on the sofa! Good evening.'

'Mr. Podgers, I must insist on your giving me a straightforward answer to a question I am going to put to you.'

'Another time, Lord Arthur, but the Duchess is anxious. I am afraid I must go.'

'You shall not go. The Duchess is in no hurry.'

'Ladies should not be kept waiting, Lord Arthur,' said Mr. Podgers, with his sickly smile.

'The fair sex is apt to be impatient.'

Lord Arthur's finely-chiselled lips curled in petulant disdain. The poor Duchess seemed to him of very little importance at that moment. He walked across the room to where Mr. Podgers was standing, and held his hand out.

'Tell me what you saw there,' he said. 'Tell me the truth. I must know it. I am not a child.'

Mr. Podgers's eyes blinked behind his gold-rimmed spectacles, and he moved uneasily from one foot to the other, while his fingers played nervously with a flash watch-chain.

'What makes you think that I saw anything in your hand, Lord Arthur, more than I told you?'

'I know you did, and I insist on your telling me what it was. I will pay you. I will give you a cheque for a hundred pounds.'

The green eyes flashed for a moment, and then became dull again.

'Guineas?'[19] said Mr. Podgers at last, in a low voice.

'Certainly. I will send you a cheque to-morrow. What is your club?'

'I have no club. That is to say, not just at present. My address is –, but allow me to give you my card;' and producing a bit of gilt-edged pasteboard from his waistcoat pocket, Mr. Podgers handed it, with a low bow, to Lord Arthur, who read on it,

---

MR. SEPTIMUS R. PODGERS

Professional Cheiromantist

103a West Moon Street

'My hours are from ten to four,' murmured Mr. Podgers mechanically, 'and I make a reduction for families.'

'Be quick,' cried Lord Arthur, looking very pale, and holding his hand out.

Mr. Podgers glanced nervously round, and drew the heavy *portière*[20] across the door.

'It will take a little time, Lord Arthur, you had better sit down.'

'Be quick, sir,' cried Lord Arthur again, stamping his foot angrily on the polished floor.

Mr. Podgers smiled, drew from his breast-pocket a small magnifying glass, and wiped it carefully with his handkerchief.

'I am quite ready,' he said.

II

Ten minutes later, with face blanched by terror, and eyes wild with grief, Lord Arthur Savile rushed from Bentinck House, crushing his way through the crowd of fur-coated footmen that stood round the large striped awning, and seeming not to see or hear anything. The night was bitter cold, and the gas-lamps round the square flared and flickered in the keen wind; but his hands were hot with fever, and his forehead burned like fire. On and on he went, almost with the gait of a drunken man. A policeman looked curiously at him as he passed, and a beggar, who slouched from an archway to ask for alms, grew frightened, seeing misery greater than his own. Once he stopped under a lamp, and looked at his hands. He thought he could detect the stain of blood already upon them, and a faint cry broke from his trembling lips.

Murder! that is what the cheiromantist had seen there. Murder! The very night seemed to know it, and the desolate wind to howl it in his ear. The dark corners of the streets were full of it. It grinned at him from the roofs of the houses.

First he came to the Park,[21] whose sombre woodland seemed to fascinate him. He leaned wearily up against the railings, cooling his brow against the wet metal, and listening to the tremulous silence of the trees. 'Murder! murder!' he kept repeating, as though iteration could dim the horror of the word. The sound of his own voice made him shudder, yet he almost hoped that Echo might hear him, and wake the slumbering city from its dreams. He felt a mad desire to stop the casual passer-by, and tell him everything.

Then he wandered across Oxford Street into narrow, shameful alleys. Two women with painted faces mocked at him as he went by. From a dark courtyard came a sound of oaths and blows, followed by shrill screams, and, huddled upon a damp doorstep, he saw the crook-backed forms of poverty and eld.[22] A strange pity came over him. Were these children of sin and misery predestined to their end, as he to his? Were they, like him, merely the puppets of a monstrous show?

And yet it was not the mystery, but the comedy of suffering that struck him; its absolute uselessness, its grotesque want of meaning. How incoherent everything seemed! How lacking in all harmony! He was amazed at the discord between the shallow optimism of the day, and the real facts of existence. He was still very young.

After a time he found himself in front of Marylebone Church. The silent roadway looked like a long riband of polished silver, flecked here and there by the dark arabesques of waving shadows. Far into the distance curved the line of flickering gas-lamps, and outside a little walled-in house stood a solitary hansom,[23] the driver asleep inside. He walked hastily in the direction of Portland Place, now and then looking round, as though he feared that he was being followed. At the corner of Rich Street stood two men, reading a small bill upon a hoarding. An odd feeling of curiosity stirred him, and he crossed over. As he came near, the word 'Murder,' printed in black letters, met his eye. He started, and a deep flush came into his cheek. It was an advertisement offering a reward for any information leading to the arrest of a man of medium height, between thirty and forty years of age, wearing a billy-cock hat,[24] a black coat, and check trousers, and with a scar upon his right cheek. He read it over and over again, and wondered if the wretched man would be caught, and how he had been scarred. Perhaps, some day, his own name might be placarded on the walls of London. Some day, perhaps, a price would be set on his head also.

The thought made him sick with horror. He turned on his heel, and hurried on into the night.

Where he went he hardly knew. He had a dim memory of wandering through a labyrinth of sordid houses, of being lost in a giant web of sombre streets, and it was bright dawn when he found himself at last in Piccadilly Circus. As he strolled home towards Belgrave Square, he met the great waggons on their way to Covent Garden. The white-smocked carters, with their pleasant sunburnt faces and coarse curly hair, strode sturdily on, cracking their whips, and calling out now and then to each other; on the back of a huge grey horse, the leader of a jangling team, sat a chubby boy, with a bunch of primroses in his battered hat, keeping tight hold of the mane with his little hands, and laughing; and the great piles of vegetables looked like masses of jade against the morning sky, like masses of green jade against the pink petals of some marvellous rose. Lord Arthur felt curiously affected, he could not tell why. There was something in the dawn's delicate loveliness that seemed to him inexpressibly pathetic, and he thought of all the days that break in beauty, and that set in storm. These rustics, too, with their rough, good-humoured voices, and their nonchalant ways, what a strange London they saw! A London free from the sin of night and the smoke of day, a pallid, ghost-like city, a desolate town of tombs! He wondered what they thought of it, and whether they knew anything of its splendour and its shame, of its fierce, fiery-coloured joys, and its horrible hunger, of all it makes and mars from morn to eve.[25] Probably it was to them merely a mart where they brought their fruits to sell, and where they tarried for a few hours at most, leaving the streets still silent, the houses still asleep. It gave him pleasure to watch them as they went by. Rude as they were, with their heavy, hobnailed shoes, and their awkward gait, they brought a little of Arcady[26] with them. He felt that they had lived with Nature, and that she had taught them peace. He envied them all that they did not know.

By the time he had reached Belgrave Square the sky was a faint blue, and the birds were beginning to twitter in the gardens.

III

When Lord Arthur woke it was twelve o'clock, and the mid-day sun was streaming through the ivory-silk curtains of his room. He got up and looked out of the window. A dim haze of heat was hanging over the great city, and the roofs of the houses were like dull silver. In the flickering green of the square below some children were flitting about like white butterflies, and the pavement was crowded with people on their way to the Park. Never had life seemed lovelier to him, never had the things of evil seemed more remote.

Then his valet brought him a cup of chocolate on a tray. After he had drunk it, he drew aside a heavy *portière* of peach-coloured plush, and passed into the bathroom. The light stole softly from above, through thin slabs of transparent onyx, and the water in the marble tank glimmered like a moonstone. He plunged hastily in, till the cool ripples touched throat and hair, and then dipped his head right under, as though he would have wiped away the stain of some shameful memory. When he stepped out he felt almost at peace. The exquisite physical conditions of the moment had dominated him, as indeed often happens in the case of very finely-wrought natures, for the senses, like fire, can purify as well as destroy.

After breakfast, he flung himself down on a divan, and lit a cigarette.[27] On the mantel-shelf, framed in dainty old brocade, stood a large photograph of Sybil Merton, as he had seen her first at Lady Noel's ball. The small, exquisitely-shaped head drooped slightly to one side, as though the thin, reed-like throat could hardly bear the burden of so much beauty; the lips were slightly parted, and seemed made for sweet music; and all the tender purity of girlhood looked out in wonder from the dreaming eyes. With her soft, clinging dress of *crêpe-de-chine*,[28] and her large leaf-shaped fan, she looked like one of those delicate little figures men find in the olive-woods near Tanagra;[29] and there was a touch of Greek grace in her pose and attitude. Yet she was not *petite*. She was simply perfectly proportioned – a rare thing in an age when so many women are either over life-size or insignificant.

Now as Lord Arthur looked at her, he was filled with the terrible pity that is born of love. He felt that to marry her, with the doom of murder hanging over his head, would be a betrayal like that of Judas, a sin worse than any the Borgia[30] had ever dreamed of. What happiness could there be for them, when at any moment he might be called upon to carry out the awful prophecy written in his hand? What manner of life would be theirs while Fate still held this fearful fortune in the scales? The marriage must be postponed, at all costs. Of this he was quite resolved. Ardently though he loved the girl, and the mere touch of her fingers, when they sat together, made each nerve of his body thrill with exquisite joy, he recognised none the less clearly where his duty lay, and was fully conscious of the fact that he had no right to marry until he had committed the murder. This done, he could stand before the altar with Sybil Merton, and give his life into her hands without terror of wrongdoing. This done, he could take her to his arms, knowing that she would never have to blush for him, never have to hang her head in shame. But done it must be first; and the sooner the better for both.

Many men in his position would have preferred the primrose path of dalliance to the steep heights of duty; but Lord Arthur was too conscientious to set pleasure above principle. There was more than mere passion in his love; and Sybil was to him a symbol of all that is good and noble. For a moment he had a natural repugnance against what he was asked to do, but it soon passed away. His heart told him that it was not a sin, but a sacrifice; his reason reminded him that there was no other course open. He had to choose between living for himself and living for others, and terrible though the task laid upon him undoubtedly was, yet he knew that he must not suffer selfishness to triumph over love. Sooner or later we are all called upon to decide on the same issue – of us all, the same question is asked. To Lord Arthur it came early in life – before his nature had been spoiled by the calculating cynicism of middle-age, or his heart corroded by the shallow, fashionable egotism of our day, and he felt no hesitation about doing his duty. Fortunately also, for him, he was no mere dreamer, or idle dilettante. Had he been so, he would have hesitated, like Hamlet, and let irresolution mar his purpose. But he was essentially practical. Life to him meant action, rather than thought. He had that rarest of all things, common sense.

The wild, turbid feelings of the previous night had by this time completely passed away, and it was almost with a sense of shame that he looked back upon his mad wanderings from street to street, his fierce emotional agony. The very sincerity of his sufferings made them seem unreal to him now. He wondered how he could have been so foolish as to rant and rave about the inevitable. The only question that seemed to trouble him was, whom to make away with; for he was not blind to the fact that murder, like the religions of the Pagan world, requires a victim as well as a priest. Not being a genius, he had no enemies, and indeed he felt that this was not the time for the gratification of any personal pique or dislike, the mission in which he was engaged being one of great and grave solemnity. He accordingly made out a list of his friends and relatives on a sheet of notepaper, and after careful consideration, decided in favour of Lady Clementina Beauchamp, a dear old lady who lived in Curzon Street, and was his own second cousin by his mother's side. He had always been very fond of Lady Clem, as every one called her, and as he was very wealthy himself, having come into all Lord Rugby's property when he came of age, there was no possibility of his deriving any vulgar monetary advantage by her death. In fact, the more he thought over the matter, the more she seemed to him to be just the right person, and, feeling that any delay would be unfair to Sybil, he determined to make his arrangements at once.

The first thing to be done was, of course, to settle with the cheiromantist; so he sat down at a small Sheraton[31] writing-table that stood near the window, drew a cheque for £105, payable to the order of Mr. Septimus Podgers, and, enclosing it in an envelope, told his valet to take it to West Moon Street. He then telephoned to the stables for his hansom, and dressed to go out. As he was leaving the room, he looked back at Sybil Merton's photograph, and swore that, come what may, he would never let her know what he was doing for her sake, but would keep the secret of his self-sacrifice hidden always in his heart.

On his way to the Buckingham,[32] he stopped at a florist's, and sent Sybil a beautiful basket of narcissi, with lovely white petals and staring pheasants' eyes, and on arriving at the club, went straight to the library, rang the bell, and ordered the waiter to bring him a lemon-and-soda, and a book on Toxicology. He had fully decided that poison was the best means to adopt in this troublesome business. Anything like personal violence was extremely distasteful to him, and besides, he was very anxious not to murder Lady Clementina in any way that might attract public attention, as he hated the idea of being lionised at Lady Windermere's, or seeing his name figuring in the paragraphs of vulgar society-newspapers. He had also to think of Sybil's father and mother, who were rather old-fashioned people, and might possibly object to the marriage if there was anything like a scandal, though he felt certain that if he told them the whole facts of the case they would be the very first to appreciate the motives that had actuated him. He had every reason, then, to decide in favour of poison. It was safe, sure, and quiet, and did away with any necessity for painful scenes, to which, like most Englishmen, he had a rooted objection.

Of the science of poisons, however, he knew absolutely nothing, and as the waiter seemed quite unable to find anything in the library but Ruff's *Guide* and Bailey's *Magazine*, he examined the book-shelves himself, and finally came across a handsomely-bound edition of the *Pharmacopoeia*, and a copy of Erskine's *Toxicology*, edited by Sir Mathew Reid,[33] the President of the Royal College of Physicians, and one of the oldest members of the Buckingham, having been elected in mistake for somebody else; a *contretemps* that so enraged the Committee, that when the real man came up they black-balled him unanimously. Lord Arthur was a good deal puzzled at the technical terms used in both books, and had begun to regret that he had not paid more attention to his classics at Oxford, when in the second volume of Erskine, he found a very interesting and complete account of the properties of aconit-ine,[34] written in fairly clear English. It seemed to him to be exactly the poison he wanted. It was swift – indeed, almost immediate, in its effect – perfectly painless, and when taken in the form of a gelatine capsule, the mode recommended by Sir Mathew, not by any means unpalatable. He accordingly made a note, upon his shirt-cuff, of the amount necessary for a fatal dose, put the books back in their places, and strolled up St. James's Street, to Pestle and Humbey's, the great chemists. Mr. Pestle, who always attended personally on the aristocracy, was a good deal surprised at the order, and in a very deferential manner murmured something about a medical certificate being necessary. However, as soon as Lord Arthur explained to him that it was for a large Norwegian mastiff that he was obliged to get rid of, as it showed signs of incipient rabies, and had already bitten the coachman twice in the calf of the leg, he expressed himself as being perfectly satisfied, complimented Lord Arthur on his won-derful knowledge of Toxicology, and had the prescription made up immediately.

Lord Arthur put the capsule into a pretty little silver *bonbonnière* that he saw in a shop-window in Bond Street, threw away Pestle and Humbey's ugly pill-box, and drove off at once to Lady Clementina's.

'Well, *monsieur le mauvais sujet*,'[35] cried the old lady, as he entered the room, 'why haven't you been to see me all this time?'

'My dear Lady Clem, I never have a moment to myself,' said Lord Arthur, smiling.

'I suppose you mean that you go about all day long with Miss Sybil Merton, buying *chiffons* and talking nonsense? I cannot understand why people make such a fuss about being married. In my day we never dreamed of billing and cooing in public, or in private for that matter.'

'I assure you I have not seen Sybil for twenty-four hours, Lady Clem. As far as I can make out, she belongs entirely to her milliners.'

'Of course; that is the only reason you come to see an ugly old woman like myself. I wonder you men don't take warning. *On a fait des folies pour moi*,[36] and here I am, a poor, rheumatic creature, with a false front and a bad temper. Why, if it were not for dear Lady Jansen, who sends me all the worst French novels she can find, I don't think I could get through the day. Doctors are no use at all, except to get fees out of one. They can't even cure my heartburn.'

'I have brought you a cure for that, Lady Clem,' said Lord Arthur gravely. 'It is a wonderful thing, invented by an American.'

'I don't think I like American inventions, Arthur. I am quite sure I don't. I read some American novels[37] lately, and they were quite nonsensical.'

'Oh, but there is no nonsense at all about this, Lady Clem! I assure you it is a perfect cure. You must promise to try it;' and Lord Arthur brought the little box out of his pocket, and handed it to her.

'Well, the box is charming, Arthur. Is it really a present? That is very sweet of you. And is this the wonderful medicine? It looks like a *bonbon*. I'll take it at once.'

'Good heavens! Lady Clem,' cried Lord Arthur, catching hold of her hand, 'you mustn't do anything of the kind. It is a homoeopathic medicine, and if you take it without having heartburn, it might do you no end of harm. Wait till you have an attack, and take it then. You will be astonished at the result.'

'I should like to take it now,' said Lady Clementina, holding up to the light the little transparent capsule, with its floating bubble of liquid aconitine. 'I am sure it is delicious. The fact is that, though I hate doctors, I love medicines. However, I'll keep it till my next attack.'

'And when will that be?' asked Lord Arthur eagerly. 'Will it be soon?'

'I hope not for a week. I had a very bad time yesterday morning with it. But one never knows.'

'You are sure to have one before the end of the month then, Lady Clem?'

'I am afraid so. But how sympathetic you are to-day, Arthur! Really, Sybil has done you a great deal of good. And now you must run away, for I am dining with some very dull people, who won't talk scandal, and I know that if I don't get my sleep now I shall never be able to keep awake during dinner. Good-bye, Arthur, give my love to Sybil, and thank you so much for the American medicine.'

'You won't forget to take it, Lady Clem, will you?' said Lord Arthur, rising from his seat.

'Of course I won't, you silly boy. I think it is most kind of you to think of me, and I shall write and tell you if I want any more.'

Lord Arthur left the house in high spirits, and with a feeling of immense relief.

That night he had an interview with Sybil Merton. He told her how he had been suddenly placed in a position of terrible difficulty, from which neither honour nor duty would allow him to recede. He told her that the marriage must be put off for the present, as until he had got rid of his fearful entanglements, he was not a free man. He implored her to trust him, and not to have any doubts about the future. Everything would come right, but patience was necessary.

The scene took place in the conservatory of Mr. Merton's house, in Park Lane, where Lord Arthur had dined as usual. Sybil had never seemed more happy, and for a moment Lord Arthur had been tempted to play the coward's part, to write to Lady Clementina for the pill, and to let the marriage go on as if there was no such person as Mr. Podgers in the world. His better nature, however, soon asserted itself, and even when Sybil flung herself weeping into his arms, he did not falter. The beauty that stirred his senses had touched his conscience also. He felt that to wreck so fair a life for the sake of a few months' pleasure would be a wrong thing to do.

He stayed with Sybil till nearly midnight, comforting her and being comforted in turn, and early the next morning he left for Venice, after writing a manly, firm letter to Mr. Merton about the necessary postponement of the marriage.

IV

In Venice he met his brother, Lord Surbiton, who happened to have come over from Corfu in his yacht. The two young men spent a delightful fortnight together. In the morning they rode on the Lido, or glided up and down the green canals in their long black gondola; in the afternoon they usually entertained visitors on the yacht; and in the evening they dined at Florian's, and smoked innumerable cigarettes on the Piazza.[38] Yet somehow Lord Arthur was not happy. Every day he studied the obituary column in the *Times*, expecting to see a notice of Lady Clementina's death, but every day he was disappointed. He began to be afraid that some accident had happened to her, and often regretted that he had prevented her taking the aconitine when she had been so anxious to try its effect. Sybil's letters, too, though full of love, and trust, and tenderness, were often very sad in their tone, and sometimes he used to think that he was parted from her for ever.

After a fortnight Lord Surbiton got bored with Venice, and determined to run down the coast to Ravenna, as he heard that there was some capital cock-shooting in the Pinetum.[39] Lord Arthur, at first, refused absolutely to come, but Surbiton, of whom he was extremely fond, finally persuaded him that if he stayed at Danielli's[40] by himself he would be moped to death, and on the morning of the 15th they started, with a strong nor'-east wind blowing, and a rather sloppy sea. The sport was excellent, and the free, open-air life brought the colour back to Lord Arthur's cheeks, but about the 22nd he became anxious about Lady Clementina, and, in spite of Surbiton's remonstrances, came back to Venice by train.

As he stepped out of his gondola on to the hotel steps, the proprietor came forward to meet him with a sheaf of telegrams. Lord Arthur snatched them out of his hand, and tore them open. Everything had been successful. Lady Clementina had died quite suddenly on the night of the 17th!

His first thought was for Sybil, and he sent her off a telegram announcing his immediate return to London. He then ordered his valet to pack his things for the night mail, sent his gondoliers about five times their proper fare, and ran up to his sitting-room with a light step and a buoyant heart. There he found three letters waiting for him. One was from Sybil herself, full of sympathy and condolence. The others were from his mother, and from Lady Clementina's solicitor. It seemed that the old lady had dined with the Duchess that very night, had delighted every one by her wit and *esprit*, but had gone home somewhat early, complaining of heartburn. In the morning she was found dead in her bed, having apparently suffered no pain. Sir Mathew Reid had been sent for at once, but, of course, there was nothing to be done, and she was to be buried on the 22nd at Beauchamp Chalcote. A few days before she died she had made her will, and left Lord Arthur her little house in Curzon Street, and all her furniture, personal effects, and pictures, with the exception of her collection of miniatures, which was to go to her sister, Lady Margaret Rufford, and her amethyst necklace, which Sybil Merton was to have. The property was not of much value; but Mr. Mansfield the solicitor was extremely anxious for Lord Arthur to return at once, if possible, as there were a great many bills to be paid, and Lady Clementina had never kept any regular accounts.

Lord Arthur was very much touched by Lady Clementina's kind remembrance of him, and felt that Mr. Podgers had a great deal to answer for. His love of Sybil, however, dominated every other emotion, and the consciousness that he had done his duty gave him peace and comfort. When he arrived at Charing Cross, he felt perfectly happy.

The Mertons received him very kindly, Sybil made him promise that he would never again allow anything to come between them, and the marriage was fixed for the 7th June. Life seemed to him once more bright and beautiful, and all his old gladness came back to him again.

One day, however, as he was going over the house in Curzon Street, in company with Lady Clementina's solicitor and Sybil herself, burning packages of faded letters, and turning out drawers of odd rubbish, the young girl suddenly gave a little cry of delight.

'What have you found, Sybil?' said Lord Arthur, looking up from his work, and smiling.

'This lovely little silver *bonbonnière*, Arthur. Isn't it quaint and Dutch? Do give it to me! I know amethysts won't become me till I am over eighty.'

It was the box that had held the aconitine.

Lord Arthur started, and a faint blush came into his cheek. He had almost entirely forgotten what he had done, and it seemed to him a curious coincidence that Sybil, for whose sake he had gone through all that terrible anxiety, should have been the first to remind him of it.

'Of course you can have it, Sybil. I gave it to poor Lady Clem myself.'

'Oh! thank you, Arthur; and may I have the *bonbon* too? I had no notion that Lady Clementina liked sweets. I thought she was far too intellectual.'

Lord Arthur grew deadly pale, and a horrible idea crossed his mind.

'*Bonbon*, Sybil? What do you mean?' he said, in a slow, hoarse voice.

'There is one in it, that is all. It looks quite old and dusty, and I have not the slightest intention of eating it. What is the matter, Arthur? How white you look!'

Lord Arthur rushed across the room, and seized the box. Inside it was the amber-coloured capsule, with its poison-bubble. Lady Clementina had died a natural death after all!

The shock of the discovery was almost too much for him. He flung the capsule into the fire, and sank on the sofa with a cry of despair.

V

Mr. Merton was a good deal distressed at the second postponement of the marriage, and Lady Julia, who had already ordered
her dress for the wedding, did all in her power to make Sybil
break off the match. Dearly, however, as Sybil loved her mother,
she had given her whole life into Lord Arthur's hands, and
nothing that Lady Julia could say could make her waver in her
faith. As for Lord Arthur himself, it took him days to get over his
terrible disappointment, and for a time his nerves were completely
unstrung. His excellent common sense, however, soon asserted
itself, and his sound, practical mind did not leave him long in
doubt about what to do. Poison having proved a complete
failure, dynamite,[41] or some other form of explosive, was obviously
the proper thing to try.

He accordingly looked again over the list of his friends and
relatives, and, after careful consideration, determined to blow up
his uncle, the Dean of Chichester. The Dean, who was a man of
great culture and learning, was extremely fond of clocks, and had
a wonderful collection of timepieces, ranging from the fifteenth
century to the present day, and it seemed to Lord Arthur that
this hobby of the good Dean's offered him an excellent opportunity for carrying out his scheme. Where to procure an explosive
machine was, of course, quite another matter. The London Direc-
tory gave him no information on the point, and he felt that there
was very little use in going to Scotland Yard[42] about it, as they
never seemed to know anything about the movements of the
dynamite faction till after an explosion had taken place, and not
much even then.

Suddenly he thought of his friend Rouvaloff, a young Russian
of very revolutionary tendencies,[43] whom he had met at Lady
Windermere's in the winter. Count Rouvaloff was supposed to be
writing a life of Peter the Great, and to have come over to
England for the purpose of studying the documents relating to
that Tsar's residence in this country as a ship carpenter;[44] but it
was generally suspected that he was a Nihilist agent, and there
was no doubt that the Russian Embassy did not look with any

favour upon his presence in London. Lord Arthur felt that he was just the man for his purpose, and drove down one morning to his lodgings in Bloomsbury, to ask his advice and assistance.

'So you are taking up politics seriously?' said Count Rouvaloff, when Lord Arthur had told him the object of his mission; but Lord Arthur, who hated swagger of any kind, felt bound to admit to him that he had not the slightest interest in social questions, and simply wanted the explosive machine for a purely family matter, in which no one was concerned but himself.

Count Rouvaloff looked at him for some moments in amazement, and then seeing that he was quite serious, wrote an address on a piece of paper, initialled it, and handed it to him across the table.

'Scotland Yard would give a good deal to know this address, my dear fellow.'

'They shan't have it,' cried Lord Arthur, laughing; and after shaking the young Russian warmly by the hand he ran downstairs, examined the paper, and told the coachman to drive to Soho Square.

There he dismissed him, and strolled down Greek Street, till he came to a place called Bayle's Court. He passed under the archway, and found himself in a curious cul-de-sac, that was apparently occupied by a French Laundry, as a perfect network of clothes-lines was stretched across from house to house, and there was a flutter of white linen in the morning air. He walked right to the end, and knocked at a little green house. After some delay, during which every window in the court became a blurred mass of peering faces, the door was opened by a rather rough-looking foreigner, who asked him in very bad English what his business was. Lord Arthur handed him the paper Count Rouvaloff had given him. When the man saw it he bowed, and invited Lord Arthur into a very shabby front parlour on the ground-floor, and in a few moments Herr Winckelkopf, as he was called in England, bustled into the room, with a very wine-stained napkin round his neck, and a fork in his left hand.

'Count Rouvaloff has given me an introduction to you,' said Lord Arthur, bowing, 'and I am anxious to have a short interview with you on a matter of business. My name is Smith, Mr. Robert Smith, and I want you to supply me with an explosive clock.'

'Charmed to meet you, Lord Arthur,' said the genial little German, laughing. 'Don't look so alarmed, it is my duty to know everybody, and I remember seeing you one evening at Lady Windermere's. I hope her ladyship is quite well. Do you mind sitting with me while I finish my breakfast? There is an excellent *pâté*, and my friends are kind enough to say that my Rhine wine is better than any they get at the German Embassy,' and before Lord Arthur had got over his surprise at being recognised, he found himself seated in the back-room, sipping the most delicious Marcobrünner[45] out of a pale yellow hock-glass marked with the Imperial monogram, and chatting in the friendliest manner possible to the famous conspirator.

'Explosive clocks,' said Herr Winckelkopf, 'are not very good things for foreign exportation, as, even if they succeed in passing the Custom House, the train service is so irregular, that they usually go off before they have reached their proper destination. If, however, you want one for home use, I can supply you with an excellent article, and guarantee that you will be satisfied with the result. May I ask for whom it is intended? If it is for the police, or for any one connected with Scotland Yard, I'm afraid I cannot do anything for you. The English detectives are really our best friends, and I have always found that by relying on their stupidity, we can do exactly what we like. I could not spare one of them.'

'I assure you,' said Lord Arthur, 'that it has nothing to do with the police at all. In fact, the clock is intended for the Dean of Chichester.'

'Dear me! I had no idea that you felt so strongly about religion, Lord Arthur. Few young men do nowadays.'

'I am afraid you overrate me, Herr Winckelkopf,' said Lord Arthur, blushing. 'The fact is, I really know nothing about theology.'

'It is a purely private matter then?'

'Purely private.'

Herr Winckelkopf shrugged his shoulders, and left the room, returning in a few minutes with a round cake of dynamite about the size of a penny, and a pretty little French clock, surmounted by an ormolu figure of Liberty trampling on the hydra[46] of Despotism.

Lord Arthur's face brightened up when he saw it. 'That is just what I want,' he cried, 'and now tell me how it goes off.'

'Ah! there is my secret,' answered Herr Winckelkopf, contemplating his invention with a justifiable look of pride; 'let me know when you wish it to explode, and I will set the machine to the moment.'

'Well, to-day is Tuesday, and if you could send it off at once –'

'That is impossible; I have a great deal of important work on hand for some friends of mine in Moscow. Still, I might send it off to-morrow.'

'Oh, it will be quite time enough!' said Lord Arthur politely, 'if it is delivered to-morrow night or Thursday morning. For the moment of the explosion, say Friday at noon exactly. The Dean is always at home at that hour.'

'Friday, at noon,' repeated Herr Winckelkopf, and he made a note to that effect in a large ledger that was lying on a bureau near the fireplace.

'And now,' said Lord Arthur, rising from his seat, 'pray let me know how much I am in your debt.'

'It is such a small matter, Lord Arthur, that I do not care to make any charge. The dynamite comes to seven and sixpence, the clock will be three pounds ten, and the carriage about five shillings. I am only too pleased to oblige any friend of Count Rouvaloff's.'

'But your trouble, Herr Winckelkopf?'

'Oh, that is nothing! It is a pleasure to me. I do not work for money; I live entirely for my art.'[47]

Lord Arthur laid down £4:2:6 on the table, thanked the little German for his kindness, and, having succeeded in declining an invitation to meet some Anarchists at a meat-tea[48] on the following Saturday, left the house and went off to the Park.

For the next two days he was in a state of the greatest excitement, and on Friday at twelve o'clock he drove down to the Buckingham to wait for news. All the afternoon the stolid hall-porter kept posting up telegrams from various parts of the country giving the results of horse-races, the verdicts in divorce suits, the state of the weather, and the like, while the tape[49] ticked out wearisome details about an all-night sitting in the House of Commons, and a small panic on the Stock Exchange. At four o'clock the evening papers came in, and Lord Arthur disappeared into the library with the *Pall Mall*, the *St. James's*, the *Globe*, and the *Echo*, to the immense indignation of Colonel Goodchild, who wanted to read the reports of a speech he had delivered that morning at the Mansion House, on the subject of South African Missions, and the advisability of having black Bishops in every province, and for some reason or other had a strong prejudice against the *Evening News*. None of the papers, however, contained even the slightest allusion to Chichester, and Lord Arthur felt that the attempt must have failed. It was a terrible blow to him, and for a time he was quite unnerved. Herr Winckelkopf, whom he went to see the next day, was full of elaborate apologies, and offered to supply him with another clock free of charge, or with a case of nitro-glycerine bombs at cost price. But he had lost all faith in explosives, and Herr Winckelkopf himself acknowledged that everything is so adulterated nowadays, that even dynamite can hardly be got in a pure condition. The little German, however, while admitting that something must have gone wrong with the machinery, was not without hope that the clock might still go off, and instanced the case of a barometer that he had once sent to the military Governor at Odessa, which, though timed to explode in ten days, had not done so for something like three months. It was quite true that when it did go off, it merely succeeded in blowing a housemaid to atoms, the Governor having gone out of town six weeks before, but at least it showed that dynamite, as a destructive force, was, when under the control of machinery, a powerful, though a somewhat unpunctual agent. Lord Arthur was a little consoled by this reflection, but even here he was destined to disappointment, for two days afterwards, as he was going upstairs, the Duchess called him into her boudoir, and showed him a letter she had just received from the Deanery.

'Jane writes charming letters,' said the Duchess; 'you must really read her last. It is quite as good as the novels Mudie[50] sends us.'

Lord Arthur seized the letter from her hand. It ran as follows:—

'The Deanery, Chichester,
'27th May.

'My Dearest Aunt,

'Thank you so much for the flannel for the Dorcas Society,[51] and also for the gingham. I quite agree with you that it is nonsense their wanting to wear pretty things, but everybody is so Radical and irreligious nowadays, that it is difficult to make them see that they should not try and dress like the upper classes. I am sure I don't know what we are coming to. As papa has often said in his sermons, we live in an age of unbelief.

'We have had great fun over a clock that an unknown admirer sent papa last Thursday. It arrived in a wooden box from London, carriage paid; and papa feels it must have been sent by some one who had read his remarkable sermon, "Is Licence Liberty?" for on the top of the clock was a figure of a woman, with what papa said was the cap of Liberty[52] on her head. I didn't think it very becoming myself, but papa said it was historical, so I suppose it is all right. Parker unpacked it, and papa put it on the mantelpiece in the library, and we were all sitting there on Friday morning, when just as the clock struck twelve, we heard a whirring noise, a little puff of smoke came from the pedestal of the figure, and the goddess of Liberty fell off, and broke her nose on the fender! Maria was quite alarmed, but it looked so ridiculous, that James and I went off into fits of laughter, and even papa was amused. When we examined it, we found it was a sort of alarum clock, and that, if you set it to a particular hour, and put some gunpowder and a cap under a little hammer, it went off whenever you wanted. Papa said it must not remain in the library, as it made a noise, so Reggie carried it away to the schoolroom, and does nothing but have small explosions all day long. Do you think Arthur would like one for a wedding present? I suppose they are quite fashionable in London. Papa says they should do a great deal of good, as they show that Liberty can't last, but must fall down. Papa says Liberty was invented at the time of the French Revolution.[53] How awful it seems!

'I have now to go to the Dorcas, where I will read them your most instructive letter. How true, dear aunt, your idea is, that in their rank of life they should wear what is unbecoming. I must say it is absurd, their anxiety about dress, when there are so many more important things in this world, and in the next. I am so glad your flowered poplin turned out so well, and that your lace was not torn. I am wearing my yellow satin, that you so kindly gave me, at the Bishop's on Wednesday, and think it will look all right. Would you have bows or not? Jennings says that every one wears bows now, and that the underskirt should be frilled. Reggie has just had another explosion, and papa has ordered the clock to be sent to the stables. I don't think papa likes it so much as he did at first, though he is very flattered at being sent such a pretty and ingenious toy. It shows that people read his sermons, and profit by them.

'Papa sends his love, in which James, and Reggie, and Maria all unite, and, hoping that Uncle Cecil's gout is better, believe me, dear aunt, ever your affectionate niece,

'Jane Percy

'P.S. – Do tell me about the bows. Jennings insists they are the fashion.'

Lord Arthur looked so serious and unhappy over the letter, that the Duchess went into fits of laughter.

'My dear Arthur,' she cried, 'I shall never show you a young lady's letter again! But what shall I say about the clock? I think it is a capital invention, and I should like to have one myself.'

'I don't think much of them,' said Lord Arthur, with a sad smile, and, after kissing his mother, he left the room.

When he got upstairs, he flung himself on a sofa, and his eyes filled with tears. He had done his best to commit this murder, but on both occasions he had failed, and through no fault of his own. He had tried to do his duty, but it seemed as if Destiny herself had turned traitor. He was oppressed with the sense of the barrenness of good intentions, of the futility of trying to be fine. Perhaps, it would be better to break off the marriage altogether. Sybil would suffer, it is true, but suffering could not really mar a nature so noble as hers. As for himself, what did it matter? There is always some war in which a man can die, some cause to which a man can give his life, and as life had no pleasure for him, so death had no terror. Let Destiny work out his doom. He would not stir to help her.

At half-past seven he dressed, and went down to the club.

Surbiton was there with a party of young men, and he was obliged to dine with them. Their trivial conversation and idle jests did not interest him, and as soon as coffee was brought he left them, inventing some engagement in order to get away. As he was going out of the club, the hall porter handed him a letter. It was from Herr Winckelkopf, asking him to call down the next evening, and look at an explosive umbrella, that went off as soon as it was opened. It was the very latest invention, and had just arrived from Geneva. He tore the letter up into fragments. He had made up his mind not to try any more experiments. Then he wandered down to the Thames Embankment, and sat for hours by the river. The moon peered through a mane of tawny clouds, as if it were a lion's eye, and innumerable stars spangled the hollow vault, like gold dust powdered on a purple dome. Now and then a barge swung out into the turbid stream, and floated away with the tide, and the railway signals changed from green to scarlet as the trains ran shrieking across the bridge. After some time, twelve o'clock boomed from the tall tower at Westminster, and at each stroke of the sonorous bell the night seemed to tremble. Then the railway lights went out, one solitary lamp left gleaming like a large ruby on a giant mast, and the roar of the city became fainter.

At two o'clock he got up, and strolled towards Blackfriars. How unreal everything looked! How like a strange dream! The houses on the other side of the river seemed built out of darkness. One would have said that silver and shadow had fashioned the world anew. The huge dome of St. Paul's loomed like a bubble through the dusky air.

As he approached Cleopatra's Needle he saw a man leaning over the parapet, and as he came nearer the man looked up, the gas-light falling full upon his face.

It was Mr. Podgers, the cheiromantist! No one could mistake the fat, flabby face, the gold-rimmed spectacles, the sickly feeble smile, the sensual mouth.

Lord Arthur stopped. A brilliant idea flashed across him, and he stole softly up behind. In a moment he had seized Mr. Podgers by the legs, and flung him into the Thames. There was a coarse oath, a heavy splash, and all was still. Lord Arthur looked anxiously over, but could see nothing of the cheiromantist but a tall hat, pirouetting in an eddy of moonlit water. After a time it also sank, and no trace of Mr. Podgers was visible. Once he thought that he caught sight of the bulky misshapen figure striking out for the staircase by the bridge, and a horrible feeling of failure came over him, but it turned out to be merely a reflection, and when the moon shone out from behind a cloud it passed away. At last he seemed to have realised the decree of destiny. He heaved a deep sigh of relief, and Sybil's name came to his lips.

'Have you dropped anything, sir?' said a voice behind him suddenly.

He turned round, and saw a policeman with a bull's-eye lantern.[54]

'Nothing of importance, sergeant,' he answered, smiling, and hailing a passing hansom, he jumped in, and told the man to drive to Belgrave Square.

For the next few days he alternated between hope and fear. There were moments when he almost expected Mr. Podgers to walk into the room, and yet at other times he felt that Fate could not be so unjust to him. Twice he went to the cheiromantist's address in West Moon Street, but he could not bring himself to ring the bell. He longed for certainty, and was afraid of it.

Finally it came. He was sitting in the smoking-room of the club having tea, and listening rather wearily to Surbiton's account of the last comic song at the Gaiety,[55] when the waiter came in with the evening papers. He took up the *St. James's*, and was listlessly turning over its pages, when this strange heading caught his eye:

SUICIDE OF A CHEIROMANTIST.

He turned pale with excitement, and began to read. The paragraph ran as follows: –

Yesterday morning, at seven o'clock, the body of Mr. Septimus R. Podgers, the eminent cheiromantist, was washed on shore at Greenwich, just in front of the Ship Hotel. The unfortunate gentleman had been missing for some days, and considerable anxiety for his safety had been felt in cheiromantic circles. It is supposed that he committed suicide under the influence of a temporary mental derangement, caused by overwork, and a verdict to that effect was returned this afternoon by the coroner's jury. Mr. Podgers had just completed an elaborate treatise on the subject of the Human Hand, that will shortly be published, when it will no doubt attract much attention. The deceased was sixty-five years of age, and does not seem to have left any relations.

Lord Arthur rushed out of the club with the paper still in his hand, to the immense amazement of the hall-porter, who tried in vain to stop him, and drove at once to Park Lane. Sybil saw him from the window, and something told her that he was the bearer of good news. She ran down to meet him, and, when she saw his face, she knew that all was well.

'My dear Sybil,' cried Lord Arthur, 'let us be married to-morrow!'

'You foolish boy! Why the cake is not even ordered!' said Sybil, laughing through her tears.

VI

When the wedding took place, some three weeks later, St. Peter's was crowded with a perfect mob of smart people. The service was read in a most impressive manner by the Dean of Chichester, and everybody agreed that they had never seen a handsomer couple than the bride and bridegroom. They were more than handsome, however – they were happy. Never for a single moment did Lord Arthur regret all that he had suffered for Sybil's sake, while she, on her side, gave him the best things a woman can give to any man – worship, tenderness, and love. For them romance was not killed by reality. They always felt young.

Some years afterwards, when two beautiful children had been born to them, Lady Windermere came down on a visit to Alton Priory, a lovely old place, that had been the Duke's wedding present to his son; and one afternoon as she was sitting with Lady Arthur under a lime-tree in the garden, watching the little boy and girl as they played up and down the rose-walk, like fitful sunbeams, she suddenly took her hostess's hand in hers, and said, 'Are you happy, Sybil?'

'Dear Lady Windermere, of course I am happy. Aren't you?'

'I have no time to be happy, Sybil. I always like the last person who is introduced to me; but, as a rule, as soon as I know people I get tired of them.'

'Don't your lions satisfy you, Lady Windermere?'

'Oh dear, no! lions are only good for one season. As soon as their manes are cut, they are the dullest creatures going. Besides, they behave very badly, if you are really nice to them. Do you remember that horrid Mr. Podgers? He was a dreadful impostor. Of course, I didn't mind that at all, and even when he wanted to borrow money I forgave him, but I could not stand his making love to me. He has really made me hate cheiromancy. I go in for telepathy now. It is much more amusing.'

'You mustn't say anything against cheiromancy here, Lady Windermere; it is the only subject that Arthur does not like people to chaff about. I assure you he is quite serious over it.'

'You don't mean to say that he believes in it, Sybil?'

'Ask him, Lady Windermere, here he is;' and Lord Arthur came up the garden with a large bunch of yellow roses in his hand, and his two children dancing round him.

'Lord Arthur?'

'Yes, Lady Windermere.'

'You don't mean to say that you believe in cheiromancy?'

'Of course I do,' said the young man, smiling.

'But why?'

'Because I owe to it all the happiness of my life,' he murmured, throwing himself into a wicker chair.

'My dear Lord Arthur, what do you owe to it?'

'Sybil,' he answered, handing his wife the roses, and looking into her violet eyes.

'What nonsense!' cried Lady Windermere. 'I never heard such nonsense in all my life.'

The Sphinx Without a Secret

An etching[1]

One afternoon I was sitting outside the Café de la Paix, watching the splendour and shabbiness of Parisian life, and wondering over my vermouth at the strange panorama of pride and poverty that was passing before me, when I heard some one call my name. I turned round, and saw Lord Murchison. We had not met since we had been at college together, nearly ten years before, so I was delighted to come across him again, and we shook hands warmly. At Oxford we had been great friends. I had liked him immensely, he was so handsome, so high-spirited, and so honourable. We used to say of him that he would be the best of fellows, if he did not always speak the truth, but I think we really admired him all the more for his frankness. I found him a good deal changed. He looked anxious and puzzled, and seemed to be in doubt about something. I felt it could not be modern scepticism, for Murchison was the stoutest of Tories, and believed in the Pentateuch[2] as firmly as he believed in the House of Peers; so I concluded that it was a woman, and asked him if he was married yet.

'I don't understand women well enough,' he answered.

'My dear Gerald,' I said, 'women are meant to be loved, not to be understood.'

'I cannot love where I cannot trust,' he replied.

'I believe you have a mystery in your life, Gerald,' I exclaimed; 'tell me about it.'

'Let us go for a drive,' he answered, 'it is too crowded here. No, not a yellow carriage, any other colour – there, that dark-green one will do;' and in a few moments we were trotting down the boulevard in the direction of the Madeleine.

'Where shall we go to?' I said.

'Oh, anywhere you like!' he answered – 'to the restaurant in the Bois;[3] we will dine there, and you shall tell me all about yourself.'

'I want to hear about you first,' I said. 'Tell me your mystery.'

He took from his pocket a little silver-clasped morocco case, and handed it to me. I opened it. Inside there was the photograph of a woman. She was tall and slight, and strangely picturesque with her large vague eyes and loosened hair. She looked like a *clairvoyante*, and was wrapped in rich furs.

'What do you think of that face?' he said; 'is it truthful?'

I examined it carefully. It seemed to me the face of some one who had a secret, but whether that secret was good or evil I could not say. Its beauty was a beauty moulded out of many mysteries – the beauty, in fact, which is psychological, not plastic – and the faint smile that just played across the lips was far too subtle to be really sweet.

'Well,' he cried impatiently, 'what do you say?'

'She is the Gioconda in sables,'[4] I answered. 'Let me know all about her.'

'Not now,' he said; 'after dinner;' and began to talk of other things.

When the waiter brought us our coffee and cigarettes I reminded Gerald of his promise. He rose from his seat, walked two or three times up and down the room, and, sinking into an armchair, told me the following story: –

'One evening,' he said, 'I was walking down Bond Street about five o'clock. There was a terrific crush of carriages, and the traffic was almost stopped. Close to the pavement was standing a little yellow brougham,[5] which, for some reason or other, attracted my attention. As I passed by there looked out from it the face I showed you this afternoon. It fascinated me immediately. All that night I kept thinking of it, and all the next day. I wandered up and down that wretched Row,[6] peering into every carriage, and waiting for the yellow brougham; but I could not find *ma belle inconnue*,[7] and at last I began to think she was merely a dream. About a week afterwards I was dining with Madame de Rastail. Dinner was for eight o'clock; but at half-past eight we were still waiting in the drawing-room. Finally the servant threw open the door, and announced Lady Alroy. It was the woman I had been looking for. She came in very slowly, looking like a moon-beam in grey lace, and, to my intense delight, I was asked to take her in to dinner. After we had sat down I remarked quite innocently, "I think I caught sight of you in Bond Street some time ago, Lady Alroy." She grew very pale, and said to me in a low voice, "Pray do not talk so loud; you may be overheard." I felt miserable at having made such a bad beginning, and plunged recklessly into the subject of the French plays. She spoke very little, always in the same low musical voice, and seemed as if she was afraid of some one listening. I fell passionately, stupidly in love, and the indefinable atmosphere of mystery that surrounded her excited my most ardent curiosity. When she was going away, which she did very soon after dinner, I asked her if I might call and see her. She hesitated for a moment, glanced round to see if any one was near us, and then said, "Yes; to-morrow at a quarter to five." I begged Madame de Rastail to tell me about her; but all that I could learn was that she was a widow with a beautiful house in Park Lane, and as some scientific bore began a dissertation on widows, as exemplifying the survival of the matrimonially fittest, I left and went home.

'The next day I arrived at Park Lane punctual to the moment, but was told by the butler that Lady Alroy had just gone out. I went down to the club quite unhappy and very much puzzled, and after long consideration wrote her a letter, asking if I might be allowed to try my chance some other afternoon. I had no answer for several days, but at last I got a little note saying she would be at home on Sunday at four, and with this extraordinary postscript: "Please do not write to me here again; I will explain when I see you." On Sunday she received me, and was perfectly charming; but when I was going away she begged of me, if I ever had occasion to write to her again, to address my letter to "Mrs. Knox, care of Whittaker's Library, Green Street." "There are reasons," she said, "why I cannot receive letters in my own house."

'All through the season I saw a great deal of her, and the atmosphere of mystery never left her. Sometimes I thought that she was in the power of some man, but she looked so unapproach-able that I could not believe it. It was really very difficult for me to come to any conclusion, for she was like one of those strange crystals that one sees in museums, which are at one moment clear, and at another clouded. At last I determined to ask her to be my wife: I was sick and tired of the incessant secrecy that she imposed on all my visits, and on the few letters I sent her. I wrote to her at the library to ask her if she could see me the following Monday at six. She answered yes, and I was in the seventh heaven of delight. I was infatuated with her: in spite of the mystery, I thought then – in consequence of it, I see now. No; it was the woman herself I loved. The mystery troubled me, mad-dened me. Why did chance put me in its track?'

'You discovered it, then?' I cried.

'I fear so,' he answered. 'You can judge for yourself.'

'When Monday came round I went to lunch with my uncle, and about four o'clock found myself in the Marylebone Road. My uncle, you know, lives in Regent's Park. I wanted to get to Piccadilly, and took a short cut through a lot of shabby little streets. Suddenly I saw in front of me Lady Alroy, deeply veiled and walking very fast. On coming to the last house in the street, she went up the steps, took out a latch-key, and let herself in. "Here is the mystery," I said to myself; and I hurried on and examined the house. It seemed a sort of place for letting lodgings. On the doorstep lay her handkerchief, which she had dropped. I picked it up and put it in my pocket. Then I began to consider what I should do. I came to the conclusion that I had no right to spy on her, and I drove down to the club. At six I called to see her. She was lying on a sofa, in a tea-gown of silver tissue looped up by some strange moonstones that she always wore. She was looking quite lovely. "I am so glad to see you," she said; "I have not been out all day." I stared at her in amazement, and pulling the handkerchief out of my pocket, handed it to her. "You dropped this in Cumnor Street this afternoon, Lady Alroy," I said very calmly. She looked at me in terror, but made no attempt to take the handkerchief. "What were you doing there?" I asked. "What right have you to question me?" she answered. "The right of a man who loves you," I replied; "I came here to ask you to be my wife." She hid her face in her hands, and burst into floods of tears. "You must tell me," I continued. She stood up, and, looking me straight in the face, said, "Lord Murchison, there is nothing to tell you." – "You went to meet some one," I cried; "this is your mystery." She grew dreadfully white, and said, "I went to meet no one." – "Can't you tell the truth?" I exclaimed. "I have told it," she replied. I was mad, frantic; I don't know what I said, but I said terrible things to her. Finally I rushed out of the house. She wrote me a letter the next day; I sent it back unopened, and started for Norway with Alan Colville. After a month I came back, and the first thing I saw in the *Morning Post* was the death of Lady Alroy. She had caught a chill at the Opera, and had died in five days of congestion of the lungs.[8] I shut myself up and saw no one. I had loved her so much, I had loved her so madly. Good God! how I had loved that woman!'

'You went to the street, to the house in it?' I said.

'Yes,' he answered.

'One day I went to Cumnor Street. I could not help it; I was tortured with doubt. I knocked at the door, and a respectable-looking woman opened it to me. I asked her if she had any rooms to let. "Well, sir," she replied, "the drawing-rooms are supposed to be let; but I have not seen the lady for three months, and as rent is owing on them, you can have them." – "Is this the lady?" I said, showing the photograph. "That's her, sure enough," she exclaimed; "and when is she coming back, sir?" – "The lady is dead," I replied. "Oh, sir, I hope not!" said the woman; "she was my best lodger. She paid me three guineas a week merely to sit in my drawing-rooms now and then." – "She met some one here?" I said; but the woman assured me that it was not so, that she always came alone, and saw no one. "What on earth did she do here?" I cried. "She simply sat in the drawing-room, sir, reading books, and sometimes had tea," the woman answered. I did not know what to say, so I gave her a sovereign and went away. Now, what do you think it all meant? You don't believe the woman was telling the truth?'

'I do.'

'Then why did Lady Alroy go there?'

'My dear Gerald,' I answered, 'Lady Alroy was simply a woman with a mania for mystery. She took these rooms for the pleasure of going there with her veil down, and imagining she was a heroine. She had a passion for secrecy, but she herself was merely a Sphinx without a secret.'

'Do you really think so?'

'I am sure of it,' I replied.

He took out the morocco case, opened it, and looked at the photograph. 'I wonder?' he said at last.

The Canterville Ghost

A Hylo-Idealistic Romance[1]

I

When Mr. Hiram B. Otis, the American Minister, bought Canterville Chase, every one told him he was doing a very foolish thing, as there was no doubt at all that the place was haunted. Indeed, Lord Canterville himself, who was a man of the most punctilious honour, had felt it his duty to mention the fact to Mr. Otis when they came to discuss terms.

'We have not cared to live in the place ourselves,' said Lord Canterville, 'since my grand-aunt, the Dowager Duchess[2] of Bolton, was frightened into a fit, from which she never really recovered, by two skeleton hands being placed on her shoulders as she was dressing for dinner, and I feel bound to tell you, Mr. Otis, that the ghost has been seen by several living members of my family, as well as by the rector of the parish, the Rev. Augustus Dampier, who is a Fellow of King's College, Cambridge. After the unfortunate accident to the Duchess, none of our younger servants would stay with us, and Lady Canterville often got very little sleep at night, in consequence of the mysterious noises that came from the corridor and the library.'

'My Lord,' answered the Minister, 'I will take the furniture and the ghost at a valuation. I come from a modern country, where we have everything that money can buy; and with all our spry young fellows painting the Old World red, and carrying off your best actors and prima-donnas, I reckon that if there were such a thing as a ghost in Europe, we'd have it at home in a very short time in one of our public museums, or on the road as a show.'

'I fear that the ghost exists,' said Lord Canterville, smiling, 'though it may have resisted the overtures of your enterprising impresarios. It has been well known for three centuries, since 1584 in fact, and always makes its appearance before the death of any member of our family.'

'Well, so does the family doctor for that matter, Lord Canterville. But there is no such thing, sir, as a ghost, and I guess the laws of Nature are not going to be suspended for the British aristocracy.'

'You are certainly very natural in America,'[3] answered Lord Canterville, who did not quite understand Mr. Otis's last observation, 'and if you don't mind a ghost in the house, it is all right. Only you must remember I warned you.'

A few weeks after this, the purchase was concluded, and at the close of the season the Minister and his family went down to Canterville Chase. Mrs. Otis, who, as Miss Lucretia R. Tappan, of West 53rd Street, had been a celebrated New York belle, was now a very handsome, middle-aged woman, with fine eyes, and a superb profile. Many American ladies on leaving their native land adopt an appearance of chronic ill-health, under the impression that it is a form of European refinement, but Mrs. Otis had never fallen into this error. She had a magnificent constitution, and a really wonderful amount of animal spirits. Indeed, in many respects, she was quite English, and was an excellent example of the fact that we have really everything in common with America nowadays, except, of course, language. Her eldest son, christened Washington by his parents in a moment of patriotism, which he never ceased to regret, was a fair-haired, rather good-looking young man, who had qualified himself for American diplomacy by leading the German[4] at the Newport Casino for three successive seasons, and even in London was well known as an excellent dancer. Gardenias and the peerage were his only weaknesses. Otherwise he was extremely sensible. Miss Virginia E. Otis was a little girl of fifteen, lithe and lovely as a fawn, and with a fine freedom in her large blue eyes. She was a wonderful amazon,[5] and had once raced old Lord Bilton on her pony twice round the park, winning by a length and a half, just in front of the Achilles statue, to the huge delight of the young Duke of Cheshire, who proposed for her on the spot, and was sent back to Eton that very night by his guardians, in floods of tears. After Virginia came the twins, who were usually called 'The Stars and Stripes,' as they were always getting swished. They were delightful boys, and with the exception of the worthy Minister the only true republicans of the family.

As Canterville Chase is seven miles from Ascot, the nearest railway station, Mr. Otis had telegraphed for a waggonette to meet them, and they started on their drive in high spirits. It was a lovely July evening, and the air was delicate with the scent of the pinewoods. Now and then they heard a wood pigeon brooding over its own sweet voice, or saw, deep in the rustling fern, the burnished breast of the pheasant. Little squirrels peered at them from the beech-trees as they went by, and the rabbits scudded away through the brushwood and over the mossy knolls, with their white tails in the air. As they entered the avenue of Canterville Chase, however, the sky became suddenly overcast with clouds, a curious stillness seemed to hold the atmosphere, a great flight of rooks passed silently over their heads, and, before they reached the house, some big drops of rain had fallen.

Standing on the steps to receive them was an old woman, neatly dressed in black silk, with a white cap and apron. This was Mrs. Umney, the housekeeper, whom Mrs. Otis, at Lady Canterville's earnest request, had consented to keep on in her former position. She made them each a low curtsey as they alighted, and said in a quaint, old-fashioned manner, 'I bid you welcome to Canterville Chase.' Following her, they passed through the fine Tudor hall into the library, a long, low room, panelled in black oak, at the end of which was a large stained-glass window. Here they found tea laid out for them, and, after taking off their wraps, they sat down and began to look round, while Mrs. Umney waited on them.

Suddenly Mrs. Otis caught sight of a dull red stain on the floor just by the fireplace and, quite unconscious of what it really signified, said to Mrs. Umney, 'I am afraid something has been spilt there.'

'Yes, madam,' replied the old housekeeper in a low voice, 'blood has been spilt on that spot.'

'How horrid,' cried Mrs. Otis; 'I don't at all care for blood-stains in a sitting-room. It must be removed at once.'

The old woman smiled, and answered in the same low, mysterious voice, 'It is the blood of Lady Eleanore de Canterville, who was murdered on that very spot by her own husband, Sir Simon de Canterville, in 1575. Sir Simon survived her nine years, and disappeared suddenly under very mysterious circumstances. His body has never been discovered, but his guilty spirit still haunts the Chase. The blood-stain has been much admired by tourists and others, and cannot be removed.'

'That is all nonsense,' cried Washington Otis; 'Pinkerton's Champion Stain Remover and Paragon Detergent will clean it up in no time,' and before the terrified housekeeper could interfere he had fallen upon his knees, and was rapidly scouring the floor with a small stick of what looked like a black cosmetic. In a few moments no trace of the blood-stain could be seen.

'I knew Pinkerton would do it,' he exclaimed triumphantly, as he looked round at his admiring family; but no sooner had he said these words than a terrible flash of lightning lit up the sombre room, a fearful peal of thunder made them all start to their feet, and Mrs. Umney fainted.

'What a monstrous climate!' said the American Minister calmly, as he lit a long cheroot. 'I guess the old country is so over-populated that they have not enough decent weather for everybody. I have always been of opinion that emigration is the only thing for England.'

'My dear Hiram,' cried Mrs. Otis, 'what can we do with a woman who faints?'

'Charge it to her like breakages,' answered the Minister; 'she won't faint after that;' and in a few moments Mrs. Umney certainly came to. There was no doubt, however, that she was extremely upset, and she sternly warned Mr. Otis to beware of some trouble coming to the house.

'I have seen things with my own eyes, sir,' she said, 'that would make any Christian's hair stand on end, and many and many a night I have not closed my eyes in sleep for the awful things that are done here.' Mr. Otis, however, and his wife warmly assured the honest soul that they were not afraid of ghosts, and, after invoking the blessings of Providence on her new master and mistress, and making arrangements for an increase of salary, the old housekeeper tottered off to her own room.

II

The storm raged fiercely all that night, but nothing of particular note occurred. The next morning, however, when they came down to breakfast, they found the terrible stain of blood once again on the floor. 'I don't think it can be the fault of the Paragon Detergent,' said Washington, 'for I have tried it with everything. It must be the ghost.' He accordingly rubbed out the stain a second time, but the second morning it appeared again. The third morning also it was there, though the library had been locked up at night by Mr. Otis himself, and the key carried upstairs. The whole family were now quite interested; Mr. Otis began to suspect that he had been too dogmatic in his denial of the existence of ghosts, Mrs. Otis expressed her intention of joining the Psychical Society,[6] and Washington prepared a long letter to Messrs. Myers and Podmore on the subject of the Permanence of Sanguineous Stains when connected with Crime. That night all doubts about the objective existence of phantasmata were removed for ever.

The day had been warm and sunny; and, in the cool of the evening, the whole family went out to drive. They did not return home till nine o'clock, when they had a light supper. The conversation in no way turned upon ghosts, so there were not even those primary conditions of receptive expectation which so often precede the presentation of psychical phenomena. The subjects discussed, as I have since learned from Mr. Otis, were merely such as form the ordinary conversation of cultured Americans of the better class, such as the immense superiority of Miss Fanny Davenport over Sara Bernhardt[7] as an actress; the difficulty of obtaining green corn, buckwheat cakes, and hominy,[8] even in the best English houses; the importance of Boston in the development of the world-soul; the advantages of the baggage check system in railway travelling; and the sweetness of the New

York accent as compared to the London drawl. No mention at all was made of the supernatural, nor was Sir Simon de Canterville alluded to in any way. At eleven o'clock the family retired, and by half-past all the lights were out. Some time after, Mr. Otis was awakened by a curious noise in the corridor, outside his room. It sounded like the clank of metal, and seemed to be coming nearer every moment. He got up at once, struck a match, and looked at the time. It was exactly one o'clock. He was quite calm, and felt his pulse, which was not at all feverish. The strange noise still continued, and with it he heard distinctly the sound of footsteps. He put on his slippers, took a small oblong phial out of his dressing-case, and opened the door. Right in front of him he saw, in the wan moonlight, an old man of terrible aspect.[9] His eyes were as red burning coals; long grey hair fell over his shoulders in matted coils; his garments, which were of antique cut, were soiled and ragged, and from his wrists and ankles hung heavy manacles and rusty gyves.

'My dear sir,' said Mr. Otis, 'I really must insist on your oiling those chains, and have brought you for that purpose a small bottle of the Tammany Rising Sun Lubricator. It is said to be completely efficacious upon one application, and there are several testimonials to that effect on the wrapper from some of our most eminent native divines. I shall leave it here for you by the bedroom candles, and will be happy to supply you with more should you require it.' With these words the United States Minister laid the bottle down on a marble table, and, closing his door, retired to rest.

For a moment the Canterville ghost stood quite motionless in natural indignation; then, dashing the bottle violently upon the polished floor, he fled down the corridor, uttering hollow groans, and emitting a ghastly green light. Just, however, as he reached the top of the great oak staircase, a door was flung open, two little white-robed figures appeared, and a large pillow whizzed past his head! There was evidently no time to be lost, so, hastily adopting the Fourth Dimension of Space as a means of escape, he vanished through the wainscoting, and the house became quite quiet.

On reaching a small secret chamber in the left wing, he leaned up against a moonbeam to recover his breath, and began to try and realise his position. Never, in a brilliant and uninterrupted career of three hundred years, had he been so grossly insulted. He thought of the Dowager Duchess, whom he had frightened into a fit as she stood before the glass in her lace and diamonds; of the four housemaids, who had gone off into hysterics when he merely grinned at them through the curtains of one of the spare bed-rooms; of the rector of the parish, whose candle he had blown out as he was coming late one night from the library, and who had been under the care of Sir William Gull ever since, a perfect martyr to nervous disorders; and of old Madame de Tremouillac, who, having wakened up one morning early and seen a skeleton seated in an armchair by the fire reading her diary, had been confined to her bed for six weeks with an attack of brain fever, and, on her recovery, had become reconciled to the Church, and broken off her connection with that notorious sceptic Monsieur de Voltaire.[10] He remembered the terrible night when the wicked Lord Canterville was found choking in his dressing-room, with the knave of diamonds half-way down his throat, and confessed, just before he died, that he had cheated Charles James Fox out of £50,000 at Crockford's[11] by means of that very card, and swore that the ghost had made him swallow it. All his great achieve-ments came back to him again, from the butler who had shot himself in the pantry because he had seen a green hand tapping at the window pane, to the beautiful Lady Stutfield,[12] who was always obliged to wear a black velvet band round her throat to hide the mark of five fingers burnt upon her white skin, and who drowned herself at last in the carp-pond at the end of the King's Walk. With the enthusiastic egotism of the true artist he went over his most celebrated performances, and smiled bitterly to himself as he recalled to mind his last appearance as 'Red Reuben, or the Strangled Babe,' his *début* as 'Gaunt Gibeon, the Blood-sucker of Bexley Moor,' and the *furore* he had excited one lovely June evening by merely playing ninepins with his own bones upon the lawn-tennis ground. And after all this, some wretched modern Americans were to come and offer him the Rising Sun Lubricator, and throw pillows at his head! It was quite unbearable. Besides, no ghost in history had ever been treated in this manner. Accordingly, he determined to have vengeance, and remained till daylight in an attitude of deep thought.

III

The next morning, when the Otis family met at breakfast, they discussed the ghost at some length. The United States Minister was naturally a little annoyed to find that his present had not been accepted. 'I have no wish,' he said, 'to do the ghost any personal injury, and I must say that, considering the length of time he has been in the house, I don't think it is at all polite to throw pillows at him' – a very just remark, at which, I am sorry to say, the twins burst into shouts of laughter. 'Upon the other hand,' he continued, 'if he really declines to use the Rising Sun Lubricator, we shall have to take his chains from him. It would be quite impossible to sleep, with such a noise going on outside the bedrooms.'

For the rest of the week, however, they were undisturbed, the only thing that excited any attention being the continual renewal of the blood-stain on the library floor. This certainly was very strange, as the door was always locked at night by Mr. Otis, and the windows kept closely barred. The chameleon-like colour, also, of the stain excited a good deal of comment. Some mornings it was a dull (almost Indian) red, then it would be vermilion, then a rich purple, and once when they came down for family prayers, according to the simple rites of the Free American Reformed Episcopalian Church, they found it a bright emerald-green. These kaleidoscopic changes naturally amused the party very much, and bets on the subject were freely made every evening. The only person who did not enter into the joke was little Virginia, who, for some unexplained reason, was always a good deal distressed at the sight of the blood-stain, and very nearly cried the morning it was emerald-green.

The second appearance of the ghost was on Sunday night. Shortly after they had gone to bed they were suddenly alarmed by a fearful crash in the hall. Rushing downstairs, they found that a large suit of old armour had become detached from its stand, and had fallen on the stone floor, while, seated in a high-backed chair, was the Canterville ghost, rubbing his knees with an expression of acute agony on his face. The twins, having brought their pea-shooters with them, at once discharged two pellets on him, with that accuracy of aim which can only be attained by long and careful practice on a writing-master, while the United States Minister covered him with his revolver, and called upon him, in accordance with Californian etiquette, to hold up his hands! The ghost started up with a wild shriek of rage, and swept through them like a mist, extinguishing Washington Otis's candle as he passed, and so leaving them all in total darkness. On reaching the top of the staircase he recovered himself, and determined to give his celebrated peal of demoniac laughter. This he had on more than one occasion found extremely useful. It was said to have turned Lord Raker's wig grey in a single night, and had certainly made three of Lady Canterville's French governesses give warning before their month was up. He accordingly laughed his most horrible laugh, till the old vaulted roof rang and rang again, but hardly had the fearful echo died away when a door opened, and Mrs. Otis came out in a light blue dressing-gown. 'I am afraid you are far from well,' she said, 'and have brought you a bottle of Dr. Dobell's tincture. If it is indigestion, you will find it a most excellent remedy.' The ghost glared at her in fury, and began at once to make preparations for turning himself into a large black dog, an accomplishment for which he was justly renowned, and to which the family doctor always attributed the permanent idiocy of Lord Canterville's uncle, the Hon. Thomas Horton. The sound of approaching footsteps, however, made him hesitate in his fell purpose, so he contented himself with becoming faintly phosphorescent, and vanished with a deep churchyard groan, just as the twins had come up to him.

On reaching his room he entirely broke down, and became a prey to the most violent agitation. The vulgarity of the twins, and the gross materialism of Mrs. Otis, were naturally extremely annoying, but what really distressed him most was, that he had been unable to wear the suit of mail. He had hoped that even modern Americans would be thrilled by the sight of a Spectre In

Armour, if for no more sensible reason, at least out of respect for their national poet Longfellow,[13] over whose graceful and attractive poetry he himself had whiled away many a weary hour when the Cantervilles were up in town. Besides, it was his own suit. He had worn it with great success at the Kenilworth tournament, and had been highly complimented on it by no less a person than the Virgin Queen herself.[14] Yet when he had put it on, he had been completely overpowered by the weight of the huge breast-plate and steel casque, and had fallen heavily on the stone pavement, barking both his knees severely, and bruising the knuckles of his right hand.

For some days after this he was extremely ill, and hardly stirred out of his room at all, except to keep the blood-stain in proper repair. However, by taking great care of himself, he recovered, and resolved to make a third attempt to frighten the United States Minister and his family. He selected Friday, the 17th of August, for his appearance, and spent most of that day in looking over his wardrobe, ultimately deciding in favour of a large slouched hat with a red feather, a winding-sheet frilled at the wrists and neck, and a rusty dagger. Towards evening a violent storm of rain came on, and the wind was so high that all the windows and doors in the old house shook and rattled. In fact, it was just such weather as he loved. His plan of action was this. He was to make his way quietly to Washington Otis's room, gibber at him from the foot of the bed, and stab himself three times in the throat to the sound of slow music. He bore Washington a special grudge, being quite aware that it was he who was in the habit of removing the famous Canterville blood-stain, by means of Pinkerton's Paragon Detergent. Having reduced the reckless and foolhardy youth to a condition of abject terror, he was then to proceed to the room occupied by the United States Minister and his wife, and there to place a clammy hand on Mrs. Otis's forehead, while he hissed into her trembling husband's ear the awful secrets of the charnel-house. With regard to little Virginia, he had not quite made up his mind. She had never insulted him in any way, and was pretty and gentle. A few hollow groans from the wardrobe, he thought, would be more than sufficient, or, if that failed to wake her, he might grabble at the counterpane with palsy-twitching fingers. As for the twins, he was quite determined to teach them a lesson. The first thing to be done was, of course, to sit upon their chests, so as to produce the stifling sensation of nightmare. Then, as their beds were quite close to each other, to stand between them in the form of a green, icy-cold corpse, till they became paralysed with fear, and finally, to throw off the winding-sheet, and crawl round the room, with white, bleached bones and one rolling eyeball, in the character of 'Dumb Daniel, or the Suicide's Skeleton,' a *rôle* in which he had on more than one occasion produced a great effect, and which he considered quite equal to his famous part of 'Martin the Maniac, or the Masked Mystery.'

At half-past ten he heard the family going to bed. For some time he was disturbed by wild shrieks of laughter from the twins, who, with the light-hearted gaiety of schoolboys, were evidently amusing themselves before they retired to rest, but at a quarter past eleven all was still, and, as midnight sounded, he sallied forth. The owl beat against the window panes, the raven croaked from the old yew-tree, and the wind wandered moaning round the house like a lost soul; but the Otis family slept unconscious of their doom, and high above the rain and storm he could hear the steady snoring of the Minister for the United States. He stepped stealthily out of the wainscoting, with an evil smile on his cruel, wrinkled mouth, and the moon hid her face in a cloud as he stole past the great oriel window, where his own arms and those of his murdered wife were blazoned in azure and gold. On and on he glided, like an evil shadow, the very darkness seeming to loathe him as he passed. Once he thought he heard something call, and stopped; but it was only the baying of a dog from the Red Farm, and he went on, muttering strange sixteenth-century curses, and ever and anon brandishing the rusty dagger in the midnight air. Finally he reached the corner of the passage that led to luckless Washington's room. For a moment he paused there, the wind blowing his long grey locks about his head, and twisting into grotesque and fantastic folds the nameless horror of the dead man's shroud. Then the clock struck the quarter, and he felt the time was come. He chuckled to himself, and turned the corner; but no sooner had he done so, than, with a piteous wail of terror, he fell back, and hid his blanched face in his long, bony hands. Right in front of him was standing a horrible spectre, motionless as a carven image, and monstrous as a madman's dream! Its head was bald and burnished; its face round, and fat, and white; and hideous laughter seemed to have writhed its features into an eternal grin. From the eyes streamed rays of scarlet light, the mouth was a wide well of fire, and a hideous garment, like to his own, swathed with its silent snows the Titan form.[15] On its breast was a placard with strange writing in antique characters, some scroll of shame it seemed, some record of wild sins, some awful calendar of crime, and, with its right hand, it bore aloft a falchion[16] of gleaming steel.

Never having seen a ghost before, he naturally was terribly frightened, and, after a second hasty glance at the awful phantom, he fled back to his room, tripping up in his long winding sheet as he sped down the corridor, and finally dropping the rusty dagger into the Minister's jack-boots, where it was found in the morning by the butler. Once in the privacy of his own apartment, he flung himself down on a small pallet-bed, and hid his face under the clothes. After a time, however, the brave old Canterville spirit asserted itself, and he determined to go and speak to the other ghost as soon as it was daylight. Accordingly, just as the dawn was touching the hills with silver, he returned towards the spot where he had first laid eyes on the grisly phantom, feeling that, after all, two ghosts were better than one, and that, by the aid of his new friend, he might safely grapple with the twins. On reaching the spot, however, a terrible sight met his gaze. Something had evidently happened to the spectre, for the light had entirely faded from its hollow eyes, the gleaming falchion had fallen from its hand, and it was leaning up against the wall in a strained and uncomfortable attitude. He rushed forward and seized it in his arms, when, to his horror, the head slipped off and rolled on the floor, the body assumed a recumbent posture, and he found himself clasping a white dimity[17] bed-curtain, with a sweeping-brush, a kitchen cleaver, and a hollow turnip lying at his feet! Unable to understand this curious transformation, he clutched the placard with feverish haste, and there, in the grey morning light, he read these fearful words: –

> ## YE OTIS GHOSTE.
>
> *Ye Onlie True and Originale Spook.*
> *Beware of Ye Imitationes.*
> *All others are Counterfeite.*

The whole thing flashed across him. He had been tricked, foiled, and outwitted! The old Canterville look came into his eyes; he ground his toothless gums together; and, raising his withered hands high above his head, swore, according to the picturesque phraseology of the antique school, that when Chanticleer[18] had sounded twice his merry horn, deeds of blood would be wrought, and Murder walk abroad with silent feet.

Hardly had he finished this awful oath when, from the red-tiled roof of a distant homestead, a cock crew. He laughed a long, low, bitter laugh, and waited. Hour after hour he waited, but the cock, for some strange reason, did not crow again. Finally, at half-past seven, the arrival of the housemaids made him give up his fearful vigil, and he stalked back to his room, thinking of his vain oath and baffled purpose. There he consulted several books of ancient chivalry, of which he was exceedingly fond, and found that, on every occasion on which his oath had been used, Chanticleer had always crowed a second time. 'Perdition seize the naughty fowl,' he muttered, 'I have seen the day when, with my stout spear, I would have run him through the gorge, and made him crow for me an 'twere in death!' He then retired to a comfortable lead coffin, and stayed there till evening.

IV

The next day the ghost was very weak and tired. The terrible excitement of the last four weeks was beginning to have its effect. His nerves were completely shattered, and he started at the slightest noise. For five days he kept his room, and at last made up his mind to give up the point of the blood-stain on the library floor. If the Otis family did not want it, they clearly did not deserve it. They were evidently people on a low, material plane of existence, and quite incapable of appreciating the symbolic value of sensuous phenomena. The question of phantasmic apparitions, and the development of astral bodies, was of course quite a different matter, and really not under his control. It was his solemn duty to appear in the corridor once a week, and to gibber from the large oriel window on the first and third Wednesdays in every month, and he did not see how he could honourably escape from his obligations. It is quite true that his life had been very evil, but, upon the other hand, he was most conscientious in all things connected with the supernatural. For the next three Saturdays, accordingly, he traversed the corridor as usual between midnight and three o'clock, taking every possible precaution against being either heard or seen. He removed his boots, trod as lightly as possible on the old worm-eaten boards, wore a large black velvet cloak, and was careful to use the Rising Sun Lubricator for oiling his chains. I am bound to acknowledge that it was with a good deal of difficulty that he brought himself to adopt this last mode of protection. However, one night, while the family were at dinner, he slipped into Mr. Otis's bedroom and carried off the bottle. He felt a little humiliated at first, but afterwards was sensible enough to see that there was a great deal to be said for the invention, and, to a certain degree, it served his purpose. Still, in spite of everything, he was not left unmolested. Strings were continually being stretched across the corridor, over which he tripped in the dark, and on one occasion, while dressed for the part of 'Black Isaac, or the Huntsman of Hogley Woods,' he met with a severe fall, through treading on a butter-slide, which the twins had constructed from the entrance of the Tapestry Chamber to the top of the oak staircase. This last insult so enraged him, that he resolved to make one final effort to assert his dignity and social position, and determined to visit the insolent young Etonians the next night in his celebrated character of 'Reckless Rupert, or the Headless Earl.'

He had not appeared in this disguise for more than seventy years; in fact, not since he had so frightened pretty Lady Barbara Modish by means of it, that she suddenly broke off her engagement with the present Lord Canterville's grandfather, and ran away to Gretna Green with handsome Jack Castleton, declaring that nothing in the world would induce her to marry into a family that allowed such a horrible phantom to walk up and down the terrace at twilight. Poor Jack was afterwards shot in a duel by Lord Canterville on Wandsworth Common, and Lady Barbara died of a broken heart at Tunbridge Wells before the year was out, so, in every way, it had been a great success. It was, however, an extremely difficult 'make-up,' if I may use such a theatrical expression in connection with one of the greatest mysteries of the supernatural, or, to employ a more scientific term, the higher-natural world, and it took him fully three hours to make his preparations. At last everything was ready, and he was very pleased with his appearance. The big leather riding-boots that went with the dress were just a little too large for him, and he could only find one of the two horse-pistols, but, on the whole, he was quite satisfied, and at a quarter past one he glided out of the wainscoting and crept down the corridor. On reaching the room occupied by the twins, which I should mention was called the Blue Bed Chamber, on account of the colour of its hangings, he found the door just ajar. Wishing to make an effective entrance, he flung it wide open, when a heavy jug of water fell right down on him, wetting him to the skin, and just missing his left shoulder by a couple of inches. At the same moment he heard stifled shrieks of laughter proceeding from the four-post bed. The shock to his nervous system was so great that he fled back to his room as hard as he could go, and the next day he was laid up with a severe cold. The only thing that at all consoled him in the whole affair was the fact that he had not brought his head with him, for, had he done so, the consequences might have been very serious.

He now gave up all hope of ever frightening this rude American family, and contented himself, as a rule, with creeping about the passages in list slippers,[19] with a thick red muffler round his throat for fear of draughts, and a small arquebuse,[20] in case he should be attacked by the twins. The final blow he received occurred on the 19th of September. He had gone downstairs to the great entrance-hall, feeling sure that there, at any rate, he would be quite unmolested, and was amusing himself by making satirical remarks on the large Saroni photographs[21] of the United States Minister and his wife, which had now taken the place of the Canterville family pictures. He was simply but neatly clad in a long shroud, spotted with churchyard mould, had tied up his jaw with a strip of yellow linen, and carried a small lantern and a sexton's spade. In fact, he was dressed for the character of 'Jonas the Graveless, or the Corpse-Snatcher of Chertsey Barn,' one of his most remarkable impersonations, and one which the Canter-villes had every reason to remember, as it was the real origin of their quarrel with their neighbour, Lord Rufford. It was about a quarter past two o'clock in the morning, and, as far as he could ascertain, no one was stirring. As he was strolling towards the library, however, to see if there were any traces left of the blood-stain, suddenly there leaped out on him from a dark corner two figures, who waved their arms wildly above their heads, and shrieked out 'BOO!' in his ear.

Seized with a panic, which, under the circumstances, was only natural, he rushed for the staircase, but found Washington Otis waiting for him there with the big garden-syringe; and being thus hemmed in by his enemies on every side, and driven almost to bay, he vanished into the great iron stove, which, fortunately for him, was not lit, and had to make his way home through the flues and chimneys, arriving at his own room in a terrible state of dirt, disorder, and despair.

After this he was not seen again on any nocturnal expedition. The twins lay in wait for him on several occasions, and strewed the passages with nutshells every night to the great annoyance of their parents and the servants, but it was of no avail. It was quite evident that his feelings were so wounded that he would not appear. Mr. Otis consequently resumed his great work on the history of the Democratic Party, on which he had been engaged for some years; Mrs. Otis organised a wonderful clam-bake,[22] which amazed the whole county; the boys took to lacrosse, euchre,[23] poker, and other American national games; and Vir-ginia rode about the lanes on her pony, accompanied by the young Duke of Cheshire, who had come to spend the last week of his holidays at Canterville Chase. It was generally assumed that the ghost had gone away, and, in fact, Mr. Otis wrote a letter to that effect to Lord Canterville, who, in reply, expressed his great pleasure at the news, and sent his best congratulations to the Minister's worthy wife.

The Otises, however, were deceived, for the ghost was still in the house, and though now almost an invalid, was by no means ready to let matters rest, particularly as he heard that among the guests was the young Duke of Cheshire, whose grand-uncle, Lord Francis Stilton, had once bet a hundred guineas[24] with Colonel Carbury that he would play dice with the Canterville ghost, and was found the next morning lying on the floor of the card-room in such a helpless paralytic state, that though he lived on to a great age, he was never able to say anything again but 'Double Sixes.' The story was well known at the time, though, of course, out of respect to the feelings of the two noble families, every attempt was made to hush it up; and a full account of all the circumstances connected with it will be found in the third volume of Lord Tattle's *Recollections of the Prince Regent and his Friends*. The ghost, then, was naturally very anxious to show that he had not lost his influence over the Stiltons, with whom, indeed, he was distantly connected, his own first cousin having been married *en secondes noces*[25] to the Sieur de Bulkeley, from whom, as every one knows, the Dukes of Cheshire are lineally descended. Accordingly, he made arrangements for appearing to Virginia's little lover in his celebrated impersonation of 'The Vampire Monk, or, the Bloodless Benedictine,' a performance so horrible that when old Lady Startup saw it, which she did on one fatal New Year's Eve, in the year 1764, she went off into the most piercing shrieks, which culminated in violent apoplexy, and died in three days, after disinheriting the Cantervilles, who were her nearest relations, and leaving all her money to her London apothecary. At the last moment, however, his terror of the twins prevented his leaving his room, and the little Duke slept in peace under the great feathered canopy in the Royal Bedchamber, and dreamed of Virginia.

V

A few days after this, Virginia and her curly-haired cavalier went out riding on Brockley meadows, where she tore her habit so badly in getting through a hedge, that, on their return home, she made up her mind to go up by the back staircase so as not to be seen. As she was running past the Tapestry Chamber, the door of which happened to be open, she fancied she saw some one inside, and thinking it was her mother's maid, who sometimes used to bring her work there, looked in to ask her to mend her habit. To her immense surprise, however, it was the Canterville Ghost himself! He was sitting by the window, watching the ruined gold of the yellowing trees fly through the air, and the red leaves dancing madly down the long avenue. His head was leaning on his hand, and his whole attitude was one of extreme depression. Indeed, so forlorn, and so much out of repair did he look, that little Virginia, whose first idea had been to run away and lock herself in her room, was filled with pity, and determined to try and comfort him. So light was her footfall, and so deep his melancholy, that he was not aware of her presence till she spoke to him.

'I am so sorry for you,' she said, 'but my brothers are going back to Eton to-morrow, and then, if you behave yourself, no one will annoy you.'

'It is absurd asking me to behave myself,' he answered, looking round in astonishment at the pretty little girl who had ventured to address him, 'quite absurd. I must rattle my chains, and groan through keyholes, and walk about at night, if that is what you mean. It is my only reason for existing.'

'It is no reason at all for existing, and you know you have been very wicked. Mrs. Umney told us, the first day we arrived here, that you had killed your wife.'

'Well, I quite admit it,' said the Ghost petulantly, 'but it was a purely family matter, and concerned no one else.'

'It is very wrong to kill any one,' said Virginia, who at times had a sweet Puritan gravity, caught from some old New England ancestor.

'Oh, I hate the cheap severity of abstract ethics! My wife was very plain, never had my ruffs properly starched, and knew nothing about cookery. Why, there was a buck I had shot in Hogley Woods, a magnificent pricket, and do you know how she had it sent up to table? However, it is no matter now, for it is all over, and I don't think it was very nice of her brothers to starve me to death, though I did kill her.'

'Starve you to death? Oh, Mr. Ghost, I mean Sir Simon, are you hungry? I have a sandwich in my case. Would you like it?'

'No, thank you, I never eat anything now; but it is very kind of you, all the same, and you are much nicer than the rest of your horrid, rude, vulgar, dishonest family.'

'Stop!' cried Virginia, stamping her foot, 'it is you who are rude, and horrid, and vulgar, and as for dishonesty, you know you stole the paints out of my box to try and furbish up that ridiculous blood-stain in the library. First you took all my reds, including the vermilion, and I couldn't do any more sunsets, then you took the emerald-green and the chrome-yellow, and finally I had nothing left but indigo and Chinese white, and could only do moonlight scenes, which are always depressing to look at, and not at all easy to paint. I never told on you, though I was very much annoyed, and it was most ridiculous, the whole thing; for who ever heard of emerald-green blood?'

'Well, really,' said the Ghost, rather meekly, 'what was I to do? It is a very difficult thing to get real blood nowadays, and, as your brother began it all with his Paragon Detergent, I certainly saw no reason why I should not have your paints. As for colour, that is always a matter of taste: the Cantervilles have blue blood, for instance, the very bluest in England; but I know you Americans don't care for things of this kind.'

'You know nothing about it, and the best thing you can do is to emigrate and improve your mind. My father will be only too happy to give you a free passage,[26] and though there is a heavy duty on spirits of every kind, there will be no difficulty about the Custom House, as the officers are all Democrats. Once in New York, you are sure to be a great success. I know lots of people there who would give a hundred thousand dollars to have a grandfather, and much more than that to have a family ghost.'

'I don't think I should like America.'

'I suppose because we have no ruins and no curiosities,' said Virginia satirically.

'No ruins! no curiosities!' answered the Ghost; 'you have your navy and your manners.'[27]

'Good evening; I will go and ask papa to get the twins an extra week's holiday.'

'Please don't go, Miss Virginia,' he cried; 'I am so lonely and so unhappy, and I really don't know what to do. I want to go to sleep and I cannot.'

'That's quite absurd! You have merely to go to bed and blow out the candle. It is very difficult sometimes to keep awake, especially at church, but there is no difficulty at all about sleeping. Why, even babies know how to do that, and they are not very clever.'

'I have not slept for three hundred years,' he said sadly, and Virginia's beautiful blue eyes opened in wonder; 'for three hundred years I have not slept, and I am so tired.'

Virginia grew quite grave, and her little lips trembled like rose-leaves. She came towards him, and kneeling down at his side, looked up into his old withered face.

'Poor, poor Ghost,' she murmured; 'have you no place where you can sleep?'

'Far away beyond the pine woods,' he answered, in a low dreamy voice, 'there is a little garden. There the grass grows long and deep, there are the great white stars of the hemlock flower, there the nightingale[28] sings all night long. All night long he sings, and the cold, crystal moon looks down, and the yew-tree spreads out its giant arms over the sleepers.'

Virginia's eyes grew dim with tears, and she hid her face in her hands.

'You mean the Garden of Death,' she whispered.

'Yes, Death. Death must be so beautiful. To lie in the soft brown earth, with the grasses waving above one's head, and listen to silence. To have no yesterday, and no to-morrow. To forget time, to forgive life, to be at peace. You can help me. You can open for me the portals of Death's house, for Love is always with you, and Love is stronger than Death is.'

Virginia trembled, a cold shudder ran through her, and for a few moments there was silence. She felt as if she was in a terrible dream.

Then the Ghost spoke again, and his voice sounded like the sighing of the wind.

'Have you ever read the old prophecy on the library window?'

'Oh, often,' cried the little girl, looking up; 'I know it quite well. It is painted in curious black letters, and it is difficult to read. There are only six lines:

> When a golden girl can win
> Prayer from out the lips of sin,
> When the barren almond bears,
> And a little child gives away its tears,
> Then shall all the house be still
> And peace come to Canterville.

But I don't know what they mean.'

'They mean,' he said sadly, 'that you must weep with me for my sins, because I have no tears, and pray with me for my soul, because I have no faith, and then, if you have always been sweet, and good, and gentle, the Angel of Death will have mercy on me. You will see fearful shapes in darkness, and wicked voices will whisper in your ear, but they will not harm you, for against the purity of a little child the powers of Hell cannot prevail.'

Virginia made no answer, and the Ghost wrung his hands in wild despair as he looked down at her bowed golden head. Suddenly she stood up, very pale, and with a strange light in her eyes. 'I am not afraid,' she said firmly, 'and I will ask the Angel to have mercy on you.'

He rose from his seat with a faint cry of joy, and taking her hand bent over it with old-fashioned grace and kissed it. His fingers were as cold as ice, and his lips burned like fire, but Virginia did not falter, as he led her across the dusky room. On the faded green tapestry were broidered little huntsmen. They blew their tasselled horns and with their tiny hands waved to her to go back. 'Go back! little Virginia,' they cried, 'go back!' but the Ghost clutched her hand more tightly, and she shut her eyes against them. Horrible animals with lizard tails, and goggle eyes, blinked at her from the carven chimney-piece, and murmured 'Beware! little Virginia, beware! we may never see you again,' but the Ghost glided on more swiftly, and Virginia did not listen. When they reached the end of the room he stopped, and muttered some words she could not understand. She opened her eyes, and saw the wall slowly fading away like a mist, and a great black cavern in front of her. A bitter cold wind swept round them, and she felt something pulling at her dress. 'Quick, quick,' cried the Ghost, 'or it will be too late,' and, in a moment, the wainscoting had closed behind them, and the Tapestry Chamber was empty.

VI

About ten minutes later, the bell rang for tea, and, as Virginia did not come down, Mrs. Otis sent up one of the footmen to tell her. After a little time he returned and said that he could not find Miss Virginia anywhere. As she was in the habit of going out to the garden every evening to get flowers for the dinner-table, Mrs. Otis was not at all alarmed at first, but when six o'clock struck, and Virginia did not appear, she became really agitated, and sent the boys out to look for her, while she herself and Mr. Otis searched every room in the house. At half past six the boys came back and said that they could find no trace of their sister anywhere. They were all now in the greatest state of excitement, and did not know what to do, when Mr. Otis suddenly remembered that, some few days before, he had given a band of gipsies permission to camp in the park. He accordingly at once set off for Blackfell Hollow, where he knew they were, accompanied by his eldest son and two of the farm-servants. The little Duke of Cheshire, who was perfectly frantic with anxiety, begged hard to be allowed to go too, but Mr. Otis would not allow him, as he was afraid there might be a scuffle. On arriving at the spot, however, he found that the gipsies had gone, and it was evident that their departure had been rather sudden, as the fire was still burning, and some plates were lying on the grass. Having sent off Washington and the two men to scour the district, he ran home, and despatched telegrams to all the police inspectors in the county, telling them to look out for a little girl who had been kidnapped by tramps or gipsies. He then ordered his horse to be brought round, and, after insisting on his wife and the three boys sitting down to dinner, rode off down the Ascot road with a groom. He had hardly, however, gone a couple of miles, when he heard somebody galloping after him, and, looking round, saw the little Duke coming up on his pony, with his face very flushed and no hat. 'I'm awfully sorry, Mr. Otis,' gasped out the boy, 'but I can't eat any dinner as long as Virginia is lost. Please, don't be angry with me; if you had let us be engaged last year, there would never have been all this trouble. You won't send me back, will you? I can't go! I won't go!'

The Minister could not help smiling at the handsome young scapegrace, and was a good deal touched at his devotion to Virginia, so leaning down from his horse, he patted him kindly on the shoulders, and said, 'Well, Cecil, if you won't go back I suppose you must come with me, but I must get you a hat at Ascot.'

'Oh, bother my hat! I want Virginia!' cried the little Duke, laughing, and they galloped on to the railway station. There Mr. Otis inquired of the station-master if any one answering to the description of Virginia had been seen on the platform, but could get no news of her. The station-master, however, wired up and down the line, and assured him that a strict watch would be kept for her, and, after having bought a hat for the little Duke from a linen-draper, who was just putting up his shutters, Mr. Otis rode off to Bexley, a village about four miles away, which he was told was a well-known haunt of the gipsies, as there was a large common next to it. Here they roused up the rural policeman, but could get no information from him, and, after riding all over the common, they turned their horses' heads homewards, and reached the Chase about eleven o'clock, dead-tired and almost heart-broken. They found Washington and the twins waiting for them at the gate-house with lanterns, as the avenue was very dark. Not the slightest trace of Virginia had been discovered. The gipsies had been caught on Brockley meadows, but she was not with them, and they had explained their sudden departure by saying that they had mistaken the date of Chorton Fair, and had gone off in a hurry for fear they might be late. Indeed, they had been quite distressed at hearing of Virginia's disappearance, as they were very grateful to Mr. Otis for having allowed them to camp in his park, and four of their number had stayed behind to help in the search. The carp-pond had been dragged, and the whole Chase thoroughly gone over, but without any result. It was evident that, for that night at any rate, Virginia was lost to them; and it was in a state of the deepest depression that Mr. Otis and the boys walked up to the house, the groom following behind with the two horses and the pony. In the hall they found a group of frightened servants, and lying on a sofa in the library was poor Mrs. Otis, almost out of her mind with terror and anxiety, and having her forehead bathed with eau-de-cologne by the old housekeeper. Mr. Otis at once insisted on her having something to eat, and ordered up supper for the whole party. It was a melancholy meal, as hardly any one spoke, and even the twins were awestruck and subdued, as they were very fond of their sister. When they had finished, Mr. Otis, in spite of the entreaties of the little Duke, ordered them all to bed, saying that nothing more could be done that night, and that he would telegraph in the morning to Scotland Yard for some detectives to be sent down immediately. Just as they were passing out of the dining-room, midnight began to boom from the clock tower, and when the last stroke sounded they heard a crash and a sudden shrill cry; a dreadful peal of thunder shook the house, a strain of unearthly music floated through the air, a panel at the top of the staircase flew back with a loud noise, and out on the landing, looking very pale and white, with a little casket in her hand, stepped Virginia. In a moment they had all rushed up to her. Mrs. Otis clasped her passionately in her arms, the Duke smothered her with violent kisses, and the twins executed a wild war-dance round the group.

'Good heavens! child, where have you been?' said Mr. Otis, rather angrily, thinking that she had been playing some foolish trick on them. 'Cecil and I have been riding all over the country looking for you, and your mother has been frightened to death. You must never play these practical jokes any more.'

'Except on the Ghost! except on the Ghost!' shrieked the twins, as they capered about.

'My own darling, thank God you are found; you must never leave my side again,' murmured Mrs. Otis, as she kissed the trembling child, and smoothed the tangled gold of her hair.

'Papa,' said Virginia quietly, 'I have been with the Ghost. He is dead, and you must come and see him. He had been very wicked, but he was really sorry for all that he had done, and he gave me this box of beautiful jewels before he died.'

The whole family gazed at her in mute amazement, but she was quite grave and serious; and, turning round, she led them through the opening in the wainscoting down a narrow secret corridor, Washington following with a lighted candle, which he had caught up from the table. Finally, they came to a great oak door, studded with rusty nails. When Virginia touched it, it swung back on its heavy hinges, and they found themselves in a little low room, with a vaulted ceiling, and one tiny grated window. Imbedded in the wall was a huge iron ring, and chained to it was a gaunt skeleton, that was stretched out at full length on the stone floor, and seemed to be trying to grasp with its long fleshless fingers an old-fashioned trencher and ewer, that were placed just out of its reach. The jug had evidently been once filled with water, as it was covered inside with green mould. There was nothing on the trencher but a pile of dust. Virginia knelt down beside the skeleton, and, folding her little hands together, began to pray silently, while the rest of the party looked on in wonder at the terrible tragedy whose secret was now disclosed to them.

'Hallo!' suddenly exclaimed one of the twins, who had been looking out of the window to try and discover in what wing of the house the room was situated. 'Hallo! the old withered almond-tree has blossomed. I can see the flowers quite plainly in the moonlight.'

'God has forgiven him,' said Virginia gravely, as she rose to her feet, and a beautiful light seemed to illumine her face.

'What an angel you are!' cried the young Duke, and he put his arm round her neck, and kissed her.

VII

Four days after these curious incidents a funeral started from Canterville Chase at about eleven o'clock at night. The hearse was drawn by eight black horses, each of which carried on its head a great tuft of nodding ostrich-plumes, and the leaden coffin was covered by a rich purple pall, on which was embroidered in gold the Canterville coat-of-arms. By the side of the hearse and the coaches walked the servants with lighted torches, and the whole procession was wonderfully impressive. Lord Canterville was the chief mourner, having come up specially from Wales to attend the funeral, and sat in the first carriage along with little Virginia. Then came the United States Minister and his wife, then Washington and the three boys, and in the last carriage was Mrs. Umney. It was generally felt that, as she had been frightened by the ghost for more than fifty years of her life, she had a right to see the last of him. A deep grave had been dug in the corner of the churchyard, just under the old yew-tree, and the service was read in the most impressive manner by the Rev. Augustus Dampier. When the ceremony was over, the servants, according to an old custom observed in the Canterville family, extinguished their torches, and, as the coffin was being lowered into the grave, Virginia stepped forward, and laid on it a large cross made of white and pink almond-blossoms. As she did so, the moon came out from behind a cloud, and flooded with its silent silver the little churchyard, and from a distant copse a nightingale began to sing. She thought of the ghost's description of the Garden of Death, her eyes became dim with tears, and she hardly spoke a word during the drive home.

The next morning, before Lord Canterville went up to town, Mr. Otis had an interview with him on the subject of the jewels the ghost had given to Virginia. They were perfectly magnificent, especially a certain ruby necklace with old Venetian setting, which was really a superb specimen of sixteenth-century work, and their value was so great that Mr. Otis felt considerable scruples about allowing his daughter to accept them.

'My lord,' he said, 'I know that in this country mortmain[29] is held to apply to trinkets as well as to land, and it is quite clear to me that these jewels are, or should be, heirlooms in your family. I must beg you, accordingly, to take them to London with you, and to regard them simply as a portion of your property which has been restored to you under certain strange conditions. As for my daughter, she is merely a child, and has as yet, I am glad to say, but little interest in such appurtenances of idle luxury. I am also informed by Mrs. Otis, who, I may say, is no mean authority upon Art – having had the privilege of spending several winters in Boston when she was a girl – that these gems are of great monetary worth, and if offered for sale would fetch a tall price. Under these circumstances, Lord Canterville, I feel sure that you will recognise how impossible it would be for me to allow them to remain in the possession of any member of my family; and, indeed, all such vain gauds and toys, however suitable or necessary to the dignity of the British aristocracy, would be completely out of place among those who have been brought up on the severe, and I believe immortal, principles of Republican simplicity. Perhaps I should mention that Virginia is very anxious that you should allow her to retain the box, as a memento of your unfortunate but misguided ancestor. As it is extremely old, and consequently a good deal out of repair, you may perhaps think fit to comply with her request. For my own part, I confess I am a good deal surprised to find a child of mine expressing sympathy with mediaevalism in any form, and can only account for it by the fact that Virginia was born in one of your London suburbs shortly after Mrs. Otis had returned from a trip to Athens.'

Lord Canterville listened very gravely to the worthy Minister's speech, pulling his grey moustache now and then to hide an involuntary smile, and when Mr. Otis had ended, he shook him cordially by the hand, and said, 'My dear sir, your charming little daughter rendered my unlucky ancestor, Sir Simon, a very important service, and I and my family are much indebted to her for her marvellous courage and pluck. The jewels are clearly hers, and, egad, I believe that if I were heartless enough to take them from her, the wicked old fellow would be out of his grave in a fortnight, leading me the devil of a life. As for their being heirlooms, nothing is an heirloom that is not so mentioned in a will or legal document, and the existence of these jewels has been quite unknown. I assure you I have no more claim on them than your butler, and when Miss Virginia grows up I daresay she will be pleased to have pretty things to wear. Besides, you forget, Mr. Otis, that you took the furniture and the ghost at a valuation, and anything that belonged to the ghost passed at once into your possession, as, whatever activity Sir Simon may have shown in the corridor at night, in point of law he was really dead, and you acquired his property by purchase.'

Mr. Otis was a good deal distressed at Lord Canterville's refusal, and begged him to reconsider his decision, but the good-natured peer was quite firm, and finally induced the Minister to allow his daughter to retain the present the ghost had given her, and when, in the spring of 1890, the young Duchess of Cheshire was presented at the Queen's first drawing-room on the occasion of her marriage, her jewels were the universal theme of admiration. For Virginia received the coronet, which is the reward of all good little American girls,[30] and was married to her boy-lover as soon as he came of age. They were both so charming, and they loved each other so much, that every one was delighted at the match, except the old Marchioness of Dumbleton, who had tried to catch the Duke for one of her seven unmarried daughters, and had given no less than three expensive dinner-parties for that purpose, and, strange to say, Mr. Otis himself. Mr. Otis was extremely fond of the young Duke personally, but, theoretically, he objected to titles, and, to use his own words, 'was not without apprehension lest, amid the enervating influences of a pleasure-loving aristocracy, the true principles of Republican simplicity should be forgotten.' His objections, however, were completely overruled, and I believe that when he walked up the aisle of St. George's, Hanover Square, with his daughter leaning on his arm, there was not a prouder man in the whole length and breadth of England.

The Duke and Duchess, after the honeymoon was over, went down to Canterville Chase, and on the day after their arrival they walked over in the afternoon to the lonely churchyard by the pine-woods. There had been a great deal of difficulty at first about the inscription on Sir Simon's tombstone, but finally it had been decided to engrave on it simply the initials of the old gentleman's name, and the verse from the library window. The Duchess had brought with her some lovely roses, which she strewed upon the grave, and after they had stood by it for some time they strolled into the ruined chancel of the old abbey. There the Duchess sat down on a fallen pillar, while her husband lay at her feet smoking a cigarette and looking up at her beautiful eyes. Suddenly he threw his cigarette away, took hold of her hand, and said to her, 'Virginia, a wife should have no secrets from her husband.'

'Dear Cecil! I have no secrets from you.'

'Yes, you have,' he answered, smiling, 'you have never told me what happened to you when you were locked up with the ghost.'

'I have never told any one, Cecil,' said Virginia gravely.

'I know that, but you might tell me.'

'Please don't ask me, Cecil, I cannot tell you. Poor Sir Simon! I owe him a great deal. Yes, don't laugh, Cecil, I really do. He made me see what Life is, and what Death signifies, and why Love is stronger than both.'

The Duke rose and kissed his wife lovingly.

'You can have your secret as long as I have your heart,' he murmured.

'You have always had that, Cecil.'

'And you will tell our children some day, won't you?'

Virginia blushed.

The Model Millionaire

A note of admiration

Unless one is wealthy there is no use in being a charming fellow. Romance is the privilege of the rich, not the profession of the unemployed. The poor should be practical and prosaic. It is better to have a permanent income than to be fascinating. These are the great truths of modern life which Hughie Erskine never realised. Poor Hughie! Intellectually, we must admit, he was not of much importance. He never said a brilliant or even an ill-natured thing in his life. But then he was wonderfully good-looking, with his crisp brown hair, his clear-cut profile, and his grey eyes. He was as popular with men as he was with women, and he had every accomplishment except that of making money. His father had bequeathed him his cavalry sword, and a *History of the Peninsular War* in fifteen volumes. Hughie hung the first over his looking-glass, put the second on a shelf between Ruff's *Guide* and Bailey's *Magazine*,[1] and lived on two hundred a year that an old aunt allowed him. He had tried everything. He had gone on the Stock Exchange for six months; but what was a butterfly to do among bulls and bears?[2] He had been a tea-merchant for a little longer, but had soon tired of pekoe and souchong.[3] Then he had tried selling dry sherry. That did not answer; the sherry was a little too dry. Ultimately he became nothing, a delightful, ineffectual young man with a perfect profile and no profession.[4]

To make matters worse, he was in love. The girl he loved was Laura Merton, the daughter of a retired Colonel who had lost his temper and his digestion in India, and had never found either of them again. Laura adored him, and he was ready to kiss her shoe-strings. They were the handsomest couple in London, and had not a penny-piece between them. The Colonel was very fond of Hughie, but would not hear of any engagement.

'Come to me, my boy, when you have got ten thousand pounds of your own, and we will see about it,' he used to say; and Hughie looked very glum on those days, and had to go to Laura for consolation.

One morning, as he was on his way to Holland Park, where the Mertons lived, he dropped in to see a great friend of his, Alan Trevor. Trevor was a painter. Indeed, few people escape that nowadays. But he was also an artist, and artists are rather rare. Personally he was a strange rough fellow, with a freckled face and a red ragged beard. However, when he took up the brush he was a real master, and his pictures were eagerly sought after. He had been very much attracted by Hughie at first, it must be acknowledged, entirely on account of his personal charm. 'The only people a painter should know,' he used to say, 'are people who are *bête* and beautiful, people who are an artistic pleasure to look at and an intellectual repose to talk to. Men who are dandies and women who are darlings rule the world,[5] at least they should do so.' However, after he got to know Hughie better, he liked him quite as much for his bright buoyant spirits and his generous reckless nature, and had given him the permanent *entrée* to his studio.

When Hughie came in he found Trevor putting the finishing touches to a wonderful life-size picture of a beggar-man. The beggar himself was standing on a raised platform in a corner of the studio. He was a wizened old man, with a face like wrinkled parchment, and a most piteous expression. Over his shoulders was flung a coarse brown cloak, all tears and tatters; his thick boots were patched and cobbled, and with one hand he leant on a rough stick, while with the other he held out his battered hat for alms.

'What an amazing model!' whispered Hughie, as he shook hands with his friend.

'An amazing model?' shouted Trevor at the top of his voice; 'I should think so! Such beggars as he are not to be met with every day. A *trouvaille, mon cher*;[6] a living Velasquez! My stars! what an etching Rembrandt would have made of him!'

'Poor old chap!' said Hughie, 'how miserable he looks! But I suppose, to you painters, his face is his fortune?'

'Certainly,' replied Trevor, 'you don't want a beggar to look happy, do you?'

'How much does a model get for sitting?' asked Hughie, as he found himself a comfortable seat on a divan.

'A shilling an hour.'

'And how much do you get for your picture, Alan?'

'Oh, for this I get two thousand!'

'Pounds?'

'Guineas. Painters, poets, and physicians always get guineas.'

'Well, I think the model should have a percentage,' cried Hughie, laughing; 'they work quite as hard as you do.'

'Nonsense, nonsense! Why, look at the trouble of laying on the paint alone, and standing all day long at one's easel! It's all very well, Hughie, for you to talk, but I assure you that there are moments when Art almost attains to the dignity of manual labour. But you mustn't chatter; I'm very busy. Smoke a cigarette, and keep quiet.'

After some time the servant came in, and told Trevor that the frame-maker wanted to speak to him.

'Don't run away, Hughie,' he said, as he went out, 'I will be back in a moment.'

The old beggar-man took advantage of Trevor's absence to rest for a moment on a wooden bench that was behind him. He looked so forlorn and wretched that Hughie could not help pitying him, and felt in his pockets to see what money he had. All he could find was a sovereign and some coppers. 'Poor old fellow,' he thought to himself, 'he wants it more than I do, but it means no hansoms for a fortnight;' and he walked across the studio and slipped the sovereign into the beggar's hand.

The old man started, and a faint smile flitted across his withered lips. 'Thank you, sir,' he said, 'thank you.'

Then Trevor arrived, and Hughie took his leave, blushing a little at what he had done. He spent the day with Laura, got a charming scolding for his extravagance, and had to walk home.

That night he strolled into the Palette Club about eleven o'clock, and found Trevor sitting by himself in the smoking-room drinking hock and seltzer.[7]

'Well, Alan, did you get the picture finished all right?' he said, as he lit his cigarette.

'Finished and framed, my boy!' answered Trevor; 'and, by-the-bye, you have made a conquest. That old model you saw is quite devoted to you. I had to tell him all about you – who you are, where you live, what your income is, what prospects you have –'

'My dear Alan,' cried Hughie, 'I shall probably find him waiting for me when I go home. But of course you are only joking. Poor old wretch! I wish I could do something for him. I think it is dreadful that any one should be so miserable. I have got heaps of old clothes at home – do you think he would care for any of them? Why, his rags were falling to bits.'

'But he looks splendid in them,' said Trevor. 'I wouldn't paint him in a frock-coat for anything. What you call rags I call romance. What seems poverty to you is picturesqueness to me. However, I'll tell him of your offer.'

'Alan,' said Hughie seriously, 'you painters are a heartless lot.'

'An artist's heart is his head,' replied Trevor; 'and besides, our business is to realise the world as we see it, not to reform it as we know it. *A chacun son métier.*[8] And now tell me how Laura is. The old model was quite interested in her.'

'You don't mean to say you talked to him about her?' said Hughie.

'Certainly I did. He knows all about the relentless colonel, the lovely Laura, and the £10,000.'

'You told that old beggar all my private affairs?' cried Hughie, looking very red and angry.

'My dear boy,' said Trevor, smiling, 'that old beggar, as you call him, is one of the richest men in Europe. He could buy all London to-morrow without overdrawing his account. He has a house in every capital, dines off gold plate, and can prevent Russia going to war when he chooses.'

'What on earth do you mean?' exclaimed Hughie.

'What I say,' said Trevor. 'The old man you saw to-day in the studio was Baron Hausberg. He is a great friend of mine, buys all my pictures and that sort of thing, and gave me a commission a month ago to paint him as a beggar. *Que voulez-vous? La fantaisie d'un millionnaire!*[9] And I must say he made a magnificent figure in his rags, or perhaps I should say in my rags; they are an old suit I got in Spain.'

'Baron Hausberg!' cried Hughie. 'Good heavens! I gave him a sovereign!' and he sank into an armchair the picture of dismay.

'Gave him a sovereign!' shouted Trevor, and he burst into a roar of laughter. 'My dear boy, you'll never see it again. *Son affaire c'est l'argent des autres.*'[10]

'I think you might have told me, Alan,' said Hughie sulkily, 'and not have let me make such a fool of myself.'

'Well, to begin with, Hughie,' said Trevor, 'it never entered my mind that you went about distributing alms in that reckless way. I can understand your kissing a pretty model, but your giving a sovereign to an ugly one – by Jove, no! Besides, the fact is that I really was not at home to-day to any one; and when you came in I didn't know whether Hausberg would like his name mentioned. You know he wasn't in full dress.'

'What a duffer he must think me!' said Hughie.

'Not at all. He was in the highest spirits after you left; kept chuckling to himself and rubbing his old wrinkled hands together. I couldn't make out why he was so interested to know all about you; but I see it all now. He'll invest your sovereign for you, Hughie, pay you the interest every six months, and have a capital story to tell after dinner.'

'I am an unlucky devil,' growled Hughie. 'The best thing I can do is to go to bed; and, my dear Alan, you mustn't tell any one. I shouldn't dare show my face in the Row.'[11]

'Nonsense! It reflects the highest credit on your philanthropic spirit, Hughie. And don't run away. Have another cigarette, and you can talk about Laura as much as you like.'

However, Hughie wouldn't stop, but walked home, feeling very unhappy, and leaving Alan Trevor in fits of laughter.

The next morning, as he was at breakfast, the servant brought him up a card on which was written, 'Monsieur Gustave Naudin, *de la part de*[12] M. le Baron Hausberg.' 'I suppose he has come for an apology,' said Hughie to himself; and he told the servant to show the visitor up.

An old gentleman with gold spectacles and grey hair came into the room, and said, in a slight French accent, 'Have I the honour of addressing Monsieur Erskine?'

Hughie bowed.

'I have come from Baron Hausberg,' he continued. 'The Baron —'

'I beg, sir, that you will offer him my sincerest apologies,' stammered Hughie.

'The Baron,' said the old gentleman with a smile, 'has commissioned me to bring you this letter;' and he extended a sealed envelope.

On the outside was written, 'A wedding present to Hugh Erskine and Laura Merton, from an old beggar,' and inside was a cheque for £10,000.

When they were married Alan Trevor was the best-man, and the Baron made a speech at the wedding-breakfast.

'Millionaire models,' remarked Alan, 'are rare enough; but, by Jove, model millionaires are rarer still!'

Poems in Prose

The Artist

One evening there came into his soul the desire to fashion an image of *The Pleasure that abideth for a Moment*. And he went forth into the world to look for bronze. For he could only think in bronze.

But all the bronze of the whole world had disappeared, nor anywhere in the whole world was there any bronze to be found, save only the bronze of the image of *The Sorrow that endureth for Ever*.

Now this image he had himself, and with his own hands, fashioned, and had set it on the tomb of the one thing he had loved in life. On the tomb of the dead thing he had most loved had he set this image of his own fashioning, that it might serve as a sign of the love of man that dieth not, and a symbol of the sorrow of man that endureth for ever. And in the whole world there was no other bronze save the bronze of this image.

And he took the image he had fashioned, and set it in a great furnace, and gave it to the fire.

And out of the bronze of the image of *The Sorrow that endureth for Ever* he fashioned an image of *The Pleasure that abideth for a Moment*.

The Doer of Good

It was night-time and He was alone.

And He saw afar-off the walls of a round city and went towards the city.

And when He came near He heard within the city the tread of the feet of joy, and the laughter of the mouth of gladness and the loud noise of many lutes. And He knocked at the gate and certain of the gate-keepers opened to Him.

And He beheld a house that was of marble and had fair pillars of marble before it. The pillars were hung with garlands, and within and without there were torches of cedar. And He entered the house.

And when He had passed through the hall of chalcedony and the hall of jasper, and reached the long hall of feasting, He saw lying on a couch of sea-purple one whose hair was crowned with red roses and whose lips were red with wine.

And He went behind him and touched him on the shoulder and said to him, 'Why do you live like this?'

And the young man turned round and recognised Him, and made answer and said, 'But I was a leper once, and you healed me. How else should I live?'

And He passed out of the house and went again into the street.

And after a little while He saw one whose face and raiment were painted and whose feet were shod with pearls. And behind her came, slowly as a hunter, a young man who wore a cloak of two colours. Now the face of the woman was as the fair face of an idol, and the eyes of the young man were bright with lust.

And He followed swiftly and touched the hand of the young man and said to him, 'Why do you look at this woman and in such wise?'

And the young man turned round and recognised Him and said, 'But I was blind once, and you gave me sight. At what else should I look?'

And He ran forward and touched the painted raiment of the woman and said to her, 'Is there no other way in which to walk save the way of sin?'

And the woman turned round and recognised Him, and laughed and said, 'But you forgave me my sins, and the way is a pleasant way.'

And He passed out of the city.

And when He had passed out of the city He saw seated by the roadside a young man who was weeping.

And He went towards him and touched the long locks of his hair and said to him, 'Why are you weeping?'

And the young man looked up and recognised Him and made answer, 'But I was dead once and you raised me from the dead. What else should I do but weep?'

The Disciple

When Narcissus[1] died the pool of his pleasure changed from a cup of sweet waters into a cup of salt tears, and the Oreads[2] came weeping through the woodland that they might sing to the pool and give it comfort.

And when they saw that the pool had changed from a cup of sweet waters into a cup of salt tears, they loosened the green tresses of their hair and cried to the pool and said, 'We do not wonder that you should mourn in this manner for Narcissus, so beautiful was he.'

'But was Narcissus beautiful?' said the pool.

'Who should know that better than you?' answered the Oreads. 'Us did he ever pass by, but you he sought for, and would lie on your banks and look down at you, and in the mirror of your waters he would mirror his own beauty.'

And the pool answered, 'But I loved Narcissus because, as he lay on my banks and looked down at me, in the mirror of his eyes I saw ever my own beauty mirrored.'

The Master

Now when the darkness came over the earth Joseph of Arimathea,[3] having lighted a torch of pinewood, passed down from the hill into the valley. For he had business in his own home.

And kneeling on the flint stones of the Valley of Desolation he saw a young man who was naked and weeping. His hair was the colour of honey, and his body was as a white flower, but he had wounded his body with thorns and on his hair had he set ashes as a crown.

And he who had great possessions said to the young man who was naked and weeping, 'I do not wonder that your sorrow is so great, for surely He was a just man.'

And the young man answered, 'It is not for Him that I am weeping, but for myself. I too have changed water into wine, and I have healed the leper and given sight to the blind. I have walked upon the waters, and from the dwellers in the tombs I have cast out devils. I have fed the hungry in the desert where there was no food, and I have raised the dead from their narrow houses, and at my bidding, and before a great multitude of people, a barren fig-tree withered away. All things that this man has done I have done also. And yet they have not crucified me.'

The House of Judgment

And there was silence in the House of Judgment, and the Man came naked before God.

And God opened the Book of the Life of the Man.

And God said to the Man, 'Thy life hath been evil, and thou hast shown cruelty to those who were in need of succour, and to those who lacked help thou hast been bitter and hard of heart. The poor called to thee and thou didst not hearken, and thine ears were closed to the cry of My afflicted. The inheritance of the fatherless thou didst take unto thyself, and thou didst send the foxes into the vineyard of thy neighbour's field. Thou didst take the bread of the children and give it to the dogs to eat, and My lepers who lived in the marshes, and were at peace and praised Me, thou didst drive forth on to the highways, and on Mine earth out of which I made thee thou didst spill innocent blood.'

And the Man made answer and said, 'Even so did I.'

And again God opened the Book of the Life of the Man.

And God said to the Man, 'Thy life hath been evil, and the Beauty I have shown thou hast sought for, and the Good I have hidden thou didst pass by. The walls of thy chamber were painted with images, and from the bed of thine abominations thou didst rise up to the sound of flutes. Thou didst build seven altars to the sins I have suffered, and didst eat of the thing that may not be eaten, and the purple of thy raiment was broidered with the three signs of shame. Thine idols were neither of gold nor of silver that endure, but of flesh that dieth. Thou didst stain their hair with perfumes and put pomegranates in their hands. Thou didst stain their feet with saffron and spread carpets before them. With antimony thou didst stain their eyelids and their bodies thou didst smear with myrrh. Thou didst bow thyself to the ground before them, and the thrones of thine idols were set in the sun. Thou didst show to the sun thy shame and to the moon thy madness.'

And the Man made answer and said, 'Even so did I.'

And a third time God opened the Book of the Life of the Man.

And God said to the Man, 'Evil hath been thy life, and with evil didst thou requite good, and with wrongdoing kindness. The hands that fed thee thou didst wound, and the breasts that gave thee suck thou didst despise. He who came to thee with water went away thirsting, and the outlawed men who hid thee in their tents at night thou didst betray before dawn. Thine enemy who spared thee thou didst snare in an ambush, and the friend who walked with thee thou didst sell for a price, and to those who brought thee Love thou didst ever give Lust in thy turn.'

And the Man made answer and said, 'Even so did I.'

And God closed the Book of the Life of the Man, and said, 'Surely I will send thee into Hell. Even into Hell will I send thee.'

And the Man cried out, 'Thou canst not.'

And God said to the Man, 'Wherefore can I not send thee to Hell, and for what reason?'

'Because in Hell have I always lived,' answered the Man.

And there was silence in the House of Judgment.

And after a space God spake, and said to the Man, 'Seeing that I may not send thee into Hell, surely I will send thee unto Heaven. Even unto Heaven will I send thee.'

And the Man cried out, 'Thou canst not.'

And God said to the Man, 'Wherefore can I not send thee unto Heaven, and for what reason?'

'Because never, and in no place, have I been able to imagine it,' answered the Man.

And there was silence in the House of Judgment.

The Teacher of Wisdom

From his childhood he had been as one filled with the perfect knowledge of God, and even while he was yet but a lad many of the saints, as well as certain holy women who dwelt in the free city of his birth, had been stirred to much wonder by the grave wisdom of his answers.

And when his parents had given him the robe and the ring of manhood he kissed them, and left them and went out into the world, that he might speak to the world about God. For there were at that time many in the world who either knew not God at all, or had but an incomplete knowledge of Him, or worshipped the false gods who dwell in groves and have no care of their worshippers.

And he set his face to the sun and journeyed, walking without sandals, as he had seen the saints walk, and carrying at his girdle a leathern wallet and a little water-bottle of burnt clay.

And as he walked along the highway he was full of the joy that comes from the perfect knowledge of God, and he sang praises unto God without ceasing; and after a time he reached a strange land in which there were many cities.

And he passed through eleven cities. And some of these cities were in valleys, and others were by the banks of great rivers, and others were set on hills. And in each city he found a disciple who loved him and followed him, and a great multitude also of people followed him from each city, and the knowledge of God spread in the whole land, and many of the rulers were converted, and the priests of the temples in which there were idols found that half of their gain was gone, and when they beat upon their drums at noon none, or but a few, came with peacocks and with offerings of flesh as had been the custom of the land before his coming.

Yet the more the people followed him, and the greater the number of his disciples, the greater became his sorrow. And he knew not why his sorrow was so great. For he spake ever about God, and out of the fulness of that perfect knowledge of God which God had Himself given to him.

And one evening he passed out of the eleventh city, which was a city of Armenia, and his disciples and a great crowd of people followed after him; and he went up on to a mountain and sat down on a rock that was on the mountain, and his disciples stood round him, and the multitude knelt in the valley.

And he bowed his head on his hands and wept, and said to his Soul, 'Why is it that I am full of sorrow and fear, and that each of my disciples is as an enemy that walks in the noonday?'

And his Soul answered him and said, 'God filled thee with the perfect knowledge of Himself, and thou hast given this knowledge away to others. The pearl of great price thou hast divided, and the vesture without seam thou hast parted asunder. He who giveth away wisdom robbeth himself. He is as one who giveth his treasure to a robber. Is not God wiser than thou art? Who art thou to give away the secret that God hath told thee? I was rich once, and thou hast made me poor. Once I saw God, and now thou hast hidden Him from me.'

And he wept again, for he knew that his Soul spake truth to him, and that he had given to others the perfect knowledge of God, and that he was as one clinging to the skirts of God, and that his faith was leaving him by reason of the number of those who believed in him.

And he said to himself, 'I will talk no more about God. He who giveth away wisdom robbeth himself.'

And after the space of some hours his disciples came near him and bowed themselves to the ground and said, 'Master, talk to us about God, for thou hast the perfect knowledge of God, and no man save thee hath this knowledge.'

And he answered them and said, 'I will talk to you about all other things that are in heaven and on earth, but about God I will not talk to you. Neither now, nor at any time, will I talk to you about God.'

And they were wroth with him and said to him, 'Thou hast led us into the desert that we might hearken to thee. Wilt thou send us away hungry, and the great multitude that thou hast made to follow thee?'

And he answered them and said, 'I will not talk to you about God.'

And the multitude murmured against him and said to him, 'Thou hast led us into the desert, and hast given us no food to eat. Talk to us about God and it will suffice us.'

But he answered them not a word. For he knew that if he spake to them about God he would give away his treasure.

And his disciples went away sadly, and the multitude of people returned to their own homes. And many died on the way.

And when he was alone he rose up and set his face to the moon, and journeyed for seven moons, speaking to no man nor making any answer. And when the seventh moon had waned he reached that desert which is the desert of the Great River. And having found a cavern in which a Centaur[4] had once dwelt, he took it for his place of dwelling, and made himself a mat of reeds on which to lie, and became a hermit. And every hour the Hermit praised God that He had suffered him to keep some knowledge of Him and of His wonderful greatness.

Now, one evening, as the Hermit was seated before the cavern in which he had made his place of dwelling, he beheld a young man of evil and beautiful face who passed by in mean apparel and with empty hands. Every evening with empty hands the young man passed by, and every morning he returned with his hands full of purple and pearls. For he was a Robber and robbed the caravans of the merchants.

And the Hermit looked at him and pitied him. But he spake not a word. For he knew that he who speaks a word loses his faith.

And one morning, as the young man returned with his hands full of purple and pearls, he stopped and frowned and stamped his foot upon the sand, and said to the Hermit: 'Why do you look at me ever in this manner as I pass by? What is it that I see in your eyes? For no man has looked at me before in this manner. And the thing is a thorn and a trouble to me.'

And the Hermit answered him and said, 'What you see in my eyes is pity. Pity is what looks out at you from my eyes.'

And the young man laughed with scorn, and cried to the Hermit in a bitter voice, and said to him, 'I have purple and pearls in my hands, and you have but a mat of reeds on which to lie. What pity should you have for me? And for what reason have you this pity?'

'I have pity for you,' said the Hermit, 'because you have no knowledge of God.'

'Is this knowledge of God a precious thing?' asked the young man, and he came close to the mouth of the cavern.

'It is more precious than all the purple and the pearls of the world,' answered the Hermit.

'And have you got it?' said the young Robber, and he came closer still.

'Once, indeed,' answered the Hermit, 'I possessed the perfect knowledge of God. But in my foolishness I parted with it, and divided it amongst others. Yet even now is such knowledge as remains to me more precious than purple or pearls.'

And when the young Robber heard this he threw away the purple and the pearls that he was bearing in his hands, and drawing a sharp sword of curved steel he said to the Hermit, 'Give me, forthwith, this knowledge of God that you possess, or I will surely slay you. Wherefore should I not slay him who has a treasure greater than my treasure?'

And the Hermit spread out his arms and said, 'Were it not better for me to go unto the uttermost courts of God and praise Him, than to live in the world and have no knowledge of Him? Slay me if that be your desire. But I will not give away my knowledge of God.'

And the young Robber knelt down and besought him, but the Hermit would not talk to him about God, nor give him his Treasure, and the young Robber rose up and said to the Hermit, 'Be it as you will. As for myself, I will go to the City of the Seven Sins, that is but three days' journey from this place, and for my purple they will give me pleasure, and for my pearls they will sell me joy.' And he took up the purple and the pearls and went swiftly away.

And the Hermit cried out and followed him and besought him. For the space of three days he followed the young Robber on the road and entreated him to return, nor to enter into the City of the Seven Sins.

And ever and anon the young Robber looked back at the Hermit and called to him, and said, 'Will you give me this knowledge of God which is more precious than purple and pearls? If you will give me that, I will not enter the city.'

And ever did the Hermit answer, 'All things that I have I will give thee, save that one thing only. For that thing it is not lawful for me to give away.'

And in the twilight of the third day they came nigh to the great scarlet gates of the City of the Seven Sins. And from the city there came the sound of much laughter.

And the young Robber laughed in answer, and sought to knock at the gate. And as he did so the Hermit ran forward and caught him by the skirts of his raiment, and said to him: 'Stretch forth your hands, and set your arms around my neck, and put your ear close to my lips, and I will give you what remains to me of the knowledge of God.' And the young Robber stopped.

And when the Hermit had given away his knowledge of God, he fell upon the ground and wept, and a great darkness hid from him the city and the young Robber, so that he saw them no more.

And as he lay there weeping he was aware of One who was standing beside him; and He who was standing beside him had feet of brass and hair like fine wool. And He raised the Hermit up, and said to him: 'Before this time thou hadst the perfect knowledge of God. Now thou shalt have the perfect love of God. Wherefore art thou weeping?' And He kissed him.

Appendix

As I indicated in 'A Note on the Texts', this appendix prints one relatively unknown text, a manuscript fragment of a poem in prose.

'Elder-tree' (fragment)

Elder-tree, there stands a neglected grave. The grass grows thick and rank around it, and the weeds have covered it all over. No bird ever sings there, and even the sunbeams seem to avoid the spot. Yet in that lonely grave the most beautiful woman in the world lies asleep. Her throat is like a reed of ivory, and her mouth is like a ripe pomegranate. Like threads of fine gold are the threads of her flowing hair, and the turquoise is not so blue as her blue eyes.

Notes

Wilde extensively re-worked a group of themes throughout his creative life, and his *oeuvre* draws heavily upon largely unacknowledged self-quotation. In the following notes I have tried to indicate the extent of this self-borrowing. Occasionally Wilde's spelling of names in his texts is not entirely accurate. I have not made any corrections to the text, but in the explanatory notes the correct (or modernized) forms have been used; so, for example, the Venetian hotel in 'Lord Arthur Savile's Crime' which in the text is spelt 'Danielli' is silently corrected to 'Danieli' in the appropriate explanatory note.

References to Wilde's other works are abbreviated as follows:
The Picture of Dorian Gray, ed. Isobel Murray (Oxford, 1974): *DG*.
Lady Windermere's Fan, ed. Ian Small (London, 1980): *LWF*.
A Woman of No Importance, ed. Ian Small (London, 1993): *WNI*.
An Ideal Husband, ed. Russell Jackson (London, 1980): *IH*.
The Importance of Being Earnest, ed. Russell Jackson (London, 1993): *IBE*.

Other abbreviations:
Horst Schroeder, *Annotations to Oscar Wilde, 'The Portrait of Mr. W. H.'* (Braunschweig, 1986): *Annotations*.
Oxford English Dictionary: *OED*.

The Happy Prince and Other Tales

1 *Dedication* (p. 1) Carlos Blacker (1859–1928) was an expatriate Englishman who lived mainly abroad, particularly in Paris, and who first met Wilde on his trips there.

NOTES

THE HAPPY PRINCE

1 *Charity Children* (p. 3) The pupils of Charity Schools, institutions supported by endowments and bequests for the education of children of the poor.

2 *Sans-Souci* (p. 5) I.e., without care. 'Sans-Souci' was the name given to King Frederick the Great's Palace in Potsdam.

3 *Second Cataract* (p. 7) This and other details of the journey of the swallow's friends (such as the reference to the Temple of Baalbec, below) are taken from Émile Gautier's poem 'Ce que disent les hirondelles' in *Émauxs et Camées*.

4 *Memnon* (p. 7) The reference is to the statue of Memnon at Thebes and the legend that it emits musical notes when struck by the rays of the sun.

5 *beryls* (p. 7) Transparent precious pale-green stones.

6 *King of the Mountains of the Moon* (p. 9) The Mountains of the Moon are a range of mountains in what is now Uganda.

7 *As he is no longer beautiful, he is no longer useful* (p. 11) A comment that pointedly refers to a contemporary debate about art and utility. The immediate target is the socialist critic William Morris, who held that the Victorian opposition between utility and beauty was misplaced and that a notion of beauty should embrace utility. Wilde's view of the matter was more succinctly expressed in the 'Preface' to *DG*: 'All art is quite useless.'

THE NIGHTINGALE AND THE ROSE

1 *she is all style, without any sincerity* (p. 15) A contrast which was to find frequent expression in later works; cf. Gwendolen's comment in *IBE*: 'In matters of grave importance, style, not sincerity, is the vital thing' (III, 28–9).

2 *Echo* (p. 16) In classical mythology a mountain nymph who possessed only the power to repeat the last words uttered by someone else; see also note 20 to p. 113.

THE DEVOTED FRIEND

1 *Gilly-flowers ... the Flower-de-luce* (p. 25) Wilde's list of flowers has been chosen more for its verbal picturesqueness than horticultural accuracy. Gilly-flower was a name already out of date in the nine-

teenth century, and formerly applied to a variety of flowers, including wallflowers. Shepherds' Purse is a common cruciferous weed (*Capsella bursa pastoris*) with small white flowers. Fair-maids of France are a double-flowered variety of Crowfoot or ranunculus. Ladysmock is a common name for the Cuckoo-flower. Flower-de-luce is an obselete form of fleur-de-lis, a lily.

2 *Lots of people act well ... thing of the two* (p. 27) An idea that Wilde used again in 'The Critic as Artist' in *Intentions* (1891): 'it is more difficult to talk about a thing than to do it, and ... to do nothing is the most difficult thing in the world.'

3 *story with a moral ... dangerous thing to do* (p. 34) The Victorian preoccupation with the moral purpose of literature was a constant butt of Wilde's humour. Cf. the 'Preface' to *DG*: 'There is no such thing as a moral or immoral book.'

THE REMARKABLE ROCKET

1 *Pyrotechnist* (p. 36) I.e., one skilled in the making of fireworks.

2 *Aurora Borealis ... more natural* (p. 36) The Aurora Borealis are the northern lights. Wilde enjoyed playing with concepts of naturalness and artificiality, most famously perhaps in 'The Decay of Lying', where a sunset is described as a 'second-rate Turner ... with all the painter's faults exaggerated.'

3 *Pylotechnic* (p. 38) A nonce-word.

4 *Bengal light* (p. 38) A firework producing a steady and vivid blue-coloured light, used for signals (*OED*).

5 *glee-club* (p. 42) Singing or musical club.

6 *I often have long conversations ... I don't understand a single word of what I am saying* (p. 43) A joke that underwent many repetitions; cf. Lord Goring's exchange with his father in *IH*: '*Lord Caversham*: Do you always really understand what you say, sir? *Lord Goring*: Yes, father, if I listen attentively' (III, 136–7).

7 *hard work ... whatever to do* (p. 44) An idea which Wilde polished into an aphorism in 'Phrases and Philosophies for the Use of the Young': 'The condition of perfection is idleness'.

8 *Gold Stick ... Court dignitaries* (p. 45) The reference is to the gilt rod carried on state occasions by a colonel of the Life Guards.

The Portrait of Mr. W. H.

In the following notes I have drawn extensively upon Horst Schroeder's thorough and informed work of scholarship, *Annotations to Oscar Wilde, 'The Portrait of Mr. W. H.'* (Braunschweig, 1986). This volume and its companion, *Oscar Wilde, 'The Portrait of Mr. W. H.' – Its Composition, Publication and Reception* (Braunschweig, 1984) deserve far greater recognition by Wilde scholars in Britain and the United States than has hitherto been the case.

1 *Birdcage Walk* (p. 49) A street on the south of St James's Park, and so one of the fashionable milieux of London that so many of Wilde's characters inhabit.

2 *Macpherson, Ireland and Chatterton* (p. 49) Three literary forgers. James Macpherson (1736–96) published what he alleged were translations of Ossian; William Henry Ireland (1777–1835) forged Shakespeare manuscripts; and Thomas Chatterton (1752–70) forged medieval manuscripts. Wilde had lectured on Chatterton; the manuscript of his talk, ironically and unashamedly plagiarized from the work of others, is in the William Andrews Clark Memorial Library in the University of California, Los Angeles.

3 *to realise one's own personality on some imaginative plane* (p. 49) This represents one of Wilde's earliest statements of what was to become a central concern in both his critical and creative works – the proposition that the main function of art or criticism or (on some occasions) certain modes of behaviour, such as that exemplified by the dandy, was to express the individual.

4 *Cyril Graham* (p. 50) The name Graham recurs in *LWF*; Wilde's elder son was called Cyril and he used the name again in *Intentions*.

5 *François Clouet's later work* (p. 50) François Clouet (1520–72) was a distinguished French court portraitist. The work of Clouet and his father Jean Clouet, also a portraitist, had been popularized by Le Comte de Laborde in *La Renaissance des arts à la cour de France* in 1855. It was Jean Clouet, rather than (as Wilde implies in his phrase the 'great Flemish master') François, who was Flemish born.

6 *Lord Pembroke* (p. 51) William Herbert, third Earl of Pembroke (1580–1630), was the patron of many poets; he was the dedicatee of the first folio of Shakespeare's work and thought by many to be the 'Mr. W. H.' of Shakespeare's Sonnets.

7 *the Penshurst portraits* (p. 51) An error. Penshurst was the birthplace of

Sir Philip Sidney. The Wilton portraits of Lord Pembroke (of which Wilde was thinking) are by Daniel Mytens and Van Dyck.

8 *Mary Fitton* (p. 51) A maid of honour to Elizabeth I and mistress of William Herbert; identified in 1886 by Thomas Tyler as the original 'Dark Lady' of the Sonnets.

9 *the playing fields at Eton* (p. 51) In a saying attributed to the Duke of Wellington, 'the battle of Waterloo was won on the playing fields of Eton'; Wilde is mocking attributes of character such as earnestness.

10 *A.D.C.* (p. 52) The Amateur Dramatic Company at the University of Cambridge from which (as Wilde indicates later) women were excluded; they continued to be so until well into the twentieth century.

11 *better to be good-looking than to be good* (p. 52) A sentiment which Wilde was to repeat in *DG*: 'it is better to be beautiful than to be good' (p. 194).

12 *Philistines* (p. 52) A term used by Matthew Arnold (particularly in 1869 in *Culture and Anarchy*) to identify middle-class values, and adopted by Wilde to denote materialist (and anti-intellectual) British culture.

13 *read for the diplomatic* (p. 53) I.e., for the public examinations for foreign and colonial services. In *WNI* Lord Illingworth refuses a career in diplomacy despite being 'offered Vienna'.

14 *It is always a silly thing to give advice, but to give good advice is absolutely fatal* (p. 53) Once more a theme that underwent modification and variation and is best known in a speech by Lord Goring to his father in *IH*: 'I always pass on good advice. It is the only thing to do with it. It is never of any use to oneself' (I, 623–5).

15 *overlooking the Green Park* (p. 53) A location also used in 'The Critic as Artist' in *Intentions*.

16 *Lord Southampton* (p. 54) Henry Wriothesley (1573–1624), the third Earl of Southampton; like Pembroke, he was a patron of poets, including Shakespeare and, also like Pembroke, he was thought by many to be the subject of Shakespeare's sonnets.

17 *Meres* (p. 54) Francis Meres (1565–1647) who published in 1598 *Palladis Tamia, Wit's Treasury*, a history of English literature from Chaucer's time to his own.

18 *preface is from the publisher's hand* (p. 55) The initials 'T. T.' in the dedication of the Sonnets stand for Thomas Thorpe, in whose name they were entered in the *Stationers' Registers* in 1609.

19 *Lord Buckhurst ... Mr. Sackville* (p. 55) Thomas Sackville (1536–1608) became the first Earl of Dorset and Baron Buckhurst in 1567.

Robert Allott's anthology *England's Parnassus*, containing contributions by Sackville (under the initial 'M.') was published in 1600.

20 *Elizabeth Vernon* (p. 55) Cousin of the second Earl of Essex, Vernon was Southampton's mistress and later his wife.

21 *Mr. W. Hall ... Mr. W. H. the writer and not the subject of the dedication* (p. 55) These explanations of the Sonnets had, in fact, been suggested by Shakespearean scholars in the 1850s and 1860s (and in particular by Andrew Brae and Samuel Neill). William Hathaway was Shakespeare's brother-in-law.

22 *W. H. .... "Mr. William Himself"* (p. 56) An idea suggested by D. Barnstorff in *Schlüssel zu Shakespeares Sonnetten* in 1860. For details of this idea and many others, Wilde was indebted to Edmund Dowden's *The Sonnets of William Shakespeare* (1881).

23 *Drayton* (p. 56) I.e., the poet Michael Drayton (1563–1631).

24 *John Davies of Hereford* (p. 56) Another identification made earlier in the century by Henry Brown in *The Sonnets of Shakespeare Solved* (1870).

25 *philosophical allegory ... Catholic Church* (p. 56) Once again, details of these particular accounts of the Sonnets were available from Dowden's *The Sonnets of William Shakespeare*.

26 *Viola and Imogen, Juliet and Rosalind, Portia and Desdemona, and Cleopatra* (p. 57) I.e., the heroines of *Twelfth Night, Cymbeline, Romeo and Juliet, As You Like It, The Merchant of Venice, Othello* and *Antony and Cleopatra* respectively.

27 *Willie Hughes* (p. 57) The identification of Mr. W. H. with Willie Hughes was neither Wilde's (nor Graham's), but was suggested by the eighteenth-century critic Thomas Tyrwhitt, and recorded by Edmund Malone in his *Supplement to the Edition of Shakespeare's Plays ... by Samuel Johnson and George Steevens* (1780).

28 *eighth line* (p. 57) An error, for the line is in fact the seventh.

29 *Chapman's plays* (p. 58) I.e., the dramatist George Chapman (?1559–1634), a detail to be found in William Minto, *Characteristics of English Poets from Chaucer to Shirley* (1875) and in Dowden's *The Sonnets of William Shakespeare*.

30 *Philistine* (p. 59) See note 12 to p. 52.

31 *Alleyn MSS at Dulwich ... the papers of the Lord Chamberlain* (p. 59) The papers of Edward Alleyn, the famous Elizabethan actor, at Dulwich College, which he built and endowed; the Public Record Office; and the Office of the Lord Chamberlain, whose Examiner of Plays was, until 1968, the state censor of theatrical performances.

32 *the gaunt Palace* (p. 63) The description best fits Buckingham Palace, but it could refer to St James's.

33 *petit-pain* (p. 64) I.e., a bread-roll.

34 *Rosalind to Juliet . . . Beatrice to Ophelia* (p. 64) For Rosalind and Juliet, see note 26 to p. 57; Beatrice and Ophelia are the heroines of *Much Ado About Nothing* and *Hamlet*.

35 *Thomas Thorpe* (p. 66) See notes 18 to p. 55.

36 *'slight Muse', as he calls them* (p. 67) In Sonnet 38.13.

37 *Marlowe* (p. 70) An idea proposed originally by Robert Cartwright in *The Sonnets of William Shakespeare* (1859) and by Gerald Massey in *Shakespeare's Sonnets and his Private Friends* (1866).

38 *Mephistopheles of his Doctor Faustus* (p. 70) In Christopher Marlowe's *Dr Faustus* Mephistopheles seduces Faustus into eternal damnation; this identification was discussed by Massey in *Shakespeare's Sonnets*.

39 *Blackfriars' Theatre* (p. 70) An error of detail, for Shakespeare's company did not appear at the Blackfriars until 1608.

40 *Gaveston of his Edward II* (p. 70) In Marlowe's *Edward II*, the king's (homosexual) partiality for his favourite, Piers Gaveston, in part causes his downfall and the play's tragedy.

41 *Red Bull Tavern* (p. 70) The Red Bull, a playhouse in St John Street in Clerkenwell, thought originally to have been an inn, where plays could have indeed been performed in the 'open yard'. *Edward II* was performed there.

42 *King Edward's delicate minion* (p. 70) I.e., Gaveston in *Edward II*.

43 *The Lover's Complaint* (p. 71) In fact, *A Lover's Complaint*.

44 *a wonderfully graphic account . . . Thomas Knell* (p. 72) In his *Annotations*, Horst Schroeder suggests that this passage is taken 'almost verbatim' from Gerald Massey's *Shakespeare's Sonnets and his Private Friends*, and points out that it is not the work of Thomas Knell, as Wilde and Massey suggest, but of Essex's secretary, Edward Waterhouse. (See Schroeder, *Annotations*, p. 29.)

45 *Sidney's Stella* (p. 72) Penelope Devereux, the daughter of the first Earl of Essex, was later married to Lord Rich. The suggestion that she was the subject of Philip Sidney's sonnet-sequence *Astrophel and Stella* was made by Massey in 1866, and rehearsed by Edmund Dowden later in the century.

46 *Hews was an Elizabethan name* (p. 72) As the scholar Frederick Furnivall had noted as early as 1876 in the academic periodical *Notes and Queries*.

47 *Margaret Hews, whom Prince Rupert so madly loved* (p. 72) I.e., Mrs Margaret Hughes. She was Prince Rupert's mistress, bearing him a

daughter who was christened Ruperta and to whom the Prince left all his estate in trust. Margaret Hughes appeared as Desdemona in December 1660.

48 *those English actors who in 1604 ... Court of that strange Elector of Brandenburg* (p. 73) The sources available to Wilde describe how a company of English actors travelled to Germany in the early years of the seventeenth century and perhaps performed before Duke Henry Julius of Brunswick-Lüneburg, and how in 1617 English comedians appeared before the Elector of Brandenburg. The other details of the episodes appear to be Wilde's invention.

49 *Aufklarung* (p. 73) The most obvious immediate source of the term '*Aufklärung*' was Walter Pater's story 'Duke Carl of Rosenmold' in *Imaginary Portraits* (1887), which Wilde had reviewed in *The Pall Mall Gazette* in June 1887. There he drew attention to Pater's use of the term (which Pater translated as 'the Enlightening') and its use in relation to the work of Lessing, Herder and Goethe.

50 *Friedrich Schroeder* (p. 73) I.e., Friedrich Ulrich Schröder (1744–1816), the first manager to introduce Shakespeare to the German stage.

51 *mimae quidem ex Britannia ... slain at Nuremberg* (p. 73) Horst Schroeder points out that 'although the history of the early English actors at Nuremberg is well documented, an incident like the one related is not recorded' (*Annotations*, p. 60). He goes on to suggest that Wilde's anecdote is fictitious.

52 *the sorrows of Dionysos that Tragedy sprang* (p. 74) A theme that Wilde probably found in 'A Study of Dionysus', an essay by Walter Pater, who had been a formative influence at Oxford. Pater's essay was published in 1876 in the *Fortnightly Review* and posthumously in *Greek Studies* (1895). At one point Wilde seems to echo Pater directly: 'It is out of the sorrows of Dionysus, then; – of Dionysus in winter – that all Greek tragedy grows' (*Greek Studies* (1895; 1901), p. 40).

53 *Bithynian slave ... yellow hills of Cerameicus ... Antinous ... Charmides in philosophy* (p. 74) The Bithynian slave was Antinöus, the beautiful page of the Roman emperor Hadrian and a favourite subject of sculptors; Cerameicus is a quarter of Athens; Charmides was a beautiful Athenian youth who appears in Plato's dialogue of that name. Wilde's theme is the age-old one of the permanence of beauty in art; but it is significant that the examples he gives are of classical male beauty.

54 *Globe Theatre* (p. 76) Erected in 1599 in Southwark for the Burbages. Shakespeare acted there, but Wilde seems to have forgotten that the

narrator has made the same point about the Blackfriars and assumes his readers were aware of the relationship between the two playhouses.

55 *Cannes* (p. 77) The popularity of Cannes as a resort dates from its virtual colonization by British visitors from the midnineteenth century onwards.

56 *night-mail from Charing Cross* (p. 77) Charing Cross was the station serving cross-Channel traffic until the 1920s.

57 *not a Clouet, but an Ouvry* (p. 78) As Horst Schroeder suggests in *Oscar Wilde, 'The Portrait of Mr. W. H.' – Its Composition, Publication and Reception*, the reference to Ouvry is in all likelihood an error for Oudry, the French painter in the school of Jean Clouet; an exhibition of Oudry's work in 1888 in London had attracted considerable interest.

A House of Pomegranates

1 *Dedication* (p. 81) Constance Wilde (née Lloyd) was Wilde's wife.

THE YOUNG KING

1 *Dedication* (p. 83) Margaret de Windt (1849–1936) married in 1869 Sir Charles Johnson Brooke, the second Rajah of Sarawak. Wilde probably met her in Paris in 1891.

2 *Faun* (p. 83) In Greek mythology a rural demigod, represented as a man with horns and the tail of a goat.

3 *Joyeuse* (p. 84) 'Joyeuse' was the epithet used to describe (and denigrate) members of Henri III's court. Wilde used it again in *DG*.

4 *Adonis* (p. 85) In Greek legend a beautiful youth favoured by Aphrodite, whose name became a bye-word for male beauty.

5 *Bithynian slave of Hadrian* (p. 85) I.e., Antinöus, the beautiful page of the Roman emperor Hadrian; see note 53 to p. 74.

6 *Endymion* (p. 85) Once more male beauty is being alluded to, for in Greek legend Endymion was a beautiful young shepherd whom Selene (the moon) visited each night as he slept in an eternal sleep. Endymion was familiar to nineteenth-century readers through the poem by John Keats.

7 *Narcissus* (p. 86) A favourite classical reference used by Wilde to denote vain male beauty; see note 20 to p. 113 and note 1 to p. 246.

8 *lateen sail* (p. 88) 'A triangular sail suspended by a long yard at an angle of about 45° to the mast' (*OED*).

9 *Ormuz* (p. 89) A famously wealthy city in the Persian Gulf, mentioned by Milton in *Paradise Lost* (II, 2).

10 *Tartary* (p. 90) In the Middle Ages, the land of the Mongols and Tartars of Central Asia, who under Genghis Khan overran much of Europe; Wilde's emphasis is upon the Tartars' legendary violence.

11 *Isis and Osiris* (p. 91) Isis was the Egyptian goddess of the sky and wife of Osiris, the god of fertility and the underworld.

12 *Death leaped upon his red horse and galloped away* (p. 91) Wilde's treatment of Death, Avarice and Plague draws heavily on the description of the Apocalypse in the Revelation of St John the Divine.

13 *pleasaunce* (p. 92) A pleasure-ground, usually attached to a mansion.

14 *dreamer of dreams* (p. 95) A quotation from William Morris's verse-romance *The Earthly Paradise*, where the poet calls himself a 'Dreamer of dreams'.

15 *the dead staff blossomed* (p. 95) An allusion to the Tannhäuser story, given its most popular expression in the nineteenth century by Richard Wagner in his opera *Tannhäuser* (1861). In it Tannhäuser confesses to the Pope his love for Venus, but is refused absolution until the Pope's staff blossoms. Tannhäuser goes back to Venusberg, and the Pope's 'dead staff' does indeed blossom. In *De Profundis*, his long prison-letter to Lord Alfred Douglas, Wilde explicitly associated Tannhäuser with Christ.

16 *monstrance* (p. 96) Gold or jewelled vessel containing the consecrated Host.

THE BIRTHDAY OF THE INFANTA

1 *Infanta* (p. 97) Technically the eldest daughter of the king and queen of Spain who is not heir to the throne.

2 *Dedication* (p. 97) Mrs William H. Grenville and her husband (Lord and Lady Desborough), of Taplow Court in Buckinghamshire, were members of a group calling themselves 'The Souls'. Wilde was a frequent visitor to Taplow Court.

3 *Mi reina!* (p. 99) I.e., My queen!

4 *Papal Nuncio* (p. 99) A permanent official representative of the Roman see at a foreign court.

5 *Escurial* (p. 99) The chief palace of the Spanish kings, about thirty miles from Madrid.

6 *auto-da-fé* (p. 99) The ceremonial delivery of heretics condemned by the Spanish Inquisition to the secular arm to be burned at the stake.

7 *vrai sourire de France* (p. 100) I.e., 'the true smile of France'.

8 *moue* (p. 100) I.e., A pout.

9 *hidalgo and grandee* (p. 101) An inaccurate conjunction of terms: hidalgo refers to the lower ranks of the nobility and grandee to the highest.

10 *Camerera-Mayor* (p. 101) The chief keeper of the Queen's wardrobe.

11 *Bravo toro!* (p. 101) I.e., 'bravo (or well done) bull!'

12 *the semi-classical tragedy of Sophonisba* (p. 102) Sophonisba was the daughter of the Carthaginian general Hasdrubal; her fate formed the subject of numerous European dramas.

13 *Tritons* (p. 106) Here statues of sea-monsters of semi-human form represented as a bearded man with the hind-parts of a fish, holding a trident and a shell-trumpet.

14 *Pan* (p. 108) In classical mythology Pan was an Arcadian deity who invented and played on the 'pipes of Pan'; as Wilde's allusion suggests, he came to be regarded as the personification of Nature, and, perhaps ironically here, was associated with fertility.

15 *tabouret* (p. 111) A low seat or stool.

16 *Holbein's Dance of Death* (p. 111) A series of woodcuts by Hans Holbein the Younger executed in the 1520s, in which Death is depicted as an unwelcome democratic leveller robbing every class and profession of their pride and status.

17 *Lucca damask* (p. 112) A figured cloth. Wilde reviewed Ernest Lefébure's *Embroidery and Lace* in *Woman's World* in December 1888, calling it 'a fascinating book'. The book not only provided details of embroidery here, but also for Chapter 9 of *DG*.

18 *Faun* (p. 112) See note 2 to p. 83.

19 *Venus* (p. 113) In classical mythology the goddess of love.

20 *Echo* (p. 113) In classical mythology an oread whom Hera deprived of speech, except for the power to repeat the last words uttered by someone else. She fell in love with Narcissus (see note 7 to p. 86), but when her affection was not returned she pined away until only her voice was left. In another version of the legend, Echo was a nymph loved by Pan (thus taking up the identification of the dwarf with Pan on p. 108).

21 *petit monstre* (p. 114) I.e., little monster.

THE FISHERMAN AND HIS SOUL

1 *Dedication* (p. 115) Alice Heine (1858–1925), widow of the Duc de Richelieu, married Prince Albert of Monaco in 1889. She was a

patron of art and artists. Wilde seems to have met her first in Paris in 1891. H.S.H. stands for 'Her Serene Highness'.

2 *Tritons* (p. 116) See notes 13 to p. 106.

3 *filigrane* (p. 116) Delicate, thread-like forms.

4 *Sirens* (p. 116) In Homer's *Odyssey* (12.39,184), sea-songstresses living on an island near Scylla and Charybdis who charm sailors to their deaths – an ironic portent of the fate of the fisherman.

5 *nautilus* (p. 117) A reference to a sea-creature (a cephalopod) that has a beautiful and delicate chambered shell and webbed dorsal arms, which it was formerly believed to use as a sail.

6 *Kraken* (p. 117) A mythical sea-monster of enormous size, the subject of a poem by Tennyson.

7 *baskets of plaited osier* (p. 117) I.e., baskets made of stripped and woven willow branches.

8 *Fauns* (p. 119) See note 2 to p. 83.

9 *leman* (p. 119) An archaic word meaning lover or spouse.

10 *samphire* (p. 120) A maritime rock plant whose leaves are used in pickles.

11 *vervain* (p. 123) A plant reputedly possessing medicinal qualities.

12 *targe* (p. 123) A light shield.

13 *Judas tree* (p. 125) The leguminous tree (*Cercis siliquastrum*) from which Judas was supposed to have hanged himself; it normally has purple flowers.

14 *Tartars* (p. 127) See note 10 to p. 90.

15 *Gryphons* (p. 128) Mythical animals which had the head and wings of an eagle and the body and hindquarters of a lion. The following paragraphs contain a mixture of names of real peoples and places (such as Tyre and Sidon) and the completely fictitious (such as the Agazonbae, Laktroi and Krimnians).

16 *selenites* (p. 131) I.e., moonstones.

17 *galbanum and nard* (p. 133) Galbanum is a gum resin; nard is an aromatic balsam. Both denote exoticism, an important element in decadent literature.

18 *wine of Schiraz* (p. 133) I.e., Shiraz, a city in Persia, famous for its wine.

19 *palanquin* (p. 134) 'A covered litter for one person, carried by four or six men by means of poles projecting before and behind' (*OED*).

20 *Circassian* (p. 134) A gentile or non-Jew. Again the exotic is being invoked.

21 *aloes* (p. 135) Plants with fragrant resin and bitter juices.

22 *ger-falcon* (p. 135) A species of large falcon.

23 *porphyry* (p. 136) I.e., a beautiful red stone with a high polish. As with the earlier reference to a 'purfled' (or decoratively braided) silk napkin, Wilde's emphasis is once more on conspicuous and exotic luxury, a common feature of decadent literature.

24 *chalcedonies and sards* (p. 137) Sard is a variety of chalcedony; both are semi-transparent quartz stones. A knowledge of gems and precious stones is a feature of both English and French decadent writing. Cf. *DG* and Joris-Karl Huysmans's *A Rebours* (1884). For his knowledge of the subject Wilde was greatly indebted to William Jones, *History and Mystery of Precious Stones* (1880).

25 *stibium* (p. 143) A black antimony cosmetic, used for blackening the eyelids and eyebrows.

26 *Field of the Fullers* (p. 146) In the Bible (2 Kings) the Fullers' Field is a spot just outside the walls of Jerusalem. The trade of fulling, or processing cloth, used alkalis and caused offensive smells and was thus carried out at some distance from habitations. Hence the spot in which the Fisherman and the Mermaid are buried is not only unhallowed, but also contaminated (and thus sterile).

27 *monstrance* (p. 147) See note 16 to p. 96.

28 *alb and the girdle, the maniple and the stole* (p. 147) Details of ecclesiastical dress: an alb is a tunic of white cloth worn by priests, the maniple is a Eucharistic vestment worn over the arm and a stole is a narrow strip of silk worn over the shoulders.

THE STAR-CHILD

1 *Dedication* (p. 149) Margot Tennant was a friend from Dublin and was shortly to become the wife of Herbert Henry Asquith, the Home Secretary and the future Prime Minister.

2 *haggard* (p. 154) An Irish term for a stack-yard.

3 *carlots* (p. 157) Peasants.

4 *Giaours* (p. 159) A term used by Turks for non-Christians, familiarized in the nineteenth century by *The Giaour*, a poem by Byron.

Lord Arthur Savile's Crime and Other Stories

LORD ARTHUR SAVILE'S CRIME

1 *Lady Windermere* (p. 167) Wilde's use of names is never without significance. As the later reference to Debrett's *Peerage* hints, he had

to be especially careful to avoid specific reference to living members of the aristocracy. The titles Windermere, Fermor, Jedburgh, and Plymdale are used again in later works.

2 *Speaker's Levée* (p. 167) I.e., the speaker of the House of Commons whose levées are traditionally held in court dress, hence the Cabinet Ministers' 'stars and ribands'. The reference (and the later allusions to Princess Sophia and the Royal Academy) locates the social milieu of the tale. An easy movement between the public arenas of political and diplomatic life, semi-public artistic institutions such as the Royal Academy and the private world of the aristocracy and upper middle classes (here represented by Bentinck House) was a feature of late nineteenth-century London society.

3 *political economist* (p. 167) I.e., a specialist in political economy, a doctrine which informed much nineteenth-century social and political thought, and a favourite target for Wilde.

4 *Or pur* (p. 167) I.e., pure gold.

5 *saint, with not a little of the fascination of a sinner* (p. 168) An interest in psychological types is a common feature of Wilde's works, as is the reversal of Victorian moral stereotypes (such as 'saint' and 'sinner'). The sentiments here are repeated in the Society Comedies and in particularly in *DG*.

6 *cheiromantist* (p. 168) I.e., palmist. Palmistry was fashionable in the 1880s and 1890s, but as the reactions of Lady Windermere's guests makes clear, the term cheiromancy was not a particularly common nineteenth-century usage. Wilde's interest in cheiromancy was prompted in part by his friend Edward Heron-Allen's essay 'The Cheiromancy of Today' in *Lippincott's Monthly Magazine* in 1890.

7 *Providence can resist temptation by this time* (p. 169) A joke which, with variations, Wilde was to re-use; cf. *IH*: '*Lord Goring*: Doesn't that sound rather like tempting Providence? *Mrs Cheveley*: Oh! surely Providence can resist temptation by this time' (III, 378–9).

8 *on a fait le monde ainsi* (p. 170) Broadly translated, 'that's the way of the world'.

9 *rascette* (p. 170) Lines at the junction of the wrists and hand.

10 *spatulate* (p. 171) I.e., broadened and rounded.

11 *lions better than collie dogs* (p. 171) In late nineteenth-century literary culture, to 'lionize' meant both to fête and champion an individual writer.

12 *Bayswater* (p. 172) The significance of areas of London has changed since the late nineteenth century. In Wilde's work addresses denote social status and are thus very important. Most of his work is set

either in country estates or in the fashionable milieux of London, principally Mayfair and what Henry Arthur Jones called 'our little parish of St James'. As a fairly recent suburban development, Bayswater was outside this élite world.

13 *The proper basis for marriage is a mutual misunderstanding* (p. 172) This line was taken virtually verbatim from Henry James's novel, *The Portrait of a Lady* (1881), but it represents the basis for many jokes in Wilde's later work; cf. *IH*: 'In married life affection comes when people thoroughly dislike each other' (III, 211–12).

14 *Morning Post* (p. 172) A popular nineteenth-century newspaper, and the preferred medium for news about London Society. In *IH*, Lord Caversham asks Lord Goring whether he reads *The Times*, and Goring replies: 'Certainly not. I only read *The Morning Post*. All that one should know about modern life is where the Duchesses are; anything else is quite demoralising' (IV, 35–6).

15 *moue* (p. 172) See note 8 to p. 100.

16 *General Boulanger* (p. 174) A topical allusion: Boulanger was the French minister of war.

17 *Nemesis . . . shield of Pallas . . . Gorgon's head* (p. 174) In Greek mythology, Nemesis was the Greek goddess who measured out happiness and misery to mortals. The armed goddess Pallas Athene had on her shield a Gorgon head (which turned to stone those who looked on it). Wilde's meaning is that Lord Arthur's fate is such as to turn his countenance to stone.

18 *Guildenstern . . . Hamlet . . . Prince Hal* (p. 175) Guildenstern is a minor character in *Hamlet*; Prince Hal is the reckless prince who later becomes king in *Henry V*.

19 *guineas* (p. 176) I.e., twenty-one shillings in pre-decimal coinage; one pound and five pence in current coinage. The professions invariably charged fees in guineas; Podgers is indicating that he should be treated as a member of a profession (such as a lawyer or doctor).

20 *portière* (p. 176) A curtain hung over a door to give protection from draughts or to act as a screen.

21 *the Park* (p. 177) I.e., Hyde Park. Lord Arthur goes north from an area around Belgrave Square, and then south-east, a social as well as a physical journey.

22 *eld* (p. 177) I.e., age; the word was archaic well before the 1890s.

23 *hansom* (p. 178) A type of two-wheeled horse-drawn cab, a very common vehicle on the streets of London in the nineteenth century. They were usually vehicles for hire, but occasionally (as with this one) privately owned.

24 *billy-cock hat* (p. 178) A kind of bowler hat.

25 *A London free from the sin ... morn to eve* (p. 179) Elsewhere Wilde admired the spectacle of metropolitan life but regretted the social and economic inequality which made it possible. Cf. Hester Worsley's outburst in *WNI*: 'You rich people in England, you don't know how you are living. How could you? You shut out from your society the gentle and the good. You laugh at the simple and the poor. Living, as you do, on others and by them, you sneer at self-sacrifice, and if you throw bread to the poor, it is merely to keep them quiet for a season' (II, 260–65).

26 *Arcady* (p. 179) Arcadia, in Greek legend the ideal region of pastoral simplicity and contentment.

27 *cigarette* (p. 180) Cigarette smoking was more of a marker of fashion in the late nineteenth century than it is now. It is used by Wilde to indicate a 'modern' or decadent consciousness: most of his heroes and some of his 'fast' women are made to smoke.

28 *crêpe-de-chine* (p. 180) A white or coloured textured silk.

29 *delicate little figures ... near Tanagra* (p. 180) Small statuettes of terracotta found in the last decades of the nineteenth century in tombs dating from the late fourth and third centuries BC at Tanagra in Greece. In the stage directions for Act I of *IH*, Wilde indicates Mabel Chiltern's delicacy and innocence by comparing her to a Tanagra statuette.

30 *the Borgia* (p. 180) Cesare Borgia, son of Rodrigo Borgia, Pope Alexander VI, became notorious for his crimes, and is said to have inspired Machiavelli's *The Prince*.

31 *Sheraton* (p. 182) A style of furniture developed in England in the late eighteenth century, chiefly by Thomas Sheraton.

32 *Buckingham* (p. 182) I.e., a London club. Clubs were all-male preserves. Membership of them was an index of social prestige: Podgers does not belong to a club.

33 *Ruff's Guide and Bailey's Magazine ... the Pharmacopoeia ... Erskine's Toxicology* (p. 183) I.e., *Ruff's Guide to the Turf* and *Bailey's Magazine of Sports and Pastimes*, both contemporary sporting journals; the *Pharmacopoeia* was (and – as the *British Pharmacopoeia* – is) an officially published book listing drugs and medicinal substances with directions for use and identification. Sir Mathew Reid's edition of Erskine's *Toxicology* is an invention.

34 *aconitine* (p. 183) A deadly poison whose manufacture began in 1847 and which in its naturally occurring (and less toxic) form is monk's-hood or wolf's-bane.

35 *monsieur le mauvais sujet* (p. 183) I.e., you scoundrel (or rascal).

36 *On a fait des folies pour moi* (p. 184) I.e., men lost their heads over me.

37 *American novels* (p. 184) A favourite butt for Wilde's humour. Cf. the exchange in *DG*: '"Dry-goods! What are American dry-goods?" asked the Duchess, raising her large hands in wonder and accentuating the verb. "American novels," answered Lord Henry' (p. 38).

38 *Lido . . . Florian's . . . Piazza* (p. 186) The Lido is an island resort off Venice; Florian's is a café on the Piazza San Marco. Venice was extremely popular among the British leisured class in the late nineteenth century.

39 *Pinetum* (p. 186) The pine forest of Ravenna.

40 *Danielli's* (p. 186) Danieli's is a fashionable hotel in Venice, near the Piazza San Marco and overlooking the lagoon, well-known to nineteenth-century British travellers.

41 *dynamite* (p. 189) In fact, a fairly recent invention of 1867 by the Swede Alfred Nobel.

42 *Scotland Yard* (p. 189) A street off Whitehall which gave its name to the headquarters of the Metropolitan Police until 1890 when it was moved to New Scotland Yard on the Thames Embankment.

43 *revolutionary tendencies* (p. 189) The subject of Russian revolutionary politics was a topical one and had preoccupied Wilde in his play, *Vera; Or, the Nihilists* (1880), and the 'Soul of Man Under Socialism'. Nihilism (mentioned slightly later in the text) was a Russian terrorist movement aimed at destroying the Tsarist state.

44 *Tsar . . . ship's carpenter* (p. 189) An allusion to the embassy sent by Peter I to Western countries for advice on modernizing the Russian navy. Peter himself went on the embassy as a volunteer sailor – under the name of Peter Mikhailov – and learned about shipbuilding at Deptford.

45 *Marcobrünner* (p. 191) Marcobrünn in the Erbach region is one of the great vineyards of the Rheingau. Fine wines figured prominently in both Wilde's work and his life. Rhine wines (known generically in English as hock) were a particular favourite.

46 *hydra* (p. 192) In Greek mythology the fabulous many-headed snake whose heads grew as fast as they were cut off.

47 *I live entirely for my art* (p. 192) The idea that art and criminality were linked in some way was one that fascinated Wilde. It formed the subject of the essay 'Pen, Pencil, and Poison' in *Intentions* (1891), and is a theme of *DG*.

48 *meat-tea* (p. 192) Wilde is generally very precise about matters of social etiquette. For one of Lord Arthur's rank, tea would be a light

refreshment taken at four in the afternoon. In *IBE* it includes cucumber sandwiches. A meat-tea would be a more substantial meal, taken rather later; hence the references to different types of meal is being used as an indicator of class behaviour.

49 *tape* (p. 193) I.e., ticker tape, a continuous paper tape which printed out telegraphic messages, most usually from news agencies and the Stock Exchange. Ticker tape machines were invented by Edison in the early 1870s in the United States and were fairly common by the late 1880s.

50 *Mudie* (p. 193) Mudie's circulating library was one of the most famous nineteenth-century subscription libraries; it later merged with W. H. Smith's circulating library.

51 *Dorcas Society* (p. 194) A ladies' association (in a church) for making and providing clothes for the poor. It is mentioned again in *WNI*, and is meant to indicate worthy (if tedious) charitable service.

52 *cap of Liberty* (p. 194) The cap worn by the Jacobins in the French Revolution was known as the 'cap of liberty'. More recently and more locally it had also been worn by some members of the Chartist movement in Britain in the 1830s and 1840s.

53 *Liberty ... French Revolution* (p. 194) The centenary of the French Revolution in 1889 and the celebratory gift of the Statue of Liberty from France to the United States made the Revolution a topical subject. Wilde's specific reference is the ideal of liberty embodied in the Revolution's appeal to 'Liberty, Equality and Fraternity'.

54 *bull's-eye lantern* (p. 197) A lantern with a lens (the bull's-eye) which focused its light into a beam.

55 *Gaiety* (p. 197) A West-End theatre noted for musical comedies. See Ray Mander and Joe Mitchenson, *Lost Theatres of London* (2nd edn, London, 1976).

THE SPHINX WITHOUT A SECRET

1 *Title* (p. 200) One of Wilde's best-known poems is 'The Sphinx', which was in turn a nickname he gave to his friend Ada Leverson. The story's title is reminiscent of an exchange in *WNI*: '*Mrs Allonby*: Define us as a sex. *Lord Illingworth*: Sphinxes without secrets' (I, 439–40). The subtitle – 'an etching' – recalls Wilde's practice of subtitling his poems in terms taken from other art-forms, particularly music and painting.

2 *believed in the Pentateuch* (p. 200) I.e., the first five books of the Old Testament. During the course of the nineteenth century the authority

of the Bible had been challenged by scientific questioning of the historical accuracy of the book of Genesis: Murchison's old-fashioned virtues are being alluded to.

3 *Madeleine ... the Bois* (p. 201) St Madeleine is a church in the 8th Arrondissement of Paris, between the Opéra and the Champs Elysées. The woods of the Bois de Boulogne are to the east of it.

4 *Gioconda in sables* (p. 201) Leonardo da Vinci's portrait, now more popularly known as the Mona Lisa, was assiduously discussed in the last decades of the nineteenth century, particularly in a 'purple passage' by Walter Pater in *The Renaissance* (1873).

5 *brougham* (p. 201) A one-horse, closed carriage.

6 *that wretched Row* (p. 201) Rotten Row, a fashionable promenading place in Hyde Park.

7 *ma belle inconnue* (p. 201) I.e., my beautiful unknown (woman).

8 *congestion of the lungs* (p. 204) Congestion of the lungs is (as Wilde implies here) a symptom of pneumonia.

THE CANTERVILLE GHOST

1 *A Hylo-Idealistic Romance* (p. 260) Hylo-Idealism was the doctrine of the Birmingham poet, Constance Naden, whom Wilde admired. The doctrine identified the spiritual as part of the material realm.

2 *Dowager Duchess* (p. 206) A dowager is a widow who enjoys the property or title that has come to her via her husband. Dowagers – whether duchesses or not – form a significant part of the comic world of Wilde's plays.

3 *You are certainly very natural in America* (p. 207) The contrast between naturalness (represented by America) and civilization (represented by Europe) is a theme common in Wilde's works, as indeed is an ironic tone towards things American. Cf. *DG* and *WNI*, where Hester Worsley, an American heiress on holiday in Britain, is said by another character to be 'painfully natural'.

4 *leading the German* (p. 207) A dance, similar to the cotillon.

5 *amazon* (p. 207) In classical legend, Amazons were a race of female warriors.

6 *Psychical Society* (p. 210) A topical allusion: the Society for Psychical Research was founded in 1882.

7 *Fanny Davenport over Sara Bernhardt* (p. 210) Fanny Davenport was a popular contemporary American actress; Sara Bernhardt was a French actress who attained great celebrity all over Europe and the United States, and was particularly famous for her voice. Wilde was

reported (by Vincent O'Sullivan) to have said that he would have married Sara Bernhardt; she was to play the title-role in *Salomé* in 1892 before the play was banned.

8 *green corn, buckwheat cakes, and hominy* (p. 210) Varieties of American cereals.

9 *old man of terrible aspect* (p. 211) An allusion to a line from Dante's *Vita Nuova*, III. 3: 'd'uno segnore di pauroso aspette' – in Dante Gabriel Rossetti's translation, 'O Lord of terrible aspect' (*Dante and his Circle*, 1874).

10 *Monsieur de Voltaire* (p. 212) The French satirist, historian, moralist and free-thinker who was exiled to England from 1726 to 1729 (when he presumably could have met the family of the Canterville ghost).

11 *Crockford's* (p. 212) A famous gambling club established in 1827 in St James's Street in London by William Crockford. Charles James Fox, the great Whig statesman, died in 1806, and so was hardly likely to have gambled at Crockford's.

12 *Lady Stutfield* (p. 212) Like Lady Windermere, a character-name that recurs in other works.

13 *Longfellow* (p. 215) Henry Wadsworth Longfellow, the American poet, whom Wilde had met on his American tour in 1882. The allusion is to Longfellow's 'The Skeleton in Armour'.

14 *the Virgin Queen herself* (p. 215) Elizabeth I.

15 *Titan form* (p. 217) Although Wilde frequently alludes to classical sources, the term here simply means 'colossal' or 'gigantic' rather than signifying Greek deities.

16 *falchion* (p. 217) A broad curved sword.

17 *dimity* (p. 217) A stout cotton cloth which is used undyed for a bedding material.

18 *Chanticleer* (p. 218) The cock in *Reynard the Fox* and in Chaucer's 'The Nun's Priest's Tale' in *The Canterbury Tales*.

19 *list slippers* (p. 220) Traditionally worn by stage 'ghosts' to give them a silent tread.

20 *arquebuse* (p. 220) An early type of portable gun where the barrel is supported by a tripod or forked rest.

21 *large Saroni photographs* (p. 221) Napoleon Sarony (1821–96) moved from his native Canada to begin work on photography in Birmingham, England. He returned to North America to open what became a highly successful New York studio in 1866 and was reputed to have photographed over 30,000 actors and actresses. He took publicity portraits of Wilde at the beginning and end of his American lecture tour.

22 *clam-bake* (p. 221) In the United States, a picnic party to eat baked clams.

23 *euchre* (p. 221) An American card game played with thirty-two cards.

24 *guineas* (p. 222) See note 19 to p. 176.

25 *en secondes noces* (p. 222) I.e., as a second wife.

26 *free passage* (p. 224) An ironic reference to the schemes for assisted emigration to the British colonies or to the USA, often for 'fallen' women or reformed prostitutes, which Wilde was to mock in *WNI*.

27 *no ruins and no curiosities . . . navy and your manners* (p. 225) A variation on a much used joke; cf. the exchange in *WNI* on the British aristocracy and American life: '*Lady Caroline*: There are a great many things you haven't got in America, I am told, Miss Worsley. They say you have no ruins, and no curiosities. *Mrs Allonby*: . . . What nonsense! They have their mothers and their manners. *Hester Worsley*: The English aristocracy supply us with our curiosities, Lady Caroline. They are sent over every summer, regularly, in the steamers, and propose to us the day after they land' (II, 245–53).

28 *hemlock . . . nightingale* (p. 225) The poisonous hemlock plant (*Conium maculatum*) has white flowers (which are usually small, however), and is traditionally associated with drowsiness and death. The nightingale was a Romantic symbol, used by Shelley and particularly Keats, and connoting the oblivion achieved through art.

29 *mortmain* (p. 231) A legal term referring to land held in perpetuity by a family or institution.

30 *Virginia received the coronet . . . reward of all good little American girls* (p. 233) Another topic freely re-used; cf. *WNI*: 'These American girls carry off all the good matches. Why can't they stay in their own country?' (I, 206–7).

THE MODEL MILLIONAIRE

1 *Ruff's Guide and Bailey's Magazine* (p. 235) See note 33 to p. 183.

2 *butterfly to do among bulls and bears* (p. 235) A dense set of allusions. The term butterfly connotes irreverence – James McNeill Whistler, Wilde's friend from the early 1880s (and with whom he later quarrelled) signed his picture with a butterfly motif. A bull market is Stock Exchange jargon for a market which is rising, whereas a bear market is one which is falling.

3 *pekoe and souchong* (p. 235) Types of tea.

4 *ineffectual young man with a perfect profile and no profession* (p. 235) Cf. 'Phrases and Philosophies for the Use of the Young': 'There is

something tragic about the enormous number of young men there are in England at the present moment who start life with a perfect profile, and end by adopting some useful profession.' The lines were read out in court during Wilde's trials.

5 *Men who are dandies and women who are darlings rule the world* (p. 236) A familiar sentiment. Cf. Lord Illingworth in *WNI*: 'The future belongs to the dandy. It is the exquisites who are going to rule' (III, 56–7); and 'A Few Maxims for the Instruction of the Over-Educated': 'Dandyism is the assertion of the absolute modernity of Beauty'.

6 *trouvaille, mon cher* (p. 236) I.e., a find, my dear fellow.

7 *hock and seltzer* (p. 237) See note 45 to Marcobrünner, p. 191.

8 *A chacun son métier* (p. 238) I.e., to each his trade, or, more colloquially, each to his own.

9 *Que voulez-vous? La fantaisie d'un millionaire!* (p. 238) I.e., 'What do you want? The fantasy of a millionaire!'

10 *Son affaire c'est l'argent des autres* (p. 239) I.e., 'his business is other people's money'.

11 *Row* (p. 239) See note 6 to p. 201.

12 *de la part de* (p. 239) on behalf of.

Poems in Prose

1 *Narcissus* (p. 246) In the Greek legend, to which Wilde's story gives an ironic twist, Narcissus was caused by Nemesis to become enamoured of his own image reflected in the waters of a spring. He pined away and was changed into the flower which bears his name.

2 *Oreads* (p. 246) Mountain nymphs of classical mythology.

3 *Joseph of Arimathea* (p. 246) Who in the Gospels took the body of Christ for burial.

4 *Centaur* (p. 252) A mythical beast with the head, trunk and arms of a man, and the body and legs of a horse.

PENGUIN ONLINE